D0389098

A MADNESS OF ANGELS

A MADNESS OF ANGELS

Or, The Resurrection of Matthew Swift

KATE GRIFFIN

www.orbitbooks.net

New York London

Orbit
Hachette Book Group
237 Park Avenue, New York, NY 10017
Visit our Web site at www.HachetteBookGroup.com

First North American Edition: April 2009

Orbit is an imprint of Hachette Book Group. The Orbit name and logo are trademarks of Little, Brown Book Group Limited.

ISBN 978-0-316-04125-6
LCCN 2009921408

10 9 8 7 6 5 4 3 2 1

RRD-IN

Printed in the United States of America

Magic is life. Where there is magic, there is life; the two cannot be separated. They shadow each other's nature, reflect each other's faces, centres and moods. The echoes of a word shouted in anger, the warmth left behind by the touch of skin, the traceries of breath, these are all parts of the lingering concept we loosely define as "magic". And in this new time, the magic is no longer of the vine and the tree; magic now focuses itself where there is most life, and that life burns neon.

R.J. Bakker, "The Changing Concept of Magic" – Urban Magic Magazine, vol. 3, March 1994

We be light, we be life, we be fire!
We sing electric flame, we rumble underground wind, we dance heaven!
Come be we and be free!
We be blue electric angels.

Anonymous spam mail, source unknown

Prelude: The Trouble with Telephones

In which a summoning is almost (but not quite) perfect, some new friends are made, and some old enemies remembered.

Not how it should have been.

Too long, this awakening, floor warm beneath my fingers, itchy carpet, thick, a prickling across my skin, turning rapidly into the red-hot feeling of burrowing ants; too long without sensation, everything weak, like the legs of a baby. I said twitch, and my toes twitched, and the rest of my body shuddered at the effort. I said blink, and my eyes were two half-sucked toffees, uneven, sticky, heavy, pushing back against the passage of my eyelids like I was trying to lift weights before a marathon.

All this, I felt, would pass. As the static blue shock of my wakening, if that is the word, passed, little worms of it digging away into the floor or crawling along the ceiling back into the telephone lines, the hot blanket of their protection faded from my body. The cold intruded like a great hungry worm into every joint and inch of skin, my bones suddenly too long for my flesh, my muscles suddenly too tense in their relaxed form to tense ever again, every part starting to quiver as the full shock of sensation returned.

I lay on the floor naked as a shedding snake, and we contemplated our situation.

runrunrunrunrunRUNRUNRUNRUN! hissed the panicked voice inside me, the one that saw the bed legs an inch from my nose as the feet of an ogre, heard the odd swish of traffic through the rain outside as the spitting of venom down a forked tongue, felt the thin neon light drifting through the familiar dirty window pane as hot as noonday glare through a hole in the ozone layer.

I tried moving my leg and found the action oddly giddying, as if this was the ultimate achievement for which my life so far had been spent in training, the fulfilment of all ambition. Or perhaps it was simply that we had pins and needles and, not entirely knowing how to deal with pain, we laughed through it, turning my head to stick my nose into the dust of the carpet to muffle my own inane giggling as I brought my knee up towards my chin, and tears dribbled around the edge of my mouth. We tasted them, curious, and found the saltiness pleasurable, like the first, tongue-clenching, moisture-eating bite of hot, crispy bacon. At that moment finding a plate of crispy bacon became my one guiding motivation in life, the thing that overwhelmed all others, and so, with a mighty heave and this light to guide me, I pulled myself up, crawling across the end of the bed and leaning against the chest of drawers while waiting for the world to decide which way down would be for the duration.

It wasn't quite my room, this place I found myself in. The inaccuracies were gentle, superficial. It was still my paint on the wall, a pale, inoffensive yellow; it was still my window with its view out onto the little parade of shops on the other side of the road, unmistakable: the newsagent, the off-licence, the cobbler and all-round domestic supplier, the launderette, and, red lantern still burning cheerfully in the window, Mrs Lee Po's famous Chinese takeaway. My window, my view; not my room. The bed was new, an ugly, polished thing trying to pretend to be part of a medieval bridal chamber for a princess in a pointy hat. The mattress, when I sat on it, was so hard I ached within a minute from being in contact with it; on the wall hung a huge, gold-framed mirror in which I could picture Marie Antoinette having her curls perfected; in the corner there were two wardrobes, not one. I waddled across to them, and leant against the nearest to recover my breath from the epic distance covered. Seeing by the light seeping under the door, and the neon glow from outside, I opened the first one and surveyed jackets of rough tweed, long dresses in silk, white and cream-coloured shirts distinctively tailored, pointed black leather shoes, high-heeled sandals composed almost entirely of straps and no real protective substance, and a handbag the size of a feather pillow, suspended with a heavy, thick gold chain. I opened the handbag and rifled through the contents. A purse, containing £50, which I took, a couple of credit cards, a library membership to the local Dulwich Portakabin, and a small but orderly handful of thick white business cards. I pulled one out and in the dull light read the name – "Laura Linbard, Business Associate, KSP". I put it on the bed and opened the other wardrobe.

This one contained trousers, shirts, jackets and, to my surprise, a large pair of thick yellow fisherman's oils and sailing boots. There was a small, important-looking box at the bottom of the wardrobe. I opened it and found a stethoscope, a small first-aid kit, a thermometer and several special and painful-looking metal tools whose nature I dared not speculate on. I pulled a white cotton shirt off its hanger and a pair of grey trousers. In a drawer I found underpants which didn't quite fit comfortably, and a pair of thick black socks. Dressing, I felt cautiously around my left shoulder and ribcage, probing for damage, and finding that every bone was properly set, every inch of skin correctly healed, not even a scar, not a trace of dry blood.

The shirt cuff reached roughly to the point where my thumb joint aligned with the rest of my hand; the trousers dangled around the balls of my feet. The socks fitted perfectly, as always seems the way. The shoes were several sizes too small; that perplexed me. How is it possible for someone to have such long arms and legs, and yet wear shoes for feet that you'd think would have to have been bound? Feeling I might regret it later, I left the shoes.

I put the business card and the £50 in my trouser pockets and headed for the door. On the way out, we caught sight of our reflection in the big mirror and stopped, stared, fascinated. Was this now us? Dark brown hair heading for the disreputable side of uncared for – not long enough to be a bohemian statement, not short enough to be stylish. Pale face that freckled in the sun, slightly over-large nose for the compact features that surrounded it, head plonked as if by accident on top of a body made all the more sticklike by the ridiculous oversized clothes it wore. It was not the flesh we would have chosen, but I had long since given up dreams of resembling anyone from the movies and, with the pragmatism of the perfectly average, come to realise that this was me and that was fine.

And this was me, looking back out of the mirror.

Not quite me.

I leant in, turning my head this way and that, running my fingers through my hair – greasy and unwashed – in search of blood, bumps, splits. Turning my face this way and that, searching for bruises and scars. An almost perfect wakening, but there was still something wrong with this picture.

I leant right in close until my breath condensed in a little grey puff on the glass, and stared deep into my own eyes. As a teenager it had bothered me how round my eyes had been, somehow always imagining that small eyes = great intelligence, until one day at school the thirteen-year-old Max Borton had pointed out that round dark eyes were a great way to get the girls. I blinked and the reflection in the mirror blinked back, the bright irises reflecting cat-like the orange glow of the washed-out street lamps. My eyes, which, when I had last had cause to look at them, had been brown. Now they were the pale, brilliant albino blue of the cloudless winter sky, and I was no longer the only creature that watched from behind their lens.

runrunrunrunrunrunRUNRUNRUNRUNRUNRUNRUNRUN!

I put my head against the cold glass of the mirror, fighting the sudden terror that threatened to knock us back to the floor. The trick was to keep breathing, to keep moving. Nothing else mattered. Run long and hard enough, and perhaps while you're running you might actually come up with a plan. But nothing mattered if you were already dead.

My legs thought better than my brain, walked me out of the room. My fingers eased back the door and I blinked in the shocking light of the hundred-watt bulb in the corridor outside. The carpet here was thick and new, the banisters polished, but it was a painting on the wall, a print of a Picasso I'd picked up for a fiver – too many years ago – all colour and strange, scattered proportions – which stole our attention. It still hung exactly where I'd left it. I felt almost offended. We were fascinated: an explosion of visual wonder right there for the same price as a cheap Thai meal, in full glory. Was everything like this? I found it hard to remember. I licked my lips and tasted blood, dry and old. Thoughts and memories were still too tangled to make clear sense of them. All that mattered was moving, staying alive long enough to get a plan together, find some answers.

From downstairs I heard laughter, voices, the chink of glasses, and a door being opened. Footsteps on the tiles that led from living room to kitchen, a *clink* where they still hadn't cemented in the loose white one in the centre of the diamond pattern; the sound of plates; the roar of the oven fan as it pumped out hot air.

I started walking down. The voices grew louder, a sound of polite gossipy chit-chat, dominated by one woman with a penetrating voice and a laugh that started at the back of her nose before travelling down to the lungs and back up again, and who I instinctively disliked. I glanced down the corridor to the kitchen and saw a man's back turned to me, bent over something that steamed and smelt of pie. The urge to eat anything, everything, briefly drowned out the taste of blood in my mouth. Like a bewildered ghost who can't understand that it has died, I walked past the kitchen and pushed at the half-open door to the living room.

There were three of them, with a fourth place set for the absent cook, drinking wine over the remnants of a salad, around a table whose top was made of frosted glass. As I came in, nobody seemed to notice me, all attention on the one woman there with the tone and look of someone in the middle of a witty address. But when she turned in my direction with "George, the pie!" already half-escaped from her lips, the sound of her dropped wineglass shattering on the table quickly redirected the others' attention.

They stared at me, I stared at them. There was an embarrassed silence that only the English can do so well, and that probably lasted less than a second, but felt like a dozen ticks of the clock. Then, as she had to, as things probably must be, one of the women screamed.

The sound sent a shudder down my spine, smashed through the horror and incomprehension in my brain, and at last let me understand, let me finally realise that this was no longer my house, that I had been gone too long, and that to these people I was the intruder, they the rightful owners. The scream slammed into my brain like a train hitting the buffers and tore a path through my consciousness that let everything else begin to flood in: the true realisation that if my house was not mine, my job, my friends, my old life would not be mine, nor my possessions, my money, my debts, my clothes, my shoes, my films, my music; all gone in a second, things I had owned since a scrawny teenager, the electric toothbrush my father had given me in a fit of concern for my health, the photos of my friends and the places I'd been, the copy of *Calvin and Hobbes* my first girlfriend had given me as a sign of enduring friendship the Christmas after we'd split up, my favourite pair of slippers, the holiday I was planning to the mountains of northern Spain, all, everything I had worked for, everything I had owned and wanted to achieve, vanished in that scream.

I ran. We didn't run from the sound, that wasn't what frightened us. I ran to become lost, and wished I had never woken in the first place, but stayed drifting in the blue.

Once upon a time, a not-so-long time ago, I had sat with my mad old gran on a bench beside a patch of cigarette-butt grass that the local council had designated "community green area", watching the distant flashes of the planes overhead, and the turning of the orange-stained clouds across a sullen yellow moon. She'd worn a duffel coat, a faded blue nightdress and big pink slippers. I'd worn my school uniform and my dad's big blue jacket, that Mum had unearthed one day from a cardboard box and had been about to burn. I'd cried, an eleven-year-old kid not sure why I cared, until she'd saved it for me.

We'd sat together, my gran and me, and the pigeons had clustered in the gutters and on the walls, hopped around my gran's slippered feet, wobbled on half a torn-off leg, flapped with broken, torn-feathered wings, peered with round orange unblinking eyes, like glass sockets in their tiny heads, unafraid. I had maths homework which I had no intention of doing, and a belly full of frozen peas and tomato ketchup. Winter was coming, but tonight the air was a clean, dry cold, sharp, not heavy, and the lights were on in all the houses of the estate. I was a secret spy, a boy sitting in the darkness of the bench, watching Mr Paswalah in number 27 ironing his shirts, Jessica and Al in number 32 rowing over the cleaning, old Mrs Gregory in 21 flicking through 300 TV channels in search of something loud and violent that when her husband had been alive she had felt too ashamed to watch, it not being correct for a lady raised in the 1940s to enjoy the *Die Hard* films.

So I sat, my gran by my side, as we sat many nights on this bench; just her, me, the pigeons and our stolen world of secret windows.

My gran was silent a long while. Sitting here on this bench, with the pigeons, was almost the only time she seemed content. Then she turned to me, looked me straight in the eye and said, "Boy?"

"Yes, Gran?" I mumbled.

Her lips were folded in over her bright pink gums, her false teeth inside the house beside her little single bed. She chewed on the inward turn of them a long while, head turning to the sky, then back to the ground, and then slowly round to me. "You sing beautiful in the choir, boy?"

"Yes, Gran," I lied. I may have cried to save my father's coat, but I had enough teenage self-respect to not be caught dead singing in the school choir.

"Boy?"

"Yes, Gran?"

"You cheat at tests?"

"Yes, Gran."

"I told 'em, I told 'em, but the old ladies all said . . . Angelina has a problem with her left ear, you know? You cheat at tests, boy?"

"No, Gran."

"Always gotta keep your pencils sharp before the ink runs dry!"

"Yes, Gran."

Silence a long, long while. I remember staring at my gran's legs, where they stuck out beneath the nightdress. They were grey, riddled with bright blue veins, large and splayed, like some sort of squashed rotting cheese grown from the mould inside a pair of slippers.

"Boy?" she said at last.

"Yes, Gran?"

"The shadow's coming, boy," she sighed, fumbling at her jacket pockets for a tissue to wipe her running nose. "The shadow's coming. Not here yet. Not for a while. But it's coming. It's going to eat you up, boy."

"Yes, Gran."

She hit me around the ear then, a quick slap like being hit with a thin slice of uncooked meat. "You listen!" she snapped. "The pigeons seen it! They seen it all! The shadow's coming. Young people never listen. He's coming for you, boy. Not yet, not yet . . . you'll have to sing like the angels to keep him away."

"Yes, Gran."

I looked into her fading, thick-covered eyes then, and saw, to my surprise, that tears were building up in them. I took her hand in sudden, real concern, and said, "Gran? You all right?"

"I ain't mad," she mumbled, wiping her nose and eyes on a great length of snot-stained sleeve. "I ain't crazy. They seen it coming. The pigeons know best. They seen it coming." Then she grinned, all gum spiked with the tiny remains of hanging flesh where teeth had once been. She stood up, wobbling on her feet a moment, the pigeons scattering from around her. She pulled me up, my hands in hers, and started to dance, pushing me ungainly back and forth as, with the grace and ease of a drunken camel, we waltzed beneath the sodium light of the city. All the time she sang in a little tuneless, weedy voice, "We be light, we be life, we be fire, te-dum, te-dum! We sing electric flame te-dum, we rumble underground wind te-dum, we dance heaven! Come be we and be free . . ."

Then she stopped, so suddenly that I bounced into her, sinking into the great roll of her curved shoulders. "Too early to sing," she sighed, staring into my eyes. "You ain't ready yet, boy. Not yet. A while. Then you'll sing like an angel. The pigeons don't have the brains to lie."

And then she kept right on dancing, a hunched singing sprite in the night, until Mum called us in for bed.

Looking back, I realise now that the problem wasn't that my gran knew more than she was saying. The truth of the matter was, she said exactly and honestly what it was she knew, and I just didn't have the brains to see it.

I stopped running when my feet began to bleed. I didn't know where I was, nor what route I'd taken to get there. I knew only what I saw: the edge of a common or a small public park, a dark night in what felt like early spring or late autumn. Leaves falling from the giant plane trees round the edge of the green – autumn, then. It was drizzling, that strange London drizzle that is at once cold and wet, yet somehow imperceptible against the background of the pink-orange street lights, more of a heavy fog drifting through the air than an actual rain. I couldn't think in coherent words; it was too early for that. Instead, as my brain registered all my losses, panic immersed it like the splashing of a hot shower, preventing any reasoning of where I might go next or what I might do.

I found a dim, neon-lit passage leading under a railway line, that no beggar or homeless wanderer had colonised for that night, and sank down against the cold, dry paving with my knees against my chin. For a long while I did no more, but shivered and cowered and tried to seize control of my own thoughts. The taste of blood in my mouth was maddening, like the lingering dryness of cough medicine that couldn't be washed away. I played again the bright blue eyes of a stranger reflected in my reflection, tried to put those eyes in my face. The memories didn't bring physical pain; the mind is good at forgetting what it doesn't want to recall. But each thought brought with it the fear of pain, a recollection of things that had been and which I would move to some uninhabited rock away from all sodium lamps and men to escape again.

For a brief moment, I contemplated this idea, telling myself that the loss of everything was in fact a liberation in disguise. What would the Buddha do? Walk barefoot through the mud of an unploughed field and rejoice at rebirth, probably. I thought of worms between my toes, fat wriggling pink-grey bodies, cold as the rain that fed them, and we changed our mind. We would run; but not so far.

Instinctively, as it had always been when afraid, I let my senses drift. It was an automatic reflex, imparted as almost the first lesson of my training, the first time my teacher had...

...my teacher had...

Give me life!

...a shadow is coming...

runrunrunrunrunRUNRUNRUNRUNRUNRUNRUNRUNRUN

Breathing was strength, the wall was safety. I pressed my spine into it, my head against it. Fingers would not grow out of the wall, claws would not sprout from the shadows. The more of me was in contact with something solid, the fewer places there were for the darkness to crawl, the better it would be. I imagined a great barking dog, all teeth and slobber, squatting by my side to keep me safe, a loyal pet to stand guard when I grew too tired. There were things which could be done, almost as good as a guard dog; but I didn't know if they would attract too much attention.

And so, again, as my breathing slowed, my senses wandered, gathering information. Smell of electricity from the railway overhead, of urine being washed away by the rain, of spilt beer and dry mortar dust. Sound of the distant clatter of a late-night commuter train, carrying sleepy one-a-row passengers to the suburbs and beyond. A bus splashing through a puddle swollen around a blocked drain, somewhere in the distance. A door slamming in the night. The distant wail of a police siren. As a child, the sound of sirens had comforted me. I had thought of them as proof that we were being protected, by guardians all in blue out to keep us safe from the night. I had never made the connection between protection and something we had to be protected *from*. Now the sirens sang again, and I wondered if they sang for me.

My clothes were too thin for the night. The drizzle made them soggy, clinging, itchy and cold to my skin. I could feel damp goose bumps up the length of my arms. We were fascinated by them, rolling up our sleeve to stare at the distortion of our flesh, and the little hairs standing to attention as if they were stiff with static. Even the cold interested us, how disproportionate it made our senses, our freezing feet too large for the space they inhabited, our numbed fingers huge pumpkin splatters across our thoughts; and it occurred to us that the human body was a very unreliable tool indeed.

Crispy bacon.

The smell of pie.

Taste of blood.

Memories of . . .

. . . *of* . . .

Half-close your eyes and it'll be there, all yellow teeth and blue eyes, looking down at you; press your eyes shut all the way and the blood will roll once again over your skin, pool and crackle across your back and sides, tickle against the sole of your foot, thicken in the lining of your socks.

You really want to remember all that?

Didn't think so.

Don't close your eyes.

I rolled my sleeve back down, tucked my chin deeper into my knees, wrapped my hands around myself, folded my feet one on top of the other.

There were other senses waiting to report in.

A little look, a quick gander, where was the harm? No one would ever know; breathe it in and maybe it will be all right, despite the shadows?

I inhaled, let the air of the place wash deep into my lungs, play its revelations through my blood and brain. Here it comes . . .

The feel of that place where I huddled like a child had a sharp, biting quality, thin on the ground, not so heavy as in other places where life moves more often and more densely, but carrying traces of other areas drifting in the air, snatched across the city in tendrils that clung to the commuter trains rattling overhead. What power and texture I could feel had a strong smell, but a slippery touch, retreating from too firm a command like a frightened bird. It gave me comfort, and a little warmth.

I pulled myself up and looked at the white-painted walls, examining the graffiti on them. Most of it was the usual stuff – "J IS GAY!" or "P & N FOR EVER" – but there was across one wall an orange swish of paint, all loops and sudden turns, that I recognised. It felt warm when I pressed my fingers to it, and tingled to the touch like slow-moving sand. A beggar's mark, delineating the edge of a clan's territory. It was good to find my senses still sensitive to such things – or even, I had to wonder, more sensitive than they'd been before? Though we could see the advantages, the thought did not comfort me.

I staggered down the tunnel, examining now in careful detail each splash of paint and scratch across the whitewashed walls. Messages like:

DON'T LET THE SYSTEM GET YOU DOWN

or:

⊠⊠ULTRAS⊠⊠

or:

Don't lick the brushes

melted into each other over the cemented, painted surface of the bricks.

One splash of paint at the far end of the tunnel caught my attention, and held it. It had none of the usual trappings of protection that most who understood such things used to defend their territory, but was written in crude capital letters across the wall in simple black spray-paint. It said: "MAK ME SHADOW ON DA WAL".

It made me uneasy, but other things that evening were taking priority on my list of concerns, so I ignored it. I had no paint, but dribbled my fingers in the sharp sense of that place and, in the middle of the tunnel, started to draw my own mark on the wall, feeling even that slight movement give me comfort as I made the long shape of the protection symbol, my own ward against evil and harm. Not quite a guard dog; but close enough.

When I had finished, my head ached, and my fingers shook. Even something so small took too much out of me, the last vestige of strength left in my limbs. A warmth inside me suggested a hollowness that time, perhaps, might repair, and the weakness was not so much one of exhaustion, but of inexperience, as if every finger was freshly grown, the muscle untested, not yet conditioned to its former use. I slumped against the opposite wall and waited.

It took only a few seconds before the shape I'd drawn started to burn and hiss on the wall, its lines emerging in thin black swirls. I slid back onto the paving stones, tucked my knees up to my chin and shivered. The white strip lights overhead buzzed quietly; I could taste the electricity in them. Lesson one for anyone in my profession was always about electricity.

I took a risk, and with the tips of my fingers snatched a little warmth and light out of one of them, which died into darkness as I drew its energy to myself. The pea-sized ball of light and heat I managed to drag from it was like a match held between two fingers – shockingly hot when I brought my skin close to it, but not enough on which to sustain life. Uncertain which was likely to cause more pain, the cold or the failure of my own strength, I risked pulling down more light, and a few degrees more heat, caressing it into the sphere between my fingers, until almost all the lights overhead were extinguished, leaving just one at either end of the tunnel. The effort left me in a cold sweat, breathless and with a nasty case of tinnitus, but it also left me clutching a fat bubble of white light the size of a small, immaterial football. I lay down and curled myself around it like it was a bag of pure gold, feeling it warm me through and drive some of the wetness out of my clothes, and closed my eyes.

We did not want to sleep – our thoughts raced, our senses strayed out as far as we could reach, into the scuttling of a rat's claws under the street, the snuffling nose of a ragged-tailed urban fox, while we tried to pick out every shape and sense of life around us. But I was tired – too tired – and regardless of what we wanted, I had to sleep. I felt my eyes sink like an executioner's blade.

Taste of blood.

Yellow teeth and watery, weak blue eyes.

Give me life give me life give me life give me life GIVE ME . . .

Not quite sleep.

Distant siren, distant cars. Someone was out tonight looking for someone else; crawling through the gutters, talking to the pigeons, stealing the nose of the orange fox seeking its hamburger supper.

We did not enjoy sleep. Our dreams were mixed in with our reality, the world seen through a haze of blue. I had always loved nights like this, when the rain bubbled in the gutter. It gave everything a clean, clear quality, and allowed the mind to roam far and easily without becoming obstructed by the haze of crowded life and busy sense that too often obscures the wandering vision. Thoughts without words.

I couldn't have slept for more than a few hours. When I woke, the warmth in my hands had slipped away back into the lights, which glowed with their earlier harsh whiteness. On the edge of my senses I was distracted by a faint *drip drip drip drip*.

At one end of the tunnel, the beggars' orange-painted mark was running down the wall in trickles, like blood from a nosebleed. It caught on a chip in the wall, pooled, then overflowed, dripping with a tiny, regular rhythm into a sad stain on the ground. I looked over at my own protective mark, the swirl of burnt paint at the other end of the tunnel, and saw that it too was starting to wobble round the edges, the lines of its power shimmering as if caught in a heat haze, the very bottom of the sign starting to liquefy.

I pulled myself up onto my feet, which immediately reported that they wanted nothing to do with the rest of me, and throbbed with a dull ache to prove the point. Blood and dirt had mixed into a dull brown stain. Hobbling to the end of the tunnel, I looked out into the dark. It was still night, or at least that dead time of morning before the dwindling gloom can muster any outline on the horizon. The rain was giving its all, pocking the ground with tiny silver craters, and turning the pavement into a reflective sheen of ebony blackness, pink-orange neon and flashing puddles.

I let my senses wander, and felt uneasy, a shuddering across my skin more than just the cold. There was a smell cutting through the rain, a blunt assault on the senses, a taste as much as a stench, that forced itself to the back of the nose and activated every receptor at once so that the brain was overwhelmed with so much information it couldn't even begin to decipher the component parts of the smell to say that this is orange peel and that wet cardboard. It was the smell of warm, wet rubbish, left to rot and moulder in interesting ways in a tight, dark, compressed area, before being let out into the air. And it was getting stronger.

I listened for dustbin trucks, scavengers and thieves.

Nothing.

Just the slow hiss of melting paint and the pattering of the rain.

I am not given to paranoia, but recent experience had altered my perspective. It seemed unlikely that paint could melt and the air smell of litter – no, of something *more* than litter, a bite sharper than disgust – without there being some direct and unpleasant connection. I turned away from the stench and started walking as quickly as my battered feet would allow me, down the tunnel and out into the rain, letting it wash over me and enjoying the shock as it ran into my eyes and washed out the sleep; even as the rest of my senses came up to scratch and reported.....

. . . the smell of rubbish . . .

. . . taste of mould . . .

. . . touch of rain . . .

. . . empty street of strange shadows . . .

. . . sound of footsteps . . .

. . . edge of dry, hot ozone, getting closer, getting stronger . . .

I started jogging, uncomfortably, each landing on the soles of my feet a reminder that the human form actually weighed a lot, and that this burden was supported by a very small area relative to the mass. What a ridiculous form our flesh took, we decided. What a ridiculous species to have conquered the world.

There was a sound in the road behind me like newspaper blowing across sand. I broke into a run, suddenly not caring about the pain, but overwhelmed by a desire to be somewhere else, fast. The noise behind me grew louder, and so did the smell, and with it came a strange, low rumble, like the engine of a very old diesel car just before it explodes in a cloud of steam.

I saw an alley between two houses, full of dirty rubbish bags and oily puddles, and turned into it, racing for the wall at the end. Somehow being hemmed in comforted me – I had no way out, but whatever was behind me had only one way in, and I could face it properly, my back safe from claws and yellow teeth. I reached the wall at the far end and turned, pressing against a high wooden gate that presumably led into someone's back garden. I stretched my fingers out on either side of me, braced myself against the reassurance of a solid surface behind and started dragging power to me. It was slow, too slow, too long since I had last tried this – I hadn't had need for so many years! Still I pulled, thickening the air with it until the walls either side seemed to ripple with the pressure I was building up, cocooning myself inside a wall of force, ready to throw it at anyone or anything that might be looking for me. No such thing as coincidence. Not tonight.

At the end of the alley, nothing. I strained and heard a faint *cling cling*, and then a noise like the slurping of thick cake mixture being slopped up from the bottom of the bowl. Then that too stopped, and there was only my breathing, and the madman's certain feeling of being watched.

I didn't move. If it was going to come down to a battle of wills between me and whatever was out there, I was more than prepared to stay exactly like this, at the end of the alley until dawn or dusk, rather than expose myself to an unknown danger.

My head snapped up as a pair of pigeons exploded up from a nearby roof gutter. For a moment I considered borrowing their eyes and looking down on the world, but decided against it. Staying upright was demanding enough; multitasking was out of the question.

I waited.

It could have been a minute, it could have been ten; I didn't know, didn't care, and the adrenalin in my system wasn't about to let me judge.

I heard a can rattling on the alley floor. I looked across at the bin bags thrown against a wall. One of them was split, and its contents had poured out, into the stagnant puddle I'd waded through to reach the safety of the rear wall. Lank, torn crisp packets and broken banana skins floated in it; dead tissues, toilet-roll tubes, cardboard boxes for ready-cook meals, stained kitchen cloths, the broken handle of a cup, ripped foil, scrunched cling film, compressed orange-juice cartons and bent pints of semi-skimmed milk, all had spilt out of the bag, and all were, very gently, and without any explanation, starting to shake like popcorn in the pan.

The small, pale finger of dread levelled its tip in my direction and offered a suggestion. I knew what this was. It had been too easy.

Old plastic bags, torn-up junk mail, broken CD cases, they bounced through the tear in the bag, ripping it further, to let more rubbish spill out. They shook on the floor of the alley, and then, the lightest first, shopping bags caught in the breeze, remnants of ham packages, the sleeve that had held some piece of cheese, started to rise, straight upwards as if gravity were just some passing fad. Then the heavier pieces of rubbish – the cardboard box that had held a new portable radio, the remnants of a half-gutted lemon, a pile of orange peel that unwound upwards like a stretching snake in one unbroken piece. I watched them drift up from the torn rubbish bag in a slow, leisurely fashion, sheets of cling film each unscrunching and spreading as they ascended, bread sacks inflating like hot-air balloons and rising, bottom down, nothing rushed, nothing dramatic, all to a gentle hissing and rustling of old litter.

They rose towards a single spot, a shadow on the edge of one of the houses, clinging to the corner where wall met drainpipe, and as it all rose, it seemed to mingle with the shadow's form, a crisp packet reflecting with silver foil off what might have been an arm, a sliver of cardboard coating what could perhaps be described as a belly. It looked like some sort of organic gargoyle, dripping strange thick liquid waste from one of its clinging limbs, still, patient, lumpen.

Then it turned its head, and its eyes glowed with the dying embers of two cigarette stubs. When it exhaled, its nose, the broken end of a car exhaust pipe, gouted smoke; when it raised one arm off the wall it clung to, its paw came away with the suction sound of well-chewed gum sticking, and its claws gleamed with the shattered razor-edges of old Coke cans and soup tins. Its thighs were composed of old hosepipe left in the street by some builders after a water-main repair job, its middle was covered over with old pieces of tin and card, bent traffic signs and abandoned boxes, to create an armoured underbelly beneath its hulked form, under which I could smell, and through cracks between its surface skin, see, a squelching heart of dead fruit, apple cores, chips, half-eaten hamburgers and abandoned Chinese takeaway, all crunched together into a brown mass beneath its surface armour, like a belly without the skin. Its teeth, when it opened its mouth, were reflective green glass from a broken bottle, its face was covered over with old newsprint and abandoned magazines, its arms shone with the reflective coat of foil, its wings were two translucent thin spreads of cling film that rose up behind it with a thin, sharp snap across the air, the joins woven together with fuse wire spun like tendons throughout its body. As it clung with its gummed paws to the wall of the house above me, the rubbish from the split bag settled into its flesh, spread itself across its arched back, wrapped itself around the backward-jointed bend of its knee. If it had been a living creature, I would have said it resembled a giant hyena, larger than a man, but hunched and feral, the shape its body made was arched and ready for a strike. But since it was not living, and its very breath was hot with the power that sustained it, I took it for what it was: a litterbug.

It had all been too easy.

I should have guessed that something like this would have to happen sooner or later. I'd just been counting a little too optimistically on later.

It stretched its jaw of green glass and rotting sandpaper tongue wide and hissed a tumbling gout of black exhaust into the air. The last broken plastic straw and burnt-out light bulb drifted up from the alley floor, settling into the litterbug's flesh, making it bigger, stronger. I saw its back arch, cling-film wings shimmering with the rainwater running across their surface, as with the hiss of a dying carburettor it stretched its razor-tin claws for my face, opened its mouth to emit a gout of fumes, kicked off with its back legs and tried to take my head off.

Instinct rather than conscious decision saved my life.

I let go the wall of force I had been building. It slammed into the litterbug mid-leap, propelled it backwards, threw it up against the wall, sending an explosion of dirty newspaper and mouldy organic spatter out from its flesh, and dropped it into the alley in a pile of torn foil and cling film. I had no interest in seeing whether this was going to stop it, I was pretty sure that it wouldn't, so without further ado I turned, slammed my shoulder into the high wooden gate until the lock tore away from the door, and ran into the garden beyond. Behind me, the litterbug pulled itself onto its hind legs, the torn remnants of its skin flowing back into its flesh, and advanced after me, snorting loudly through its rusting nose.

I ran across the soggy garden lawn, climbed over the back wall without looking back and slipped down the long drop to the railway line below on my backside, which, compared to my feet, had had an easy time so far. Bracken and broken shopping trolleys, which always seemed to find their way into railway cuttings, tore at my skin and clothes; nettles stung me, and a family of rats scuttled for cover in the destructive wake of my passage. I hit the hard ballast of the railway line with a bang and sprawled across it, catching myself on one of the railway tracks, smooth and silver on the top surface, rusted thick brown on the sides. Getting back on my feet was perhaps worse than the descent down the embankment: every muscle screamed indignation, every inch of skin featured a cut or a bruise or a stung bubble of inflamed flesh. I hobbled along the side of the railway track in that dry muddy space where ballast met slope, not caring where I was going, so long as it was somewhere else. Litterbugs did not just randomly stalk the streets of Dulwich; they had purpose, direction, intent, and it didn't take any thought to know that tonight, it wanted us. Behind me, I could hear the low wailing hunting-cry of the creature, a sound like the shriek of ancient bus brakes. I didn't have the courage to look back, but kept on hobbling along the railway line.

It was hard to say how far I went. I stopped only when I reached a station: North Dulwich. It was locked, the lights on its high yellow-brick walls casting odd shadows. I crawled onto the platform close by the safety of its heavy doors, and didn't care that the CCTV camera was watching. I lay down on my back and shook and felt in pain and generally sorry for myself.

When I had my breathing under control and some of the fire in my skin had died down to just a dull ache, we cast our awareness into every inch of ourself, feeling the shape and pressure of every cut and bruise. We were oddly fascinated by it, by the reality of it, even though we were surprised and appalled at the indignity of pain. We lay, and felt the cold rough surface of the concrete beneath us, and the cold rain drying on our face in the breeze that drifted along the railway track. For a moment, the overwhelming torrent of sense from every inch of our body, from every nerve in our skin, the coldness of the rain, the hotness of our muscles, the dryness of our tongue, the wetness of our hair, the gentle bleeding of our scratches and the tightness in our bruising, was fascinating, real, alive. For a moment, we wanted to laugh, although I wasn't sure if it mightn't be wiser to cry.

Then I smelt the rubbish.

Getting up on my feet was a triumphant act of will – staggering to the closed exit a shocking realisation of weakness, leaning against it a second of reprieve. I whispered imploring words to the lock and caressed it with my fingertips until it gave up and clicked; pulled back the heavy door even as, beyond the circle of neon light on the platform, I saw the glowing reddish embers of the litterbug's eyes. It slunk out of the dark, taller than ever, its skin now glowing with pieces of broken glass snatched up from the railway embankment, mosaicked across its flesh like royal jewellery.

I staggered out of the station, and it followed. The moment of reprieve had given me time to think, remember; I knew what I needed. It didn't take me long to find it as I ran through the tight uphill streets. The first was the lid of a black dustbin, painted with "Flat 5" in yellow letters. The second was a bank of green wheelie bins, left by the local council outside a chemist on a small shopping parade, and thank all the powers in the heavens, they weren't too full. The litterbug was not far behind me, but it was too big to run as fast as the fear could carry us; not that it would give up for such a simple reason.

I opened all the lids on the wheelie bins, checking that there weren't any containing split rubbish bags – and tonight my luck held: every bin looked clean. I held the black dustbin lid I had taken from Flat 5 like a shield, pushing my right hand as far as I could through its handle, until it rested just above my wrist, wedged onto my arm. But by the time I was ready the creature was in sight, padding up the middle of the road and wading through the rainwater that poured downhill, with the slow, laborious and inevitable purpose of a sidewinder crossing the desert.

Here, the rain pouring off my face and seeping into my clothes, and, I hoped, washing some of the stench away, I turned and faced the monster.

We regarded its approach curiously, watching the care with which it advanced towards us, and with what single-minded purpose. It seemed almost a pity to destroy it, since we could probably have learned a lot from its structure, its form of life, but the preservation of ourself took priority.

As it came on, I stood my ground, hefting my dustbin lid in front of me, waiting. It advanced more cautiously than I expected, and before reaching me it stopped, raised its snout and emitted a strange shriek, like the scrape of old tyres skidding on a wet road. It did this three times and then sunk onto all fours, eyeing me up with its unblinking red embers. I felt that if I blinked it would pounce, and was immediately aware of my own eyes and the need to blink, as if, by thinking about it, the unconscious part of me that controlled this action could no longer function, and every blink and every breath had to be a deliberate, demanding thought-process. Still the monster didn't attack, and it took me too long – embarrassingly so – to work out why. The shrill call wasn't a challenge or an expression of pain – it was a call for reinforcements.

So much for this.

I looked around the street for a source of heat and found a fragment clinging to the wet surface of the chemist's bright green and white shop sign. Raising my left hand, I dragged it into my fingertips, crunching it down into a small penny shape between my fingers. The light, sucked dry of its energy, flickered and whined in indignation. I turned to the litterbug. It sensed my intentions, shifted uneasily, rose up a little, flexing the metal shards of one of its paws and emitting puffs of smoke. I pinched the penny of heat between my thumb and forefinger, and it winked out. For a second, nothing happened. Then the cigarette embers in the creature's eyes glowed brighter, burnt yellow, and exploded into flame. The spitting fire caught the newspaper of its head and burrowed into the soggy mass, sparks digging down through its skull to the dry ash and paper that formed the bulk of its long, snoutish head.

It screamed with the sound of a thousand screeching brakes as flames burst up through the mesh of wire and old laundry line that had spun a frame around its head, gouts leaping out through its nose, mouth, eyes and ears, spreading down the dry rope of its spine and melting the thin fuse wire of its wings, turning their cling-film sheen black and liquid, dripping hot plastic onto the ground. The flames burst out between the metal plates of its belly, glowed red-hot in the joints at its knees and elbows, spat out angry sparks between its clawlike fingers, made the chewing-gum pads of its paws dribble and smoke with a sickly smell, sent gouts of steam exploding off its surface—

But didn't kill it.

Instead, with a furious roar, it drew itself back on its hind legs, tensed its blazing back, and sprang.

I dropped onto one knee as it leapt, raising the dustbin lid up over my head to protect myself, and braced for the impact. Its bulk blocked out the light; its smell made my eyes run, twisted a knot in my stomach and sent a shudder through my belly. When it hit, it was like bricks falling in an earthquake. I tucked my chin into my chest, hunched my shoulders towards my stomach and put my arms, with the bin lid across them, over my head. Around me, rubbish showered down, and a thin gout of smoke stretched into the darkness. I heard a low moaning sound and peeked up from under my makeshift shield. The litterbug lay on one side, half an arm missing and a small hole gouged in the side of its chest. Around it litter drifted, displaced by the impact with my shield. I staggered upright, head spinning from the shock, and raised the dustbin lid against it. It rolled over and stood, moving awkwardly, its mass now off balance, belched smoke and ash, and threw itself at me. This time I raised the shield high over my head and willed what was left of my strength into it, until the plastic burnt against my skin. As the litterbug drew up to its full height, towering overhead, almost as high as the upper windows of the houses around us, I shoved the bin lid up towards it.

It roared with the blare of a hundred car horns, and smashed one claw down towards the bin lid with the weight of a wrecking ball. The force of the collision nearly knocked me off my feet. Around my shield a shower of bright orange sparks flew out in an umbrella shape, and litter rained down. The monster reared back in agony, clinging to the remnants of its shattered paw. As it did, distracted by whatever it was that counted for pain in such a creature, I threw my shield aside and leapt at it. I punched through a piece of cardboard that made up its loose underbelly, into the sticky, hot, rotten mass of its chest, while it flailed at me with shattered, stumpy arms. Fire snapped at my sleeve as I drove my arm into its middle, up to the shoulder; jagged metal parts, that seemed to float inside the foul core of mouldering food and other remains, slashed at my skin. My fingers closed over something small, that felt frozen, at the exact same moment that the litterbug, swaying precariously, wobbled onto one foot and with the other delivered a clawed kick that threw me backwards across the pavement, spraying organic spattered remains and soggy cardboard as I went.

The litterbug stood, its insides dripping, its head steaming as the rainwater competed with the smouldering flames of its eyes, and looked confused. Its gaze settled on my hands, where, with the creature's slime dripping off it in a thick black sludge, I held a single scrunched-up ball of paper, ice-cold to the touch. I unfolded it. Underneath the scrawl of symbols, summonings and incantations drawn in black felt-tip pen, I saw the words:

...local borough initiative...

...recycling boxes provided...

...collection **Monday, Thursday**...

...glass, tin, paper and all organic...

...making a **BETTER** *environment...*

...for the people of...

The ink started to run in the rain. The litterbug screeched, with its strange, mechanical, metal voice. I crawled onto my feet. My eyes fell on the open, waiting wheelie bins. So did the monster's. It started to run, ready to throw itself into my path. I began to run too, slipping onto the pavement and reaching out for the bins, the icy piece of paper growing soggy in my fingers. Just as I reached the nearest bin, the litterbug reached out to slam its lid, and I was suddenly trapped between the bin and the monster's on-coming burning bulk. I closed my eyes instinctively, ready for the life to be crushed out of me, and dropped the piece of paper into the bin.

There was a bang, and I felt a sudden warm, enveloping sensation. I heard the sound of the rain, and a rustle of falling paper, felt the gentle passage of sticky rotting goo run down the back of my legs and the tickling brush of old newsprint and bits of plastic floating down around me as, without a sound, the litterbug collapsed. Its cardboard skin slid off its rotting flesh with a great wet splat, its wings drifted like angels' feathers to the floor, bits of hosepipe slid out of its mass like the splattering of intestines falling from a gutted fish. The embers in its eyes went out, the cigarette butts falling with sad little *plop plops* onto the soaking ground.

I pressed myself against the wheelie bins, forgetting to breathe as the drifts of rubbish settled around me. A few loose plastic bags caught in the wind and floated down the street. A ball of compressed newspaper rolled into the gutter and got stuck between the bars of a drain. A few embers were burning out in a puddle, a crunched Coke can bounced loudly against the wall. I opened the wheelie bin's lid an inch and peered inside. The inscribings on the piece of paper, the symbols of invocation and command that were the core of any construct and the heart of the creature, were gently burning themselves into ash inside the bin, powerless and contained.

I dropped the lid and turned, rubbish shifting at knee height all around me. Back down the hill, a few hundred yards away, a car was parked directly across the middle of the street. It hadn't been there before. A man got out of the passenger door. Then two more climbed out of the back, and a fourth, probably a woman, it was hard to tell in the light, got out of the driver's door. They started walking towards me. Reinforcements, I guessed. They'd heard the litterbug's wail.

I leant against the wheelie bin and half-closed my eyes, struggling to retain control. We were tired, in pain, and angry. We had not come here for this; this was not how things were meant to be, the wrong kind of living. Everything, we realised, but everything, was wrong.

I was too tired to care.

We opened our eyes. The world was bright blue in our vision; electric fire.

We stepped forward through the swirling remnants of dirt and monster. We opened our arms and let the blue fire spread between our fingers. It was so good, so easy! We thrilled in it.

"Do you wish to fight us?" we yelled towards the advancing men. "Do you think you will live so long?"

They stopped, hesitated, drew back in the middle of the road, and I could have just sat down in the filth of the street, stopped, could have, but that the fire was now burning behind my eyes. Beautiful, brilliant blue fire. "Do you not relish what life you have?" we called, letting the flames burn across our skin. "Do you not live for every breath, dance every moment to the rhythm of your own heartbeat, have you not seen the fire that burns in every sight?"

We tightened our fingers, ever so slightly, pulling them into the shape of a fist. Above us, the neon lights of the street lamps exploded, the burglar alarms on the sides of the shops popped, spraying metal, the water in the gutter bubbled, twisted, turned, like it was being sucked down into a vortex. "If all you see in life is its end," we called, "then join us!"

It was so easy, now we were willing to try, the power felt so good, that brilliant, sacred word we hadn't dared to whisper since I had first reopened my eyes, the magic of the streets, *my* streets, our magic . . .

Lights started turning on; there were voices in the houses; car alarms started to wail in the street. I didn't want to be caught, I so badly didn't want that to deal with on top of everything else now, please not now. I wanted to sleep. We wanted them gone.

Neither, it seemed, were they prepared to stay. They started backing away; then turned and ran, scuttling into their car, and firing the engine. We let the power slip from our fingers, although I knew, so easily, I knew that just a thought could burst their brakes or shatter their windows or twist their pipes or burn their fuel, we knew we still had that strength inside us, so simple, so easy to just . . .

I let the power go, let the built-up magic between my fingers slip away; and it hurt. There was so much of it, just letting it go without bursting into flame made my head ache and my heart pound. Inside, I knew that we loved it. We loved that fire in our fingers, we loved that victory against the monster, we loved the rain and the rubbish and the night and the noise, and we would never, entirely, let it go.

As the first person started shouting from their window, "What the fuck is . . ."

. . . I turned, and walked away, into the night.

That was the first night.

By the end of everything, I missed the calm of those hours in Dulwich.

I had fifty stolen pounds in my pocket. I sat on a bench until dawn, a slippery grey turning from monochrome to colour crawling up from the east. I didn't have to wait long. Sleeping was out of the question; we wouldn't let our mind stop, wouldn't shut our eyes, although I so wanted to sleep.

At sunrise, I took the first bus that came along, to the first tube station I could find. The man behind the counter couldn't see my bare feet, so didn't ask; but I knew I still smelled and looked wild because even through the plastic glass that separated us, he recoiled when I approached.

He was, I now realise, the first person I had spoken to in nearly two and a half years. The daily *Metro*, newly delivered to the newspaper rack inside the station, gave me the date; the man behind the window gave me conversation.

The date should have appalled me.

But I suppose the night had brought me time to think, to reconcile myself to the worst of all possibilities, and when I read it, I was almost relieved to find it hadn't been longer since I had last held a newspaper.

The man selling tickets said, "What d'you want?"

"An Oyster card."

"You OK?"

"OK?"

"Um . . . yeah. OK?"

"I had a rough night."

"Oyster card, right?"

"With a travelcard. Monthly, zones one to six."

He named a price. I was duly appalled – two years had not been kind to inflation. But we weren't about to care about the cost of travelcards, not yet, so let it go.

"What can I get with what I've got?" I asked, pushing the fifty pounds through the copper-plated hollow between us.

He gave me a weekly travelcard, and not much change. I hoped a week would be long enough.

It would be two more hours before the shops would open. I waddled down to the platform. The escalator felt warm, the slats an unusual sensation between my toes. I curled my feet over their edge as I rode down; and then, since the feeling had seemed so strange, we rode up again, and down one more time, trailing our fingers along the polished metal surface in the middle of the escalator shaft, or leaning against the black rubber handrail as it moved at a slightly different speed from the stair itself, dragging our body faster than the stairway could carry us.

I caught the first train of the morning, almost empty, travelling north beneath the river. I went to Great Portland Street station, and walked along Marylebone Road. Even at this early hour, with the sun reflecting grey-silver-gold across the wet pavement, the road was busy, cars stopping every hundred yards to wait for that elusive green light to ripple from one end of the system to the other. On Marylebone High Street the houses were big, pale stone or red brick, with high windows and large glass doors or shopfronts on their lower floors. The street woke slowly, lorries crawling away from offloading their goods into the small supermarkets just as the one-way system started to feed its first cars of the day south, towards the West End. People avoided me as I walked by. I was a mess; but not threatening enough to justify calling the police. I radiated humility and harmlessness, a good-natured insanity, and they let me be.

I camped out on the pavement like a beggar in front of the shop I'd had in mind until it opened, and was looked at strangely by the young shop assistant – new since I'd last been here – as I wandered in.

It was a charity shop, one of the biggest of its kind. I drifted past second-hand books, old alarm clocks and newly laundered dresses in all the oddest sizes on the scale, to the shoe section. More battered and flattened creatures I had not seen; they were exactly what I wanted.

I tried on a pair of trainers, that had once been bright blue and white and were now faded blue and muddy grey. The padding still fitted snugly, but it was thin enough underfoot for me to feel the texture of whatever surface I walked on. The laces didn't match, and the trim at the back of one shoe was torn; they were perfect. Buying them, and breakfast, took the last of my change.

Breakfast was crispy bacon, egg swimming in grease, potato waffles containing mostly cardboard-tasting white powder, suspicious sausage, baked beans overboiled, and tea. It was ambrosia on our tongue, an explosion of sense and memory, a delight unlike any we had experienced before. It made me, for a moment, feel as if nothing had changed, and that all could, perhaps, be well.

Fed and finally shod, the question arose of what I should do next. We desperately wanted to go walking, to explore the city and find what two years had done to it, see how it was different in daylight, eat the food, drink the drink, revel in every street and sight like a tourist, seeing it all for the first time outside the hazy mess of my memories.

But our feet were in pain and our safety was uncertain, our clothes stank of litter and urban rain, stained a thin beige-brown. Besides, I had a long list of questions that needed to be asked, and until I knew the answers, I felt that I would not be safe.

For the sake of decency and security, I needed new clothes. I would attract too much attention in my current garb, and if the litterbug had demonstrated anything, it was that there would be people looking for me.

I needed money.

Begging was an option, but I wasn't sure if I had the time. We certainly did not have the patience, not when there were more . . . exciting solutions to our problem.

I wandered up Marylebone High Street in my new, blissful shoes, until I found a phone box, bright red, a hangover from a bygone pre-mobile-phone era, preserved by the local council in the name of heritage and tourism. The interior of the phone box stank of piss and beer, also in keeping with London tradition, and, as the ultimate in old-timey heritage, the back wall of the box was covered with a selection of little cards.

"LOOKING FOR A GOOD TIME?" was the least imaginative and least biologically explicit of the cards on offer, but in keeping with its neighbours it had a picture of a woman with what I could only assume still medically qualified as breasts protruding monumentally from beneath the tag line.

"!!!HOT HOT HOT!!!" proclaimed its neighbour while, below, a number of cards offered services ranging from exotic through to mind-blowing, all with attached telephone numbers for ease of booking your special encounter. At random I picked one that had been stuck up with bits of old chewing gum, all the while with my eyes half-closed. Anything close to taste or discernment in these circumstances made me feel dirtier than I already was. "**SEXY ASIAN BABE**" was its motto, and even as I put it in my pocket we were glancing this way and that in case someone, anyone, was watching us in our moment of shame. I walked with this card to the nearest bank, just opening up for the morning. The security guard watched me from the door to the counter and kept on watching, face dark and eyes narrow, waiting for me to make a move. I picked up one of the counter pens on its little beaded chain, and started to write on the back of the card. I wrote four sets of four numbers, relieved that I could remember them after so long. It was possible that someone in the credit card industry would be watching, studying their computer screens for the sacred numbers that could charm any ATM in any corner of the world to flash across the transaction board, ready to trace their user; but then, that was exactly the point. These digits, which so neatly resembled an account number, could be used anywhere, at any time and, like any black ant on a dark night, their use would get lost in the volume of data, too dense even for the sharpest magician to see.

That at least was my hope, though even as I finished inscribing the card I knew what a risk I was taking.

I left the bank before the security guard could try to arrest me on whatever premise he felt necessary, and kept on walking. Three streets away there was another bank, with an ATM planted firmly in the concrete wall outside. I walked up to it, checked over my shoulder for any passing watchers, pulled my SEXY ASIAN BABE card out of my pocket, and pushed it, careful not to bend the cardboard, into the debit card slot of the machine.

The screen went black.

I waited.

A single 1 appeared in the top right-hand corner, then quickly expanded into a mad marathon of numbers and figures tumbling over the screen. A warning sign appeared and for a brief moment my fears were realised – someone was watching the banks, looking for the sacred numbers that could access an account – then it was gone again, and the message appeared, *PLEASE SELECT THE SERVICE YOU REQUIRE.*

I chose cash withdrawal.

The machine said:

£10	£*shadowrun* 100
£30 *burnburnburnburn*	£*damnedsouldealdealdeal?*
£50	£200
£80	£ *Any Other Amount*

I chose any other amount, and took out £500.

The notes rolled out reluctantly, my cardboard card was returned.

With a sad little squelch, the machine rolled out a receipt. It was black all over, soggy with ink, and tore itself apart in my fingers with the weight of liquid spilt across the thin paper.

I took my money and ran.

By 10 a.m., Chapel Street Market already smelt of cheese, fish, Chinese fast food and McDonald's. It was a market defined by contrast. At the Angel end of the street, punk rock music pounded out from the stall selling pirate DVDs; from the French food stall, more of a van with a rumbling engine at its back, there sounded a recording of a man singing a nasal dirge about love, and Paris when it rained; at the cannabis stall (for no other name could do justice to the array of pipes, T-shirts, posters, burners and facial expressions that defined it, everything on display except the weed itself), Bob Marley declared himself deeply in love to the passing hooded youngsters from the estate down at Kings Cross. Outside the chippy, where the man with inch-wide holes in his ears served up cod to the security guards from the local shopping mall, a gaggle of schoolgirls from the local secondary bopped badly in high-heeled shoes to a beat through their headphones of *shuung-shuung-shuung-shuung* and shouted nicknames at their passing school friends in high voices that didn't slow down for the eardrum. Fishmongers chatted with the purveyors of suspicious rotting fruit, sellers of ripped-off designer gear gossiped with the man who sold nothing but size-seven shoes, while all around shoppers drifted from the tinned shelves of Iceland to the rich smell of the bakery, wedged in between the TV shop and the tattooist's parlour.

I wandered down the middle of the market, sidestepping the wind-blown papers, dead plastic bags, vegetables and fruit splattered on the road, chubby young mothers with prams, and impatient vendors flapping over their wares, between stalls selling wrapping paper, cheese, mushrooms, batteries, pirate films, pirate CDs, second-hand books (including numberless Mills and Boon titles for 50p a shot), cakes, bread, personal fans, portable radios, miniature TVs, scarves, dresses, boots, jeans, shirts and odd pieces of spider-web-thin fashion that looked like they were too light even to billow in the wind. My clothes here were no problem; there were too many sights and smells for people to care a damn about me.

I checked out the army surplus store, full of hunky boots, camouflage netting and men who loved to own both, the discount fashion store, the cobbler's, the baker's, the art shop and finally the costumiers, guarded by a fat black-and-white cat that sat on a wicker chair outside its door, the ceiling heavy with clothes drooping down from the roof so you had to duck to get through the doorway and heave your path clear between the shelves; walls lined with socks and shoes and antlers and old board games and prints of 1930s sporting events and wizard's hats and all the wonders of the world, in miniature, discount form, hiding somewhere in the dust.

At the army surplus store I bought two pairs of socks, a warm-looking navy-blue jumper with only a few holes in it, a Swiss Army knife replete with more gadgets than there could be use for, including such classics as the fish descaler, impossible-to-use tin-opener, and a strange spike with a hole through the top whose use I had never been able to fathom. At the fashion discount store I bought a plain satchel, which I suspected would earn me the scorn of the shrieking schoolgirls outside the chippy but had the feel of a thing that would never die. At the cobbler's, with a lot of persuading, I bought a set of ten blank keys for the most common locks in the city and a keyring to hang them on, as well as a small digital watch that could also dangle from the ring; in the art shop, I bought three cans of overpriced spray paint. At the costumiers, I bought my coat.

It was an excellent coat. It was long, grey, suspiciously blotched, smelt faintly of dust and old curries, went all the way down to my knees and overhung my wrists even when I stretched out my arms. It had big, smelly pockets, crunchy with crumbs, it boasted the remnants of a waterproof sheen, was missing a few buttons, and had once been beige. It was the coat that detectives down the ages had worn while trailing a beautiful, dangerous, presumably blond suspect in the rain, the coat that no one noticed, shapeless, bland and grey – it suited my purpose perfectly.

I paid, and tried it out. Back on Chapel Market, I turned up the collar, slung my satchel laden with its goodies over my shoulder, and walked through the crowds. No one paid me the slightest attention. I walked up to the cannabis stall, where I picked up a large plastic pipe with a picture on it of the Pope and three pot leaves against the flag of Jamaica. Slowly and deliberately, I opened my satchel and put it inside. As I walked away, no one even looked. Feeling on the edge of elation,

I went over to the discount shampoo store, and put the pipe down on the counter. I leant across towards the tired-looking Chinese man who ran the store and said very loudly, "Boo!"

He jumped, hands flying up instinctively. "Uh?" he squeaked, staring at me with frightened eyes.

I nearly danced on the spot. We wanted to play with electricity, we wanted to throw fire and whoop with joy, delighted to find that the power still worked, that the instinctive use of that magic was still there, binding itself into my clothes, my skin, completing me just as it had in the old days, making me, if not invisible, then utterly anonymous at will: simply not worth noticing. I pointed at the pot pipe on his table and said, "Present."

Before he had time to ask embarrassing questions, I turned, and sauntered away. We could have whistled.

Eleven a.m. brought us to the Cally Road swimming baths.

What Islington Council had thought would come of putting a swimming pool inside a corrugated-iron shed halfway between a railway terminal and a prison, I could not fathom. What mattered was that within these dark brown iron walls, besides the swimming pool inhabited by complaining children being forced through their weekly lesson by the bald, hook-nosed swimming master, there was a hot shower to be had for no more than £4.99 a throw.

We had thought heaven was some superficial construct of an ignorant humanity.

Standing in the shower, the stench of the litterbug being washed out of our skin, our hair, our bones, we realised this was not so. Heaven was on the Caledonian Road, smelt faintly of chlorine and was blasted out of a slightly grimy tap at 44 degrees Celsius under high pressure. We could have stayed there all day and all night, head turned into the water, but as always the driving fear of staying in one place too long, the memory of what might await me if I was found before I was ready, kept me moving.

By lunchtime, hair clinging damply to our face and new clothes pressed like the cloth of gold to our skin, I was ready.

I went in search of some old friends.

*

My old friends could not be found.

I tried calling from phone boxes, picking numbers out of the haze of memory. I tried Awan first, a good, solid old man who'd always been kind to me in his dryly tolerant way. The number was disconnected. I moved on to Akute, with whom I had once shared a not very serious and rather drunken kiss on Waterloo Bridge, before discovering that she preferred blonds. An old lady answered the phone and informed me, no, sorry, never heard of her. A man shouted abuse at me from the number that should have been Patel's; and because Pensley's office was only a few minutes' walk from the Caledonian Road, set back behind York Way, I went to find him in person, and found the place had been converted into a bathroom warehouse.

Uncertain, and getting desperate, I tried dialling Dana Mikeda's house.

A man answered; not a good start.

"Yes?"

"I'm looking for Dana Mikeda."

"Who's calling?"

"I'm . . . an old friend."

"What's your name, please?"

"I need to speak to Dana Mikeda."

"Who shall I tell her is calling?"

"I'm . . ." I bit back on the edge of saying my name, not safe, not yet, not until we knew for certain. "Please. It's really important."

"Where are you?" asked the man firmly, a posh, determined voice used to barrelling its way through all objection by shock and stubbornness. "Who is this?"

I slammed the phone down. My hand was shaking. The fear was back again, the terrible, biting certainty of eyes in the street, barely diminished by the bright merriness of the sun. There was one other number I could try, but the thought of it made my stomach turn and twist, threaded terror like a doctor's wire through every vein and blocked the flow of hot blood.

There was only one place left to go.

In the heart of London, in the area defined by Wigmore Street to the north and Oxford Street to the south, there is a network of little weaving, half-hearted roads and tiny, crabbed alleyways, the remnants of a time when almost every street in the city snuggled up to its neighbours like fleas to skin, compressing the people between its walls into ever tighter and darker corners. Some of these streets had become gentrified over the years, offering a posher flavour of tea or a higher-cut boot than the discount bargain shops and the giant department chains that squatted on Oxford Street itself, like sullen hulking mounds looming over a river of wealth. Others had retained that darker edge of cut-price squalor that defined much of Oxford Street's commercial goods – strange recycled computers, odd-tasting pizza with the fur left on, unusual lingerie shops for the woman who understands both work and play; suspicious acupuncture clinics and uncredited "Schools of English", clustered in the shadows between the streets.

Amongst them, and I was pleased to see it hadn't gone, was the "Cave of Wonders, Mysteries and Miracles", advertised by a small wooden sign swinging above an open door through which the overwhelming smell of cheap incense and musty carpets hit the nose like it wanted a pillow fight. It lurked between a small bookshop and a pub with frosted windows and dark paintwork, looking embarrassed to be there. I felt embarrassed going into it. But I told myself it was for the best, took a deep breath of fresh air before entering, and began my descent.

What began as a bright stairwell with white walls was suddenly transformed. Beyond a hanging covered with mystic-esque symbols it became a dull stairwell of dark maroon walls and polished wooden floors, tormented by an eerie, nasal background droning from tiny speakers high up on the walls. The feel of the place changed too. The buzz of magic was stiller, quieter, an elusive black-silk touch across the senses rather than the shock of sensation I always used to associate with the Cave. Immediately, that made me suspicious.

The reception area had always been a makeshift affair, with plastic benches and tatty editions of last year's *Magic and Miracles* – "**THE GUIDE TO TRUTH!!!!** – Featuring an exclusive interview with ****Endless Might**** on the rewards of proper summoning technique!!!"

These quaintly unpleasant items had been replaced with black leather sofas and a silver cigarette tray containing stress balls. I walked up to the receptionist, a sour-faced man wearing tight leather trousers and not much besides, and said, "I'm here to see Khan."

"Uh?" His attention was fixed on a magazine which seemed to be all about What Brad Did Next, and breasts.

I tried again. "I'm here to see Khan – what are the stress balls for?"

He had a tattoo across his bare, bronzed back of a Pegasus spreading its wings. Down one arm someone had inscribed in black and red ink: "*WIZARD*".

"Excuse me?" I repeated patiently. "Why do you have stress balls?"

His eyes didn't leave an article dedicated to "How I Pulled Cheryl!!" as he replied, "Clear your aura for the reading."

"Clear my what?"

"Your aura. You got an appointment?"

"No."

"You'll need to make an appointment."

"I just want to see Khan – what do you mean 'clear my aura'?"

"You gotta be in the zen to do a reading. Gotta have a clear head for the truth that'll unfold, see?" he mumbled through his disdain.

I thought about it, and reached the only conclusion to be had from a lifetime of magical experience and several years of extracurricular mystic activity. "But . . . that's bollocks," I said, hoping he might be inclined to agree.

"Not my problem. Wanna make an appointment?"

"No, I want to see Khan."

"No one here called Khan."

"He owns this place."

"Uh-uh. Sorry, mate, you'll be wanting somewhere else. No Khan here."

He still wasn't paying us attention. We were not prepared to tolerate disrespect. We leant across the counter, grabbed him by the throat with one hand, pulled his face an inch from ours and hissed, "We want to see whoever is in charge *now*!"

He made a wheezing noise and pawed at my wrist. We wanted to see his eyes bulge a little further from his face, but I relaxed my grip and pushed him back. I smiled, in a manner that I hoped was apologetic but firm. "Perhaps I should just go through," I offered.

He pawed at his neck and made gagging sounds. I nodded politely, and swept past reception and through the curtains leading to the gloom beyond.

The irritating nasal droning was even louder in the shadows beyond the curtains, and the smell of cheap incense almost giddying; its thick smoke spilled out of every corner and tickled the eyeballs. There was only one source of light: on a table in the centre of the room a crystal ball was glowing white. It didn't really emit light, so much as hug the shadows, defining a tight area of space against which the darkness pressed. I didn't bother with it, since its colour and texture felt entirely mains-powered, rather than anything worth the name of magical. From beyond the next curtain, of a thick black velvet, a voice like snow swishing across a mountainside said, "Since you've come so far, you are welcome."

I pushed the curtain back.

Half lost in a cloud of incense, the woman sat at the back of the room on a chair upholstered in red silk. Her hands were folded neatly in her lap, and a deck of cards lay on the table in front of her. She was wearing more gold medallions and fake gold chain than I had ever seen on a single living creature. The jewellery hung from a headpiece resting precariously on her dyed-black hair, dangled over her heavily made-up face, swept across her shoulders and down her arms, tinkled along her fingertips, drooped down her front and spread out in waves around her ankles and across her bare feet and polished toenails. When she moved, each motion a delicate twitch, she jingled, she glinted, she glowed.

She said, not raising her eyes from the cards, "Will you not sit, since you are so eager to hear your fortune told?"

I said, spreading my arms wide in disbelief, "What the bloody hell is this?!"

"The mystical often takes us by surprise..."

"No, but seriously, what the bloody hell is going on? Where's Khan? What's all the shiny stuff for, why do you have a glow-in-the-dark crystal ball, who's the man in the tight trousers, what's up with all the incense, I mean really and right now? What kind of establishment is this meant to be?"

For a moment, just a moment, she looked surprised. Then her

expression reset itself into one of semi-divine entrancement, her hands drifting up around her face in the swirling patterns of the smoke she disturbed, a beatific smile settling over her bright scarlet lips. "I am the seer of the future," she intoned, "I am here to grant to you..."

"Where's Khan?"

"I am here to grant you a vision into..."

"Bugger a vision into the unknown mists of fucking whatever, I want to see Khan, and I want to see him right bloody now!"

She hesitated, a flicker of something real passing over her serene features for a moment, and in a slightly more sensible voice, tinged with a hint of Peckham, she enquired, "Why would you seek this man?"

"Do you know who Khan is?"

"A king, an emperor, a lord..."

"We are not here to play games!"

She froze, and this time made no effort to recover, the surprise clear on her face. I glared at her, daring her to mumble a single line more of inane waffle, itching to throw something. Finally, with a little breath, half a laugh, half a start of surprise, she said in a much clearer, sharper voice, "Why are you here? What do you know about Khan?"

"Alfred bloody Khan," I snapped. "Seer of the bloody future. Something, may I add, which you are not."

There was a flash of anger behind her eyes. She stood up, gathering her skirts in a single sweeping, practised gesture, and exclaimed, "Be careful. You were not invited here."

Then, to our surprise, she stepped right up close to us, and stared at our eyes. She drew in a long breath between her teeth and whispered, "Well then..."

She reached up to touch my face, and instinctively I caught her wrist, the metal across it cold and uncomfortable. "Tell me" – I struggled to keep our voice tame – "where Khan is."

She hesitated, then smiled a thin, humourless smile. "Alfred Khan died two years ago," she said flatly. "You are behind with the news. Anything else I can do for you, sir – aura cleansing, mystic divination, unfolding of the sacred secrets? No?"

I let go of her wrist, before I could forget that I held it. We were not entirely surprised; nevertheless I didn't know what to do, what to say, how, exactly, I should behave. So we did nothing, but waited to see if an emotion would strike, curious to know how we responded to such news, whether we cried or shouted or became angry or felt nothing at all. We hoped we would cry; it was the most human response. My eyes remained firmly dry, my mouth empty of any words.

The woman was staring at us, waiting to see how we reacted. We sat down on a padded stool covered in silk. In that close space, she towered over us, a proud tilt to her chin. I guessed she was in her mid-thirties, that the yellowish colour of her eyes came from a pair of tinted contact lenses, and that somewhere underneath that headdress the roots of her hair were blond. She waited for the news to settle, and the flat waters of incomprehension to start bubbling into a sea of embarrassing self-pity, before she said, "You knew Khan well?"

"Sort of."

"Former client?"

"He once read me my future in the flight of a plastic bag," I replied with a shrug. "He derived the secrets of time in the patterns of vapour trails in the sky, or the drifting of scum on the surface of the canal. Sounded like a load of pretentious balls at the time, but I guess, in retrospect..."

"What did he tell you?" she asked.

I smiled despite myself, ran my hands nervously through my drying hair. "He said, 'Hey man, you're like, totally going to die.'"

"That sounds like him," she conceded. "Tact is not part of the service."

"He was right," I scowled. "He was bloody right."

Silence a while.

Then she said, "You really didn't know? That's he's dead?"

"No. I've been away."

"It was two years ago," she repeated. "I run this place now."

"You're not a seer," I snapped. "How can you even breathe in all this bloody incense?"

She shrugged. "I understand what people want to hear, I have a good enough brain to see things, an excellent manner and a husky, sensual voice."

"Is that the qualification, these days?" I asked.

"And I know things," she added, firmer.

"Any useful things?"

"I know how to spot a magician."

I looked up sharply, found her staring straight back down at me. "Yeah," I said at last. "I bet you can. But you're still not quite hitting the money, are you?"

"You come here to have your fortune read, magician, or is it something else you're looking for?"

I found myself forcing a smile. "I was never a believer in having your fortune read, even by Khan. It was all too fatalistic."

"Even the best-told fortunes can be evaded," she said with a shrug and a jangling of metal. "I don't take kindly to anyone barging in, by the way, magician or not. It's rude, and it's unprofessional."

"It's not been a good day."

"A poor excuse. Stand up, I want to look at you."

"Why?"

"You have interesting eyes."

"I do?"

"Very blue."

We were surprised she had noticed; not a total fool, then. Perhaps she could see in our eyes a signal, to all who dared look, of our true nature. "That interests you?" I asked, for want of anything more intelligent to say, and to buy time.

"I am interested in all unusual things."

Then, and I was too numb by now to resist, she grabbed my wrists with the same forceful gesture by which I'd grabbed hers, and turned my hands over. She studied my palms, my fingers, my knuckles, my nails, the veins in my wrists. Having turned my hands this way and that, she then tossed them aside like rotten potatoes. She took hold of my face, with the same unsympathetic grip the doctor uses when examining a swelling, and turned it this way and that, scrutinised the colour of my eyes, the shape of my ears, even the condition of my teeth, smelt my breath.

Suddenly her fingers were at my throat, digging in, pushing my chin up as the tips of her nails drew half-moon rims of blood. We half-choked, reached instinctively to find the electric fires that always burnt inside. But her fingers went no deeper, and I held back, uncertain.

She hissed, her face an inch from mine, "*Sorcerer.*"

"How'd you tell?" I asked through the pressure of her fingers on my neck.

"I told you – I know things. I know the smell of magics; and you don't just dabble, you swim in it, you *breathe* it. An urban sorcerer, in my shop? Who are you?" When I didn't answer, her grip tightened, sending a wave of heat into my head as the blood strained in its arteries. "I am not defenceless," she added. "As I'm sure you can imagine."

"Very much so," I croaked. "Are you like this with everyone you meet?"

"Your name!"

"Swift," I said, and was pleased at how easily the remembrance of it came to me. "My name is Matthew Swift."

Her grip relaxed for a moment; surprise, not intent. "Matthew Swift?" she echoed flatly.

"That's me. Ta-da!"

"You want to tell me that you're Matthew Swift."

"Is this a bad thing?"

"You are a dead man, Matthew Swift."

"You must have customers flocking to hear your predictions."

"It was a statement of fact, of *history*."

"It pays for prophets to be cryptic, particularly in this litigious age," I wheezed.

"You misunderstand," she said gently, her breath tickling my skin. "Now, right now, as we are talking, your corpse is rotting in the earth."

I shrugged weakly. "Clearly, it isn't."

"Matthew Swift," she said, slowly, "the sorcerer called Matthew Swift, died two years ago."

"Question!" I said, raising one meek hand. "Did you actually see the body?"

She hesitated.

"Well, there you go."

"Nothing bleeds that much and lives."

We wound our fingers carefully around hers, started unpicking them from our throat. "Then consider this. If, hypothetically, I am the same Matthew Swift who was attacked two years ago and who lay expiring in his own blood while his killer walked away, happy with the thought that no doctor nor hospital in the world could repair such a hole in the heart, such a tear in the lung, such a rip in the chest – if, say, I happen to be the kind of man who can survive that to stand here now, shouldn't you be more concerned about threatening me?"

We detached her last finger from our neck, pushed her hand carefully back to her side. She stood in front of us, jingling faintly with the weight of breath she drew. Finally: "How would Swift survive?"

"Precariously."

"It's not possible to . . ."

"No," I said firmly. "It isn't. Now will you tell me what happened to Khan?"

Silence.

I smiled my most beatific smile. A kind of serenity was settled over me. I knew now, standing in that stench of incense and beneath that endless nasal drone, that things had got just about as bad as they could conceivably get. Therefore it stood to reason that things could get no worse; therefore I was finally almost calm.

"His throat was cut," she said flatly, after a pause. "He saw it coming, and couldn't stop it. That's power – to kill a man even when he knows every detail of his own demise – that's truly a cruel death. If you are Swift, where have you been for two years?"

"Around."

"I deal in cryptic answers every day, Mr Swift; don't try and distract me with my own devices."

"Fair enough. I will not play with you and invent some story; I will simply not tell you where I went or how I got there. Is that satisfactory?"

"No."

"Well, shucks."

"Can you prove you're who you say?"

I thought about this. "No."

"No," she repeated with a nasty twist to her lip. "Of course you can't."

"I can't prove it," I growled through my teeth, "because I own nothing that was my own. Everything that I thought I had, everyone I knew . . . no, I can't prove anything." I added, "You are a *terrible* prophet."

"My opinion of you is hardly in the stratosphere," she retorted. "Why did you want to see Khan?"

"That's my business."

"You... wanted his help?"

"That's not important."

"Then what do you *want*?"

When we answered, we spoke without my noticing, with a word that slipped out as naturally as breath.

"Revenge." Once spoken, it seemed so right, so honest and comforting, that I was amazed I hadn't said it before. "I want revenge."

"Against...?"

"The one who attacked me. Who left me to die. And... And against the one who brought us back."

She hesitated, her narrow eyes flicking to and fro, her fingers dancing a tiny rhythm at her side, their jewellery jangling like wind chimes. "Where have you been?" she murmured. I had the feeling it wasn't a question intended for me. Then, clearer, "Do you have a plan?"

"Not yet."

"Does anyone know that you're... that you claim to be Swift?"

"No. And if you tell anyone..."

"If I tell?" she snapped, defiant.

"We will kill you," we said gently. "You are nothing before us. We can stamp you out like a whisper of static in the wire. We *will* kill you. I'm sorry about it, but that's just how it is."

She didn't seem frightened by this, more curious. She put her head on one side and breathed, "Interesting."

"Really?"

"You keep on saying 'we'."

I shrugged.

"I may be able to help you, possibly – Matthew Swift."

"How?"

"I have... friends. People who share a common interest."

"Why would you help me?"

She smiled. "Even if you aren't Matthew Swift, you could be of use."

"I thought you were helping me."

"There could be mutual benefits."

"I'm not really interested." I turned to go, seizing the curtain. She reached out and grabbed my arm, her fingers digging into my skin. Instinctively we shied back, flexing our fingers for the feel of the power, ready to strike; but, sensing our fear, she snatched her hand back. "Matthew Swift and Alfred Khan are not the only ones who died these last years. Do you know that? Have you asked? If you want to know who else is dead, and why, go to the Eye tonight, at nine. Things have changed; perhaps you do not know. There are new rules, new . . . dangers."

"I'll work it out."

"Do you know Robert James Bakker?" I was halfway out of the door and her words stopped me dead. "I think you do."

"What is your interest in Bakker?"

"If you want to know more about Bakker, what he has done, what he has become, we are the ones to talk to. We can be of great use to you."

I forced a smile. "And I to you, yes?" Her cold expression was answer enough. I said, "I'll think about it. Good afternoon, miss. Remember what we said."

And walked away.

Whether or not I had any interest in the fortune-teller's proposition, a few things she said had got my thoughts moving.

Without really knowing why, I found myself going towards the river. I walked through Middle Temple Inn, a place of old trees, high brick buildings, sash windows, cobbled streets, enclosed courtyards, lawyers, and film actors, in costumes from roughly 1580 to the present day, at work on some new historical drama (usually Dickens). I made my way towards Blackfriars Bridge, and into the gloomy concrete zone of wiggling, covered alleys, traffic-filled streets, tunnels and pedestrian walkways that link Blackfriars and London Bridges on the north side of the river. I wandered under dull yellow neon lights, watching my shadow stretch across the walls as I walked, listening to the distant rumble of cars passing through the maze of one-way systems and underpasses that had sprung up after the Blitz between what was left of the area's history and the new, ugly, squared-off buildings compressing the winding byways of the city into ever more unlikely shapes. The Circle line sent up a hum through the pavement as it rattled towards Monument and, overhead, the train to Farringdon wheezed its way through a tunnel of nail-tight buildings pressed up against the railway.

I came to the tiny yard of flagstones and half-hearted container shrubs that jutted out between a giant converted warehouse and an office with walls of black-green glass, and sat down on a bench looking out past a row of iron railings to the river. At low tide, the water lapped against a wide beach of pebbles and brown sand embedded with plastic bags and dropped bottles. Within a few hours, the tide could rise up the tall stone wall on which my courtyard sat, where a green line of weed defined the high-tide mark, a metre or so below my feet.

A part of me was disappointed at how unchanged the place seemed, now that I sat and contemplated my situation while I watched the tide rise. There wasn't a plaque of remembrance, nor a bunch of wilting flowers tied to the railing, nor even a lurid stain on the flagstones where so much of my blood had been spilled. Even the telephone box hiding in a corner, as if embarrassed to be seen in the mobile phone age, didn't have a sign inside saying in childish script, "i was ere". Instead it had the usual cards, advertising sex and, this being the City with a definite article and its own coat of arms, yoga stress support groups for the harried banker, probably at a slightly higher rate than the cruder alternative.

Out of curiosity I picked up the receiver. There wasn't even a dialling tone, let alone the sounds I'd heard last time I was here. The booth smelled of pee and neglect. I was disappointed that my fingers, scrabbling up its side in desperation as I had tried to dial, hadn't left scratch marks for posterity. I kicked the telephone with the heel of my foot until it reluctantly gave up £2.40 worth of change into the returned-coins slot. Returning to my bench I contemplated what this could buy me. In this city, I decided, not much.

The tide rose, and the shadows changed direction. I only got up and left when it started drizzling again, the cold raising goosebumps across my skin. I didn't know if visiting the place of my previous demise had been a good idea; probably it had to be done sooner or later, if only to experience the full reality of my own absence. Here, all unremembered, was where Matthew Swift crawled across the wet paving stones to the telephone booth, dragging most of his exposed organs with him, and where in the morning they found only bloody clothes and pieces of skin.

There could, we decided, be advantages to my former self having been forgotten, even though it seemed that the sorcerer I used to be still had a name worth remembering. Certainly, seeing the place where I had died made what we wanted to do that bit easier.

I spent the rest of the day in the local library, reading newspapers. The world had changed in some ways that I found almost impossible to grasp: regimes different, governments fallen, icons dead, new stars, new soaps, new orders, new ideas. Phones were smaller, computers faster, lives more packed, worlds more messed in together. In other ways it remained constant. The temperature was still rising, and the complaints – tax, the NHS, transport, scandal – were still the same.

And at 9 p.m. I found myself at the London Eye.

At no point had I decided that this was where I wanted to be. Perhaps I simply had nowhere better to go.

I paid for a ride and queued with all the tourists curious to see the city at night. The crowd was dense – the day's drizzle had cleaned the air so that tonight, at the summit of the giant, white-and-silver ferris wheel, you could see all the way to the North Downs in one direction, and to Alexandra Palace in the other.

I didn't bother looking for whoever might want to speak to me. If they were worth any conversation, they'd find me. Meanwhile, I would not have been there were it not for the crowds. There is a protection of sorts in numbers – so long as the other bugger is playing by the rules.

I found myself in a capsule with a small flock of Japanese tourists who exclaimed as the floodlit Houses of Parliament dropped away beneath us, marvelled at the watery reflection of the lights on Victoria Embankment, photographed the pools of light sprawling out northwards to the dark splotch of Primrose Hill, ogled the purple and green lit-up walls of the National Theatre, pointed at Tower Bridge and pushed past each other to see the BT Tower sticking up from the West End; there was also a family from, judging by the accent, somewhere in south-east England, whose youngest child was only now discovering her fear of heights.

As for us, we sat on the bench in the middle of the capsule and watched our city expand beneath us, and felt like God. We had never seen anything so beautiful, and could not conceive of more magic in the world.

By the time the ride had started its descent, the staff below were already closing up the capsules ahead of us and turning away the public for the night. On our arrival at the embarkation platform, while the tourists shuffled out through the door, I didn't move; nor did anyone ask me to.

I heard footsteps on the capsule floor and the swish of the door closing behind me. The river began to drop away again, the capsule making another trip skywards.

Behind me a voice said, "Lovely night, isn't it? Enough to move a sentimental man to verse, I find."

I shrugged, wrapping my coat tighter around myself and watching the patterns of neon spread out underneath me once more. By the sound of their steps, there were two of them. The one who spoke had a heavy, breathless voice like the deep snorts of a walrus. It was a cultured voice, well-educated to the point of being overly so. Knowledge so intense it drowns out all common sense. The man also brought with him a smell. It tingled on the edge of my senses: a deep, subtle shade of magic that tasted of cream crackers and the colour of shining oil. However, it wasn't coming from him, I realised, but from his companion, whose reflection I saw in the glass of the capsule against the night outside – a young Asian man in a smart suit, hands folded in front of him, who stood by the shut door like it was the gateway to a treasury, eyeing me up in my own reflection even as I watched him.

The man who'd spoken sat down on the bench beside me; so I figured that, whatever strange aromas the younger man gave off, he was merely the sidekick to this man's central act.

He said, "I hope you haven't minded the delay."

"No."

"It is intolerably rude to make someone wait for an appointment. But I fear these are not such civilised times, Mr Swift. I blame the mobile phone, naturally."

I turned to look at him properly. He was fat – there was no other way to describe it – a belly contained by a shiny waistcoat like a straining bulkhead, any second about to explode a shrapnel of buttons. His suit was a subtle pinstripe, finely cut to disguise the sheer scale of his form. His face, emerging out of the rolling slope of his neck, was friendly, with bright eyes peering from under gigantic eyebrows, the only hair on an otherwise polished pale head. He had a ring on his wedding finger and a pair of black leather shoes, but otherwise no possessions with him worth the name. He studied me as I studied him, and at roughly the same instant I was reaching my conclusions about him, he said, "My, yes, but the resemblance is extraordinary, isn't it?"

"Resemblance?"

"To our sadly departed dead sorcerer, Matthew Swift."

"Ah."

"Although as far as I know, he had no brothers."

"I don't."

"Of course, of course," he said. "You don't. In fact, if I recall correctly, you have no living relatives?"

"I have a grandmother in a nursing home." A sudden pang of guilt that I hadn't even thought of her until now; alive, dead?

"Do you?"

"I did when I last checked."

"See her often?"

"She only likes talking to the pigeons," I replied, honestly enough.

"I see. Such a shame."

"The pigeons let her fly with them. They bring her all the news. It is not sad."

He smiled again, but this time the smile was tighter: less friendly but somehow more honest for it. "Indeed, indeed," he mumbled. "But forgive me; I'm going about this terribly rudely. We should introduce ourselves before digressing to personal matters."

"You know who I am."

"I know who you say you are. And I know what you appear to be, which is quite different. But for the now let me say that I am Dudley Sinclair, and that it is my honour to make your acquaintance."

He held out his hand. I shook it, after only a moment's doubt. The cold clamminess of his grip clenched hard around my fingers and lingered a second longer than politeness required. We pulled our fingers away.

"You know the fortune-teller?"

"Dear boy, I know *everybody*. It's my business, you see?"

I didn't have anything to say to that, so resumed my quiet study of the two men's reflection against the glory of the city.

"Yes, yes," he muttered, not particularly for my attention. "Of course." The smile reasserted itself, broad, but somehow not revealing any teeth as it ran from ear to ear. "Well, yes, this is a remarkably fortuitous encounter. Indeed. Shall we dispense with the boring questions for now and say that yes, indeed, you are Matthew Swift, a sorcerer in every form, way, and guise. Yes, I think this is best, don't you?"

I shrugged.

"A man of few words; I can respect that, although personally I find you can discover a lot about a fellow even in the meaningless detritus with which he may litter his speech, an unconscious, perhaps, symptom of who he really may be, beneath his conscious mind. But you, sir, seem to play a close game – well, good. Yes, very good."

"There was talk of mutual benefit," I said. "The fortune-teller said . . . there were people who can help me."

"And, I believe, there was talk of revenge, yes?"

"I can manage my own affairs."

"Of course you can, yes! A very capable gentleman, certainly – indeed, to be Matthew Swift and to have survived when so many others have died would suggest quite how capable you may indeed be!"

"Who died?"

A flicker in the eyes, a tiny movement around the corners of his mouth. "I take it you are unfamiliar with current events."

"I've read some newspapers."

"I was thinking of events within that . . . special area in which you and I both happen to dabble."

"You dabble, but he" – I nodded at the silent young man by the door – "does a bit more than that, I think."

A moment's hesitation; hard to tell whether the tightening around his eyes was surprise, or pleasure, or both. The young man showed no feeling – we could have been talking about a dead stranger as far as he seemed to care. "A man of insight, sir," murmured Dudley Sinclair finally, his voice quieter and deeper than before. "I can see why she thought you curious."

"Who died?" I repeated. "I tried calling some . . . who died?"

"A list? Crude, certainly crude, but perhaps necessary. Very well – as far as I'm aware, you – I mean Matthew Swift – were the first, although we do not entirely know whether your death fits the pattern since, as of course you know, no body was ever found. Alfred Khan died shortly after – the theory goes he had visions of your death, and of his, and knew what was coming for him, but could not stop it. Imagine that, if you will; imagine that."

I said nothing.

"Patel went missing, but they assumed he was dead when they identified his thumb and part of his left hand by its fingerprint. Awan was found partially flayed – thankfully, I believe, the shock killed him first; Koshdel had been strangled with his own intestines; Akute's head was discovered on her bedroom floor, we're not entirely sure where the rest of the body went; Pensley was set on fire. Ah, now Dhawan managed to put up a bit of a fight, which unfortunately collapsed the entire building he was in, making identification a tricky process – dental records, eventually. Did you know Foster? A young sorceress, perhaps not really in your circle, but her death was by . . ."

"Did the same person kill them all?" I asked breathlessly, the words running like sand between my fingers.

"We assume so."

"Why?"

"Oh, the violence of the crime, the focus on practitioners of the art, the ritualistic nature of the death, the prolonged . . ."

"I meant why kill them?"

"We don't know. We have theories."

"Who's 'we'?"

His eyes shifted away to the city, his right hand twitched. "We are . . . concerned citizens."

"Urban magicians?"

"Some of us, yes."

"Why do you think they were all killed?"

"Now that's really very tricky to say."

"Try."

His eyes flashed for a moment, glancing at me and away. If he'd felt anger, though, he hid it well. "You must have views yourself. You were one of them – until today."

"I have an idea of who may have had motive."

"Then you must have an idea who sent the litterbug after you this morning."

That surprised me – that he could have known, and so soon. I tried to hide it, but I'm sure he saw through my half-hearted grunt and tight expression to my unease.

"We found the burnt core," he explained, almost nicely, "and the local council was inundated with complaints about rubbish on the streets near one of its stations. I'm sure you understand why we made the leap of judgement – there are only so many practitioners of our unique profession who understand the summoning of such a creature, or indeed know the best way to break such a powerful spell."

When I didn't say anything he shifted his weight slightly and said, "May I suggest something to you? I don't wish to influence your own personal views in any way, or even imply a course of action. I merely wish to throw an idea out, sir, and see if you find it in any way conducive."

"Well?"

He leant in close until his breath almost tickled my ear and whispered, "Robert James Bakker," and leant back with a smile to see how I reacted.

I rocked the sole of my left shoe idly across the floor of the capsule. I ran the index finger of my right hand in and out of the dips between the knuckles of my left. I watched the city. I said not a word.

Not a word seemed ample, for Mr Sinclair. "Very good," he said, "very good. You are a man who does not wish to be too forward with his own views – I respect that, it is an admirable quality; you wish to gather all information first, yes, of course, naturally. Perhaps, then, it would be of interest to you to know that Patel was one of Khan's closest confidants, and that if Khan revealed anything about his impending death, it would have been to that young gentleman? Awan, of course, was linked to Mr Guy Lee, who I'm sure you know of, a close associate of Mr Bakker's. Koshdel was a gentleman who had very strong, perhaps too strong, views about the appropriate use of power, and liked to get involved. Pensley, one of my closest associates, yes, indeed, a tragedy for Pensley considering he was only doing as asked – Dhawan, a sorcerer like you, I'm sure you must have met him on occasion, and of course, he too knew Bakker. Akute... remains something of a mystery, but I suspect once we've had more time to research the nature of her demise, a link of sorts will transpire. Nothing provable, of course, nothing solid, there were never any witnesses, naturally, naturally! – and you always need more than motive. Theory, you understand, conjecture, nothing more, and Bakker is, after all, such an outstanding citizen."

I raised my head slowly, for fear that if I rushed anything, I'd lose control. I looked him straight in the eye and said, "Are you hoping I'm going to say that Bakker attacked me?"

"No, no, I do not wish to impute any such suppositions to you!"

"He didn't."

"Of course not, no, I never thought..."

"I saw no one attack me."

"But you have an idea who might have..."

"Yes."

"May I be so bold as to enquire..."

"You can enquire; I don't think I'll answer yet. I don't think I know enough. I don't know you."

He let out a little tired-uncle-left-with-the-children sigh. "I take it then, you have no interest in these other deaths."

"They interest me very much. I knew some of them. And the manner of their deaths is disturbing."

He let out an impatient sigh. "Do you know, sir, why I mentioned Robert James Bakker?"

"I take it you see some connection between him and these deaths."

"All who have died are in some way linked to him; indeed, yes, it is most true. Including you, I believe? You and Robert Bakker... were very closely linked indeed, were you not?"

"Where is he now?"

"No one is entirely sure."

"What does that mean?"

"He moves around. He is very difficult to find. These last few years... he has become more than just a recluse. No one knows where he's based, or where he will be at any moment. It is suggestive, in itself. Do you know?"

"Me?"

"You knew him."

"I guess so."

"Come now, let us not be too coy, sir! I know that on the day you died, you met Robert Bakker at St Thomas's Hospital. I know you argued with him, I know that you left him and walked along the river; all this is on record, sir, all this the police themselves turned up, quite without help from me, I may add. I know that a few hours after leaving him, you were found missing, but a lot of your blood was found very much present, sir. More, sir, more, I know that the people currently inhabiting your house are employees of a company that indeed, sir, is ultimately owned by Bakker's own corporation, and that there was a good deal of external pressure from his lawyers to see your property and your assets divided as soon as possible after your presumed demise – such as there was. I'm sure, sir, why you understand my concern, yes indeed."

"You know so much, why talk to me? I've said what I have to. I don't know your reasons for being interested in Bakker, nor who you are, and I don't really care. I'm only here to find the person who attacked me, and..." I stopped myself, but too late.

Sinclair's eyes glowed with the reflected light of the city. "Yes," he said, taking a long time to get the sound out. "And of course, 'the one who brought you back'. That was the phrase you were looking for, was it not, Mr Swift? And she was right – you have most unusual eyes."

"Is that relevant?"

"You must understand, Mr Swift. I have spent a considerable amount of time studying both your demise, and the unfortunate deaths of these people I have named, among others. It is... you may say... an invested interest. In this time I feel I have come to know you, or at least know what part of yourself you chose to leave behind to posterity – which may, in truth, not be much. I know what you look like, every detail of your face; I know your habits, your dispositions. I know that when you walked into that courtyard by the Thames your eyes were brown, and now when I look at you, your eyes are very much blue. And I find myself wondering – is this the same Matthew Swift after all, or is it some fraud? Perhaps... neither? Perhaps you do not experience the kind of death that I am given to believe you did by the state of your clothes when they were found, by the blood and the mess it made – forensic science, you see, marvellous thing. Perhaps you do not experience such things and come away the same. Perhaps you change to survive, yes?"

I looked away.

"There was one thing about the death of Matthew Swift that struck me most," he explained after a pause.

"What was that?"

"His fingerprints were found, in blood, on the receiver of a telephone booth just a few metres from where we find the first pool of blood. He dragged himself to the booth, lifted the receiver, but did not dial 999. Instead, the body disappears, leaving merely the shredded remains of bloody clothes, a few loose pieces of skin and the odd vital fluid from the occasional organ."

"So you think Bakker had me attacked?"

"I do sir, indeed yes, I do. I think you may be so inclined as well – at least, your curiosity must have been aroused – unless of course you know something that I don't, in which case I would implore you to share such knowledge."

"Didn't see anyone I knew."

"But of course you saw something?" He was almost panting, the sweat trickling down his cheek. We could smell the salt in it, feel the heat from his face. "The police think that Swift took a long time to die, yes? You must have seen something!"

I thought about it. We didn't trust this man; but on the other hand, what he seemed to know already was enough to make him interesting. "It was a shadow," I said. "That's all."

"Come now! Come!" he proclaimed. "I'm sure there must be more!"

Abruptly I stood up. "Mr Sinclair," I said, "you have a lot of information. Yes, I talked with Bakker, I quarrelled with Bakker. But whether he is behind what happened to me, I will not say. Until I know more, I will not trust you. I have learnt too many lessons to take that chance, and we are still new to this game."

"We?" his voice cut in, sharp and harsh.

I ignored it. "You want my help with something. What is it?"

He got to his feet, and now there was no friendliness in his face, just a full, sweeping stare, trying to read every part of my mind and heart. "Matthew Swift," he said, slow and deliberate. "I do not know with what power you must have consorted to stay alive, when so many others died who, I think, had been more knowledgeable, powerful, careful and aware than you ever were. But if what sustains your life now becomes a threat to me, I will eliminate it, do you understand?"

We shook our head. "We are not here for you," we explained, and for a moment there was fear in his eyes. I folded my arms. "So, Mr Sinclair. Tell me. What exactly do you want?"

He thought about it, stretching up to his full, not-too-impressive height, and folding his hands behind his back in a formal posture. Finally he said, "Let us be blunt with each other. I am interested in finding out more about Mr Bakker's organisation, his friends, his purpose, his abilities and his history. I, and some other…concerned citizens…suspect that this gentleman may be exploiting his many advantages for a level of personal gain which may endanger others of my persuasion."

"And what persuasion is that?"

"Living, Mr Swift. Simply living."

"You believe Bakker is a threat to people?"

"Honestly, sir, I do. I have little proof beyond hearsay and a series of violent deaths within a certain community, but I do, sir, consider Mr Bakker to have an agenda that could be of great concern to us."

"What 'agenda'?"

"From what I understand, he is gathering to himself certain items, individuals, objects and abilities which, combined, could render him disproportionately influential, if you understand my implication."

"I think I may."

"In this light, I hope you won't consider it rude if I enquire as to the nature of your dispute with Mr Bakker?"

"I won't consider it rude; but, again, I'm afraid I will not answer."

"Will you at least concede as to whether it had any bearing on the hypothesis I have proposed?"

"I believe…I *believe* that Robert James Bakker long ago became a danger to myself and to others. Is that what you want to hear?"

"Indeed, indeed, it is close. Is it true?"

"I knew Bakker was a danger before I came to meet you."

He nodded vigorously. "Good, good, yes, of course. And, I take it, you were considering some investigation of his activities yourself?"

"Perhaps."

"Naturally, yes. The circumstances of your demise led me to assume there must be some link."

"I take it you wish in some way to limit his threat?"

The question seemed to take him aback. "Let us speak bluntly, Mr Swift. I wish him killed."

"I see."

"I take it you do not agree with this course of action?"

"I don't agree with it, no. But we think it may be necessary." I let out a breath I hadn't realised I'd been holding. "Mr Sinclair, I apologise if my behaviour appears unhelpful. I learnt a harsh lesson when . . . you are correct in thinking that these things change a man. As for the nature of my continued survival, we intend no harm. You wish to kill Bakker. I will not pull the trigger, but I will not condemn it; and, if I can, I will help you in any other way, so long as when we require assistance, you are willing to reciprocate."

The big words tumbled out of my mouth, matching him pomp for pomp.

This time the smile was real, and it was frightening for it. "Good. Good, Mr Swift. Good. Yes, indeed. I think this will be a most profitable relationship. In fact, if you would be so kind, I'd like you to meet some friends of mine."

He had a silver Mercedes parked in one of the little, squat-housed streets near Waterloo station. It had mirrored glass thick enough to be bulletproof. The young man with milk-chocolate skin drove, while we sat in the back on white leather upholstery. Dudley Sinclair offered me a Turkish delight from a silver-edged box. We were tempted; I said no. That was the end of any conversation as we drove back across the river.

We made our way north-west, past Hyde Park and Marble Arch, crawling up Edgware Road with its shopfronts in curling Arabic script, bars selling shisha, and windows full of expensive, gaudy lampshades. Five times a day Edgware Road is lined with men kneeling on mats dragged hastily out of car doors or onto the floor of restaurants, praying to Mecca, while all around the traffic edges sulkily past the congestion charge zone. We turned off into the narrower byways towards Marylebone High Street, where the red-brick terraced houses have flower-filled balconies, tall windows, spiked black railings, and wide steps leading up to their giant front doors.

In one such street we stopped, got out; and Sinclair marched, as best his bulk allowed, up a flight of steps to one such door, where a buzzer showed the house to be divided into five flats. He rang three times, twice short and once long, and the door clicked open without question. The hall beyond was wide, with black-and-white marble flooring and a thickly carpeted staircase curving upwards. Sinclair headed for a surprisingly plain lift, with a rattling metal door, and warped mirror walls that made our reflected faces look diseased. All of us – myself, Sinclair and his ever loyal, ever silent companion – piled in, an act of intimacy more than any handshake as we compressed ourselves to accommodate Sinclair's bulk, and rode the straining contraption to the top floor. It didn't open up on a shared hallway, as I had expected, but straight into a flat itself, whose walls were papered in white with a swirling reddish floral pattern, and whose pale blue carpets almost caressed our shins with their freshness. Sinclair waved us on towards a light shining beneath a door, from beyond which I could hear voices.

As I pushed open the door, all conversation stopped – a reaction I'd always hoped for in my secret dreams, but which had never happened until now.

Seven people were sitting or standing, round a glass-topped coffee table, on which stood half-eaten bowls of crisps and glasses of wine. I recognised the fortune-teller, now more comfortably attired in a dark, semi-formal dress that clung in a way that suited her. The rest were so mixed, and the odours they gave off, both natural and unnatural, so diverse, that I hardly knew where to begin.

Sinclair started for me. Sweeping into the room with a "Good, good, excellent, glad to see you all, yes . . ." he had a glass of wine in his hand before he'd finished, ". . . you all know why we're here, yes, naturally, and of course you're eager to get on."

Looking round the room, I noticed that the curtains were closed and the lights turned down. Next I became aware of the tension in one man, with a long, pale, horselike face, who sat hunched forward, knees locked together, white-knuckled fingers clasped on his lap; also how the fortune-teller glanced nervously around, looking away the instant anyone looked at her.

Only one person seemed relaxed. She was sitting in a corner with a bowl of peanuts in her hand, wearing a faded pink woollen cardigan that had every dire symptom of being hand-knitted, a grey knee-length skirt of some thick material, a woolly hat with a bobble on it and a pair of furry slippers. At her feet were a number of large plastic bags. Even from across the room, they emitted strange smells of curry and grease and, to my consternation, traffic fumes, spilling out from the largely empty space around her. She looked me over with eyes sunk deep into a face like a map of the Pyrénées, and shrilled between the gap in her front teeth, "Raisins in the bottom of the bag!" Then her eyes narrowed and in a smaller voice she added, "I sees you hiding in that skin. Heard in the wire, ain't it? Heard it go away."

We shifted uneasily in the force of her gaze.

"Hah!" she shrieked. "Bollocks arseholes!"

"Thank you, Madam Dorie," intoned Sinclair. "As always, your contribution is scintillating."

"Up yours, walrus-bottom!"

No one seemed particularly bothered by this statement – clearly Madam Dorie's contributions were often along these lines.

"Gentlemen, ladies," Sinclair ploughed on. "You all know why we're here."

"I don't," I offered.

"Is this a sorcerer?" asked one man, who wore what I assumed was some sort of African tribal costume, despite his being as pale as snow in December, and ginger. His voice was like the last hum of a fading siren. "He looks like nothing."

"You look like a twat in a dress, but you're only a warlock despite it," I retorted. I have never liked warlocks. They lack the intuition of a sorcerer and the academic aptitude or patience of your hard-working wizard. Instead, as a short cut to power, they align themselves with the ancient spirits of the city – Lady Neon, the Seven Sisters, the Beggar King, Fat Rat and so on – doing their will in exchange for a quick-fix magic trip. It's a lazy, risky profession.

The horse-faced man made a snuffling noise that might have been a laugh, hastily repressed. The fortune-teller's lips twitched, Dorie ate a handful of peanuts, Sinclair showed no reaction at all. Of the other two in the room, one was a woman in jeans, with skin the colour of roast coffee, and a tight black jacket which bulged in odd places; she looked like she was ready to set something on fire. The other, a large man in the vast trousers and jacket of someone who rode motorbikes and took it seriously, laughed so loud the glasses on the table shook.

The warlock in the tribal costume glared at him, and this just seemed to make the biker laugh even more, and exclaim through it, "Sinclair, have you found something interesting to talk about at last?"

"If you will..." Sinclair cut in, "Mr Swift is willing to help us with our mutual concern. I thought it wise for us all to meet and discuss in more depth exactly how we wish to remedy our collective problem, yes?"

"We're going to kill the bastard," offered the biker. "You OK with that, sorcerer?"

"Are we all talking about Robert Bakker?" I asked.

There was a series of grunts and nods around the room which I took to be yeses, along with Dorie's cry of "Gotta dig the bottom of the bag!"

"And what do you all have against him?"

"What do *you*?" snapped the warlock.

"My reasons for getting involved," I replied quickly, "are my own. I'd like to know yours."

"So we tell you about ourselves, and you tell us nothing?"

I glared at the warlock. "Yep. Pretty much."

"Gentlemen, gentlemen," crooned Sinclair. "This is a matter we can easily sort out. Mr Swift – you largely know my interest – I am concerned because I suspect Mr Bakker of being involved in a number of deaths, including, I believe, yours. Such things concern me, as a man who may be involved, yes? I'm sure you understand."

"Are you police?" I asked.

"Good heavens, no, no, no, that wouldn't do at all. I am, shall we say...affiliated to certain aspects of government, who are keen that, at all costs, order should be maintained. And here, I fear, I must say no more."

"A spook," added the biker dryly. "*X-Files* with cream tea."

"And you?" I looked round the room. "Are you all enemies of Bakker?"

"You must understand," soothed Sinclair, "things have changed."

"How have they changed?"

"The Tower runs things now."

I rolled my eyes, impatient. "Great. What is the Tower, what has changed, and what is Bakker's role?"

"The Tower," the fortune-teller cut in, "is an organisation of magicians, wizards, warlocks, witches and other practitioners of the art, and Bakker is their leader."

"A union? Sounds like balls to me."

"Oh, it's very real," sighed Mr Sinclair. "I believe they even have AGMs."

"Why do you sound like you don't like it?"

"Because what they cannot get, they take," snapped the fortune-teller, "and they kill when they are not obeyed."

"The magicians who are dead," explained Sinclair gently, "all in some way crossed the Tower. As I think you did."

"I've never heard of the Tower."

"It grew up shortly after your death. They are gathering things – books, knowledge, ability, magicians, items, artefacts – they are accumulating power. I think you knew Bakker had this interest... perhaps was dabbling in certain things that shouldn't be handled. I think that's why you quarrelled."

"You can think what you want," I replied. "What is he dabbling in specifically?"

"Rumours," said the warlock.

"Too many rumours for them all to be false," corrected Sinclair. "Too many, in too close proximity. Experiments, Mr Swift. We believe Bakker is experimenting on magicians, on civilians, searching, that he is looking for something powerful – presumably, something dangerous, since he keeps its nature so secret from his staff, his servants and the community at large."

"If that's so, why aren't you doing something?"

"Because Bakker's a fucking sorcerer with enough money to buy Mayfair, *duh*," intoned the warlock.

"You're a charmer, aren't you?"

"Look," he said, angry now rather than just annoying. "Getting to him is like trying to get into Fort Knox with a fucking tin-opener!"

"There are other sorcerers..."

"No," said Sinclair sharply. "There aren't."

"Don't give me that."

"You know that Dhawan is dead, and Akute. I didn't mention deMaurier, MacKinnon, Samuels, Zheng..."

"I don't believe this."

"...and if they're not dead, they've fled. Do you understand this, Matthew Swift? They've hidden, run away – people who oppose Bakker die. Do you think the litterbug just happened to turn up in Dulwich this morning? You must have been seen. It takes power to summon a creature like that; it was looking for *you*. If you are to oppose the Tower, Mr Swift, you need to do it discreetly. As we do now. You cannot simply charge in and hope to come away alive."

I looked round the room. Embarrassed faces avoided my eyes. Even Dorie sat perfectly still on her chair, studying her bowl of peanuts. Finally I said, "All right. Let's say, just for the moment, that I believe you. What exactly do you propose to do?"

There was an almost audible relaxation of breath. In her corner Dorie muttered, "Bug bug bug bug bug blue bug..."

The man with a horselike face stumbled, "We had a plan..."

"Fucking idiotic plan!" the warlock contributed.

"Moron," snapped the fortune-teller.

"Fight!" said the motorbiker with a happy smile. "Go on, fight!"

The woman in the jeans said nothing, but looked more angry than ever before.

"Ladies, gentlemen," soothed Sinclair. "Charlie, please?"

The one addressed as Charlie turned out to be Sinclair's loyal shadow, he with his dark eyes and straight black hair. At the mention of his name, he produced from behind a sofa a slim black briefcase. He entered a pair of combination codes on the clasps, snapping them back with a press of a brass button, and carefully put the whole contents of the briefcase onto the table.

Pictures, words, columns, figures, diagrams, maps – all sprawled out at Sinclair's fingertips as he arranged them across the table. "This," he said, spreading his hands above it like it was spider's silk that might drift away on a breeze, "is everything we know about the Tower: who runs it, how it works, how it stays alive."

I waited for something more.

"Anyone who tries to approach Bakker directly – assuming they can find him – fails." For a moment, his eyes were on the lady in jeans, whose scowl, if possible, deepened. "You must understand – he is not merely a dangerous practitioner of magic. He has wealth: his lawyers can protect him from the law, and should they fail to do so, he has a plane ready to take him out of the country, and money overseas. His reach is international, his friends are in the highest circles and can operate in the lowest gutter."

"He's always had power."

"Yes, yes, of course," murmured Sinclair. "But only recently has he exploited it so flagrantly. What we propose, then, is to remove as much as possible of the source of his power before we strike against him. We are not merely talking the odd curse here or there. We are talking about undermining his wealth, his reputation, his influence, removing his friends one at a time until there is nothing left, merely him, alone. Then, perhaps, he will be vulnerable, if such a thing is even possible any more."

"You have a plan?"

"Everything," he said, waving his hands over the documents, "everything is here. We will tear the Tower apart piece by piece."

I studied the papers he'd spread in front of me. The room waited. I said, "Sounds like a shitty plan to me."

"Sinclair, do we have to have shit-for-brains here?" growled the warlock. We felt flickering sapphire-blue anger.

"Mr Swift, you have an alternative? You think you can find Bakker by yourself, you think you can... undo whatever has happened here... without our help?" Mr Sinclair was still smiling, but his voice was the incantation of the bored priest administering funeral rites.

I shifted uncomfortably, looking down at the tumble of papers. "I will help you. But I will not kill Bakker unless it becomes necessary."

"You are entitled to your wish."

"What can I do?"

"Bakker has lieutenants, key people in running the Tower."

"I know some. Guy Lee, San Khay, are they who you're thinking of?"

"Also Harris Simmons, and Dana Mikeda."

"Dana Mikeda?"

"You know her?" asked the warlock sharply.

"I... did. What's her involvement?"

"I suppose, for the sake of saving time, I shall be crude. Protégée. Lover. One or the other, although perhaps it doesn't do justice to the relationship."

"How long has she been this way?"

"What way?"

"Protégée, lover, and all the other things you aren't describing."

He smiled, a rare flicker of amusement. "Approximately two years. You know her." It wasn't a question, and thus didn't require an answer.

"You're planning on killing them also?"

"If necessary."

"You have an alternative?"

"Perhaps. If they can be useful."

"I see. If there is . . ."

"Pustulant warts!" shrilled Dorie from her corner.

"For fuck's sake," groaned the warlock.

"Oh, well, bollocks to your brain," she muttered.

We hesitated, looking up from the documents on the table to where she sat, arms folded, in the corner of the room.

"Swift?" asked Sinclair quietly, seeing our expression.

We looked round the room, suddenly uneasy.

"It's nothing," I said. "Nothing."

"You're a nit when not them, aren't you?" Dorie muttered.

I stepped back from the table. I walked a few paces across the room towards her, hesitated just in front of the window, found my right hand shaking. "You know us," we said, uncertainly.

"Heard you in the wire," she said with a yellow-toothed grin. "'Come be we and be free', that's your song, ain't it, blue-eyes?"

"You have met us?"

"I like the dance you play," she admitted. "But I wouldn't stand where you do right now."

"Why?" I asked.

"Fucking shadow on the wall," she replied. "Duck!"

I ducked. I can respect formidable magical talent when I meet it, and Old Madam Dorie, the grey bag lady who smelt of curry powder and car fumes, had it in spades. She exuded skilful manipulation of primal forces just like her bags gave off the smell of mould, and if she'd said hop, I would have hopped. She, like my gran, had the look of a woman who talked to the pigeons; and in the city no one sees more than the pigeons.

I ducked, which is why the bullet from the sniper's rifle shattered the skull of the horse-faced man, who'd just been standing, rather than mine.

"Banzai!" shrilled Dorie.

The lights went out in the room – and, more than that, the power went too. I could feel the sharp loss from the walls and ceiling as the fuses were pulled, somewhere below in the rest of the house. The darkness was intense, but only for a moment, as the orange-white glare from the street lamp outside came in through the curtains. I crawled across the floor towards the horse-faced man's body, even as Dorie stood up and clapped her hands together with a cry of "Ratatatatatatat!"

Somewhere on the other side of the road, someone duly cocked a small mechanism in a big weapon, and opened fire. The bullets tore through the remnants of one window and shattered the other, peppering the rear wall and filling the room with white puffs of mortar dust. From the floor I saw Dorie scuttling out through a door, utterly unconcerned, while the corpse of the horse-faced man bounced and shook with the impact of every bullet. The line of fire puffed out the stuffing from the sofas, shattered wine glasses, sending a fine spray of red wine and crystal shards flying across the room, blasted pictures off the wall, smashed doors into splinters, ripped up curtains and punched through pillows. In the gloom I saw a pair of high-heeled feet belonging to the fortune-teller as she wriggled towards the hallway door, closely followed by the absurd robe of the warlock, while somewhere behind the remnants of the sofa, now almost reduced to a bare frame with rags hanging off it, I guessed were Sinclair, the biker and the sullen lady in jeans.

The ratatatatatat of the gun on the other side of the road stopped. In the sudden ringing silence I heard the wailing of car alarms, burglar alarms from the houses around, the screaming of people, the flapping of terrified pigeons, the running of feet. And the grinding mechanism of the lift, rising up from the ground floor.

I shouted, "They're coming upstairs for us!"

"Bedroom," came the shrill sound of the warlock. "There's a fire escape."

"If they've got any brains, they'll come up that too," muttered the fortune-teller.

"You want to take chances?"

"Some help here, please?" came the biker's voice.

I crawled on my belly round the back of the sofa. My fingers dipped into sticky blood mingling with wine; my elbows crunched on broken glass.

Behind the sofa was indeed the lady in jeans, with the biker, breathless, face spattered with blood but not his own, and what was left of Sinclair, wheezing desperately, the folders clutched to several holes in his chest and belly. Even though he was a large man, the bullets had penetrated well enough; and as he breathed, he sweated, he bled, he stank of salt and urine and death, as if his whole body was unclenching at once, every cell letting out everything within it, chemicals, blood, fluid, life and all.

The motorbiker was struggling to hold him up. "Can you do anything?" he hissed.

"Come on!" shrieked the fortune-teller. "They're coming!"

The warlock glanced at Sinclair with a brief look of pity, but kept moving.

"Shit," I muttered. "Shit."

I pulled back the front of his jacket and there were even more holes. The entire shape of his body was distorted, as if he was sand pocked by tiny meteors, and bent into the odd dips and curves of impact.

"Do something!" demanded the biker.

"I can't just fix this!" I retorted angrily.

"Fucking sorcerer!" he roared.

I heard the ping of the lift door in the hall. "Move," we hissed. "Get him to the back escape."

"It'll be watched," said the woman sharply.

"Then fight!" we replied. "Get him out of here now."

They didn't bother to ask questions. The woman snatched up the bloody folders and gracelessly stuck them down the back of her trousers, the tops protruding from behind the belt. With an almighty grunt she helped the biker raise up Sinclair's great bulk, an arm over each of their shoulders, and started dragging him towards the back door.

I crouched behind the sofa and rummaged frantically in my satchel. I heard footsteps in the corridor outside and, as our fingers closed over the first can of spray-paint, a foot kicked open the remnants of the door. White torches swept across the room, dazzling us, if only for a second.

We stood, letting the world move slowly around us. We stretched out our left hand and pinched out the light on those torches, breaking the glass of their bulbs at our will. With our other hand we threw the spray-paint can at the door and, as it bounced off the shoulder of the first man through it, we pinched that too, and turned our back.

The can exploded with the bang of a firecracker, sending out a shower of blood-red paint and twisted metal. The spray tickled the back of my neck as I ran towards the door, and a razor-sharp shard of metal nearly took my ear off as it spun past. In the doorway I heard screaming, and a familiar voice shouting, "Shoot, shoot, dammit!" San Khay, a friend of Bakker's even when I'd been one too. I'd never met him until now but, even back then, back before all the things for which I couldn't find a name, his star had been rising.

One of them got enough paint out of their eyes to find a trigger, but not enough to aim well. I dove through the bedroom door and slammed it shut, one hand already in my satchel for another can of paint. As the crowd of attackers in the other room got control of themselves again, I drew a ward across the door, big and exaggerated, stretching it over the walls in long strokes that eventually described a crude key. A foot slammed into the door, which shook, but didn't open. I murmured gentle words into my ward and backed away. Someone opened fire, the noise at this proximity almost painful, shocking to our senses, but the door didn't splinter, didn't move, didn't open. That wouldn't last long, but it was good enough. I crawled across the room, past a neatly made double bed to where a window stood open, a metal staircase visible below. I half-fell onto the cold stair, damp from the evening drizzle, and saw below the struggling shapes of the motorbiker and the woman, hauling Sinclair down towards the ground.

I scurried after them, and caught up as they managed to drag the gasping Sinclair into a small passage at ground level.

"The men?" the motorbiker asked me, with a strong grasp of the relevant.

"They'll get through eventually."

Sinclair's face was white and slick. "He needs a hospital," I muttered.

"You think?" snapped the motorbiker.

"Do you have a vehicle?"

"My bike."

"Can you get him on it?"

"Shit, you think he's in a fit state? You're a fucking sorcerer, do something!"

"It's not that simple! To repair something like this you need equipment, preparation..."

"Sorcerers can't heal," said the woman. It was the first time I'd heard her speak. Her voice was low and cold, almost dispassionate. "It's not part of their magic."

"I can fucking heal when I have the fucking equipment!" I retorted. "But no, if you're asking, we're not exactly into bringing people back from death or even the bloody edge!"

"Great," the motorbiker hissed. "You're just so grand, aren't you?"

"We can keep him alive," we snarled. "Our blood can hold him for a little; if you can get him to a place to heal."

Perhaps even the motorbiker sensed our intent – certainly he was not foolish enough to question us. I pulled out the Swiss Army knife from my satchel, the cool metal slipping in my bloody fingers. My hand was shaking; I didn't know what I was doing, nor if it would work. And if it didn't, then...

We steadied our hand, forcing ourselves to be still. We took a long, slow breath, every nerve on edge, and tried to calm our heart from its thundering in our ears. We searched, and levered out the hinged knife we needed from within the casing. Then, careful not to cause ourselves more than a shallow injury, we drew the blade across the palm of our left hand. We could feel the disgust and horror in the woman, even though her expression stayed cold, and see the surprise in the man's face. For a moment, the pain was a shocking relief, a distraction that removed the ringing in our ears, the burning in our eyes and the shaking in our limbs, and focused us entirely on the blood pooling in our cupped hand.

At first the blood was not appropriate: dark, almost black in the poor light. Just crude human fluids; ugly, temperatureless. We waited.

After a few seconds, the change began. A bright worm of blue light rose to the surface of the blood welling between our fingers, then dipped down again, like an animal breaking from the sea for air. A moment later, another shimmer of blue flashed like a static spark between two lightning rods across the surface of our blood; then another. I tried to hold back nausea as, emerging like blue maggots, the colour spread throughout the blood in my hand, a bright glow of sparks that rose up to the surface, shimmering and twisting, so bright it cast shadows across our faces, pushing back the darkness in its electric-blue glow. It wasn't just in the blood in my hand; as the writhing blueness spread, I could feel it running up inside my veins, saw my skin turning white and blue as the redness drained from it, a pallor running from my wrist up my arms, that seemed to turn my blood to ice, shuddering through my flesh like frozen electricity, rattling off my bones and making my head buzz with...

...come be...

...we be...

I closed my eyes as the blueness rose in front of my vision, burning away the darkness and covering the world with its sapphire glow. But even behind my eyelids the blueness burnt and, God help me, we loved it, revelled in it, raised our fingers and felt the electricity flash between them like every nerve carried a hundred volts, like every organ was bubbling acid feeding a spark plug inside my heart that, with every pump, set our skin on fire. In all my life I had never felt so alive, so inhuman.

We moved automatically through the fear, performing our function. We pulled back the jacket of the injured man, peeled away the remnants of his waistcoat around the worst of his injuries and tipped some of our burning blue blood onto his flesh. Where it touched, the flesh crisped, and at every drop the man jerked and moaned like he was being burnt with pincers. We poured a few drops into each of his wounds and pulled open his shirt over his heart. We waited for his breathing to become steadier, and said, "You will need to hold him."

"What are you doing?" demanded the woman.

"We will keep him alive, as long as we can without harming ourself," we said. "Our fire in his flesh."

We poured the blood over his heart. He screamed, but the man obeyed our command and held him down as we rubbed the blood into his chest, the liquid dividing into worms of blue light, each one brighter than a diamond at noonday, which wriggled across his skin for a moment and then started burrowing, digging down into his flesh, a dozen, more, of our sparks burrowing into his skin, his nervous system. Where they had entered his flesh, they left tiny, pale burn marks, and we were not sure if those would heal. However, he slowly relaxed as the last of our blood dug itself into his skin, and his breathing became more natural. Across his skin and in the palm of our hand, the smears of blood still visible gently faded back to their original dark red; carefully we tore the end off our shirt sleeve to bind around our hand and prevent further bleeding.

"Now," I said breathlessly, fighting the spinning in my head and sickness in my belly, "he'll live long enough to reach a hospital. Can you get him there?"

The motorbiker smiled. "Oh, yes," he said. "I think so."

His bike was parked in the street outside; and the street outside was deafening. Every car alarm wailed, every light was on in every house, and in those where they weren't on, burglar alarms were blaring out their distress into the night. I could hear sirens in the streets around, police cars getting closer, and one or two braver souls further from the gunfire, who perhaps hadn't worked out its context, had even opened their front doors and were peering into the street. The bike was big, with huge silver pipes and gears sprawling out of it like the tubes of some demented church organ, and with a giant leather seat and wide handlebars. We slung Sinclair across the front and the motorbiker climbed up behind him, reaching his huge arms across the other man's mercifully unconscious form, hands just resting on the handlebars, a grin on his face. "I'll be at UCH, find me," he said. "Before they do."

With that, he kicked the stand out from under the bike, and started the engine with a thick, heavy fart of fumes and a roar of the engine like the mournful wail of a dinosaur.

Left behind in the middle of the road, the woman said, "This is too easy."

"Oh, you just had to go and say it," I muttered, slinging my satchel into a better position.

"If they were determined to kill us, I'm sure they could have done it in a more efficient manner," she replied primly.

"You're jumping in there with question number two on the list."

"And question one?"

"How the hell did they find us in the first place?"

Her eyes roamed quickly across the street. "Where's the warlock? The seer woman?"

"I have no idea; let's start walking." With my least bloody hand I turned her briskly away from the house. She flinched from my touch like it burnt.

"We have to move," I hissed.

She hesitated, then nodded and started walking. I fell into step with her, face forward, breathing steady, hand now on fire, wondering if I needed another tetanus jab any time soon, or if tetanus was even applicable any more.

Our shadows bent around us.

She was right, it was easy, far too easy. I felt cold all over, the fire in my blood simmering down to leave nothing but exhaustion and pain. We felt eyes on us, tasted the same ice-cold shimmer in the air that I had sensed that day two years ago, when I'd picked up the telephone receiver with bloody hands by the river; but this time it was stronger. Was that because I was already half-looking for it, or because it had grown in my absence? The lick of its power in the air was like drinking thin black moonlight. I looked down, knowing what I would see, and felt my stomach tighten. My hands started to shake and – we could not stop it – tears in my eyes, the memory of every single cut, stab, tear, pain, every moment, every trickle of blood from my skin, every instant – it was there, real, enveloping me, drowning out sense; and though we tried to fight it down we could see our vision blurring and feel the strength going out from our bones at the thought, astonished that a mere state of mind could reduce our physical form to the consistency of wet paper, and afraid, so afraid that we were about to experience these things for ourself, about to end sensation with these sensations...

"What's wrong?"

The woman's voice was a relief, a knife through the high-pitched buzz in our ears.

We pointed with trembling hands at the pavements where, slowly and surely, our shadows, defined by the orange neon outline around us, were beginning to bend *towards* the light.

"Run," I whispered.

"What?"

"Run."

I grabbed her hand when she didn't move and though she tried to pull free, we gripped with all the strength in our bones and pulled her down the street.

We ran.

There was no sign of pursuit, no sound of running footsteps, no shouting of "Oi, you!", no sirens, no yelling, no breath at the back of our necks, no gunshot, no symptom at all of being chased. But as we ran I watched our shadows stretch out thinner and thinner, and they didn't bend with the light, they didn't move as we ducked under every lamp, didn't contract and expand they way they did when you ran through the city, moving from pool of shadow to splotch of neon, they just stretched pole-thin, dragging behind us, until my shadow felt almost like a physical weight, a cloak of lead pulling me back head first. My neck hurt with the effort of keeping my eyes forward, my shoulders creaked, every movement of my legs felt like they had sandbags tied to them. She must have noticed too – I doubt she would have kept running without the realisation that her own shadow was moving around behind her and becoming distorted, warping, the edge shimmering and melting.

That night we ran like we had run all our life, like it was all we knew, all we needed, all that there was.

We ran south, across Wigmore Street and back into the mess of alleyways where I'd first encountered the fortune-teller in Khan's old Cave of Miracles. We ran out onto Oxford Street, still busy but less so at this hour. Beggars, drunk men and skimpily dressed women paid us little attention as we crossed in front of the oncoming night buses towards the half-shut gate of Bond Street station, pushing past the large sign saying "Station Closed" and the half-asleep guard in dark blue who was writing it, and scampering down the stairs into the station proper.

"Wait a minute!" piped the guard.

The woman, with a surprising show of pragmatism, pointed to me and shouted, "He's got a gun, fucker!"

There were only two things for the guard to do in answer to a statement like that – test it or not test it. I had a feeling he wasn't paid enough to find out if I did have a gun. With an exclamation of "Fuck, shit," he turned and ran.

Bond Street station was still lit up – indeed, I doubted that the lights ever went off – but the ticket machines had black screens, and the shutters were down on all the booths. In the artificial brightness, our shadows weren't even visible, blotted out by the white strip lights across the ceiling.

"Is that it?" asked the woman.

"You wish," I muttered. "Do you have a travelcard?"

"The tube's not running. We've missed the train . . ." she began.

"This is not the time to argue," I said in my nicest voice, "just say bloody yes!"

"Yes," she muttered.

"Good. Through the barrier, now."

"But the train . . ."

"Either it will kill you or we will unless you move *now*!"

I had shouted; this surprised us all. She nodded numbly, fumbled in her pocket with bloody fingers, found the card and, without a word, shoved it into the ticket mouth of the electronic barrier.

"Not working!" she called out even as I fumbled for my Oyster card. "Shall I jump?"

"Don't bloody jump!" I snapped. "It won't work if you jump."

"What won't work?"

I ran over to the barrier, and slammed my Oyster card as hard as I could onto the card reader. Sparks raced from my hand into the machine – I hadn't even consciously tried for the spell, everything was running on adrenalin – and with a polite *beep*, the gate opened. I stepped through. "Try again!" I exclaimed at her.

There was a movement at the top of the stairs. The lights flickered on the ceiling, pushing us in and out of darkness.

"But I . . ."

"Do it now!"

She pushed her travelcard into the reader and this time it accepted and, with a beep, opened the gate. She scuttled through, and the gate shut behind her.

I turned my attention to the stairs coming down into the station. The lights at the top of the stair died with a tiny whining sound, as if they'd simply given up the ghost. Then the lights in front of those, and in front of those, and in front of those. The darkness spread down from the mouth of the staircase like a tide coming in from the sea. As it crawled across the barrier and snuffed out the illumination over our heads I reached up and snatched a glimmer of white light out of the last lamp before it could expire, clutching it between my fingertips, while the other hand was clenched tight around my Oyster card.

The darkness spread past us, running down the escalators at our back and leaving us in just a tiny spot of white light encased by shadows. An inch from me, the woman murmured, "What is it?"

"Don't let go of your ticket," I replied.

In the gloom on the other side of the barrier, a deeper patch of darkness seemed to rise up from the floor, thicken, move, open eyes the colour of star-filled night. It opened a mouth, and it was a he; and though he seemed like the withered corpse of a man, I recognised him nonetheless. In a voice like the swish of silk across polished bone, he whispered, "Hello, Matthew."

"Hello," I murmured, unable to muster anything better. "Hungry?"

"Always, always an aching belly. And hello, Matthew's fire," he added. "And such fire you are!"

He started walking towards the barrier, dragging shadow as he came. In the dull reflected light of the sphere of whiteness in my fingers, I could see his face, corpse-white, shrunken, bone protruding at every angle, a skull on which skin had been thinly draped, teeth misshapen, eyes a sickly, watery blue, almost as pale as his skin, hair a thin white rag drooping down from the uneven, pocked skin across the rough plates of his skull, just visible beneath the broad black hat he wore to shield his eyes. His neck was barely thicker than his spine, his fingers unnaturally long, and when he moved he didn't seem to lift his bare feet, with toes like stretched matchsticks and veins protruding like baby snakes between the long tendons of his legs, but glide across the shadows on the floor, pooled around him in thick oily waves. He wore a pair of thin, tattered trousers, half-rags, spattered with whitewashed stains, a loose white shirt that hung off his frame like a deflated air balloon, and a coat. I recognised the coat with a shock – long, beige, and with the faded brown stain of where my blood had seeped into it, dried, and been crudely washed out again.

He saw my expression and murmured almost petulantly between his jutting yellow teeth, "I keep something in honour of all my friends. I was going to take your heart – but when I looked again you had kept it for others!"

He neared the barrier, slowed, looking it over with a scornful air.

The woman's fingers tightened on my arm.

He hunched down in an almost animal pose, head on one side, and then without any apparent effort, leapt. As he rose, the darkness seemed to stretch around him, and for a second, his coat – *my coat*, on his body – was nothing more than a raven's wing, catching at the air, and his form stretched and shimmered like it was made of bent fog. His leap carried him up and forward. He sailed over the barrier, hit the space directly above its middle, and was, with a bang, thrown backwards. He sprawled across the floor in the darkness, and then, not showing any sign of injury or pain, picked himself up again. His eyes glowed with silvery light.

"Will you think to hold me?" he hissed.

I held up my Oyster card like a policeman's badge in front of me, pointed directly towards him, and said, "These are the terms and conditions of carriage: 'If you do not have an Oyster card with a valid season ticket and/or balance to pay as you go on it, you must have with you a valid printed ticket(s), available for the whole of the journey you are making. You may use your printed ticket in accordance with these conditions. All printed tickets . . .'"

The creature threw itself with a roar at the barrier again, his form stretching out around him until he almost filled the station; and again he was thrown back with a sharp electric bang.

"'. . . remain our property and we may withdraw or cancel any printed ticket at any time. We will only do this for a good reason, and if we do, we will give you a receipt.'"

He opened his mouth and roared, and from his throat came the smell of rotting flesh and a rolling tide of darkness, physical darkness taking shape like moths that threw themselves at the barriers and the air above them and the spaces below and, whenever they hit the middle of the barrier, shattered into little black pieces of ash that faded as they sank to the floor.

I kept speaking, lost now in the spell, thrilled with it, and as I did, the air around the barrier thickened, growing firmer with every word until the shadow of the creature on the other side of the barrier was distorted by the sheer density of magic between us and it. I yelled, revelling in the feeling of it, "'You must only buy printed tickets from official ticket outlets. If you buy a printed ticket from anyone else, it is illegal and may result in the ticket being withdrawn and the seller/you being prosecuted . . .'"

On the other side, the creature grew claws of ebony blackness and raked them across the barriers, but they didn't even wobble. I screamed, the spell burning around me, filling me from head to toe, "'The single fare that you must pay at London Underground stations or for journeys on London Underground and for journeys to places served by other operators, is the fare from the station where your journey begins to the station/Tramlink stop where . . .'"

With one last, almighty hiss of frustration, the creature launched itself at the barrier, scrabbled at the invisible wall of power suspended in its path, tore and snatched and pummelled at it and finally, wailing like an injured animal, fell back.

"'. . . where your journey finishes.'"

I realised I was out of breath, my head spinning, my entire body now feeling light to the point where if I moved, I thought I'd float off the ground.

The lights started to come on around us. They spread back up the escalator and curled round the walls, encircling the black shadow, which now looked vaguely human again, standing in the middle of the concourse.

Through the wavering wall of force between us, it said, "I'll come again, Matthew. For the blue electric fire, for your guardian angels, I'll come again."

Then, without a sound, without a sigh, it melted, darkness shimmering off its frame and boiling down to nothing but a shadow on the floor that raced away, up the stairs and into the night, as the lights all came back on.

I slid to the floor. Bewildered, I sat on the dirty tiles of Bond Street station, the slow, sneaky awareness slipping through my bones that I was alive.

The woman squatted down in front of me, keeping her distance. After a while she said, "You all right?"

"Uh?"

"Are you all right?"

"Yes. Fine."

"Can you walk?"

"What?"

"We need to leave this place."

"We do?"

"I told the guard you had a gun."

"Oh, yes, right. Walk. Sure. No problem. Give us a hand?" She hesitated, face crinkling in displeasure at the thought. "Fine," I muttered, crawling onto my hands and knees and laboriously up. I felt like I hadn't eaten for a week, or that this was the precursor to an almighty hangover. "*Fine.*"

I staggered up to the barrier and beeped myself out. She followed suit. The barrier opened and closed like the wings of a butterfly around us, no problems, no questions asked, the miracle of a valid ticket on the London Underground.

"Will it come back?" she asked, as we staggered up the stairs.

"You know," I said honestly, suddenly very tired, "I have no idea. But I doubt it. Not tonight."

"Why?"

"Because it's not used to being thwarted. Let alone twice."

"Twice?"

"Come on," I sighed and, fixing my eye on the nearest bus stop, went to find a way from that place.

On the night bus as I lay across the front seats of the top deck, she said very quietly, from the row behind me, "Twice?"

"Give it a break."

"That . . . abomination . . . knew you. It called you by your name."

"Uh-huh. It did too."

Outside, the shop lights were green, yellow, orange, white, lighting up mannequins in all the latest fashions of the day, staring out contemplatively onto the quiet street below. Even the beggars were calling it a night, opening up their pieces of cardboard in front of the shop doors and stretching out their sleeping bags at the feet of the ATMs while the day's litter – takeaway boxes and McDonald's packaging, HMV bags and the plastic wrappings of newly purchased CDs, receipts and cigarette butts – billowed in the wake of the passing night bus.

"You knew what it was. You knew that it was coming."

"We've met before," I said. "I'm sure you'll work it out."

"What was it?"

"A shadow," I said. "Just a shadow. You can call it Hunger. That's all. All there is to see."

"What was the spell that stopped it?"

"Basic warding."

"With an underground ticket?" She sounded amused, rather than surprised.

I groaned and sat up – explaining the intricacies of magical theory while sprawled across the top deck of a bus wasn't, I felt, the appropriate way to deliver the lesson. "What exactly is your part in this?" I asked flatly. "You seem to know bugger-all about magic, have sod-all feel for it. You have no . . . flavour on the air, your movements leave no colour, no smell of spice. What the hell are you doing with Sinclair and that lot?"

She smiled thinly, and looked down at her bloody hands, folded in her lap. "My disposition lies elsewhere."

"What's your name?"

"Oda. You can call me Oda."

"Matthew," I said. "You can call me pretty much anything you like."

She smiled again, lips shockingly pink in an otherwise dark, finely formed face. Her black curly hair was braided so close to her skull it had to hurt, and her eyes were wide and alert. "Very well. Explain to me – the underground ticket."

I scrunched my hands into fists and covered my eyes, trying to press some of the fatigue out of my brain. I gave it my best shot. "Everything, everyone and every place has its own unique magic. The underground's magic is defined by the rhythms that go through it. It's like a heartbeat, a pulse, the flow of life like blood through its veins, describing in every detail the shape of power in its tunnels. When you go into the underground, you buy a ticket, you pass through the barrier, you enter its tunnels, you take the train, you use your ticket, you exit through the barrier. This is part of what defines it, this is part of what makes the taste of its magic different, heavy, crowded, full of dirt and noise and *life* and strength. If you know that this magic is there, if you understand the rhythms that shaped it, it is a very simple matter to harness it to an appropriate spell that utilises to the full its unique signature. In this case–"

"An impassable barrier, to something without a ticket."

"Pretty much."

"I suppose that is clever," she admitted. "In an obscene way."

"It's sorcery," I replied with a shrug. "All that sorcery is, is a point of view."

Her eyes flashed up to me, and held, and for a second there was a fire in them that scared me. "Sorcery," she said quietly, "makes men into gods, and men were not meant to be such creatures."

"You're . . . not what people call *nice*, are you, Oda?"

"There is a distinction between being nice and being righteous," she replied primly.

I groaned and slumped back into the tattered embrace of the seats as the bus turned onto Tottenham Court Road.

University College Hospital was new, clean, busy, bright and smelt of disinfectant. The floors and walls were so bright and white they almost hurt, the glass in every window an odd, reflective bottle-green, the potted plants were cheerful plastic in full bloom, the seats padded and pale, the uniforms of the night staff bright blue. Outside the Accident and Emergency entrance was parked a very large, black motorbike.

We didn't look out of place in A and E: two bedraggled figures stained with blood, staggering in from the street. The receptionist took one look and promptly assured me that a doctor would see to me soon. We didn't ask where Sinclair was – as two bloody people, looking for a gunshot victim didn't seem the best way to go about matters. Instead we followed signs on the wall up through the hospital, endless identical-looking corridors of gleaming white and strip lighting, tried intensive care, found no one, and eventually made our way towards the operating theatres.

We found the motorbiker sitting on a bench with a can of Red Bull open in one meaty hand, outside Operating Theatre 3. He grunted as we approached and said, "You took your time."

"Were you followed?" asked Oda sharply.

"You don't follow me," he replied in a voice that left no room for argument. Then with a sudden flash of a smile, "But you'd be welcome to try, lady." Oda rolled her eyes.

There were no windows or other way of seeing into the operating room, so I sat down on the bench opposite him, every muscle exhausted, every nerve throbbing in reproach, and said, "What do they think?"

"Oh, you know. Police must be called, immense internal damage, may not make it through the night, miracle he got so far, don't understand what's keeping him alive will do everything they can so on and so forth yadder yadder yadder, you get the drift?" There was an alert gleam in the corner of the motorbiker's eye. "You get trouble?"

"A little."

"Come out OK?"

"Yes."

"Good. Well, shit, now you're here, I don't know about you but I think we should consider buggering off."

"What about Sinclair?" asked Oda quickly.

The biker burped. "He lives, he dies, we can't change it, OK? But the police are coming. And I don't want to deal with the police, do you?"

"You'll leave him to die?"

"Christ, woman, I signed him in under a false name and like I said, the police will be here soon. If the guy pulls through, he'll be safe enough."

Oda glanced at me, eyebrows raised. I said, "We'll only bring him more danger."

"I don't believe that," she replied.

"Then we will only suffer more inconvenience if we stay," I corrected, "is that better?"

She gave a snort in reply, but didn't disagree. The biker stood up in a single quick movement, slapping his thighs cheerfully as he did and tossing the empty can of drink with perfect aim into the recycling bin by the vending machine. "Right! Let's bugger off out of here before the shit really hits the fan."

The biker lived, for want of a better description, in a garage, in a scrapyard. If that wasn't bad enough, it was in Willesden.

Willesden, to most of the population of London, is a place that you pass through on your way to somewhere better. It is a composite, an area whose character is defined by the places around it – by the leafy streets of Hampstead to the east, by the broad avenues of Maida Vale to the south, by the squat, semi-detached homes of Wembley to the north, and by that strange, indefinable area sprawling out, along streets with still-young trees that aspire one day to be great oaks, from the boundary on Willesden's western edge where city becomes suburb, and stays that way for nearly fifteen miles beyond. London, indeed, can be defined as one big suburb spread around a relatively small core, and at Willesden, every aspect of this suburbia seemed to combine into a mishmash of scrapyards, railway junctions, neat terraced homes, semi-detached bungalows, tall terraced houses, giant supermarkets, strange ethnic greengrocers, synagogues, mosques and Hindu temples galore, all pressed together like they didn't quite know how they'd got there in the first place.

The biker's shed, for there wasn't a kinder way to describe the cobbled sheets of corrugated iron that enclosed his home, was near an old canal, a remnant of a more industrial past, opposite a field of dead cars and mechanised hands for crushing them. The walls of his home were hung with tools, jackets, salvaged spare parts from bikes and cars, and pictures of bikes, reminding me of a cross between a garage and a teenager's bedroom. There were no overt symbols of a mystical nature anywhere to be seen. But as he stoked the small iron stove in a corner and kicked a small electricity generator until the lights stopped flaring up and down and settled for a dull consistent glow, I tasted a certain unique spice on the air, like a flash across the senses, seen and instantly gone. I could only guess at its nature since whenever I tried to catch the sensation again, it was as elusive as a bar of wet soap slipping from my fingers.

The biker gestured at a couch covered with old, stained blankets and said, "Want coffee?"

"No," replied Oda, not bothering to sit.

"Yes," I said, slumping across the couch with the sudden, absolute certainty that coffee was the thing around which every ambition in my life revolved.

"Want to talk about what happened?"

"Yes," said Oda.

"No," I replied.

"Shit, well, I guess I'll just make the running," he said, putting an old iron kettle on top of the stove. "Any of you two think we were sold out?"

"Yes," said Oda.

"Perhaps," I whimpered, pressing my hands against my temples with the effort of staying awake.

"Want to guess whether they'll come after us again?" added the biker, cheerfully spooning a large heap of instant caffeine into a chipped brown mug.

"If they are smart," said Oda calmly.

"Perhaps," I added.

"The creature – what you call Hunger – said he would come after you, Matthew Swift," she pointed out, without any sign of concern.

"You had to remind me," I groaned.

"What creature is this?" asked the biker casually.

"Just a shadow."

"It knew the sorcerer," she corrected. "Called him by his name."

"I'll handle it," I said.

"You sure of that?"

"It's what I'm here for."

"Fair enough," muttered the biker, as the kettle started to spout hot steam. "So – what do you want to do about this shit?"

"I am here to destroy Bakker," said Oda flatly, folding her arms. "This changes nothing."

"You'll get no complaints from me on that one. Question is – how do you want to do this? We're not doing a great job right now."

Oda produced the bundle of blood-smeared documents and spread them across the rough metal floor of the shed. "We have what we need, here," she said.

I rolled over on the couch to see more clearly.

"Everything we need to destroy the Tower, to stop Bakker from whatever he plans, to rein in his power, to destroy his evil," she added, and the way she said it was more frightening than any shadow, it made my nerves itch, "is here. I am not without my friends, or my resources."

"Me neither," murmured the biker, passing a mug of coffee in my direction, though his eyes were fixed on the documents.

I picked up a picture from the pile of papers on the floor and studied it. The pale, fine features were familiar to me – indeed, I could give them a name. San Khay, Bakker's right-hand man.

I took the picture, folded it and, very carefully, slipped it into my bag.

Part 1: The Hunting of San Khay

In which the beginning of a plan unfolds, revenge is plotted, and a lot of rats decide to congregate.

At dawn, we parted company. Oda went – where, she would not say – and the biker's only contribution was that he was going to "hit the road" for a while. We agreed a time and a place to meet again, and I, with the sum effect of Sinclair's research on the Tower in my bag, went to find a safe place to sleep, and read, and think.

When the first shops opened at 8.30 a.m., I bought myself a heavy-duty box of plasters to cover the cut on my left hand, a new shirt to replace the bloody remnants of my current one, and a packet of aspirin, just in case. At 9.30 a.m. I checked myself into a small but friendly enough hotel off the Cromwell Road, in that strange, transient part of town where the mansions of the rich compete with the squalor of endless bed-and-breakfasts and their constantly migrating population. In the tiny, windowless space next to my room, I had a bath. The experience was bliss, a sudden sinking into warmth and contentment that we had not imagined possible, a moment when our fears and senses began to relax, letting go of the night's tension which, we realised, had clenched every muscle to the edge of rupture. We lowered our head underwater and stayed there until we thought we would burst, lungs burning, and emerged again with a sense of being more alive and powerful than ever before, risking death and coming away unharmed, clean, safe. Blood and dirt turned the water pinkish-grey as it floated off our skin like mist rising in the morning sun. We then wrapped ourself in towels and stood behind the net curtain in the window to watch the bright morning light cast the shadows of the trees across the street below, and felt, at last, content.

Clean and dry, I bandaged my cut hand, brushed my hair with my fingers, having forgotten to buy a comb, and examined myself in the cracked mirror above the sink. In my new shirt and stolen trousers, I looked almost dignified. An almost perfect resurrection, then, just like we'd thought, just like we'd hoped – at least physically.

My eyes were still too blue. I leant in close to the bathroom mirror and saw that the iris was tinted, as human eyes should be, with flecks of other colour, a hint of brown, a suggestion of green, a darker rim. But the overall prevalence was the colour of a summer sky. It didn't particularly suit me, and gave a disconcerting albino appearance; but I supposed, like a new haircut or a shave after a week of neglect, I would grow used to my current appearance, and forget the old. I considered being frightened, curling up at the base of my bed and whimpering in fear at what consequence this change in my appearance might bring. The mood wasn't on us, so I didn't.

I felt less than confident about painting a ward onto the door of the hotel room, so settled for a compromise and, with a biro, drew a swift protective symbol onto five pieces of hotel-headed notepad paper and left each sheet around the bed in a vague semicircle as the closest I could come to a magical defence without causing criminal damage. Then I lay down and slept. This time, we did not try to resist, and could not remember our dreams.

I woke in the mid-afternoon. Sitting on the floor at the foot of my bed, I spread out the bloodstained remnants of Sinclair's documents in front of me.

I did not care why Sinclair really wanted Bakker dead. I did not care particularly why the rest of them were involved, although I suspected Oda's reasons went beyond mere personal motives and into a more dangerous realm. We chose not to be concerned with this now, however, until we knew if it threatened our own interests.

What did I want?

What did we want?

I wanted... I wanted...

...come be we...

...to find and...

...we be fire, we be light...

...stop...

...we dance electric flame...

..."hello Matthew's fire!"...

...stop...

...we want...

. . . stop NOW.

. . .

Done?

. . .

Good.

I wanted to kill Hunger.

If that meant ploughing through more mortal creatures on the way, then so be it.

I wanted to kill the shadow.

We found it ugly, and dangerous.

I picked up Bakker's photo and studied the face. There was a bloody fingerprint, probably Sinclair's, in the top corner. If you aged the face, gave it a tropical disease, starved it of food and drink, took the fire out of its eyes and the smile away from its lips, if you looked at it with all that in mind, just out of the corner of your vision, then Bakker's face could just, perhaps, be fitted onto another creature's shoulders. For that alone, I suspected Bakker might have to die.

However, these things were easier said than done. And revenge, we decided, should be more than about dying.

I turned my attention to San Khay.

An impression of the daily life and routine of San Khay.

At 6.30 a.m. his alarm goes in his penthouse flat on the river by Victoria. If he has had romance the night before, he does not wake his sleeping partner, but walks across his white-carpeted floor to the bathroom, a thing all of mirrors and silver taps, so that, standing at any point in the room, he can see his own reflection, muscles and polished almond skin, reflected back at him. The tattoos that cover his entire body are done in deep black ink, and every six months he returns to a very special tattooist in Hong Kong, to make sure that any faded areas, around his buttocks or across his chest where they may have experienced strain, are kept up in full, ebony-coloured glory. The swirls of ink crawl around his ankles and across his toes, run round the back of his knees, spiral up his hips, curl lovingly around his belly button, sinking inside like some sort of strange root burrowing into earth, lash themselves across his back and chest, bend luxuriously down his arms and, at the wrist and neck, just below the collar line, fade gently, into nothing.

The men he takes home with him on Tuesdays and Fridays (his days for such affairs) often regard such extensive swirls of ink as kinky, but not unattractive. To the more considerate magician, such an embedding of symbols of magic into skin is as much dangerous as it is potentially rewarding. For this reason, San Khay usually keeps the ink hidden, studying his flesh all over only in the morning when he is sure he is alone in his bathroom.

In other men this relentless examination of themselves every morning would be vanity. For San Khay, the studying of his own naked form is the perusal of an investment: nine months of pain for his mother, twenty-three years of school fees at the best institutions in America, Asia and Europe for his father, and a subsequent fifteen-odd years of gym sessions, martial arts classes, dance lessons, organic food detox diets and nearly forty-eight hours of intense pain under that tattooist's needle, every six months, for himself. San Khay wishes to be assured that his investment is being well maintained, since presumably he will be reliant on its dividends for the rest of his life.

He showers in the 360-degree power shower installed by his Spanish plumber Enrico to his special request, at the highest temperature allowable, until his skin is lit up red like the end of Rudolf's nose on Christmas Eve. He then turns the shower down to its coldest temperature for a few seconds, and dries himself off with a neat white towel, fluffy as a bunny's tail, before going into the kitchen to prepare breakfast.

Although he has three staff serving his needs – a chauffeur, a maid and a personal assistant, who live in the building and are on call at any hour of the day – San Khay makes his own breakfast, a bowl of nuts and fruit that all but clatter on their way through the gut, they are so unpleasantly healthy. He dresses in his wardrobe room, itself lined with mirrors, and again it is not vanity that leaves his reflection stretched out to infinity around him, but the monitoring of an impression. When San Khay goes to work, he is not merely selling his product, he is selling himself. He wears a black suit with polished black shoes and does up every button of his smart pink shirt, his only flash of colour, to hide every trace of ink on his skin. He combs his dark hair slicked back, but shaves only on Wednesday and Monday, since his beard grows at a snail's pace anyway and he has very sensitive skin.

All this takes him no more than half an hour.

At 7 a.m. he leaves the penthouse. His chauffeur has his car – a long, black but otherwise anonymous Mercedes – waiting down in the car park. He seems to prefer it if his lover of the night does not wake before his departure, as that saves embarrassing goodbyes, but instead leaves orders with the maid, Sally, to make sure his companion has everything he wishes and is treated with the utmost courtesy, before he is shown out.

By 7.30 a.m. San Khay is at his desk, having beaten the early-morning traffic and everyone else in his office. New members of his company often attempt to beat San and turn up before he does, but find that more than a few weeks of working 7.30 a.m. to 8.30 p.m. in order to impress their boss, and be in before and out after his working hours, is beyond human endurance. The more courageous ask how he does it, but he merely smiles and assures them that he drinks a lot of water.

His office is in the heart of the City, in that area just off Bishopsgate where the giant glass towers of the megacorporations loom over the traditional guildhalls and converted old mansions of their lawyers and clerical providers. Certain names appear on every street corner as regularly as the Corporation of London bollards – Merrill Lynch, PricewaterhouseCoopers, Morgan Stanley, the National Westminster, Saudi Arabia, Credit Suisse – the bankers of the City and their lawyers, compressed into a space no more than a mile wide, within easy walking distance of each other and their favourite sandwich bars for lunch.

The firm he works for is called Amiltech, and it is based on the 24th floor of a tower. Not "the Tower", as Sinclair would probably hasten to point out were he not in critical condition with three bullets in his chest – this was not "the Tower", merely a corporate subsidiary, a security firm that had floated its very special assets and been bought, absorbed into the ever-growing conglomeration of companies and interests headed by Robert James Bakker. During San's average day, he will hold three meetings in his office, and perhaps another three outside, in locations as diverse as the café on the corner, or Pentonville

Prison, depending on what he is looking for. On his official payroll are secretaries, lawyers, administrators, accountants, press secretaries, drivers, assistants and managers. On his unofficial payroll are fortune-tellers, prophets, seers, magicians, witches, wizards, voodoo-artists, murderers, thieves, criminals, a few judges, policemen, politicians and, so Sinclair recorded with "a rumour?" written in the margin, a member of the royal family.

When asked his job description, San Khay is very vague – but usually just ends up saying "securities". Not merely insurance, he adds, but actual security. After all, he says, he is far more likely to make a profit from insurance premiums if he can absolutely guarantee that no harm will come to the client.

Needless to say, among his clients are other names that interest me:

Guy Lee, officially unemployed, wizard, benefactor of the arts, suspected of dabbling unhealthily in necromancy, vampirism and all the other much hyped, vaguely defined "dark arts". He's Bakker's enforcer in the magical community and, after San Khay, next on my list of people to have a conversation with. Amiltech provided personal security for Mr Lee, at a very reasonable rate.

Harris Simmons, Bakker's chief financial adviser. A poor and clumsy magician, from what Sinclair's files suggested of him, whose chief talent in that area lay in his vast collection of magical artefacts and other items, including, so the rumours went, Nostradamus's ashes (overrated), at least three contenders for the name of Excalibur, plus over seventeen possible candidates for the skull of King Arthur (pointless), several vials of fairy dust, and a tub of dragon blood (extracted from a pet lizard). He had also accumulated numerous protective items and enchantments whose precise nature was unclear to me, as it was to Sinclair, but which seemed to have Sinclair greatly concerned as to how easy it might or might not be to eliminate Harris Simmons. Amiltech provided security for Simmons's personal vault, and Simmons churned out money for the Tower.

Dana Mikeda. Here, I was not prepared to speculate.

San Khay has little or no contact with these others, except for occasional brief meetings with Lee in the City, or the odd telephone conversation with Harris Simmons. Dana Mikeda, as far as he and most of the rest of the corporation are concerned, doesn't exist, and probably for good reason.

At 12.30 precisely San leaves his office and goes to the gym. He works out until 1.30 to build appetite, then returns to his office, and has lunch at his desk. His lunch is a salad, sushi, and a bottle of green sludge that Sinclair swears is a kind of organic vegetable drink, and which we find interesting, in much the same way we are fascinated by the play of light across the shimmering shell of a dung beetle. All things we do not know interest us.

At 6 p.m. he has a one-hour dinner with members of his staff, in his office. The food is prepared by the catering unit three floors below. Rumour is he likes pine nuts, but I am not convinced that this isn't detail gone mad in Sinclair's notes. On Monday he dines with the finance department, on Tuesday with the executive managers, on Wednesday with the press office, on Thursday with the secretarial administrators and on Friday with the lawyers. They all turn up exactly on time, every week, without fail and without question.

Between 7 p.m. and 8.30 p.m., he either works at his desk or, if need be, travels around the city to inspect his various interests and ensure the smooth managing of business. This business can be as diverse as double-checking the vault codes on a door, or commissioning an assassin and delivering the target details. Partially for this reason, I am almost entirely certain that San Khay took the pre-emptive step of sending a litterbug after me that first night in Dulwich, perhaps with the philosophical attitude of "if you want it done, do it hard and fast". Perhaps for his arrogance, he is at the top of our list of people to see.

At 8.30 p.m. he stops work, unless there are unusual circumstances, and when his schedule does not require anything more he goes into the city, to one of the exclusive underground clubs where only the very rich dare enter, where he will buy champagne just for himself, and talk politely with the many young men and women of the City who desire his patronage. If it is a Tuesday or a Friday, he will find a man of a similar sexual inclination, and take him home. His preferred type, according to Sinclair, is broad, and dark, and probably rather shallow.

At 11.30 p.m. he goes home, and he will be asleep by 1 a.m. If he has company he will do as company does – if not, he reads until it is time to turn the light out.

Five and a half hours later, his day begins again.

I resolved to disrupt this routine.

I started relatively small.

The International Investment Bank of Tokyo had its central London office behind Paternoster Street, in a gloomy enclosure ironically known as Angel Court, where in the last century a bomb or two had clearly fallen, and the debris been replaced with architecture that was less than inspired. I went down there for 10.30 p.m., coat buttoned up as well as might be, satchel over my shoulder, well fed, well slept and ready for the fight. Riding the train to Moorgate, I let the unique taste of the underground's magic wash over me. Back on the street I shuddered with every swish of passing traffic, as with its passing, it spun the latent magic drifting through the air into eddies. In Telegraph Passage I ran my hands down the old, narrow house wedged in between two shiny new office buildings, feeling its sluggish, heavy history tingle against my fingers, its own unique power. By the time I reached Angel Court I was almost giddy on my own prepared spells and gathered forces. As I walked, I directed the CCTV cameras away from me, guiding them with the twisting of my fingers to point this way, not that, so that I might slip unobserved past the lowered traffic barrier into the lurking buildings beyond.

There was a single sleepy security guard on the front desk of the International Investment Bank of Tokyo's office. I pulled my coat and my spells tighter around myself and walked by him without stopping – he didn't even look up. I called a lift to the fourth floor, and rode up in the polished brass interior, fighting the urge to whistle.

At the fourth floor I politely asked the CCTV camera to look the other way, and stepped carefully over the ankle-height laser alarm by the front door. I walked up to the burglar alarm fitted by the first bulletproof glass door into the office there, and considered it. It required a combination that I guessed wouldn't stop at the tenth digit, and after so much effort in coaxing the CCTV cameras to look elsewhere, I doubted if I had the patience to send my thoughts into its intestines and wheedle the code out of it. Besides, we weren't there to be discreet.

So, wanting to laugh with the exhilaration of it, we pressed our palms to the glass exterior of the first door into the office, opened our mouth and hummed. We started low and quiet, then built up the hum from the back of our throat to its full strength, pushing it out of our lungs like it was water and we were drowning in it. We then took the sound, and pulled it back, into us, through us, sending the power of it down our arms so that it tickled our nerves, made our skin tremble until we were buzzing with it, let it build up just behind our wrists and kept the sound going from the very back of our mouth, until we thought we would burst. Then, with a pinch of our lips to cut off the movement of air, we let go the built-up power in our hands.

Glass shattered beneath our fingertips and we wanted to laugh, dance, as it rained down around us like diamond snowflakes. Above us, the alarm wailed, shrieking indignation, and we laughed again, letting the sound pummel us, loving the sudden change in the air as downstairs the guard woke from his reverie in a panic, as in the streets outside people jumped, the whole texture of life around shifting up a key, and through that change the magic that we fed on becoming sharper, the feel of it in our head clearer, solid, like the knives of glass falling around us.

I struggled to control our euphoria, and crunched over the glass to the next door. This one was heavy and wooden, with locks of more ordinary design. Fumbling in my satchel, I took out the blank keys on their ring, and caressed one with the tip of my index finger until its form wobbled, taking on an almost liquid quality. Seizing that moment of uncertainty, I pushed the key into the lock, felt it assume the shape of the barrel within, and twisted. The lock came undone. I repeated the procedure with two more blank keys and stepped into the office.

It was a depressing place, the weight of it heavy on my senses: dull plywood tables, grey standard-issue chairs, neat pencil pots, polished stainless-steel flat-screened computers which clearly in my two years of absence had become the fashionable thing – and strip lighting, left on every day and night of every working week and holiday, including Christmas. Regardless of my aesthetic reaction, I felt no need to burn it all to the ground nor even rearrange the furniture; a breach of security was enough to achieve what I wanted. I pulled out a black can of spray-paint, shook it vigorously, and with extreme care and caution, started to draw.

The white strip lighting had cast a faint stretched shadow from my body up the white wall; I now filled in its features with the black paint, until my shadow was a thick, dripping void plastered almost as high as the ceiling. As curses went, it wasn't the most powerful. But it was enough to make the pipes in the ceiling start to drip even before I was done, and, according to the local newspaper, the fuses in the box downstairs shorted on alternate Thursdays for six months after. Our power still seemed unpredictable, the feel of it across our fingers, something we had to remember anew, as if tasting its heady sweetness for the very first time.

I left by the fire escape, sauntering out onto Moorgate just as the first police vans started to arrive.

The bus shelters in London are, more often than not, badly designed. Roofed with thin plastic sheets that sag under any weight, curving downwards to form a slight bowl, they collect pools of rainwater on their tops, which can remain there for days. Most of these shelters are below tree height, so that fallen leaves can rot down in these pools, creating the odd muddy pond with its own fungal subculture that nothing can erase, short of a burning August drought.

The flatness of these shelters allows other things to be left on top of them. A single, decomposing sock is a common feature, or a laceless left-foot plimsoll. Half a shopping trolley has been known, or a bicycle handlebar, as have Ikea catalogues and plastic bags full of broken bananas. However, above everything else, on the top of every other bus shelter in London there is almost invariably a rotting copy of the Yellow Pages.

People tend not to ask what a copy of the Yellow Pages is doing on the roof of a bus shelter, nor how it got there, and this is probably a good thing – a poor reflection on the curiosity of the human spirit, perhaps, but an excessively useful defect for the struggling sorcerer, for inside every Yellow Pages left on the top of the shelter, and those pages only, are the exclusive listings.

I found my own copy of the fat book, with its thin, mouldering pages, on top of a shelter opposite Liverpool Street station, and sat down on the bench beneath to flick through its unique content. I ignored Witches-for-hire, Alchemists, Abjurers, Seers, Prophets, Fortune-Tellers, Magical Suppliers, Hunters, Questing Adventurers, Crusaders, Mages, Mediums, Mystic Scholars and all the other members of the magical community who sell their often suspect wares to each other through the adverts and listings in the bus-stop pages, and eventually found my way to Exorcists. I picked the biggest advert – "Evil at work? Being sent curses to your inbox? Haunted by the spirits of the deceased? Call Exorminator, guaranteed 100% success in cleansing your local magical environment!!!" – wrote the number down on my hand, tossed the Pages back onto the top of the bus stop for the next magician who might be passing, and went to find a phone box.

The man who answered sounded very cheerful for the time of night and greeted me with, "Exorminator, how can we help?"

"Hi, I'm phoning about an exorcism."

"Can I take your name?"

"I'd rather not say."

"Sure, fine, we understand. May I ask as to the nature of your problem?"

"There's a curse going round."

"Uh-huh, sure, no problem, we can handle that. Do you have any details on what kind of curse?"

"A shadow on the wall."

"Nasty. Anything more?"

"A curse of the stones of a building, of the bricks in its walls, of the earth that shelters it, the water that feeds it and the sky that guards it."

"That's a pretty solid curse, man. Haven't seen shit like that for a while. You sure of it?"

"I wrote it, I'm fairly sure of it."

"OK, you wrote it?" The exorcist had a slightly Australian tinge to his voice, and the laid-back, whatever-comes-next attitude of a man who had suddenly realised two degrees short of sunstroke that exorcism was the perfect career choice he'd never been offered at school.

"Yes."

"OK... uh... not usual we get people writing their own curses and then getting them exorcised. Some kinda accident with the spray-paint?"

"No."

"No. Uh... OK. But I'm guessing you want it removed."

"Oh, no, not at all," I said quickly. "I'm phoning to tell you that probably tomorrow morning, you or one of your associates will get a call from someone else wanting it removed, and I'm asking you not to."

"I see. Look, sorry to say this, but it's our job. We exorcise things. You know. Exorminator... no exorcism too big? Gotta pay the rent, man."

"Yes, but you'll have difficulty exorcising this one."

"Uh... we will?"

"You have to understand – this is a fundamental curse inscribed for revenge. It's more than just a bit of spray-paint. When I drew the curse, I thought of every second of pain and suffering that I'd endured and of my undying thirst for vengeance. We're way out of the holy water and garlic league. Sorry about that, by the way, it's nothing personal against *you*, it's just how it had to be done."

"Look, Mr..."

"Also," we added quietly, "if you undo the curse, then we'll come after you next."

Silence from the end of the line. "Uh..." said the man at last, "you know, mate, I'd love to help you with this, but it sounds like you've got some serious issues..."

"I'm just giving you a heads-up," I burst in. "These things are going to appear all over town, and Amiltech is going to come to exorcists to clear it up. And I'm asking you nicely not to."

"Because..."

"Amiltech is going to burn," we replied cordially. "We are going to shred them from top to toes and leave nothing but a shadow on the wall behind. And I figured... it'd be a shame for you guys to get hurt on the way."

"Are you for real?"

"Good night, Mr Exorminator."

"Jeez, *whatever*."

I hung up and walked away, feeling, all in all, that things were going rather well.

*

Between Friday evening and Sunday afternoon, I broke into a total of six offices, one penthouse suite and a small bank, and cursed them all. I cursed the stones they were built on, the bricks in their walls, the paint on their ceilings, the carpets on their floors. I cursed the nylon chairs to give their owners little electric shocks, I cursed the markers to squeak on the whiteboard, the hinges to rust, the glass to run, the windows to stick, the fans to whir, the chairs to break, the computers to crash, the paper to crease, the pens to smear; I cursed the pipes to leak, the cooler to drip, the pictures to sag, the phones to crackle and the wires to spark. And we enjoyed it. We enjoyed all the magic, the shaping of it at our fingers, the tiniest cantrip up to the most profound curse; we enjoyed the edge of danger. It made us feel alive.

Not that this was a random venting of my general dissatisfaction with life, fate and all the things it had done wrong in the last few days, months, years. I chose my targets very carefully, from Sinclair's immaculately maintained and only slightly blood-spattered list of Amiltech's favourite clients.

On Monday morning I dialled the *Financial Times* from a telephone near the Blackwall Tunnel, and politely told the receptionist to have someone check up on a spate of break-ins and look for an Amiltech connection. It was not the subtle kind of call from which journalistic myths were made, but it had its use. On Tuesday morning the *Financial Times* ran with a headline on page three reporting a damaging series of attacks on offices and properties either owned by, insured by or protected by various divisions of Amiltech Securities. By Tuesday evening the headline in much smaller form was hitting the freebie City rags, and by Wednesday morning the broadsheets had picked up on it too. Amiltech responded that it was being victimised by a systematic campaign of hatred, and that it would bring the perpetrators to justice. On the unusual painted signs left behind at all the scenes of crime, they made no comment.

On Monday afternoon I moved out of my small hotel room on the Cromwell Road, and migrated under a new name to a larger, more expensive hotel off the Strand. It seemed only a matter of time before reprisals headed my way, if they were not already en route, and I wanted to stem any more significant encounters until I felt sure of my abilities, and our readiness. We were not yet certain that we could stop

Hunger, should he come for us again; and we knew that he desired our blood. Not only was Hunger an ugly creature, offensive to all our senses; he was, perhaps, equal to all that we could be.

That frightened us.

On the Monday evening that I called the *Financial Times*, I also hit two more companies and a storage facility. The latter turned out to be housing organs in vacuum-packed bags. Some were human; some were not. In the deepest darkest corner of the basement, behind a false wall I found while looking for something to burn the place to the ground, I discovered a vault containing the relatively recently dead body of a man whose foul nails, pin-pricked veins and overgrown beard proclaimed him to be a stolen soul from the street. His skin was white and splotchy grey, not a drop of blood left in his body. Someone had cracked open his ribcage, pulled out his heart and tried to replace it with a replica of carved London clay. An experiment in necromancy; one that had gone wrong.

This time I took a waste-paper basket from upstairs, a cigarette lighter out of a desk drawer, and a bundle of old newspaper, and set the place on fire. It took three hours for the flames to catch properly and start gouting black clouds through the building's broken windows. We stood in the crowd with the other onlookers as the firemen scuttled to contain the blaze, and felt its warmth on our face and the burning intensity of it in our eyes, and that too, was beautiful.

On Thursday evening my efforts made *Watchdog* on BBC1, where the sincere, if overly groomed and sexy, presenter made an appeal in a husky, seductive voice for the unknown arsonist to come forward. I almost felt a stir of guilt as the programme unfolded, particularly for the well-meaning sergeant in his white shirt and constabulary tie who sat uncomfortably on the studio's low stool and announced, "We believe this individual could be a threat to society, and himself..." Hearing the comforting tones of his voice, I could imagine the police counsellor waiting for me down at the station, with a cup of tea and the soft-spoken phrase "So tell me about this sorcery of yours..."

On Friday, riding through the City on the 23 bus, I picked up a dropped copy of *City A.M.*, the guide to all things going on in the bankers' district, and flicked through it to see how Amiltech was doing.

Surprisingly well, was the answer. Too many people whose wealth should have taught them better were too afraid of Amiltech to kick up the ruckus I had been hoping for.

That night I went to Amiltech's office. There were three security guards in the front foyer, a towering glass thing full of potted plants and some full-grown trees, as well as a waterfall cascading down from the first-floor platform into a pool of artfully arranged pebbles. One of the guards had a whiff of magic about him, despite the identical nature of his straight black suit. He sat with nonchalant confidence by the entrance to the lift bank, one leg hooked over the other, and had the look of a man not about to be fooled by the simple cantrips I habitually spun into my coat.

Since my usual enchantments of anonymity didn't look likely to work, I adopted a different tack. At 9.30 p.m. I walked into the Amiltech foyer, went up to the reception desk and with a flick of my wrist flashed my Oyster card at the receptionist. I did this just fast enough for him to see a card being waved but too quickly for his brain to register anything but the most officious-looking credentials he'd seen in his life.

He blinked up at me, and hesitated. I jumped in before the tangles of gentle, sleepy magic woven around his head could be shaken away by full alertness, and said, "I'm here to see Adam Reiley."

"What?"

"Adam Reiley, Amiltech? He's expecting me – you should have my name."

"Uh... give me a moment."

The man tapped away at his computer. The human mind, when it works, is a marvellous thing. With all its attention diverted onto the task at hand, it becomes an abstract other, performing beyond the usual realms of self-awareness. When humans work, they frequently become unaware of their own body, their own senses, are surprised to find that their wrists ache or their backs are sore or their friend has left the building. It's as close to an out-of-body experience as can be achieved short of fifty volts, a circle of warding, a pigeon's claw cut from an albino female of purest white feathers, or a lot of mushrooms. In such a state, not only does the process of their thoughts play across their face, but the observant listener can also trace the sense of their feeling in their mind. More than just the flicker of an eye, the mind, usually such an insensitive object, opens itself, drifts, even while the conscious, controlled aspect – a tiny part of the human brain at any moment – is focused.

So it was with the receptionist, tapping through his computer; and so it was that we could almost hear the buzz of his thoughts, their deepest undercurrents, see the rich purple veins of his suppressed desires, feel the heat of his passions, locked away beneath the professionalism of the day, taste the sharp edge of his envy, a drop of vinegar on the tip of our tongue, resentments and jealousies that he himself probably didn't know he had, but which drifted in his unconsciousness, shaping how he spoke even while he didn't know why he said the words he did. The mind, so exposed, fascinated us, as we perceived the thick longing strains of his thoughts, the black oily surface of his disdain for the job, and glimpsed, just for a second, the fiery images of his dreams.

So I pulled just a little, just a tiny sliver, of magic across his eyes, blurring his vision for a moment, spinning the fatigue of his day into his nerves, so that for a second he didn't care that he had to check all people coming in and out, didn't care that his boss was insistent on security, didn't care that he hadn't really seen this guy's credentials, not really, not properly – for a moment, all he cared about was that he was in a shit job and just wanted to be left alone.

He said, "Uh . . . sure, right, yeah, whatever. You know the way?"

"Uh-huh. Thanks."

"No problem."

He gave me a paper badge in a plastic holder. I took it with a grateful smile, pinned it to the front of my coat, and walked towards the lift.

The man on guard whose merest magical presence twisted the otherwise cool, calm, pale blue sense of that place into himself, like a small moon warping the space around it, glanced up at me as I passed, and at my badge, and the edge of his consciousness scraped along my own. I kept him out instinctively, throwing up a rough wall in his mental path, focusing clearly on that one image to fill my entire consciousness and keep him from penetrating my intent. He was a crude magician – potentially powerful, I felt, but, unlike sorcerers, unlike those who can taste the magic of the city, who revel in it, his power was one of spells, incantations and gestures, a thing tamed, rather than a thing natural.

We had no fear of him, so nodded coldly in his direction as we went by, and walked on.

I rode up to the 24th floor. The lift was clear glass, on the outer wall of the building, so I could see the city drop away beneath me. As on the London Eye that night, I was astounded by the beauty of its multi-coloured spectrum: not just the sodium orange of the suburban sprawl, but the white interiors of office blocks, green traffic lights, red aircraft beacons on the taller towers, purple floodlights washing over high walls, pooling beams of silver on enclosed courtyards, shimmering blues on fountains, or in the doors of clubs, the moving snakes of traffic, defined only by headlights, brakes, or indicators flashing on and off like an endless slithering column of eyes, and the reflected pinkish glare across the ceiling of the sky, except for where an aircraft's guiding lights sent out a cone of brightness, through the black scudding clouds heavy with rain as the wind carried them towards the sea.

I could almost drink the magic of what I saw, almost lie back suspended on nothing but its intensity and float above the ground with the force of it, the sudden, overwhelming sense of it – and that, we knew, was all that sorcery was; all, perhaps, that we were. An awareness, an understanding, a point of view. Take away that sense of the city's wonder and we were no more than insects, grey figures on a grey landscape scuttling along, unable to see the daily extraordinary things. Though it was a strange emotion, we almost felt pity.

The door to the Amiltech office was more than locked – it was warded. Not the first that I'd seen on my arsonist's/burglar's progress around Amiltech's client base, but the strongest. My blank keys would not change shape to fit the lock, nor, I felt, would mere force – a bombardment with the electricity in the wires above, nor the use of sound – settle it satisfactorily until the ward itself was broken. For a ludicrous moment I wondered if there were any air ducts I could crawl through to get inside the office; but life was not like the movies. The door was pretty much immovable, not even breakable without a considerable expenditure of time and energy. So, with this in mind, I went up, to the offices of the company on the floor above – Verity – which, according to the brochure by the door, specialised in proving insurance claims wrong even if, so the small print suggested, they weren't.

They appreciated a challenge. Its door was not warded, and my keys, after the usual coaxing, fitted perfectly.

I walked through Verity's office until pretty much dead-centre, got out my all-purpose Swiss Army knife, and started cutting a square in the thin nylon and lino carpet on the floor. I pulled up a piece of flooring roughly big enough to let me step through, put it to one side and went in search of the office kitchen. I found it eventually, next to the ladies' toilets, a small space dominated by a coffee machine. I filled the kettle and set it to boil. Under the sink I found a bottle of bleach. When the kettle was done, I took it, full and steaming, back to my square of exposed floor, and poured the boiling water over the small area of concrete underneath. I dribbled a few drops of bleach onto the wet floor, at the four points of the compass, then stood back and tried to find the right spell.

Transmutation is not a strong point of mine – even if you can convince the substance in question to become what you want it to be, it tends not to be a permanent process (at least, not without ending in an explosion), and it requires a lot of time and effort to get it right.

I wasn't after perfection, and I hoped that after I'd raised the temperature of the water and mixed in one of the nastiest substances I could find in the kitchen, the liquid spilt on the floor was already halfway to a change of state. Magicians tend to have pre-written incantations and spells for these kind of things, usually calling on various dire or implausible powers (of which my favourite was "Upney, Grey Lord of Tar", who I'd heard mentioned by amateurs and who we knew to be real) to achieve their temporary wills. Sorcerers rely on will power and raw magic, and I now deployed both, snatching heat and power out of the air around me until my breath condensed with the sudden cold, and the lights above me whined and flickered. I stretched my arms out, fingers turned towards the floor, and pushed every inch of power I could get from that room, every trace of snatched breath left lingering in the air, every hum of electricity, every remnant of warmth from human skin, every smell of sweat, every half-forgotten lingering sound of shouting, all the detritus of left-over life that makes magic what it is, for life is magic, magic *is* life, the left-over life we don't even notice we're living; I drew it into me, and pushed it into the floor.

The water–bleach mixture started to bubble. Then it started to smoke, a thin, acrid white billow that made my eyes water and reminded me of the taste of hot solder. It hissed, it boiled, and for a moment – just a moment, because I couldn't sustain this intensity of concentration for long – the water on the floor became acid strong enough to eat through lead.

It ate through the exposed area of the floor in no more than sixty seconds, reducing its substance like it was made of half-baked flour. The hole in the floor spread out across the entire area where the liquid had spilt, eating into the carpet around. When I felt it was wide enough, I let the power go, jerking with the pressure of it running away between my fingers. At my feet, the hole was now human-sized, looking straight down onto floor 24.

I waited a few seconds for the acid to revert back to its watery, bleach-spotted state, then poured the rest of the kettle over it for good measure. When that had stopped dripping too much, I sat on the edge of the hole, and lowered myself down. I still got a soggy bottom and wasn't happy about the drop, but managed a survivable, if not a dignified, flop into Amiltech's London headquarters.

In cursing them, I inscribed the black shadows not just on the wall, but on the floor and across the doors. We found San Khay's office, with its wide windows looking out across the city, and, in big blue letters, wrote across the glass for all the world to see:

Come be me and be free!

Then, because I wasn't entirely sure why I had written this, I added a caveat with a biro on one of the neatly laid-out pads of papers on a conference table.

Make me a shadow on the wall.

How long until he comes for you?

Feeling that this made more sense, I wandered round the office, flicking through desk drawers and rummaging under piles of paper with no real concept of what I might be looking for, but a feeling that it was the right thing to do. It was all depressingly mundane. Lists of stationery acquisitions, tax details for the accountants, scribbled notes to remind X to talk to Y about Z and how it might affect the pension plan – not at all what I'd hoped for from an organisation that dabbled in mystic forces beyond our ken.

The most promising object, I found in the broom cupboard. Behind a pile of mops was a small security pad, clearly designed for a numerical code. It had been scribbled over with a number of protective wards in permanent red ink; but on looking closer I saw that these only covered the pad itself, and with my knife I was able to undo the screws that held it to the wall, and pull the entire thing away from the surface it rested on. Behind was a fat cable running into a small hole in the wall. I unplugged the pad from the cable, put it to one side, and snatched a small handful of static out of the nearest sleeping computer screen on an office desk, twisting it between my fingers like a cat's cradle as I contemplated how best to make it work. I tried touching my electric fingertips to the cable, then tried sending it down the wires in short bursts, and eventually – though how I did not pretend to understand – something went very quietly, *click*.

I looked round for the source of the sound, and found it in a small panel that had slid back behind the bottles of cream cleaner, with a lever in it. Never the kind of man who didn't press the button, I pulled the lever and, with a hiss of tortured hydraulics, one wall of the broom cupboard swung back. This, I felt, was much more like it; this was how things should be.

The room beyond filled with a dull bluish-white light as I stepped inside it, illuminating some extraordinarily interesting objects. One of them said, "You're not a regular fucker, are you?"

I walked up to the chin-high blue jar that suspended the thing inside it and said, "What are you then?"

The creature belched a small cloud of car fumes, which were quickly sucked up through the ventilation tube at the top of its thick jar. "Could ask you the same bloody thing," it said through the glass, which gave its voice an odd, almost mechanical resonance.

It was short, approximately four feet nothing, its skin a pale grey colour, and rough, like old tarmac on a road. Its eyes were big and round, reflective and multifaceted, and from its nose and mouth dribbled a pale brown liquid that looked for all the world like engine oil. I reached the obvious diagnosis.

"You're a troll," I said.

"Well, give the man a prize."

"What the hell are you doing in a jar?"

"I got fucking caught; what the hell do you think I'm doing in a jar?!" it wailed.

I considered the creature from every possible angle. Back in the distant dark ages, its ancestors had probably eaten the bones of men slain in anger, and bathed in the local swamp. But evolution had done its thing with trolls, like most other creatures of magic, and now the little thing probably enjoyed nothing more than a leftover hamburger and a bath in crude oil. I squatted down until my eyes were level with its own, and managed to hold its gaze despite the initial moment of revulsion as I saw the thin sheen of ethyl alcohol secreted by its tear glands to keep the black surface of its lenses clean.

"You got a name?" I said.

"Mighty Raaaarrrgghh!" it replied.

"I was thinking of something shorter and less guttural."

It shrugged and said in an embarrassed voice, "Jeremy."

"Jeremy?"

"I have endured every fucking indecency, wart-face, don't think you're getting me high with Jeremy."

"Jeremy the troll," I repeated, just to make absolutely certain I'd got it right.

"The Mighty Raaaarrrgghh!" it added for good measure. "And when I get out of here I'll suck the jelly from your eyes!"

"Why?"

"Because I'm a fucking troll!"

"I was under the impression trolls these days liked nothing more for supper than a used tea bag with a few days' mould on it."

"For you, I make an exception."

"Why? I haven't done you any harm. Surely it's Amiltech that you have the beef with."

"You have an ugly face," it replied with a leer that revealed a set of sharpened steel teeth. I do not attempt to understand evolution in the age of urban magic.

"Let me put it this way," I said patiently. "You've been trapped in a jar for I don't know how long by Amiltech and all its works, you probably want out, and I'm willing to let you out, and you're going to eat the jelly from my eyes?"

"Uh... right."

"You see where I'm going with all this?"

"I'm waiting for the catch, there's always a catch with fucking magicians, isn't there?"

"I just want to piss Amiltech off."

"Is that *it*?"

"Yes."

"Why? What's your grind?"

"You would not begin to understand," I sighed. "So, you want to be let out?"

"You're not going to ensorcel me, are you?"

"No."

"You sure?"

"Yes."

"You know, I find that really hard to believe."

"You can just stay there..."

It waved its spindly grey arms as wildly as was possible inside a jar and said, "Hey, hey, I was just asking... release away, human!"

I undid the various nuts and bolts that secured the top of the jar and with a pop of trapped pressurised air, the thing came free. The troll sprang out of its container with a single leap, and perched on the lid, grinning hugely, a whiff of car fumes trailing down from the end of its nose. "Human?" it said, the grin stretching as far as its tiny, circular ears.

"Almost."

"I get paid to stay in the jar." It leapt, fingers outstretched, teeth shining, in a perfect descending line from its perch straight towards my throat. I staggered back, raising my hands instinctively, and snatched magic into them, twisting the air around us into a wall, a whirlwind, spinning thick sheets of it across our path so that they picked up the little creature as it leapt and slammed it back against the wall of the room. Then, before it had a moment to recover, we flung our hands out and reached for the nearest amenable resource, found the cold, hard sense of iron rods running through the building, leading all the way to the foundations, and, with a twist of our fingers, made them grow.

The troll wailed, but the sound was choked off as a sharp splinter of worked iron spat itself through the wall and wound round its throat, pulling it up by the neck until it twitched and wheezed. Then another wrapped itself across the creature's convulsing legs, and a third growth of iron lodged itself under the troll's armpit, dragging it up on one side while on the other the weight of its body dragged it down, until it looked like a misshapen accident, all lopsided and moaning.

I dragged my hands down to my side with a shudder of effort and waited for the blue rage to go out of my vision, and for the blue buzzing in my skull to subside. We were angry, we were so *angry*, and it had been a moment of choice, just a second, that had stopped us from asking the iron growing out of the wall to grow straight through that creature's heart.

Around the room, there was a low, animal chitter of caged monsters, punctuated by the low, self-pitying whimper of the troll. We stabbed an accusing finger at it and spat, "If you want to live, you will be silent!"

Wisely, the troll bit its own lip until the oily black blood rolled, and made not a sound.

We looked round the room again. In various pots and jars were creatures from across the magical spectrum, fairies with their fine aluminium wings, tiny trapped elves with their burning hair, neon fireflies that sparked orange and pink as they banged angrily against the side of their jar, moths of purest moonlight, kept in a dark corner so that their strange beauty might be better admired, visible for a second only in the flap of a wing. In other jars were merely the remnants of some creatures – the concrete skull of a shambler, the steel bone of a banshee, the still-beating heart of some monster, which spat electric sparks with every pulsation across the floor of the pot it rested in. We said, for the benefit of those creatures that could understand, "You all know us. You know our dance."

There was a chitter of animal motion, a flash of wing, a blink of sullen reflective eyes.

I went first to the cage containing the three trapped fairies, their delicate foil wings glinting silvery in the dull light, their long, pale faces crowned with wreaths of woven fuse wire. I leant down so my face was level with them and pointed accusingly. "You be good fairies, capisce?"

There was a tiny squeaking, like the sound of a rusted wheel on an old trolley. I opened up the door to the cage, and with a sigh, they flapped out, and hovered uncertainly round my head. I considered my options, and said, "Amiltech imprisoned you. If you want revenge, now is the time."

Little smiles, no wider than the curved nail on my little toe, passed across the fairies' faces and, with a flap, they were out of the room.

I released every other creature in that room and listened with content to the sound of banging as they, each in their own fashion, tore through the office, ripping up computers and smashing glass, spinning their spells or simply tearing with tiny fists against the institution that had trapped them.

I nearly missed the last trapped creature in all the commotion, but my attention was drawn to it by a small squeaking sound near my foot, and looking down, I saw a single, fat black rat, its coat slimy and the end of its tail an ugly stump, looking up at me with a pair of dark, beady eyes. I knelt down next to the cage that contained it and said, "Hello."

It blinked at me, unimpressed, and unafraid. I opened the cage door and it scuttled out, crawling up my extended arm to sit happily on my shoulder, where I petted it vaguely, the slime of its coat sticking to my fingers in a thin, dirty goo. I then let it run down my arm to the floor again, where it looked up at me, squeaked once, and waddled off into the office. I followed it without too much concern, to find the floor covered with torn paper, broken glass, overturned furniture, shattered desks; the computer screens were in pieces, the hard drives of the computers spitting sparks, the light fittings spread across the floor and in some cases embedded in the walls, and everywhere chaos as the imprisoned creatures of Amiltech let go the full vent of their anger. I cleared my throat and said loudly, "No one gets hurt, understand!"

There was an audible sigh of disappointment from one or two of the monsters I'd released, but I felt that in this, at least, I could be obeyed. I looked across the floor for the rat, and saw it scuttling into San Khay's office. Suddenly curious, I followed – rats rarely do anything without good reason.

In San's office, it went straight to the desk and raised itself up on its hind legs, resting its forelegs against the lower drawer. I knelt next to it and pulled the lower drawer open a few inches – but there was nothing inside that I hadn't already seen. I closed it and the rat repeated this exercise, rearing itself up to press against the drawer and then collapsing again, then rearing, and collapsing, and after longer than I care to admit, it occurred to me that the creature wasn't trying to get into the drawer, but was, in fact, trying to move the desk. I heaved against it until it moved, and when it finally went I saw beneath it a small hole dug into the floor, leading into what looked like a series of pipes. The rat squeaked once, and vanished down the hole, probably never to be seen again.

There was, however, something more about the hole. Resting in one corner, wrapped up tight in a plastic bag to protect it, was a small, unaddressed envelope. I picked it up, and opened it.

Inside, inscribed in thin biro, was the outline of an angel on a sheet of paper. It had a crude triangular body, a circular head, and sweeping wings. All of it had been shaded in blue.

We dropped the envelope and scrambled back, shocked to our core. We knew of Bakker's interest in such things, of course; but to find that San Khay also had the image of the angel in his possession, and that perhaps he knew of its significance, disturbed us. It was too late, however – our fingers had brushed the image as we pulled it from the envelope and now, as we watched, the angel shimmered on the page, the thin blueness of its form thickening to the texture of liquid paint, and then without a sound, it caught fire, a bright blue flame that leapt up from the dropped paper and burnt ice-cold in the air until the image had been entirely scoured out of the sheet on which it was drawn. We shredded what was left of the paper, and, disturbed to think that our secrets might already be known, we left that place as fast as we could, while behind us the fairies tore it all to pieces.

In the early hours of Saturday morning, someone scried for me, and they were formidable.

I became aware of their scrying when the protective pieces of paper I'd put around the edge of my bed, warding me against harm, caught fire. The fire alarm then woke me up, and that in itself was a shock – that they'd not only scried, but had had the will to suppress my ward and suppress my own instinct, to keep me asleep while they tried to tune in to my location. I felt them the instant I was awake, a burning, crushing pressure, almost a physical weight on my back as the sheer volume of their will slammed against my senses – a sorcerer without any doubt, and there were only two sorcerers I could think of who might be even remotely interested, who might be even remotely not dead. I had grabbed my belongings and was out of the door even as the hotel manager and a porter with a fire extinguisher burst in; I was hopping down the stairs, struggling to get my shoes on, by the time the fire alarm went out, and staggering, breathless, covered in a cold sweat, into the street even before half the lights in the hotel had been turned on and the first angry voices raised.

And still that will remained, fixed straight on me, trying to push me to the ground, see through my eyes, determine through my own senses what I might have seen. Such a scrying could only be using something of my own to track me – there was no way that a spell like this could be achieved without it – but there were plenty of things, I reasoned, which could serve the purpose. My mind went to my old coat, sitting on Hunger's emaciated shoulders, and I ran, gasping for breath, into the night, searching for an underground station or, at the least, a crowded and well-lit place where I might be safe. All the while I could see my own shadow contract and increase, contract and increase like the motion of a heartbeat, as I moved from pool into pool of light. The laws of physics did not suspend themselves – the steady movement of my shadow continued without change, and no smell of litter or other magical intent tingled on my nose, despite my constant imaginings. We wanted to strike out at the sense following us, to strike out randomly into the dark and see what banged; we wanted to burn the consciousness that dared intrude on us – but it had something of ours on which to focus, and we had nothing.

The scrying broke about twenty minutes after I became first aware of it – truly, a formidable act of will on the part of my unseen enemy, considering how hard I was running and how determined I was to shake it off – and I ran for another ten minutes until I found a night bus which might as well have been going anywhere, and which I rode to the end of the route, just for good measure.

That event had scared me, and perhaps threw into a different light my disruptive antics at Amiltech. I had clearly got someone's attention, and that someone was more of a danger than I had considered – we were not ready to fight this kind of battle, and were shaken by the revelation of our own weakness. I did not sleep for the rest of that night, but rode in silence, contemplating all that had happened. And, perhaps for the first time, all that could.

In the morning I went to University College Hospital. Perhaps it was guilt.

I found Sinclair by drifting along the endless corridors of various intensive-care units and in-patient wards, glancing in through every door for a hint of plumpness. It occurred to me that I didn't even know if Sinclair had survived his operation, just like I didn't know if my gran still talked to the pigeons or if any of my friends – from back then – remembered my name, those who were still alive. Or indeed if any of them lived. Maybe it wasn't guilt that had brought me here after all – loneliness, perhaps, although we found it hard to understand how, in this city, anyone could be lonely.

Sinclair was alive. That merest fact brought a salve to my conscience, a moment of relief as a tension lifted that I hadn't even realised was there. I found him by the plain-clothes policeman sitting, half asleep in the first silvery early-morning light, outside Sinclair's room. The door was locked, but the policeman wasn't paying any attention to me or my antics, so I took a key and unlocked it, letting myself inside with a quiet click.

The room had the orangey-brown quality of light filtered through the curtains of almost all sickrooms – a warm colour that made the eyes instantly feel sleepy and relaxed, as if the walls themselves could be hypnotic. The fat man was not so fat; even in a few days his bulk had been reduced to nothing more than a distortion under the sheets, and his skin had an unhealthy pallor, visible even in the softening gloom of the room. Various devices beeped and whined around him, monitoring things I couldn't begin to guess at, while wires and tubes ran in and out of his skin. Every breath condensed a cloud onto the mask on his face; but other than that and the steady beeping of the machines around him, there was nothing to suggest that he was alive at all. The sight of him in this state horrified us: to show only the tiniest symptoms of life and yet be, somehow, still alive, trapped, motionless, unaware – the thought made us recoil. I sat down on a chair by his side, careful to stay out of the sight of the door, and said, feeling foolish but that it was also, somehow, necessary, "Hello."

The little cloud of condensation appeared and faded, appeared and faded on his mask.

"The shit's hitting the fan," I added, and watched the stillness of his eyes, not even movement beneath his lids, and the drooping utter immobility of his face. I didn't know what I was doing there or why; we just wanted to leave, to get away. This non-life frightened us, it wasn't what we were here for.

I stood quickly, and said, "Sorry," the word slipping out unconsciously before I realised I meant it. "You probably expected more."

I turned to the door, and walked straight into Charlie's fist.

Charlie. I knew his name was Charlie because that was how Sinclair had addressed him, when asking his loyal shadow to do something, and that was the name that Charlie, silently, immovably, had reacted to. I knew that he had dark eyes and black hair and wore a black suit that seemed to blur into itself; I also found that when he moved, he left a taste of thick treacle in the air, a sludgy afterglow that twined into my senses.

In the small hospital room next to Dudley Sinclair's motionless body, I learnt two more things about him. The first was that he had a fist made of reinforced steel woven into a block of concrete, disguised as four protruding, callused knuckles; the second was that he was an unstable wereman, a fact I discovered when I noticed, on my way to the floor, the silvery rat claws and pinkish withered toes, warped and stretched mimics of their previous human form, curling out beyond where they'd burst through the end of his shoes.

He clearly understood a key fact about sorcerers – while in theory we should be able to harness the primal forces of magic to our very will, it's hard to concentrate on building up a really good, three-hundred-volt smack when someone's hitting you. After the initial pain came the realisation that it wasn't about to stop. We curled in on ourselves, shivering away to the back of our senses, tucking our head into our hands and cowering, hoping to blank out the impact of a fist knocking us to the ground, a boot in the belly, a smack across the back, each one rendered with the force of a boulder hitting a wall, each one a shudder through our flesh, but unable to block out the sensations that we thought would overwhelm us, drown us in a big black pit. Only instinct remained as I slid down the wall, and it was instinct that, somewhere between the shock and the pain, grabbed his foot as it came up from the floor for another swing and, with my fingers scraping across the rat-edged claws that protruded from his feet, twisted. In an ordinary person, even under the best of circumstances, this would have broken their ankle. But Charlie was not ordinary. From the savage twist I gave his ankle, he seemed to transmit its spinning movement throughout his whole form, turning his body through three hundred and sixty degrees with a leap and landing on all fours, like a cat jumping from a tree. He crouched, shoulders hunched, eyes burning yellow, the beginning of whiskers protruding around the animal bulge of his mouth. He snarled, and it was the snarl of the fox cornered in his den, and his fingernails were claws, and the hair sprouting on the backs of his hands was tatty and grey. Slumped against the wall, I fumbled for support and in doing so, one hand fell on a mains plug: a blessed relief. I snatched the first dribble of voltage I could get out of the system and as he raised himself up on his oddly bent knees to strike, I threw my hand up, the electricity burning between my fingers, and shouted, "Pax!"

He saw the sparks running down my arm, and that, more than my speaking, made him hesitate. He crawled back on all fours, nose twitching, the corners of his mouth turned up in a bestial snarl, but there was still a glimmer of human consciousness there, watching, listening.

I licked my lips, wondering how best to keep his attention, and tasted blood. My nose felt like someone had set off a small bomb just behind the solid front of cartilage, and was streaming copiously. My back felt like it was made of jelly, my stomach like any movement would cause me to throw up: every breath was one breath away from the sick bowl. In a voice made unnatural by stress and pain, I said, "Listen to me. Just listen."

He made a little sound between his teeth, but didn't attempt to rip my throat out, which I took to be a good sign. "I tried to protect Sinclair," I began. But all this seemed to provoke was a snarl, and a shudder across his flesh as ginger fox fur and slimy grey tufts of rat hair squeezed their way up through the human softness of his skin. Weremen were not as uncommon in the city as I personally wished;

and behind the human exterior he seemed to have a bad case of the condition, a mingling of rat and fox, and perhaps just a hint of crow, boiling somewhere in his veins. Though their forest-dwelling descents, the werewolves, didn't exactly have a good reputation for personal hygiene, this latest twist on the species always upset me – unpredictable, unstable, highly territorial, and often clever in the unhealthy way of a child who devises ingenious methods of torturing a fly.

I tried to think through the now relentless aching of my bones. Being in a hospital helped a little; as with the underground, it had its own unique magics tingling on the edges of sense, and I tried to dabble my fingers in it as much as I could, while continuing to pay attention to the electricity still bound up in my right hand. "If you're thinking I sold Sinclair out," I tried again, "you're wrong, and if you give me half a chance, I'll prove it. If you're thinking I'm here to cause him harm, you're wrong, and frankly you should have worked it out by yourself. If you're thinking I abandoned him, you're wrong and again, I can prove it. And if you think we will let you harm us further or raise one more finger against us, then we will have to kill you. So... I suggest you try and get control over your more unusual nature, see if you can't coax those claws away, and I'll try very, very hard not to throw up over what's left of your shoes. How does that sound?"

He hesitated, head twisting to one side like an inquisitive pigeon. Perhaps he had some of that blood in his system as well. His mouth wrinkled like a wave was passing along it; but he didn't growl, and very slowly the hunched shoulders and odd curvature of his back relaxed a little, although the claws at his fingers showed no sign of going away.

He hissed in a voice that was a good 70 per cent human, "I was meant to protect him."

"Well, there's not much anyone can do against machine guns in the dark," I pointed out. I was pulling myself up the wall, every inch a triumph of will, every moment a conquest worthy of climbing Everest, until I was sitting nearly upright. "We were all befuddled by that."

"I have no reason to trust you."

"I'm not rosy about things myself. But put it like this – if I were your enemy, don't you think I would have fried you by now? Or Sinclair for that matter?"

"That's hardly an argument for one who looks as you do."

"Then you'll just have to make a decision on your lonesome, won't you?"

We sat on the steps of UCL's main building, a strange thing pretending to be a Greek temple behind a pair of tall wrought-iron gates, and drank cheap, thin coffee from the union shop. No one bothered with us; torn shoes were probably a question of style for the UCL students, and a blackened eye or so could be a badge of honour within the university athletics club.

I felt that it should have been drizzling, perhaps with a thundercloud or two overhead; it would have suited my mood. As it was, the day was crisp and clean, a thing of bright light and cold, empty blue skies, big and pale. I sat with my arms curled around as much of my aching body as I could comfortably achieve, and tried not to wobble a newly loosened tooth. There was probably, I knew, some spell or other that could repair the damage, but I wasn't about to try mystical dentistry and somehow felt as if the entire thing was beneath me. James Bond never had to go for emergency dental treatment; Jackie Chan never smiled a smile of gold crowns; Bruce Lee didn't spend the final credits of any kung fu film sitting with his arms wrapped round his belly like he had food poisoning, feeling sorry for himself – therefore, neither should I. Besides, from what little we knew and what we could guess, dentists were a species we wished to avoid.

Charlie said, rolling the cardboard coffee cup between the open palms of his hands, "He found me on the streets. As a child I was fascinated by the creatures in the city. They live around us all the time – foxes, pigeons, rats, crows, gulls, cats, dogs, mice – plus some you wouldn't expect. I saw a wolf once in Hyde Park; it just sat and stared at me, not the least bit scared. All those creatures that live off the rubbish we leave behind – and we leave a feast. You understand? I was fascinated by them. This whole animal world going on around us and we just ignore it. Choose not to notice.

"It wasn't all just childish curiosity, though. Some of it, somehow, got into the blood. My brother always said a rat bit me when I was a baby. I would go wandering in the night, and when I hit puberty, biology lessons weren't warning enough."

"You're not alone in that," I sighed. "Tell me about Sinclair."

"He... watches. That's his job."

"*X-Files?*"

"No. 'Concerned citizens'."

"He said that before; it sounded like a euphemism then and does now."

"It's how things work. Someone in government realises their wife has been putting a curse on their baby daughter; a rich businessman discovers that his number two prays to the neon; a patron of the arts sees an illusion come to life in the spray-paint drawing of a child. Concerned citizens with mutual interests. Sooner or later, they come together. They have influence, power; they want to make sure that these things don't get out of hand. Sinclair helps."

"And now they're concerned about Bakker?"

"Yes. The Tower has grown too big, Sinclair said. It's not just what Bakker is – and Sinclair thought he was a monster – it's what the Tower is. So big, so fast; so powerful. Its enemies die. Anyone who opposes it dies. There are concerned interests on every side. Sinclair's sponsors wished to ensure the containment of magic. There are equally those who wish to exploit it; and, perhaps, those who wish to destroy it. You can understand."

"Yes. I think I can. All right. Tell me about the others. The warlock, the fortune-teller, the biker..."

"Sinclair knew Khan. Khan helped him, saw things. When Khan died..."

"...Sinclair had the fortune-teller moved in?"

"Yes."

"Could she have betrayed us? Told Bakker where we were meeting, organised the shoot-out?"

"I doubt it."

"Why?"

"Because she was Khan's lover," he said, in a voice of surprised simplicity. "She wants Bakker dead. That's why she told Sinclair about you."

"What did she tell him?"

"That either Matthew Swift was alive, or something that was powerful enough to mimic his flesh lived in his place. Either way, Sinclair saw a possibility."

"Because he thought I wanted revenge on Bakker?"

"Don't you?" he asked sharply, eyes flashing up as he sipped from the paper cup. I didn't answer. "Sinclair wondered what you might have quarrelled about. He had a few theories. It takes a lot to abandon your teacher, I hear, when you're a sorcerer."

"You know nothing about it," I snapped. "You wouldn't understand."

"I think I do," he replied. "Sinclair taught me how to control what I am, cared for me. Isn't that what sorcerers do for each other? You are more than other magicians, you lose yourselves in the city, your minds and thoughts are so much a part of it that at rush hour you must walk because the city is moving, and at end of office hours you cannot help but feel a rush of relief and the desire to look at the sky, because that is how the city works. There are sorcerers who have lost themselves entirely to the power of it, their minds submerged for ever in the rhythms of the city, identities stripped down to nothing more than the pulsing of the traffic through the streets. You see? I understand how these things are. I can hear the creatures of this place wherever I go, all the time, and when I dream, my dreams are in the eyes of the pigeons and I wish I could never wake, and fly with them for ever. Sinclair told me, when I told him my dream, that that was sorcery."

"That's part of it," I admitted. "But just a part. What about the others? Who was the man with the horse's face?"

"The..."

"He was shot in the room. A sniper killed him as I walked in front of the window."

"His name was Edward Seaward. He was a wizard, a representative of the Long White City Clan. They're an underground movement. We usually just call them the Whites. They oppose the Tower."

"Why?"

"Because the Tower attempts to control people, to use them for its own end. The Whites protect their own people from the Tower and, unlike the Tower's protection, they don't demand services in return. They say they're 'the good guys'. I think they're just out for kicks. Don't like being told anything, get stubborn for the sake of being stubborn."

"Why haven't I heard of them?"

"They're still weak. Their last leader was murdered – betrayed from within. They vie in their own small way for influence within the community – they find individuals like me, who need their help and who keep order in their ranks, stop too many demons being summoned by people who should know better. They can cause some irritation to Guy Lee – they break his spells, disrupt his activities; but they are weak."

"What activities?"

"Glamours, illusions, enchantments, bedazzlements – these are the tricks he uses on behalf of the Tower, to bring in basic resources. He runs brothels in the city, whose walls are covered with enchantments, makes them an addiction, charges for every second of glamour-washed magic; brings back illusions of dead ghosts, runs fortune-telling parlours where the minds of the victims are ransacked for information, the better to relieve them of their wealth. The Whites find this offensive, dangerous. So do plenty of others, but they won't risk offending the Tower's agent."

"What about the warlock?"

"He was sent to us from Birmingham, where the Tower has also been attempting to move in. A pre-emptive strike, I think, was what the warlock desired. He's also been working to get the Scottish wizards on side; there's a lot of people running angry in Edinburgh and Glasgow at Bakker's ambitions."

"How about the biker?"

"His clan resents the Tower. It demanded the services of the bikers, carrying messages, goods, passengers. No one can get anywhere as fast as a biker; to them, distance, space, is simply a matter of perception. They bring the road to them when they travel."

"What went wrong?"

"The money offered wasn't much, and some of the things they were being asked to carry were . . . disturbing."

"Such as?"

"The crisis came when they were asked to transport a piece of flesh around the country perpetually. The flesh belonged to a man who had been caught in a brothel, one of Guy Lee's honey traps. They sliced off a piece of his skin from the base of his skull while he slept and kept it so that at any given moment they could curse him with his own flesh, or blind his senses with pain, or paralyse him from the neck downwards, or send dreams to his eyes. This man was an enemy of Bakker, an accountant who had somehow offended the Tower. The bikers were ordered to keep the man's flesh constantly moving, lest someone broke the Tower's hold on him. The bikers said no and burnt the flesh to break the spell – their leader was killed. It was not a pleasant death. Since then, the bikers have been moving too, never stopping, outrunning Bakker's revenge on them."

"And the biker at the meeting?"

"He calls himself Blackjack. He was sent as envoy to Sinclair to discuss the possibility of an alliance against the Tower. Don't underestimate him. To your eyes he may just look like a man in black, but I have seen what the bikers can do. Their magic is a wild, dangerous thing, it never stops moving. They can find anything, anywhere, and lose themselves at any moment, and you will never catch them."

"What about Oda?"

"I do not know anything about her. Sinclair seemed afraid of her."

"But she's not a magician."

"Perhaps... not *her*, then; but the people behind her... I do not know."

In honesty, I hadn't expected much more. "How about Dorie?"

"I think he may have feared her above all others. She is old, sorcerer. Sinclair says she was old when he first knew her, and he was younger then. She has been old for a very long time."

"Could she have betrayed us? Why was she there?"

"I don't know. Sinclair said... to understand Dorie, you have to know about the city. He called her the Bag Lady, as if that was a good thing."

"*The* Bag Lady? With a definite article and a strong emphasis?"

"I suppose so. Is it important?"

"Yes – could be." I tried a stretch and immediately regretted it, nausea filling my belly, and the taste of bile rising in my mouth. "What are you going to do?" I asked.

"I protect Sinclair."

"Has anyone come looking?"

"The police. I hid. They can't find out much from the sleeping body of a patient with no medical record, so they leave a man on the door. When he is awake, I hide as a rat and crawl through the water pipes. When he sleeps, I move like the fox so he doesn't hear me pass. I make sure that if they should return for Sinclair, they will fail. Will you kill Bakker?"

The question came so suddenly, I almost didn't hear it. "What?"

"Will you kill him? I read that Amiltech is suffering – that is, San Khay; he is loyal to Bakker. You wish harm to the Tower, but you haven't said if you'll kill him. I want you to. Kill him and destroy everything he's made. Can you?"

"We can kill Bakker," we said thoughtfully, "but it is not him who we fear."

"Then who? Who if not Bakker?"

I didn't answer.

"Kill him."

"Why?"

"He is a monster."

"Is he? I haven't seen any claws."

He flinched, but said, "If you want to know what Bakker has done, visit Carlisle."

"The city?"

"No. The care centre."

"Why? What's there?"

"If you go, you'll want to kill him."

I stood up, and that was an achievement. "If I need you, you'll be . . ."

"With Sinclair," he said firmly. "I'll see you. Although," he grinned, and the teeth were yellow and ratty, "you may not see me. Goodbye, sorcerer. Bring me some of his blood on your hands, when you make up your mind."

"You're a funny guy," I replied, and walked away.

I don't know why I let myself in for these things.

I went to Carlisle.

The care home was on the southern edge of Croydon, in a converted red-brick house with a big driveway, near a park rolling down towards the green belt and its countryside. Even here the taste of the air was different, not as sharp and strong as in the city, but hinting at that other magic, the strange magic that so few people understood these days – that of places beyond the city, the slower, sluggish, calm magic of the trees and the fields, that had, once upon a time, burnt as brightly as the neon power through which I now wandered. There were still some left who could harness it as it had once been used – druids and the odd magician out in the countryside who summoned vines instead of barbed wire from the earth – but they were few in number and generally didn't talk to their urban counterparts, whose magic they regarded as a corruption rather than an evolution of the natural order of things. It was a debate I kept well out of.

I didn't exactly know who I was there to see when I arrived at the Carlisle care home. But the question was quickly answered when I got a glimpse of the residents' book in reception. One name leapt out at me – Elizabeth Jane Bakker.

I signed myself in as Robert James Bakker, and went to meet her. They didn't question who I was, but the nurse informed me that she was delighted I had finally come to the home and that Elizabeth was showing good signs of improvement, though she still screamed at the sight of mirrors.

Elizabeth Jane Bakker sat in a wheelchair at one end of a living room full of beige furniture. She wore a white veil over her face and a bandage of white around what was left of her hands, as well as the obligatory, shameful blue pyjamas of the other residents. On her lap was a tray of untouched food – mashed potato, carrot and some kind of sausage meat in suspiciously fluorescent gravy. I sat down on a stool opposite her and said, "Hello, Elizabeth."

The veil twitched. Between its hem and the top of the pyjamas, I could see the scrambled, scarlet remnants of the burnt skin on her neck. When she spoke, her voice was distorted by the effort of shaping words with the twisted remains of her mouth, and came out almost inaudible at first, so I had to lean right in to catch it.

"I see . . . to be free . . . they say . . . be me . . ." she whispered.

"How are you?" I asked, and immediately felt stupid.

"The rats keep singing when I try to sleep. All the time, singing singing singing. But the voice in the phone went away."

"Aren't you hungry?" I tried.

Her glance moved down to the plate. With a deep grunt from the back of her throat, she seized the tray with the remnants of her hands, throwing it across the room. Mash flew out from the little plastic indents as it smashed against the far wall. The nurse hurried in from the corridor, saw the mess, and merely rolled her eyes, as if this was something regular and understandable, before cleaning it up.

Elizabeth lapsed into sullen silence. Unsure what else I could say that wouldn't be either dangerous or mad, so did I.

We stayed sitting in silence for almost ten minutes before she looked up slowly and said, "Is it free, where you are?"

I hesitated. "It's all right," I said, hoping this was a safe answer.

"Come be me," she sang, in a faint, distant voice of one remembering a nursery rhyme. "Come be me and be free!"

We felt a shudder run all the way down from the hairs on our skull to the tips of our toes. "Where did you hear that?" we asked.

"They used to burn in the telephones. I danced with them before they went away. Did you lie?"

"Did your brother hear them sing too?" we asked.

She shook her head, slowly, uncertainly, then added in a more cheerful voice, "Have your pudding and eat it, that's what they said, save the best for last, meat and two veg, do you see?"

"Did he hurt you?" I asked, as gently as possible.

"Said to dance, said to burn and we've always loved the city . . ."

"Did he do this to you?"

"He just sits in the chair that's all, nothing bad, just sits and likes to eat, watches, gets on with things, although the water doesn't taste so good any more, vodka, vodka and lick the lamp post . . ." Her shoulders were starting to shake – with a shock, we realised that she was starting to cry.

Uncertainly, I leant forward, and put my arms round her shoulders, although she was so limp that it was hard to tell what good it did. We put our mouth near her ear, and so close now we could see through the veil, the burnt, sunk flesh, the remnants of a nose, the unevenness of burnt-off lips, and murmured as quietly as we could, like a mother singing her lullaby, "We be fire, we be light, we be life, we sing electric flame, we slither underground wind, we dance heaven – come be we and be free. Come be me."

Her shaking slowly stopped. She pulled away from our hold and looked through the veil straight into our eyes. The bandaged stub of a hand brushed our cheek, sending a shudder through our skin. "So blue," she whispered. "No wonder you went away."

"Why did Bakker do this to you?" I asked quietly. "Why would he do this thing?"

"He wanted to hear the angels," she whispered. "He wanted to find them, to see the blue, but he couldn't, he couldn't, he tried and they wouldn't answer, he was too far, too quiet, they didn't come for him, he couldn't understand and he said . . . he said . . ." The bandage pressed against my cheek. *"He asked you,"* she hissed. "To find them, he asked *you*. And you said no – why did you have to say no? I would have kissed you and you said no, and he needed another sorcerer, he needed someone to give their senses and their blood and you said no so he asked me. He tried to bring them back and when I couldn't do it, when I couldn't do it, he said it was all right, he was sorry, he said he loved me, he forgave me and . . . and . . ."

And Elizabeth Jane Bakker, just like her brother, was a sorcerer, and her skin burnt my cheek to the touch, even through the bandage, and the lights spat and fizzed around her and the floor hummed like a train was passing beneath us. I grabbed her arm and whispered, "Listen to me, listen to me . . . what did Bakker want you to do?"

"He is so hungry!" she whispered. "So hungry . . ."

"Did he bring us back?" we demanded. "Does he still want the angels, did he bring us back?"

"Make me a shadow on the wall." She nearly wailed it, clung to my face like she wanted to press it into some new, better shape. "I said I was sorry, so sorry, that I wouldn't say no again and it just kept on, kept on burning, kept saying that I didn't understand, so sorry, so sorry, make me a shadow on the wall . . ."

"Bakker did this to you, because you wouldn't help him?"

"So sorry . . ."

She was shaking again. I ran my hand over the top of her head, across the white fabric of her veil and felt the odd stubble of patchy hair underneath it, and whispered soothing noises as she pressed her face into my shoulder and the humming in the floor gently started to die down and the rats scuttling in the walls began to breathe again. "It's all right," I whispered. "It's all right. We're here now."

"He wouldn't kill me, he wouldn't. He said I should feel what it's like, know how it felt, understand..."

"It's all right," we repeated, not sure what else we could say. "Shush, it'll be all right."

"So hungry," she whispered. "I'm so hungry." We leant away slowly, staring into the vague shadow of her eyes. She stared straight back, lips twitching under the veil. "He said I should live and that I would always be hungry, always be thirsty, always be ugly, always be in pain, because I didn't help. Matthew?"

"I'm here," I murmured.

"Why didn't you do what he asked you to? Why didn't you help him?"

I thought about it. "Because it was obscene," I said finally. "What he wanted was obscene."

"Missed you," she whispered. "Just like the song said. They always said the world was bigger than the current could flow, and when you'd touched every corner, you could drift away into the stars... did it hurt, your death? He said you were dead. I screamed at him and called him names. I screamed and screamed until they burnt my tongue, make me a shadow on the wall, I said, make me a shadow... I would have helped if you weren't dead. I called him murderer. He said I couldn't understand, that it wasn't... that you weren't... but they kept on and he said... they were always there and then it just stopped!"

"Shush, shush," I whispered, stroking the odd, coarse tufts of her hair. "I'm here now. We'll see you safe."

She leant up and with the rough, uneven edges of her mouth, through the veil, kissed my lips, once, gently, and put her head into my shoulder. "My angels," she whispered. "My electric angels."

I stayed with her for the rest of the day, and she didn't say anything more, and neither did I. And that, too, was sorcery.

Shortly after dusk, we left her sleeping, kissing the whisper of our voice into her tiny, lobeless ear, and went to finish San Khay.

The newspapers reported pretty much what I knew. The Amiltech office was in ruins, the staff had been sent home. It wasn't safe any more, they said, and those who stayed too long thought they saw the glimmering of aluminium wings in the fan vents, and heard the chittering of the fairies.

Clients, while sympathising greatly with the clear campaign of hate that had been taken up against Amiltech, were making tactful enquiries about switching security firms for the simple reason that Amiltech was plainly unable, in its current state, to fulfil obligations.

There was more I could do, and I knew it. A little arson, a bit of trashing – this was not enough to bring down a company permanently, this was something insurance could still cover. I could be methodical, thorough, find every blood bank and illicit financial record, burn them all, expose them all, tear Amiltech apart.

But now, we were not in the mood to wait. We wanted San Khay, we wanted to pull down the king at the top of this particular house of cards, and with him gone, we knew that even the Tower would feel the blow.

What we didn't know was whether we wanted to kill him, or if he was simply a pawn on the way to the ace in the sky – Bakker.

We knew now that we wanted to kill Bakker.

I thought about the blue drawing of a burning angel I'd found under San Khay's desk.

I remembered the taste of blood.

I remembered . . .

. . . give me life . . .

. . . be free . . .

. . . my electric angels . . .

Bakker had to die. And if that meant going through San Khay, so be it.

I needed equipment.

I spent a night and a morning in bed recovering from my encounter with Charlie. I spent the afternoon purchasing from every general store, haberdasher and art shop I could find, as much dye of every kind as I could find. Bottles of ink, capsules of fabric dye, in every conceivable colour; I purchased everything I could get my hands on and which could fit into my bag. I also went round the junk stores until I found the shattered remains of a large grandfather clock, from whose face I stole the minute and hour hands, and acquired a small bell, a set of six six-sided dice, a blanket and a very large, heavy-duty permanent marker. From the supermarket I bought a week's supply of egg and cress sandwiches, a bunch of bananas, a pair of buckets and six litres of bottled mineral water. Lastly, I went to the second-hand bookshops on Charing Cross Road and trawled up and down through their shelves until I found a copy of *The Train Journey's Companion*, published in 1934, its dusty cover red and heavy, smelling of crushed insects and dry leaves.

Then, I hired a van. The man who let it to me was willing, for £400, to ignore my lack of valid driver's licence and ID. The van stank of cabbage and cornered like a drunken elephant. It would do.

The next day I spent looking for just the right kind of place. In the newspapers, San Khay vowed to take revenge on the enemy of his company and his employees, and bring them to justice for their crimes. His share price fell by sixteen pence on the London market, and everyone expressed immense sympathy. The vice-president of the company moved his family to Cornwall, after all the walls of his house were scratched by dozens of very, very tiny aluminium fingernails. San's personal secretary complained that she couldn't sleep because the shadows kept moving on her walls, and there were voices in her head, and as a result, she'd have to take a holiday in Corfu as soon as possible while the company repaired itself.

I found what I needed eventually in a for-let garage space underneath a railway line in Camden, with solid metal doors and a single light high in the roof. I cleared out a dead fridge and half a bicycle from inside the garage, and then set to, creating my magic circle.

Circles are a very traditional form of magic; mine was no exception. With my permanent marker pen (do not be deceived by those who favour chalk – an unreliable, amateur substance) I drew a big, slightly wonky circle on the floor. Inside this I placed the buckets, and next to them I put the pile of preservative-heavy sandwiches, the six litres of water, the bananas, and the blanket, neatly folded.

Around the edge of the circle on the outside I placed the six dice, going clockwise in ascending order with the top side showing one to six as they went round, at equal distance from each other. At the top of the circle I put the salvaged hour hand, pointing inwards, and at the bottom, nearest the door, I put the minute hand, also pointing inwards, directly towards its counterpart in the north.

This done, I then did something that I do very rarely, and got down on my knees at the bottom of the circle, and prayed.

It was a summoning as much as a prayer, an invocation, that passed my lips. I knelt on that spot for the best part of an hour whispering my hopes and aspirations to the spirits of that place. The floor was hard, and my knees ached, but once embarked on such an incantation, you do not break out of it lightly. I summoned all the powers that might watch over that small garage under the railway line, begged them, cajoled them, enticed them with every inch of will and magic I had available, and half-thought that they weren't going to come – until the vibration of the train passing over my head became too long, rattling on and on and on so that I thought perhaps the train wasn't one, but a whole herd of the things, all going home for the evening, rushing along the same track.

It took a while to equate that pounding noise, the regular *cuthunkcuthunkcuthunk* of the wheels over the joins in the silvery track, to the cold breeze growing on the back of my neck, and the way my breath condensed in the air, even though it was not so cold outside. When the spirit of that place began to appear, it did so gradually, a shimmer of navy blue that flickered in and out of existence – flash and then gone – bringing with it the distant mournful whistle of a train heard in the night through a locked bedroom window. I kept on with the summoning, feeling at my side for the copy of *The Train Journey's Companion* to reassure myself, the only warm thing in the place, while I waited for the spirit of that place to come fully into being.

It appeared on the other side of the circle a bit at a time, like the Cheshire Cat, not entirely sure if it was coming or it was going, and when it was definitely *there*, even then bits of it kept focusing in and out with the faint rushing of wheels that defined it, its left arm suddenly snatched away by a cold breeze, only to be replaced a moment later by another copy, its face suddenly twisted into a fading patch of dark brown fog before it snapped back into place, its hat fading on and off its head, sometimes changing styles, at one moment big and broad and dark blue, the next tight and black, the next with a silver badge on the front, quaint and old-fashioned. Around its neck hung a small grey plastic machine with a slot for a credit card, in its hand was a book of pinkish paper tickets, in its breast pocket a multiplicity of pens and pencils, on its feet, the only thing that seemed constant about its shifting form, a pair of black leather loafers.

It was, in short, the spirit of the railway conductor, guardian of that place, and its expression, as it looked at me, was decidedly unimpressed. When it spoke, its voice was like the rushing of wind through a dark tunnel, and it said,

"All tickets, all tickets please!"

I held up *The Train Journey's Companion* and said respectfully, "Sir, I have a gift?"

The book opened itself in my hands, the pages rustling like leaves on the line, blurring the words and pictures. Then, as ethereal as the creature standing in the garage in front of me, it too began to shift, move, fade away, leaving just a cold breeze on my fingertips.

"So much is changing," the figure whispered sadly. "We are not what we were. All change, please, all change."

"Martin Mill, Hither Green, Three Bridges, Woolwich Arsenal, Mudchute, Bounds Green, Gospel Oak..." I replied, rattling off the names of the train stations as they came to mind.

Its form shifted, a hint of a big leather belt, seen and then gone, the flash of brass buttons, the gleam of a corporate badge. It seemed to smile. "They would rather just leave and arrive, leave and arrive, than take a journey. This place will fade with the rattling of the train."

"In the names of Thameslink, First Capital Connect, Southern Railway, South Western, GNER, National Express, Great Western, Chiltern Railways..."

It raised its head and said, "It is always nice to be remembered, even by little sorcerers who would rather fly. Where do you want to go today?"

"I need to keep someone here. I need to make sure they are safe and well, but cannot leave, and cannot be found by others who may come looking. Will you help me?"

"It is nice to be remembered," the figure repeated. "We will keep your magic circle, and think of you, when we pass by."

With that, it started to fade, taking with it the touch of the cold breeze from a train rushing by the platform edge, and the taste of mechanical steam.

I stayed a while longer, until the next train passed overhead, and stood up, my place now secure, my magic circle now guaranteed, and went to find San Khay.

Say what you will for San, even in times of crisis his routine was fixed. I found him on the roof of a building on the edge of the City of London, where its boundary merged with that of the City of Westminster. He was sipping champagne. The roof comprised a wide balcony, warmed by tall heaters with hatlike tops, which blasted away with the intensity of gas cookers, and a large glass conservatory. All this had been added as an afterthought onto a grand 1930s art deco building whose clean lines and simple silver curves housed grand offices beneath its exclusive roof garden. The conservatory was full of trickling fountains, ornamental trees, floodlighting and, this evening, women in little black dresses, and the hubbub of tipsy chatter. I watched it through the eyes of a pigeon circling overhead, the patterns of people's movement as they bounced from group to group; the more wealthy and senior members of the club seated at tables where their drinks were brought to them along with small dishes of olives and oil, while the aspirant and younger members circulated from table to table, easing themselves in, networking, and moving on.

San sat at his own table, flanked by two bodyguards, and politely, as always, talked to those who came to see him, and was reasonable and calm with them all. He was also shrewd; and as the evening wore on, his eyes would dart more and more to my pigeons circling above his table until at last, at 11.30 p.m., as the gossip was hotting up and the champagne was flowing yet more freely, he looked up, straight at the creatures in whose brains I was nestled, and raised one hand, as if in invitation, or as a toast. Then he leant over to one of his bodyguards, who nodded and left.

I withdrew my mind from the pigeons' and abandoned the bench on the street corner where I had been sitting while my mind drifted in their thoughts. Putting down the handful of feathers I'd collected from the street, which had given me the connection, I turned towards the doors of the building in which San waited.

In due course, the bodyguard San had spoken to appeared in the doorway. I walked up to him. He wasn't actively waving the gun wedged under his right armpit, and didn't seem up to throwing much magic, so I said, "Are you looking for me?"

"Mr Khay would like to know if you would join him," he replied politely.

"Guns such as yours make me nervous."

"He was most insistent that I didn't use it, despite, naturally, my skill in such matters," said the bodyguard smoothly. His smile dazzled.

"Was he?"

"Indeed, sir. He said, sir, that should I attempt in any way to threaten you, you would most likely explode my heart in my chest before I had a chance to remove the safety; and that, therefore, he would deal with you in person, if sir would be willing to settle this matter that way."

I thought about this, shifting the hefty weight of my satchel on my shoulder. "You hold that thought," I said. "And I'll have a drink with Mr Khay."

In real life, San Khay was taller than I expected, but that might have been the good posture with which he sat, even at eleven thirty at night, on a low bench that wasn't comfortable, but was probably art. He nodded courteously at me as I sat down opposite him on the balcony. "Drink?"

"I'm fine, thank you."

"I hope my assistant was tactful."

"Very. Didn't start shooting or anything."

"I explained to him the likely consequences. You are, after all, a man of significant power, yes?"

I hesitated. The question in his voice threw me – not necessarily in an egotistical way, since the definition of "power" was one that had been up for debate ever since my unlikely return to the waking world over a week before. It did suggest, however, that he didn't know the extent of what I could do, beyond the proof he'd seen on his walls.

I said, "You've seen what I do."

"Of course. I am, naturally, curious as to why you do it and to what end – and would be happy to hear your views on both."

He spoke in neat, clipped tones and the hint of an American accent, probably from too many years getting an expensive education. His only motion was the tiniest tapping of his little finger against the stem of his champagne glass.

"I'm afraid it's complicated," I replied.

"You are a warlock, perhaps?"

"No, no, not really."

"You are clearly a man of means."

I laughed, despite myself. "No," I said with a smile, "not that either."

"May we conclude 'capable' then, as a suitable epithet?"

"'Capable' may have to cover it."

"You understand, I cannot permit your current campaign against my business to continue. While trivial enough in itself, it is disruptive, and worst of all, bad for my reputation. Reputation, you see, in an industry such as mine, where so much has not been legislated for, is worth a hundred lawyers and all their gold watches."

"I see."

"With which in mind I will offer you a simple enough choice."

"Which is?"

"Either I employ you, or I kill you."

Surprise barely covered it. "Come again?"

"A man of your ability would be far more useful on my team than operating against me, and it would be a shame to bury your abilities entirely. If you have desires, now would be the time to name them."

"Desires?"

"I can offer you wealth, property, money – these are, though, the simple things of a corporate role. I can offer more. Magic. Secrets. Revenge. Have you ever wished for a place by the river, the lights on the water at night, or for sharing the dreams of a child, sensing the skin of another sex, hearing all with the ears of a bat, seeing with the eyes of a hawk, smelling with the nose of a dog, your thoughts in unimagined brilliant colour, or dabbling in the visions of a heroin addict on the edge of death and seeing what he sees as he passes beyond, a glimpse of something more? We can put you on the same eyeline as God. I can offer you these things: visions, wonders, comfort, security. Whatever you desire."

"Is this the standard employee package?" I asked.

"We are good to our people at Amiltech."

"Health insurance?"

"I don't see why not."

"And who pays?"

"The company."

"I meant who pays for the other things? Whose senses must I steal to have these powers, whose mind must I violate, whose house will I inhabit, whose wealth will I profit by, whose dreams will I dabble in, whose ideas will I skim for gold, who will I have to kill, who will I have to control?"

"Does it matter?"

I thought about it. "Yes," I said. "It matters to me."

"Is this your reason for coming here tonight?"

"It's part of it."

He sighed impatiently, ran one delicate finger round the rim of his champagne glass. It whined like a suffocating bat. "I think you are not interested in an amicable solution, no?"

"Not really," I admitted. "But I appreciate the offer."

"Well then, I offer you the alternative. Run, hide, magician. I've seen your face, I can recognise you now; wherever you go and whatever you do, my men can find you, follow you, track you by the prints from your fingers, and we will kill you, *I* will kill you and show your corpse to my clients and say, 'These are the dead bones you were afraid of, and look how they died. I will do this to your enemies if you name them.' I shall have your skull on my desk as a paperweight, and wish that you still had eyes to see my victory."

I waited. There wasn't any more so I said, "Tell you what, you come find me tonight, and we'll sort out this whole shebang. Sound reasonable?"

He sipped his champagne. "Very reasonable."

"Good!" I stood up, smiled at him, nodded at the two bodyguards, who also stood, and said, "I'll just get running, then. See you later, Mr Khay."

"Good evening, magician," he replied, and sipped again, and didn't move.

I smiled one last time, turned, and walked into the crowd. My heart was racing but it wasn't fear – the crowd protected me, even San wouldn't risk shooting me among that lot – it was excitement. The sense of a battle coming and, more to the point, a battle we knew we could win. I summoned the lift. When it came, I rode it to the bottom, stuck my foot into the door, and pressed every single button between the ground floor and the roof. I reasoned that while they either waited for the lift or used the stairs, I'd have the time I needed.

This done, I ran into the night, and the pigeons followed.

The place I had chosen for the night's work was Paternoster Square. It was an unusual place: the new buildings, with their clean walls and big tinted windows, wouldn't be out of place in a utopian science fiction movie; but like the best of such places, it had a darker bite to it. CCTV cameras were angled on every wall and, during the daytime at least, there were always security guards. Their presence made me suspect the existence of spies or gangsters in an office somewhere nearby, since I couldn't think why else they'd be patrolling what was ostensibly just one more London square.

What took the square out of the realm of futuristic fantasy was its neighbour: St Paul's Cathedral, half of it white from cleaning, the other still a sooty grey as the council tried to polish it up faster than the dirt could accumulate. It loomed over the mismatched shape of Paternoster Square (which had too many sides to deserve its name) like the last laugh of the past, mocking its descendants who still couldn't build grander than the dome or the figures on the cathedral roof whose eroded features gazed down Ludgate Hill. It was a strange meeting point of past and present, and at this hour of the night, almost deserted. My footsteps were too loud, the pigeons too quiet, the lights too bright in the dark – huge white floodlights smiting the cathedral walls and every angle of Paternoster Square together with the smooth marble pillar at its centre – a baby version of the Monument, complete with golden ball of flame at its top, raised in memory of the Blitz.

In that place, that strange place where the sharp bite of racing magic met with the ponderous stones of the cathedral, sluggish with its own history, every shadow contained a ghost; and that night, with no one else around and the clouds busy overhead, the ghosts watched us. We brushed a toe along the bottom step of the cathedral's west front, and we could hear the low murmuring of the priests' incantations, the high singing of the choirboys in their red and white cassocks, the footsteps of heavy heels on the marble floor, the whispers of so many thousands, millions, of people around the gallery in the cathedral's dome, feel the burning of the fire that had led to its reconstruction, taste the dust of its stones being slid into place, sense the bombs falling around it, hear the rattle of carts and carriages fade into the roar of car engines, the tones of the tourist guides in brisk Japanese, silken Italian, every language of the earth, see the shadows of so many people who'd passed through that place; you couldn't be a magician, even a concussed idiot of a magician, and not know that those stones were buzzing with time, magic. We hadn't seen any sign of a God in this world, but we could understand it if people went to that place to pray, if only to do honour to a past so magnificent.

Business called.

I blew the fuses without too much effort in every camera I could see. Then I walked round Paternoster Square, laying out my provisions. I opened all my bottles of ink and laid them out at intervals across the pavement. I cracked open the tubs of powdered dye, careful to keep my fingers out of their contents, which I sprinkled across the paving stones in long sweeps of scarlet, black, green and blue. This done, all I had to do was pace around to keep warm, coat buttoned up and hands buried in my pockets, and wait.

The bells of St Paul's announced midnight – quarter past – half past. So much for San Khay's efficiency. We nervously collected a fallen pigeon feather from the foot of a statue of Queen Anne, who looked frighteningly far too large under the fierce artificial lights, and shared the bird's gaze for a few minutes, sweeping over the rooftops and through the alleys and the streets around the square, just to make sure that San hadn't already found us, and wasn't putting snipers into place as we waited like a fool. He would have been wise to do so; but we somehow felt it wasn't right for what he wanted, and indeed, as we drifted on the air beneath us, and enjoyed the weight of our wings and the strength in our bones as we dove and swept up again on our own momentum, like a child's acrobatic kite snapping in the breeze, we saw no sign of him.

Back on the ground, we waited.

I blew into my hands to keep them warm while my thoughts followed the numb progression of absent consciousness that every ten minutes jerks into your awareness with a conclusion that you cannot trace or understand, and which fades from memory almost as soon as you've reached it. As the bell tolled quarter to one, the conclusion that seemed to have emerged most prominently from my idling brain was the desire for fish and chips, so intense we could almost smell it, the tang of the vinegar in our nose, the feeling of heat through greasy wrapping paper, the crumbling of fish on the end of little wooden forks . . .

San Khay was at one moment very much absent, and the next very much there. He was about thirty feet away, coming through the small, fake-Stuart barbican archway at the southern end of the square, and headed straight for me. He wore no shoes: I could see the swirl of inky stain that wound even around his toes like the roots of some leafless tree. He'd also removed his shirt, revealing the shiny black whorls of colour on his chest which moved as he did, rippling ever so slightly black to red with the beating of his heart, never brightening much beyond dark ebony, but still with that hint of magic in the ink. His feet should have been bleeding, his heart racing and his breath heaving – none of these were so; and he moved fast, far too fast, like a sprinter leaning at an angle for a bend in the track, moving in a long, rapid curve towards me that threw my perceptions off kilter and made it hard to judge where he might strike.

In either hand he had a knife; both were clearly designed by someone with an overactive imagination who probably enjoyed zen gardening and clean kills – curved, long, polished and so sharp I could hear their tearing of the air as he moved. The sound was louder than his shockingly, unnaturally light, quick footstep. I hadn't expected such weapons; knives complicate things, and I couldn't hope to outrun him or outfight him in close quarters. So I did the only thing that seemed appropriate, and turned out the lights.

I snuffed the lights on the pillar in the centre of the square, on shuttered restaurants and boutiques around its edges, in the tall, glass-walled offices above, in the streets around, the floodlights on the cathedral, in the shop windows, in the phone boxes, even in the few passing cars. I pressed them down to nothing with a swish of my hand through the air and grabbed the surplus light and heat they left behind, pulling it into me, around me, so that even the orange glow of the city sky was muted; and in my palm, held tightly so he couldn't see, was the tiniest speck of their brightness, compressed into a space no larger than a banana seed.

Even then, he was fast, and single-minded; still he kept coming straight for me, even though his eyes must have been confused as they struggled to adapt. I could feel the force of his moving through the air as he left the ground a few feet away and headed, knife-edge first, directly for me.

I threw myself to one side. He landed on his feet, easily as a cat, in the space I'd just left. I picked myself up gracelessly and threw a handful of the stolen heat from the lamps into his face. The force of it in the air rippled even the darkness and threw him back, making him shield his face with his hands. Anyone else would have been, at the least, temporarily blinded, and at the most, incinerated. But San had magic in his skin and, all it did was make him stagger with a grunt, the ink flaring bright across his forearms where the brunt of the heat had struck. I ran for where the dark was thickest, in an arcade of pillars on the other side of the square, aware of how loud my footsteps and breathing were compared to the easy, light and confident lope of San. In the dark I found the nearest pillar with my fingers and memory, and pressed my back into it, comforted by its solidity, and waited.

From there we heard the gentle footfall of San's movement, as he prowled like a carnivorous animal, searching, feeling his way, listening for the tiniest sound that might reveal our presence, the creak of a shoe, the rush of a breath. We could taste him more than anything else, the sharp, painful edge of his magic, a prickling across our skin, a dark rushing through our senses. We pressed our fingers into the cold stone and half-closed our eyes, and there was a whisper of...

...cart on cobbles...

diesel engine rattling in a big red bus

bells at sunset...

a smell of

...smoke from burning timber

coffee

river at low tide

at high tide

carrying salt water in...

...sewage out...

a taste of

...fresh-baked bread in a clay oven...

sparks on a hay-covered floor...

...explosives in the sky...

burning skin

mortar dust...

And San's voice. "Magician? You can't hide in this dark for long."

We opened our eyes, and the shadows looked back. Faceless remnants of the past, drifting pieces of memory and time left behind, trapped in the stones, the statues, the trees, the streets. They rippled out of the dark into the still square, crawled up from the ground and writhed their way out of the walls, shadows stretching back beyond the Fire of London, beyond the building of the cathedral, some so old they were little more than grey shimmers across the stones, some still dark and new. I pulled my coat up around my face and stepped out from behind the pillar, still hiding the light from the lamps in the palm of my hand. Seen only by the reflective orange glow of the clouds overhead, the shadows were everywhere, they filled each inch of space in a blurred mass of greyness, sometimes with a snatch of face or clothes, but more often just a glimmering form, as if they were made of pale water. I moved like one of them, circling, as they did, the pillar in the heart of the square, the golden flame on its summit the only thing that caught what light there was and gave enough reflective glow to cast a shadow.

In the middle of the ghosts stood San Khay, pushing through them, brushing them aside like they were cobwebs that disintegrated at his touch, shimmering out of existence at his movement. He scanned the mass of faceless shadows with narrowed eyes, and an intensity against which, I suspected, the simple enchantments of my coat would offer no protection. I moved faster through the silent crowds, feeling a coldness every time I passed through one of them, like the wind just before rain. I placed myself as far as possible from the turning shape of San Khay, his skin shockingly bright among the moving shadows, and waited for him to face me directly.

When he did, he was strong enough, smart enough, to see me

instantly – or perhaps he simply heard my breath. He lunged for me, ignoring the shadows in his path that broke down to nothing as he moved. I didn't wait for him to get closer, but released in an instant the bundle of light trapped in the palm of my hand.

And closed my eyes.

Every lamp, lantern, bulb, floodlight, street light, car light, shop illumination, uplight and downlight came on in an instant, explosively bright in the darkness of the square, their touch melting the shadows down to nothing like they were butter thrust into the sun. He staggered back for a second; but a second was all I gained and he was moving again – again directly for me.

I turned my palms skywards, and raised my hands – and with them, the water beneath my feet.

It responded quickly – there was a lot of power in that place. The tops blew off the drains: the circular metal lids above the sewers, the rectangular slabs covering the fireman's water taps; each blasted upwards in a geyser of cold water. The basin around the foot of the pillar glinted as the fountain inside it flowed, then gushed, splashing out over the rim in a torrent. Around it, dark lines of water crawled between the paving stones, then spilled out and over. Where the water met my coloured swirls of dye, it mingled with them and started to change.

None of this seemed to bother San Khay, so with a swat of my hand I directed the nearest geyser of water to turn and knock him to one side with its force. He rolled through it, falling where it pushed him, then out of its reach. As he did, he rolled into a bottle of black ink, spilling its contents across the paving stones and spattering the top of his left arm with dots of darkness.

It was a start, but not enough – he kept on coming, and now there was anger in his face. Hastily I stepped away from him and started snatching at the power in the air, ravelling it between my fingertips and heaving it skywards in a bundle so fat and uncontrolled it almost boomed on its way up, like a plane passing overhead. As it rose, so did the water: geysers gushing up from the pipes, puddles forming between the paving stones, even the dazzling spatter from the fountain. It wasn't just water: where it had mingled with the dyes it was blue, red, black, green, dragging up vivid hues along with sheets of clean liquid, filling the square with the effect of backwards rain, rising away from the ground in a cloudburst of cleanliness and colour.

The effort of that took the breath out of me for a moment – long enough for San Khay, dripping with the water spiralling up around us, to reach me. I didn't even see him coming. But we felt the movement of his arm through the air, and instinctively ducked under the first blow, which would have torn our throat in two. He swung next with his right arm, fast, powerful, jabbing towards our heart. We had no choice but to retreat, back-stepping as our shoes started to soak through and turn black as we stepped into a pool of half-diluted dye. And still he kept coming, right, left, an unrelenting rhythm that didn't even give us time to throw another spell, we had to turn and duck and move so fast. He didn't just advance in a straight line, but spun round the axis of his own shoulder so that at any moment death might come from left or right or above or below. We had never been so unsure of our own abilities nor, as we danced in front of his knives, so thrilled with ourselves that, second from second, we survived. We kept retreating through the upwards rain, feeling the water crawling up our chin, leaving streaks of black and red across our face as it curled up into our hair; we felt it shiver along our fingertips, running between the curves of our knuckles, staining our skin a motley bruised colour as the inky water ran across our flesh.

And little by little, San Khay started to falter.

As he advanced through them, the melded dyes and water rising from the ground now settled in the empty spaces between the lines of his tattoos. They blurred their edges, disguised their swirls with other, uglier stains of black and blue, and marred the otherwise elegant curves of ink across his skin. As they did, the magic in his flesh began to leach. I could see it, smell it: the enchantments bound into his flesh sparked into the water, flashed with motes of blackness into the rising rain around us, melting away as the patterns that defined the enchantment became distorted. He could still fight, and better than me, but he was so used to that strength in his skin that as it started to fail he began to make mistakes, not understanding his own limitations. So with one swipe he overreached, staggering right past me, and with another his fingers, shining with the water running over us both, nearly opened and dropped the knife, as if it were suddenly too heavy to hold. This was a man who hadn't used his muscles, really *used* them as themselves, for years, so that like an astronaut returning to gravity he felt his legs become weak, his breathing difficult, his skin turning to the colour of an industrial accident.

I moved back and, when he followed, he staggered, barely picking himself up. He stabbed, and I caught his wrist, the strength in his arm suddenly resistible, the speed of his movement now visible as more than just a blur. We twisted his arm back on itself, and his fingers opened automatically, dropping the blade. We pushed him back hard, and his bare feet slipped on the soaking pavement, his toes almost black from the puddles of colour we waded through. We blinked green drops of water out of our eyes and scooped up the knife in passing, moving towards him, wary that he still might have a trick to play but increasingly confident, tasting no more in his movements now than just the ordinary heat of a human passing by. He lunged at us poorly with his other blade, but his arm was an image of worm-thin wriggling splotches of colour flowing up to his shoulder and then away, skywards. We sidestepped easily, kicking down towards the back of his leg as he passed at us, and pushing his knee towards the ground. As he swung his arm back, we stepped round behind him, caught it at the elbow and wrenched it backwards, further than it wanted to bend, hard. He let out a sound between his teeth like his breath had become trapped behind his tongue, and as we put the knife against his throat, his inky face expressed nothing but pain.

Around us, the water began to fall back down from the sky in bright droplets as the spell ran out, splashing red, green, blue, black in thin swirls across the pavement, dripping off the golden flame on the top of the monument, running down windows, and plopping with a clear, regular *drip drip drip* onto the twisted metal coverings of the pipes below ground. We felt the rain soak our skin, cold and shocking.

San Khay's flesh was the colour of an infected bruise, the outline of his tattoos now marred. He hissed, "If you have sense, you will let me go!"

We leant forward sharply, pressing the tip of the knife into the hollow at the base of his throat. "If you had sense, you would not have come looking for us," we hissed. "Did you really not see what you were contending with? Could you not taste it, did you not have the wit to understand?"

"I serve the Tower," he snarled. "They will come for me and they will tear your flesh from your bones!"

"They tried that before and still we live, our blood, our skin, so alive, you cannot understand!"

He half-turned his head to look at us, and gave a forced laugh. "He will eat your heart," he whispered. "He likes to keep something to honour his friends."

We drew the blade back to cut his throat, the blue anger across our eyes, ready to finish this ignorant, arrogant thing. At the last moment I held back, forced my fingers to stop shaking, and tightened my grip, breathing slowly and steadily until our screaming, our fury at this creature too small to even see his own place in the city, too small to know his own smallness, had abated. I dropped to one knee behind him, thrusting his head back towards mine with the tip of the blade, and whispered, "Tell me what you know of the shadow."

"He will eat your heart," he repeated, voice trembling with victory, fear, rage – I couldn't tell which. San Khay was not a man used to losing.

"How long has he lived? How long has the shadow been out there?"

"Why should you care?"

"Just tell me what you know."

"No. I know what he does to his enemies."

"Whose? Hunger's – the shadow? Or to Bakker's?"

A flicker on his face. Perhaps, for a moment, he was beginning to understand. "Who are you?" he asked.

"My name is Matthew Swift."

"The name . . . seems familiar."

"I'm sure it does, and if things had been otherwise, you might have been the one they asked to hide the body."

"What body?"

"That," I said, "is the question they really should have explored. Can Bakker control it? The shadow?"

"It kills his enemies. It'll kill you eventually."

"Doesn't mean he's in charge. How do I kill it?" He didn't answer. We dug the blade into his throat until it drew a thin line of beady blood. "How do we kill it?!"

"You can't."

"Why not?"

"It is a shadow. You can never kill it."

"Then how does Bakker control it?"

"You said yourself, maybe he can't."

"How does he control Dana Mikeda?"

"How do you know Dana Mikeda?"

We pressed the knife closer until his breath wheezed. "We can rip out your thoughts," we hissed, "as you yourself would see the mind of the dying man. We can dance in your senses, as you would have played with others; we can put maggots of blue fire into your blood and feel through their eyes as they roam around your heart, your blood, your thoughts, your soul. And we will do it, we will do it and so much more in order to live, to be free in this world, not hunted, not lost, not afraid to be free. So . . . tell us. How does he control Dana Mikeda?"

"He doesn't. She controls herself."

"She wouldn't help him of her own will."

He gave a snort that was somewhere between laughter and a croak of pain. "She can't, but she would."

"Why?"

"You're not a magician, are you?" he hissed. "Not just a magician. I think you're more."

"Where is Dana Mikeda?"

"I think you're like them," he replied, eyes narrowing. "I think you feel your heart race at rush hour, that on a bank holiday you can hardly raise your head, that in the centre of the city you walk with its rhythms, and only when you are away from it do you remember your own gait, only when you close your eyes from all those lights do you remember who you are. I think you're one of them, just like Bakker, just like Mikeda. Sorcerer."

"I'm a sorcerer," I answered into his ear. We lowered our voice. "*But we are the angels.*"

He spat. Again we considered slitting his throat, ending him right now for his arrogance and his stupidity. But he was no longer a danger to us, and without the blue rage in front of our eyes, we found the thought repulsive. We could imagine the feel of the skin parting at our strength, the slickness of the blood on our hands. We felt colder now, the water no longer refreshing but bringing out stained goosebumps in the night breeze, and the idea of killing him seemed like murder. That was fine. I had prepared for this event: a magic circle drawn in Camden, with enough sandwiches and water to keep him alive for a week. Long enough to get answers. Murder might have to come eventually; but not yet.

So I pressed my hand across the back of his neck and put darkness over his thoughts until he went loose in my grip, slipping to the pavement like a dead salmon, in a pool of spreading green ink.

I left him there, and went to get the van.

When I got back with the van, approximately thirty seconds later, San Khay's heart was missing. Part of his ribcage too, although the odd shard of bone spread across the scarlet pool of his blood suggested it hadn't been taken, merely broken in the process of getting into the chest. His stomach had been split open, and the veins and arteries running down either of his neck slit straight down from ear to collarbone. I had seen death before, but never this death, in such proximity, or with myself so heavily to blame.

We got down on our knees without noticing that we fell, and threw up. Salt in our eyes and acid on our tongue, we emptied out the entire contents of our stomach in the puddles of colour around us and retched until we thought we would throw out our bones. When we were done, we sat in a pool of blue water with our arms across our knees and shook.

I saw the shadows move, but still all we could do was sit and tremble. I saw the way the shadows bent around the lights, twisting across the paving stones, the long arrow of the pillar's shade turning like the point of a sundial, shrinking and bending slightly in the middle, as if cast by something concave. When he started to rise out of the ground, dragging the darkness up with him like a blanket spread on the earth, all we could do was stare, and shake, and feel tiny.

He solidified a bit at a time, starting with his feet and spreading upwards: the whiteness of his hands, the face becoming brighter and more intense, his features growing out of the darkness into eyes, nose, and eventually, a smile of curved blue lips, and yellow teeth. He opened his arms – in greeting or an apologetic shrug, we couldn't tell which – and said,

"Hello, Matthew's fire."

I got us up off the floor somehow, on hands and knees first, pulling us up a little at a time and feeling hollow inside, as if at any moment we might collapse in on ourself. I said, "He was on your side! One of *yours*!"

"I would have taken his skin, but it isn't so beautiful any more," he murmured, drifting across the soaking ground. The water ran off his feet like droplets from a puddle of oil. "You did that."

I backed away, mind racing without my being aware of it, a background scream. Unable to think coherent thoughts, we burned with anger, fear, shame, sickness, guilt, hate.

I said, "How did you find me?"

"I heard your dance," he replied, his voice tipping over his teeth like oil popping in the pan. "I felt the electric burning. I tasted you play with shadows. I knew it was you, even from so far away. I rushed through the dark to get here, I sped across the river in the shadow of the waves blown in the wind. I thought perhaps I would be too late."

"I wasn't going to kill him!" I spat, and realised, to my surprise, that it was true. A wave of relief nearly knocked me to the ground, passing as quick as the last breath of the storm. Relief, and something riding the back of the wave: hot sharp anger.

"No," whispered Hunger. "I had to do that for you, because you were too afraid."

"You are an abomination!" we snarled.

"Such fire! What shall I call you, deepest blue?"

I bit my lip and snapped, "Do you know why I call you Hunger?"

"Yes," he said, almost preening, stretching out the unnatural length of his limbs, and uncurling his fingers to admire the black curve of his nails. "It is myself."

"Do you remember what you said when we first met?"

"No."

"You said, 'Give me life.' You tried to see if my life really did flash before my eyes as I died; you scratched at my face asking, 'Can you see yet? Can you see?' Do you remember that?"

"Yes."

"Learnt anything since then?"

The shadow thought about it. "I'm still hungry," he replied.

"We thought you might be." Bending, not taking our eyes off him, we picked up the two curved steel knives that San had carried. My hands were shaking. "And we could kill for fish and chips." We swiped the blades a few times through the air, testing their weight. "Fish and chips and *ketchup*."

The creature looked confused. "I hunger for life! What are your desires to mine?"

"*We*," we said firmly, "are living it."

His face darkened, the shadows spreading out from beneath his eyes, around his mouth. "Give it to me," he hissed.

"No," we replied.

He stretched his arms out wide, the darkness spreading around him with the movement. "*Give it to me!*"

"Get stuffed," I said, and, because the words made us feel stronger, we added, with a feeling of recklessness that made us almost dizzy, "Arsehole!" We felt like a child caught stealing sweets and wanted to laugh at the terrifying, impossible consequences we faced. Anger was heating up my skin, despite the sodden state of my clothes, and the rage across my eyes was clean, not a hint of blue, entirely mine. I raised the knives towards him, and they dragged fiery sparks through the air as I laced their edges with the heat in my heart.

Hunger grinned, and flexed its fingers. It could kill me, I was pretty confident of this, but in that moment of heady drunkenness, we didn't care.

There was a rattling.

It sounded like a hundred broken teeth being knocked around inside a metal box.

It took me a moment to realise that it had nothing to do with the shadow. Surprise must have shown on my face; suspicion was on his.

It got closer, an uneven noise of bouncing, of metal clanking. As it approached, so did the smell: a mixture of curry powder, dust, car fumes, petrol, mothballs, wool and old tea bags which was somehow familiar. Hunger's face was a picture of confusion, the darkness still warping the air around him, as he stood, ready to pounce. The rattling came nearer, the smell got stronger and with it came another sound.

The sound went like this:

"Buggery buggery bugger youth today! Buggery arseholes when *I* was young but no no no they don't listen, moving with the phones, jazz, bling, ting, zing! Fucking pigeons! Shit where's me oranges? Oranges oranges oranges gun oranges two pairs of nylons oranges..."

Hunger whispered, "Sorcery."

I said, "You have no idea."

The voice replied, "Show respect you imbecilic nit toad flea insectoid wart!" Rattling along in front of her on three wheels, her trolley heaved with ancient plastic bags as Old Madam Dorie bounced her way into Paternoster Square.

There is a story of the Bag Lady.

She isn't simply a bag lady – a lady who carries plastic bags full of the strangest scrounged items she can get her hands on – she is *The Bag Lady*, the queen of all those who scuttle in the night, gibbering to themselves, and the voices only they can hear. She is the mistress of the mad old women in their slippers who ride the buses from terminal to terminal, she is the patron of the scrapyard girls who play with the rats, she is the lady of all dirty puddles. She has been in the city since the first old woman left alone in the dark decided to tell the dark why she was crying, and she is, of course, myth, and no one believes a word of it, including me.

However, when the pigeons were nested for the night, it was to the Bag Lady that my gran would always offer her prayers.

Dorie looked at me, she looked at the shadow, she looked back to me and said, "All right, you stupid bastard, piss off out of here!"

I said, "What the bloody hell are you doing here?"

"Fucking trailing you, fucker!" she shrilled. "You dense like the kids say?"

"We didn't see you," we complained.

"That's because you've got all the brains of a concussed cod!" she shrilled, flapping her pink fingerless woollen gloves furiously in the air. "Shit, and you're supposed to be a saving fucking grace?"

"You smell of... nothing," hissed Hunger, head twisted on one side, his attention momentarily diverted. "You taste of... nothing."

"You going to smell shit in the sewer?" she asked, glaring straight into Hunger's empty eyes without even blinking. "Oi, sorcerer?"

"What, me?"

"You want to be someone else?"

"It's complicated."

"Fucking run already, nit!"

I began feebly, turning in Hunger's direction. "Evil creature, essence of darkness and undying hunger..." Already I felt like I was losing momentum overall.

Dorie's attention flashed to me in an instant, and for a moment her eyes were the colour of the pigeons', yellow-orange, intense, bright, alert. She said, in a voice as sane as I had ever heard it from her lips, "I only do this for you once, blue electric sorcerer. Next time, you'll burn."

And with that, she leant over her trolley, and opened the plastic bags.

Out of the first came the twitching nose of a rat, climbing up and over the edge of the trolley before landing with a big flop in the middle of its body onto the pavement of the square and looking round with confused, blinking eyes. Then came another rat, and another, and another, half a dozen, a dozen, two dozen; they swarmed out of the battered old Sainsbury's bag in a writhing mass of black bodies, streaming down the sides of the trolley, flopping onto the ground into a teeming, twitching mass, spreading out from her like a pool of black blood, scuttling and scampering, and still they kept coming, a hundred, two, more than I could count, crawling across the pavement, along the walls, up Dorie's legs, her middle, until her whole body was covered in rats and there wasn't a body there at all, just a heaving tower of blackness and there were more rats in the bag than could get out, a hill of rats building up around the half-obscured hub of the trolley, spilling towards me, towards Hunger.

That was one bag.

The second bag released the pigeons. They exploded upwards in a shower of feathers, one, half a dozen, two dozen, the same crowding and swiftness as the rats, and whirled overhead, and level too, the sky somehow not big enough for them, flying across my face, obscuring Dorie from my sight in moments. It snowed feathers, blinding me with the touch, smell, taste of dirt-grease pigeon as their wings beat at me, their claws scraped my shoulders, their feathers brushed my nose; while at my ankles the rats scuttled, flowing round me like I was an island in their black sea.

From the last bag came the other creatures. A swarm of big black bluebottle flies, the skulking ginger bodies of young foxes, a scampering contingent of mice that ran easily across the backs of the ratty mass like pebbles skimming the sea. Sinuous stray cats, missing a tail or half an ear, teeth bared, cruel, fur in tufts; the black feathers of crows, brown sparrows, flashing yellow breasts of a flock of great tits, even the curved necks of a pair of herons, hopping mottled frogs, the swooping shapes of swallows, the coiling gleam of a snake, teeming gleaming shells of the cockroaches, the long, arched back of a deer. They scrambled, flew, writhed, twisted, leapt, lurked or scuttled out of Dorie's bags, out of the trolley, until the world was so full of moving creatures that it was as if the sky had become a solid mass, or we were trapped in a tornado, lost in a spinning torment of feather, flesh and fur.

Dorie was lost to sight in a matter of seconds; so was Hunger. Instinctively I ducked the whirling mass of birdlife, crawling on all fours while the rats flowed up my back and across my head, and dropped down around my face like beads of fat living sweat. Little tiny pink claws bit into me and released; twitching noses snuffled through my hair, whiskers tickled over my skin, fat hairy bodies pressed down across my back. I was grateful that I had already been sick; there was nothing left inside for any worse horror. We couldn't...

we couldn't...

couldn't...

...so I did. I closed my eyes and felt the creatures around me, on hands and knees following their swirl of life which, all the powers have mercy, parted around me. Where I put my hands down, the creatures moved aside, hurried out of my way, so there was no breaking of tiny mouse bones as I pulled myself along, no squishing of snake's tail; a path opened up in front of me, its end obscured by the hurricane of creatures, but still distinctly a path. I crawled along it; then pulled back sharply, spilling a snake off my shoulder as a shadow loomed across my path: for a moment a corpse-white hand solidified out of the blackness of the paving stones, its fingers reaching up and becoming flesh, before they were swamped by the scurrying mass of creatures, that bit and scratched at the hand even before it was entirely there, until it collapsed back into whirling obscurity among the animals. I risked raising myself up and realised that, if I did not flinch from the birds swooping around my head, they would not actually hit me. At this, I straightened up and, scattering the odd clinging mouse and dripping with inky water, I ran.

I didn't know how far, nor where, they led me, until I was actually there: Ludgate Circus, where Fleet Street, Blackfriars Bridge, and Farringdon Road all run into a whirlpool of people, lights, cars, taxis and buses. Blinking, I staggered from the creatures' embrace into the sudden light of the street. The birds swooped skywards as if they'd only just discovered that up as well as sideways existed, while the land animals were halfway into the bins, drains and gutters, and the narrow places between buildings and under doors before I even realised that my escort was melting away.

I stood, alone and confused, an inky soaking figure, looking somewhere between a woad warrior and a clown; pigeon feathers stuck to my head, and tufts of fur clung to my coat. Self-consciously I picked off the worst and, as I did, felt a stirring in my coat pocket that, to my shame, made me jump. Reaching in with an imagination full of teeth, I found a small white mouse. Contentedly sitting in the palm of my hand, it was the only proof now left – apart from the general state of my appearance and smell – of the tide of vermin that had probably saved me from whatever untimely fate Hunger had had in mind.

Of Dorie, there was no sign; nor did my shadow bend. I got down on one knee and put the mouse down on the pavement. It scampered away, unconcerned, down the street towards a bus stop where, as ordinary, boring and mundane as anything we could have wished to see, a night bus was pulling up.

The driver said, "You've got to be kidding."

"I'm paying, aren't I?"

"You smell like the zoo," he replied. "And you're covered in feathers. I can't let you on this bus."

We leant forward so he could see into our eyes and said, "We've not had our most successful evening. Are you going to make it worse?"

He let us ride his bus and, content in the security of the back seat on the upper deck, we let it carry us wherever it would, and curled up in our wet clothes, and didn't sleep.

The bus terminated in Streatham, a suburb between nowhere in particular and somewhere less than distinct.

I walked through the sleeping streets of large terraced houses and wide pavements, neat and repetitive, until I found a small office building with a red fire hydrant sticking out of a side wall. I coaxed the end off, and the water on, with a little magic and a lot of hitting, stripped off my coat and shirt and knelt under the force of its pressurised gout of ice-cold water until I thought my skin would turn to stone.

I still looked like I'd been involved in an industrial accident, and was grateful that my hair was dark already so that it hid the streaks of colour running through it, although my face still resembled a tattoo job gone wrong.

I found a small area of scuffed grass with a couple of giant plane trees round the back of a vast, shed-like Homebase, stole a metal dustbin from a nearby house, emptied out its bulging black bags, put in as much old newspaper as I could carry from the local recycling bin and a few odd twigs from beneath the plane trees, and lit a fire. I huddled by it until it burnt down to nothing just before dawn, feeling the heat dry out my clothes and burn some of the ice out of my flesh. Perhaps we slept; we could not tell.

We had failed San Khay, and we were still no nearer to killing the shadow.

But perhaps we were closer to killing Bakker; and that, I felt, might well become the same thing.

As the sun rose across south London, my thoughts began to turn towards Mr Guy Lee.

Part 2: The Allies of the Kingsway Exchange

In which allies are made, enemies revealed, trains taken at late hours of the night, and an unusual use suggested for paint.

In the morning I managed, through much sweet persuasion and a hefty amount of money, to get myself into a small hotel in Merton – a place that I had always regarded as something of a fiction spread by the enemies of London and was surprised to find so real and large.

I had another shower, and scrubbed until my skin was raw and not a trace of ink or dye remained, I rubbed at my scalp until the shampoo sluicing down across my face was no longer tinted blue.

Then, at least, I felt less dirty. I went out and bought new clothes; the old ones I abandoned in a recycling bin. Even wearing my old clothes to the charity shop made me feel unclean again, their smell of rat so strong that the scrupulously polite girl behind the counter cringed at it.

I took my coat to the dry-cleaner, who offered to scrap it for free, but in the end accepted twelve pounds fifty to do a rush job on a repair. When it came back, the colour was faded and still splotched across the shoulders and cuffs – irredeemably so, the manager told me – but when I put it on again the fabric was warm and smelled clean, and for the first time that morning I felt just a bit human.

The day's headlines blamed the Amiltech stalker for the brutal murder of San Khay, but the papers made no mention of how he'd died, nor of the inks that covered his skin. I didn't know if that was the police being careful, or the Tower covering its tracks. Perhaps it was arrogant not to care, but at that moment we didn't want to think about it.

We decided to take the rest of the day off.

We had croissants, hot chocolate, coffee, jam, bread rolls and fruit salad for breakfast, and went to the cinema. We had never been to the cinema before. The plot was something about a genius arms dealer who discovered redemption, cardiac conditions and an interesting and potentially lethal use for spare missile components in a cave. It wasn't my thing. We were enthralled, and staggered out blinking from the cinema two and a half hours later with our mind full of pounding noise and our eyes aching from the overwhelming brightness, resolved to see more films as often as possible. During school hours we sneaked into an empty playground and rode the swings, so high we thought we'd fall off, then spinning on the roundabout until the world was a blur; sliding down the silver slide while trying not to whoop with glee; letting the sand in the pit trail through our fingers and, finally, resting to catch our breath at the very top of a roped climbing frame, from which we could see across a wide common of mown grass, great trees and dog walkers, all the way to the big old houses beyond the railway line. I hoped no one would see me.

We went to a bookshop, and sat reading graphic novels, fascinated by the style, the strange inhuman faces that were nevertheless so readable, the worlds in those pages made up of strange, twisted things, the buildings all out of proportion, the bright colours too bright, the dark sweeps of shade too deep – and yet, for all their fantastical properties, the pictures that we saw were somehow recognisable, and provoked in us feelings that matched the creatures in those pages.

When we were asked to move on, we took a train into the centre of the city, found a ticket booth and joined the queue. We bought a ticket for the first thing that was available, which turned out to be a musical. Still not really my thing, but we were determined to give it, anything, everything a try – and while we waited for the hour of its performance, we wandered into Chinatown and ate crispy duck with pancakes, and drank green tea and listened to the waiters chattering in Cantonese. We found that, without consciously translating, we could understand what they were saying: an unexpected side effect of our resurrection.

We saw the musical, and even though the lyrics were absurd, we came out burning with the energy of the place. We had not become lost to a spell, but with so many minds around us enthralled by what they saw, we too let our thoughts sink into that illusion. It thrilled us, the intensity of that buzz in the blood, and the light in the eyes of every face that came out from it. For a brief while, we forgot that we were wearing mortal flesh, mortal skin, mortal hurts, and were gods again, watching a world full of stories. As a treat to end our first proper day of life, we bought fish and chips, and ate it, with ketchup, on the bus back to the hotel. For the moment, we could ignore revenge, anger, pain, desire, hunger, want, fright, fear and hope; all we could hear was the gentle heartbeat of the city, and when we walked, we walked in time to its rhythm.

Next day, I went back to work. I checked out of the small hotel in Merton, and wandered up to the nearest supermarket, from one of whose dumpsters I removed a large sheet of cardboard. I also bought a tatty blue jumper, a pair of fingerless black gloves, a woolly hat, soup in a white polystyrene cup and a small packet of child's coloured chalks. Feeling pretty much equipped, I caught the bus, heading north.

My dilemma was simple. I didn't know where Bakker was. And even if I did, the knowledge wouldn't do me much good, since, if Sinclair's files were right, Amiltech was just one of the many organisations run by the Tower which protected him. While I felt perfectly comfortable tackling the lesser thugs of the institution, it was pure arrogance to assume I could handle more than one thing at a time. San Khay had died before he could tell me what I needed to know about the Tower and Bakker; that meant I would have to ask someone else. I had chosen Amiltech as my initial target because owing to its relatively high profile, I felt it would be an easier target to focus on without too many risks of reprisal than some of the other Tower-affiliated organisations. Now, my attention had been forced to move to an altogether different source of information, and danger: Guy Lee. Master of an underground network of... pick a name and it would be there, accountant through to zealot who worshipped at the altar of Lady Neon and other spirits of the city. San Khay had been arrogant enough to assume that he could handle us alone. It would be unlikely Guy Lee would make the same mistake, now that San was dead. He would be on guard; that meant I would have to change my tactics. I would need help.

I had a vague idea where to start.

The patch I'd chosen for the day's work was near Paddington station. A medley of worlds joined here – the Arab community from the Edgware Road merging into the giant white terraces and quiet mews of the wealthy, bordered in turn by the council estates and student digs overlooking the railway lines crawling in and out of the station itself, in a deep cutting, as if embarrassed to be taking up so much space and hoping no one would notice their progress.

Like all terminus stations, Paddington attracted a roving population of tourists, travellers, squatters, prostitutes, muggers, racketeers, smugglers and beggars. It was this last that interested me, because, after the pigeons and the rats, it's the beggars who tend to see the most.

So it was that on a cold, clean morning as winter was beginning to make itself known to autumn, and autumn was looking bashfully towards the door and explaining it had to go and wash its hair, I put my sheet of cardboard down in the service doorway round the side of a restaurant near St Mary's Hospital, unfolding it as protection against the hard coldness of the pavement. I pulled on my hat and gloves, dragged my coat up tight around my chin and patted my pockets for the coloured chalk. Sitting still on the pavement for hours, if you aren't properly dressed, lets the cold crawl all the way into the bones, twining itself around the spine with the grip of rooted ivy. I knew this from experience – begging for a day had been one of the things Robert James Bakker had instructed me to do; and back then, without question, I had obeyed; and back then, he'd been right.

In a small fountain outside Paddington station I had rinsed the empty polystyrene cup that had contained my soup and now put it on the ground in front of me. On the pavement I scratched in careful capital letters, *HUNGRY PLEASE HELP*, and with my coloured chalks, pale smears on the stones, I started to draw. I took my time, ignoring the footsteps of passers-by as they ignored me, using the rectangular shape of one particular paving stone as my frame, and putting in every detail of what I drew: not just in the face and clothes, but in the background, fading it from red to blue, smudging the strong colours where they met into a waving line of purple. I drew a face in profile with a curved yellow beard like some sort of inverted horn, a sharp triangular nose, a beady blue eye, and a smile – a distinctly smug smile. I filled in the tiny black diamonds on the figure's blue collar, and shaded its shoulders with red sweeps of colour to suggest the richness of its clothes; finally, I gave it a pointy crown. The drawing eventually resembled a king in a pack of playing cards, all odd angles and confusing shapes and colours. I don't know how many hours it took; but by the time I finished I'd got 57p in my polystyrene cup, and cramp in my arms from too much leaning on my elbows.

With the cup by my side, I curled up on the doorstep behind my chalk picture and my message on the floor, and waited.

There are several kinds of beggars in London. There are the lone aggressive ones, usually with thick beards and big duffle coats, who approach passing strangers with "Please, I just need 80p, please" – and sometimes that works. Perhaps it is a more honest approach; but for the ordinary passer-by, these open appeals can be as frightening as they are direct, and too often the answer no is followed by cursing that only confirms the stranger in their opinion of the beggar as frightening and dangerous.

A subcategory of this class of beggar, who perhaps inspires the greatest fear, is the stranger who comes up to you and asks for money while behind him or her, two friends lurk right in your path. It is not begging as such – there is no appeal to charity or understanding. Instead, it is a psychological mugging.

The majority of beggars are the silent huddled ones sitting alone near an ATM, or in shop doors when the shutters are drawn, or outside an expensive jewellery store until the police are called to move them on, or near the railway stations, or outside a café in the hope that enough money may become a sandwich, or a cup of coffee, or that the stranger will be more inclined to believe the cardboard sign with the words "*not on drugs, hungry, poor, please help*", or that the staff, at closing-up time, might give them a packet of something about to pass its best-before date, or let them use the bathroom. Passers-by don't just not see these people; they go out of their way both to ignore them, and then to forget that they ignored them, to drive away from their shamed recollection the shape of the huddled girl with her pet dog and tatty boots, or the image of the old man with the tangled beard who they didn't even smile at, not wanting to admit that they failed to take pity. If asked why they did not give charity, the standard reply is "They would only have spent it on drugs". Unkind as this is, the bastard's reply is even worse: "It's their fault they're here; why should I waste my money on someone who can't be saved?"

Thus, with a single swoop, the entire population of old, young, black, white, frightened, bold, subdued, cowering, cold, ill, hungry, thirsty, dirty or addicted are classified as self-destructive, and every ignored face, every shadow blotted out of the memory of the stranger on the street, can be classed by a single word – *failed*.

Perhaps they are worth saving, as people are always worth saving, sigh the compassionate.

But perhaps, whispers the voice of cynicism, lurking just below, just perhaps the beggars cannot or worse, *do not* want to be saved.

Pity and compassion walk a fine line hand in hand, but one will always be a more welcome guest than the other.

At the time, I didn't understand why Robert James Bakker made me spend a day of my education begging. By the evening of that lesson, I understood entirely.

I watched the faces of those few people who glanced at me and then quickly walked on. A beggar must be humble; must keep his eyes to the ground so as not to frighten the easily afraid. As so many people went by in shiny shoes and comfortable clothes, with big bags and big coats, concerned with how many hundreds of pounds must go out this month to pay the mortgage, rather than with how many pennies will combine to the next cup of tea, my emotions progressed slowly from chilled self-pity to anger at the faces that from four hundred yards away braced themselves to avoid meeting my eye.

It took a kindly woman wearing a dog collar to stop, squat down opposite me, look at my chalk drawing on the pavement and say, "I haven't seen you before," to prevent us from grabbing the nearest passing stranger by the ankle and tripping him nose-first to the floor. She gave me two pound fifty and asked if I'd found God. I told her no, but she still gave me a leaflet informing me that *Strength is Faith*, and directions to a Tuesday evening soup stand. The leaflet fascinated us – *why* was Strength Faith, and did it matter what you had faith in? The whole concept seemed bizarre to an unusual extreme, but we folded the paper up and put it in our coat pocket, in order to mull over its implications another time.

From that lady onwards, the anger faded, and a numb gratitude settled in at the flick of even a five-pence coin in my direction. It was no longer a burning desire to hate the majority who ignored me; it was a necessary comfort to be grateful to that minority who bothered to demonstrate kindness.

Boredom was the ignoble theme of the day.

Utter, bone-breaking, cold-biting, toe-tingling boredom.

A guy can only mull on self-pity for so long. Too quickly the needs of the body – discomfort, aches, pains, thirst, hunger – kick in so that any pretence at achieving a higher state of spiritual awareness through a day of sitting quickly succumbs to the overwhelming desire to have a pillow to sit on.

Five minutes took fifteen.

An hour was three.

Horrific, unwatched, uncared for, inescapable boredom.

By sunset, I had thirteen pounds forty-eight pence in various pieces of small change. I abandoned my post for a few minutes to buy myself a bread roll, a packet of wafer-thin turkey, an apple and a very large cup of steaming hot coffee, and when I returned my picture in chalk had been smudged over by someone's thoughtless boot. I managed to bite down the curse on the tip of our tongue before it could harm them for their carelessness. By the time I'd finished repairing the damage, the street lights were flickering on and the cold was starting to spread out with the shadows. We felt exposed on our piece of card as the darkness settled around the neon splotches on the street, unsure without four walls to protect us that the next pair of footsteps wouldn't steal our hard-won cup of coins, or scuff our picture, or prove to be a monster looking for our blood.

We had no intention of sleeping, and my bones ached too much to let instinct pull me under. Every twitch was an uncomfortable one, every surface not just hard concrete, but deliberately, overengineered, *hard* concrete whose sole purpose was to push tighter and tighter against the bones in my body, as if the door space I inhabited was closing in against me, trying to squeeze me into a cramped splotch on the floor.

The streets became quieter, my hands became colder. A man staggered down from the pub on the corner, on the other side of the street, saw me, shouted, "Ey-oi mate!" and threw up in the gutter. In a friendly way. He grinned when he was done and proclaimed to the closed windows of the street that he felt much better.

A small child being dragged to bed peered curiously at me as it passed, then waved. We waved back, not being entirely sure how else to respond to small creatures like that. A black taxi pulled up, disgorged a group of women dressed for commercial combat, in suits so tight you could see the seams warping under pressure, and drove off again while they giggled their way down the street.

I let my mind drift. We listened to the brains of the seagulls as they swept towards the river, drawn by the smell of rubbish and salt; we briefly balanced on a wall between two small gardens with terracotta-potted plants, in the mind of a stray cat with one beady yellow eye; and we lounged in the senses of a bored fox watching the bins behind the halal burger bar. But it was through our own ears that we heard the regular, unhurried footsteps approaching us up the street.

I half-opened my eyes, straining with my mundane human ears for the sound of someone nearing. The footsteps, when I eventually picked them up again, had a sharp, nail-in-sole *click* to them, and a steady, inevitable beat, as if the walker was in no great hurry, but would somehow get somewhere regardless of anything. It sounded a good kind of stride.

The owner of the footsteps stopped by my chalk drawing of the stylised king in his crown, rocking back and forward on the balls of his tattily shod feet. The feet wore a pair of once-comfortable soft loafers, now held together with so much hammering and thread, I felt my toes curl at the sight of them. The owner of the shoes said in a nasal voice, "Could be worse."

I raised my eyebrows and waited for an explanation.

"Could have rained. You wanting something?"

I looked him up and down. He wore badly patched corduroy trousers, a big puffed jacket with stuffing coming out of a clumsily sewn-up gash in the side, which gave him an inflamed, swollen appearance, a shirt that smelt of sweat and old hamburger, together with a pair of knitted gloves, a big blue scarf, and a large woollen hat with the words *Arsenal FC* in red and white across the front. His face was long and angular, not merely stretching down top to chin, but out in odd directions too, so that the tip of his grizzled jaw protruded nearly as far as the end of his nose, and his ears stuck out, even inside the hat, like he had half a lemon on either side of his head. He scratched his chin with long, dirty brown nails the texture of old wood, and surveyed me through a pair of intelligent grey eyes.

I found that after a day of silence, the words didn't come.

"New to this?" he asked.

I managed to stumble an "In a way."

"You're not one of us, then?"

"No. Not really."

"But you know about things, I'm guessing."

"Things? Yes."

"And I'm just guessing," he said, rolling his eyes with melodramatic emphasis, "that you've got an *agenda*." He spat the word between his wonky front teeth. "Everyone's got a fucking agenda these days, too easy just to give money on the street, oh no, we've got *social assets* to consider and fucking community spirit. All right. You've sat the sitting, drawn the fucking picture, whatever. What do you want, *sorcerer?*"

He didn't like the word sorcerer.

That was just fine. I was beginning to understand why it might not be popular.

"Well," I said, pulling myself up one stiff joint at a time and rubbing some of the numbness out of my arms, "ideally I want to destroy the Tower and all its works for the evil it has committed, for its own selfish acts against the magical community of the city among others, and to see the shadows of its making burnt so even the walls can no longer remember their stains. But right now, I'd settle for a cup of tea, a comfy chair and an audience with the Beggar King."

He led me to a scrapyard underneath the Westway, a great big sprawling bypass that in five minutes of motorway trundling takes the traveller from Paddington to Shepherd's Bush, above and parallel to the railway line out of the station. In the grey, smelly shadows underneath the motorway some of his flock were clustered: men in torn jackets, clumped round fires burning in old metal canisters, women with pale, lifeless skin, and thick veins standing out on the tops of their hands, eating chips and sharing a single, depressing cigarette.

He lived in an abandoned London Transport maintenance van, whose walls were insulated with more variations on a theme of flea-ridden blanket than I had ever seen. It boasted at one end a large metal safe, into which he deposited from his pockets two packs of hotel matches, presumably lifted from some expensive side table before he was thrown out, a rusted tin-opener, and some loose change amounting to roughly £27. He said, not really paying me much attention, "I accept donations."

I gave him all my day's takings. There are always rules, always prices to be paid. A day sitting in the cold; an offering of pennies and shiny five-pence pieces. These are rules so obvious, they never needed to be written down. Nothing about the Beggar King is *ever* written down.

He grunted and said, "Seen worse," turned on a tiny paraffin heater, put a tin of tomato soup onto it, and as it started to bubble in the can he sat down, cross-legged on top of a pile of thick, itchy tartan blankets and old stained trousers, scratched his chin and said, "So... I'm guessing you've got issues if you're looking for a chat with the old miser. That's the word, isn't it? We aren't allowed to say *problem* these days."

"'Issues' is fine," I said. "I think the king might even have a few in common with me."

"Such as?"

"The Tower."

"Shit, what the hell's he got to do with it? They don't bother us much."

"How little is 'much'?"

"He can't protect everyone," said the man, eyes flashing.

"From what I hear, have read, the Tower takes beggars off the street. San Khay offered me a trip in the senses of an addict on the edge of death. I can think of no better way to get that than from a beggar, alone, unnoticed, dying in the dark."

"We have... the occasional clash. These things happen."

"I saw a warehouse," I replied carefully. "It was run, maintained, by Amiltech, probably on behalf of Guy Lee. In the basement, I found the body of a beggar. Things had been done to it. Everyone knows Guy Lee has an interest in necromancy. It needs tools. Are you going to sit and wait for Guy Lee to catch an unfortunate disease off one of his badly washed bodies until you say, No more?"

"You see what happens to the enemies of the Tower?" he asked, casually scraping a thick nailful of dirt out from under his thumb.

"Yes."

"And you're still looking for a fight. Well, shit."

"I think the Beggar King would understand."

"Why?"

He wasn't looking at me, this man with his huge beard. He gave off the air of a man who just didn't care, who, above all these things, was lost in fascinated study of the dirt under his nails. Perhaps it wasn't an act. Perhaps these things really were as tiny to him as dust in the street.

I shifted uneasily, licked my lips. "Because, like the Bag Lady and the Boatman, it's not just a title, is it?" I stared at him, daring him to speak. "Sure, there's been a lot of beggar kings, a lot of dead bodies left in unmarked graves or thrown into the river. But the Beggar King, the *real* Beggar King, who comes when you draw the image of his crown on the pavement and sacrifice a day of takings to his throne, lives on, generation after generation. The Beggar King is there when the druggie dies alone in the puke and shit of his last shot, holding a bloodless hand until the last breath is gone. The Beggar King is the shadow across the street who smiles up at the window of the refuge when the homeless girl gets given her own room, and tells her it's all right, you don't have to fear the walls. The Beggar King... the *real* Beggar King... is the one you offer your prayers to when your jacket is too thin and the stones are too hard, and every penny you have has just been taken away by the spite of people who don't understand. Not just flesh and blood, yes?"

"You should know," he replied quietly. "They told me, when you went from the telephone lines."

We went cold, and my jaw felt like it was locked.

He smiled at us.

"Bright blue eyes," he murmured. "They don't suit you."

"We are... we... as... we are..."

"Tongue-tied?"

I stuttered, "Will you help me?"

"Just you? Just the little mortal wearing a dead man's flesh? Or do you want something more? What, you have to ask yourself, but what do the angels want?"

"We are... we... we want revenge."

He chuckled. "Join the queue. You get used to that too, on the streets. Gotta be polite. Gotta keep to the rules. Gotta cause no trouble, 'cause the second you're trouble" – he snapped his fingers – "no one will even try to save you." Then, "What exactly do you intend?"

"I need to find the Whites."

"Why?"

"Bakker is at the heart of the Tower, but he's protected. Guy Lee, Harris Simmons, Dana Mikeda . . ."

"San Khay?" It was an accusation as well as a question.

"I didn't kill him."

"I would have."

"I didn't."

"Nasty way to go, from what I hear; suggests a slightly loopy brain at work and frankly I . . ."

"We didn't kill him!"

He smiled, an expression of unamused interest. "Well," he said, "at least part of you is honest. Which part, though?"

"Guy Lee is master of an underworld army," we said. "His creatures prey on the ignorant, the innocent; he keeps the clans down under an iron fist, his enemies . . ."

"All enemies of the Tower disappear, little sorcerer!" he snapped. "You know this, I think? But perhaps such people should be fucking controlled, yes? By concerned citizens, maybe, making sure that those who know the secrets of these things don't go spilling them too easily to the masses? To the piss-stupid fucking people?"

"Bakker does it for his own ends, not for others."

"And what ends are those? Does anyone know?"

"I can make a good guess," I muttered.

"Can you?" He leant forward eagerly. "I'm all ears."

We met his eyes squarely. "He wants to be like you, your majesty. He wants to be an idea. He wants to outlive his own flesh."

He drew back, face darkening. "Impossible," he said. "So shit."

"You know it's not. There wasn't always a Beggar King, there wasn't always a Bag Lady. These things have to grow out of something, they have to have a vessel, a beginning, and eventually, a conclusion. He will be like you."

"You know this?"

"I know this."

"But do *you* know this?" There was an urgency to his voice, a hungry intensity. "Not *you*, little sorcerer, but *you*, do you know this?"

We recoiled, surprised at the force of his gaze, and stammered, "We are not . . . this world is still strange."

"You're just a fucking child, aren't you?" he laughed.

"I'm not."

"Sure, sure, whatever," he said, waving a casual curled, dirty fist in the air. "You've lived long enough to die. But them, the other ones with the bright blue eyes – fucking kids! Never seen nothing! Never felt nothing! Christ, and you want my help?"

"Yes," we replied. "We do."

He leant back slowly, a look of dissatisfaction on his face. Finally he said, "If I do anything for you, all my people are put at risk. I have a responsibility."

"The Tower is dangerous," I repeated.

"And you can stop it?"

"Yes."

"Why? Because Bakker's shadow slit your throat and with your dying breath you managed to slip into the blueness that he dreams of achieving?"

I felt the pain of a dozen old aches, weeks old to my mind, a life ago to the world, the burning in my skin. Taste of blood in my mouth. I thought that, with enough fish and chips, hot tea, crispy bacon, with enough new memories to wipe over the old, it would go. But there it was again, still again, the iron bite of it on my lips.

I still needed help.

So, I got down on one knee in front of him, and bowed my head in respect to the Beggar King.

"If you help me," I said, "if you would honour us," we added, "we will stop the shadow."

His eyes flashed up brightly, alert, interested. "The shadow?" he asked quickly.

"It grows out of nothing. It has yellow teeth, dead skin, watery eyes," I replied, trying not to see too clearly the images in my head. "You'll have heard of it. It says, 'Give me life.' Help us. Join us against the Tower."

He thought about it, then put his hand on my shoulder, the skin warm through my clothes. "I offer you a thought to consider, little sorcerer. If Bakker thinks he can beat his own death, have you not considered that, now you are out of the wire, it might be your very blue blood that can help him do this?"

We looked up slowly, uncertainly, and were met with an almost fatherly sigh. He patted us on the head, as if we were a young child making innocent remarks that, to a wiser audience, were laced with hidden meaning. "I suggest this, in case you're wondering who might have brought you back."

We opened our mouth to speak, but he said abruptly, "Right, can't have you lolling around here, bugger off!"

The moment passed, our mind still revolving this interesting, frightening idea. *Who brought us back? Why?* I stood up uncertainly, to occupy the space of my own silence, and said, "Will you . . ."

"Maybe. I'll think about it."

"But if . . ."

"You're going to ask the Whites, aren't you?"

"Yes."

"They will help you."

"I don't know where they are."

"Well, shit!" he laughed. "All you gotta do is follow the writing on the wall!"

We left him there, the Beggar King in his court of rags and fleas.

We navigated while my mind drifted, picking our way through the night with our eyes wandering through every flowerpot, lamp-post, fence and street sign, marvelling that however well we thought we knew these streets, when we looked again we could still find something new in them. I thought about Elizabeth Bakker, sitting with just the pigeons for company in her care home. I thought about the Beggar King, the Bag Lady, and my gran, who liked the songs that the rats sung in the night through the hole in the corner of her floor, and always fed the squirrels. Somehow, thinking about it all made me feel tired, cold, the anger of my certainty fading down to just a flat recognition of things that needed to be done, rather than things that I desired.

However, before anything more could be done, there was somewhere we had to go first.

If I was going to get help, I wasn't going to be picky about where it came from.

Subways at roundabouts and beneath busy streets are, in general, frightening places. It's not simply the basic London subway with its friendly sign in big blue letters "**POLICE PATROLS HERE**" to comfort the uneasy traveller; it's not the strange, translucent stalactites drooping down from the ceiling like warm salt icicles; it's not even the odd patch of pondlike green mould on the floor to trip the unwary passer-by. It's the enclosed, hidden nature of the place, which makes human instinct flex its fingertips in uncertainty and distress at the thought of imminent destruction, the utter confidence that whatever happens, in the subways there's no place you can run.

I arrived early, around 2 a.m. in the maze of tunnels underneath the roundabouts, one-way systems and sprawling circular roads on the edge of Aldgate, where the City becomes simply the city, and the signs point to The North as well as to Bow and Whitechapel. In London, places beyond its boundaries are always called The North or The West, too big, too vague and too Not London to merit any more detailed descriptions.

I huddled down by the specified exit, pulling my coat around me for warmth, and let the hum of the intermittent traffic – lorries full of the next day's shopping, bras, socks, shoes and a dozen different kinds of apple – travel with a buzz up my fingertips.

I was half-asleep by the time the biker sat down next to me with a loud "Oof!", stretching out his legs into the narrow concrete width of the passage and dumping a big black sports bag down at his side. "You look shitty," he said. "Not a morning person?"

"I didn't notice you," I said.

"You surprised?"

"Not entirely. No great reprisals got to you, since I saw you last?"

He gave a grunting half-laugh. "You really surprised?" he repeated. "I move too fast for any whacked-out fucker to catch."

"Not at all," we sighed.

"I hear you've been busy."

"Really?"

"San Khay."

"I didn't kill him; please let's not go down that line of enquiry."

"It wasn't you?"

"No."

"Jesus. Although – you didn't seem like the blood-drinking, heart-ripper type."

"Touching. I don't suppose you're up for lending me a hand?"

"That's why I'm sat in this shit-hole talking to you," he replied with a shrug. "Anything in particular?"

"I'm looking for help to go up against Guy Lee; are you interested?"

"Why Lee?"

"He might know things about Bakker. And even if he doesn't, he has a small army at his command. It'd be nice to know that it's not at his command, before going after the top of the Tower."

"Why do you need help? You seemed just fine with Amiltech. Swanned off all mysterious for your solo day of judgment, like something out of a fucking Clint Eastwood movie."

"That's just it," I replied, thinking of the shadow rising up from the darkness of Paternoster Square. "This time, they'll know I'm coming. Guy Lee isn't going to make the mistake San did."

"How much help?" he asked carefully. "I ain't gonna speak for the others."

"It's still all in the planning, but I thought the Whites, the beggars, the bikers, the painters, the drifters, the . . ."

"Dregs of fucking society, right?"

"Guy Lee isn't renowned for his selectivity, either, when it comes to membership."

"You think you can beat Lee?"

"Yes."

"It's not going to be like pissing around with San Khay. If Lee knows you're coming, he's not just going to sit by while you torch the office and curse the staff."

"Yes," we said. "We were thinking that."

"You must have one hell of a beef."

"It's the entire bull and the horns, since you ask."

"What makes you think you can pull this lot together? Shit, no wonder sorcerers have short life expectancies – that's some cock-arsed arrogance you must have, wobbling around inside the pink stuff in your head."

"I think they'll want to help."

"Why?"

"Because the Tower will probably make the decision for them."

"You like being a mysterious bastard, don't you?" he asked with a grin. "Sweet."

"I learnt a few nasty lessons."

"Bakker teach you any in-between classes?" he asked in an overly casual voice, and when I looked up, "Oh, yeah, I can do fucking research too, you know."

I steepled my fingers, took in a long breath of the piss-stained air of the subway tunnels, half-closed my eyes. "And you are called Blackjack, Christ knows why; you're a member of the biker clan, the men and women who specialise in living off speed, being nowhere and everywhere, who revel in their own freedom; and when they travel, the road is shorter for them than for anyone else. Your leader, if you guys can really be said to have one, was murdered, and your clan attacked. You like being unpredictable, unexpected, everywhere and nowhere, standing up for being a difficult bastard just to see the looks on people's faces, you think being normal is being shameful... shall we carry on, and see who runs out of trivia first?"

To our surprise, he grinned. "You want to know a secret?"

"Always."

"My real name is Dave."

"I see."

"This doesn't seem to amuse you."

"I met Jeremy the troll a few nights ago."

"Seriously?"

"Seriously. Also known as the Mighty Raaaarrggh! Although... I can sorta see why you changed the name. 'Dave' isn't known for its mysterious, mystic sexiness."

"What about you?"

"What about me?"

"'Matthew the sorcerer'? You weren't tempted to go for something... well... with more vowel sounds?"

"To tell the truth, the idea didn't occur to me."

A footstep at the end of the subway, loud on the wet stairs leading down. Blackjack added casually, fingering his bag, "Like I say, I got a lot of research done on you while I was wandering."

"Hum?" I asked absently. We eyed the stairwell at the end of the tunnel.

"Uh-huh. But the bird – Oda?... she's a slippery fish to pin down."

We tried in vain to decipher the layers of imagery. We opened our mouth to ask a question, and Oda was at the end of the tunnel, and Oda wasn't alone.

Sometimes, dignity is sacrificed under the weight of sheer, adrenalin-rush instinct. Instinct said fight or flight, but there wasn't anywhere to fly to in that long tiled gloom under the ring road. We stood up hastily, keeping the rumbling of the traffic still in our fingertips to be unleashed at any given moment, and said, very carefully, "We were to meet alone."

Blackjack was also on his feet, eyeing up the two men who stood flanking Oda. He had a tight, cold look on his face; at his side his fingers gently flexed.

Oda said, "Someone wants to talk to you."

The men on either side of her reached into their pockets. Their hands weren't even out before Blackjack was taking something from his bag and his fist was wrapped in a length of chain that seemed to grow at his touch into a writhing, living snake of metal links, lashing into the air and stretching as it moved. I saw guns being pulled out from the bulging jackets of the two men with Oda, and instinctively snuffed out the light, crudely swiping at the strip lights overhead with the rumbling heat still in my fingertips, bursting the bulbs with a loud static *pop* and a sprinkling of falling glass. I put my hands round my head to protect it from the crystal tinkling as the shards rained down, and turned and ran.

Somewhere in the dark I heard a loud snap, a rattling sound as of a chain scraped along a tiled wall and the crunch of tiles being pulled free from their mortar with the passage of the metal links; I heard running feet, shouting, the click of catches and gears. Perhaps in different circumstances we would have stayed and fought, we would have burnt them all for daring to challenge us – but I feared guns, I didn't like to try and stop bullets in the dark, it was too unpredictable. I stuck my hands out to feel along the wall and stumbled towards the yellow glow at the other end of the tunnel, away from Oda, Blackjack and the men in black. I heard a gunshot – it wasn't as I had expected, not a ringing blast in the dark, but a snap, more like the bursting of an air rifle than an explosion of chemicals – but whatever it was, I heard a shout in the gloom that could well have been Blackjack's voice, and for a moment thought about going back for him, pulling up all the glass pieces on the floor and throwing them down the tunnel in a wave, like a swarm of angry flies; but by now I was at the staircase at the other end and clawing my way up into the open where I could see, stand my ground, fight with more effective tools and...

"Hey, sorcerer?"

The voice came from the pavement above the mouth of the subway stairwell, out of my line of sight. That too was probably the source of the dart that impaled my back like the nose of an angry swordfish, and with it, the quick shrinking down of my world to a pinprick of yellow light that tightened, tightened and, with a sigh, went out, taking me with it.

We woke, didn't know where we were, and panicked. In our confusion we lashed out at the nearest thing we could find and shattered the front passenger seat window into a hail of safety glass with our fear, before a hot electric snap across our neck sent us lurching back into a painful blackness, from which no amount of violent dreaming could wake us.

When we next woke, we felt a tightness in our chest, an aching in our arms, a terrible pain in our shoulders, and a hot patch of blood in the small of our back, where the dart that had first knocked us into darkness had been pulled out by someone who didn't care how much it bit into our skin. We jerked on waking, the fear sweeping us; but this time awareness and control were quicker to come and with all my strength I kept my eyes shut, my breathing level, and my face empty.

That first start of surprise when we woke, though, had betrayed us, and over the sound of rushing traffic, through the flashing regular pulse of neon light racing by and the cold breath of wind through the shattered passenger window, we heard Oda's voice say, disinterestedly, "He's awake again," and that was cue enough for someone to send us back to darkness.

The last waking of that outward journey was the slowest of them all. There was no more traffic hum around me, but the pain in my joints was amplified tenfold. I came back to awareness with the slow understanding that the greyness on the edge of my vision was the beginning of sunrise, that the wetness on my face was from dew on the grass, that the cold dampness seeping through my clothes was rising up from the mud I'd been dropped on, that the pain in my shoulders came from the position of my arms, pinned behind my body, which had then fallen back, cutting off any remaining circulation to my fingertips. I felt frazzled and sick, but not entirely afraid. Perhaps the repetition of my wakings and sleepings had inured me to fear; perhaps it was simple relief at being alive, I didn't know and didn't care – the stillness of my own mind was a comfort in itself.

The world fascinated us, that I now saw at right-angles from where our head had fallen on the grass. As the pale sunlight started to sneak over the top of a chalky hill, we became aware of the smell of mud, animals, dead leaves, mould, rain, dew, cattle manure and fresh water, mixed with just a hint of burnt tyre. We heard the calls of wrens, sparrows, starlings, magpies, blackbirds, blue tits, and woodpeckers, and saw, crawling an inch from our nose through the mud, tiny flies and other insects, some no more substantial than the lightest drizzle glimpsed falling at night in front of a street lamp. We had never seen so much open nothingness, nor imagined that nothingness could be so busy in the pallid light. We searched for power to drag to our hands, to pick at the tight plastic cuffs that were rapidly causing our fingers to go numb, and though it was there, though we could sense some sort of magic, some lingering essence on the cold air, it was strange to us, like an echo of song, heard far off.

Countryside.

Bloody crappy pollen-drenched, grass-covered, dew-soaked bloody countryside.

Not a neon bulb, not a power line, not a water or gas main within half a mile all around. Nothing to arm myself with, except what little warmth was left inside our blood.

A voice said, "I take it you're not a country man."

I croaked, tasting bile in my mouth, "It's got its charms."

"But you are an *urban* magician, Mr Swift. Your disposition lies elsewhere, you find your magic in the cities, not the fields, correct?"

"Just a point of view," I whispered. "That's all."

Hands pulled me up by the elbows and shoulders, and as the world swung back into place I forced down the taste of acid in my throat, and half-closed my eyes against the sensation of spinning. I saw a pair of black leather shoes, topped by smart black trousers, a black jacket and – here was the bad news – a dog collar and a purple scarf. Never underestimate the ridiculous things that have been done in the name of religious-semantic obscurity.

The face that topped these defining features was round and smiling, friendly in the manner of all inviting alligators who only want to talk; it was the colour of rich, dark chocolate, and topped by silvery-grey curly hair, plaited at the back of the neck into dreadlocks of such solidity that I suspected they'd never be undone. The owner of this ensemble appearance spoke in a soft voice, lyrical with a gentle tone, and said, "May I put a suggestion to you, Mr Swift?"

"Where's the biker?" I asked. "What about Blackjack?"

"He's fine."

"Fine what? Finely chopped, with a stick of celery?"

"I think, considering your position, you'll have to take my word on it, Mr Swift."

I looked round cautiously. The field in which I'd been dumped was bordered by tall trees on two sides; elsewhere it stretched away into more rolling muddy shapes: a landscape devoid of any kind of help. Around me, in various poses of threatening or sceptical looming intent, were more men and women, of every colour and age; some held guns, and one or two, we noticed with something resembling disgust, were holding swords, or fireman's axes, with the look of people who not only knew how to use them, but enjoyed doing so. Oda was among them; in one hand she had a curved blade that resembled a samurai's katana, still in its ornate sheath, while over her shoulder and more to the point, I felt, was slung an automatic rifle with a sturdy wooden butt and the well-oiled look of a weapon properly cared for.

She stared at me, and there was no pity in her gaze.

I stammered, trying to keep our eyes on the silver-haired man, "You want something."

"I have a question I'd like to ask you. Or at least, I've got a question I've been asked to ask you. Personally, I find it unlikely you will survive the judgment, but these tests must still be administered, even now and to someone as shrunken as you."

"You've got my attention."

"Can you control them?"

"What?"

"It's very simple, Mr Swift. Can you keep control?"

"I don't understand."

"Please, let's not play coy with this. It is the matter on which your whole life currently depends. Should I decide that you are incapable of keeping the creatures currently inside you at bay, should I judge that you are a threat equal or even superior to that which you are attempting to destroy, I will have your head removed from your shoulders, your face shot off, your fingerprints burnt away and the remnants dumped in a variety of rivers feeding a number of fish-infested seas. So please, take me seriously when I say, I will have an answer. Can you keep control?"

I licked my lips and felt the shaking in my bones. "I'm a sorcerer. I've been taught how to . . ."

"This isn't about your sorcery!" he snapped. "Tell me about *them*."

"About who?"

He hit us with the back of his hand, across the face, and his knuckles slammed into our jaw and the pain filled us with shock and astonishment, anger flashing inside us. Hands pulled me back up and he said again,

"Can you keep control?"

"Who are you?"

He hit us on the other side of our head, and when we tried to crawl back up of our own accord he hit us again, knocking us once more to the earth. I bit down the anger turning the silver streaks of sunlight electric blue in my eyes and waited for the people there to pull me up. When they did, he said again, "You must be angry by now, Mr Swift, you must be afraid. You've died once before, and your kind can only see the flames of hell when your heart stops, when your soul leaves, so you must be afraid. Can you control them, when they think about dying, when they wonder about losing their new-found existence, can you stop them from lashing out, can you keep them under the calm waters of reason, can you persuade them not to fight, kick, scream defiance, can you stay human? Can you keep control?"

I took too long to think of an answer, tasting blood on my lips, and he hit us again and pressed his foot down across our neck, forcing our face into the mud, and leant close and hissed, "Is your blood on fire yet, can you stop it blazing?"

We snarled at him, twisting under his weight, but he just smiled and kicked us, knocking us flat to one side; and now we were angry, we were ready to take his heart and crush it until it burst, we were ready to boil the blood in its vessels, we were prepared to...

I squeezed my eyes shut against the blueness and pressed my face deeper into the earth, feeling the coldness of it against my skin and breathing rapidly, trying to purge the pain from my muscles, chill the heat away from my blood. Hands pulled me up again, and the silver-haired man came close, pulling my face up so that blood trickled down from my nose into my mouth, and leaning in until his breath tasted of coffee and too many hours without brushing his teeth. He hissed, "What are they saying now, sorcerer? Are they cowering like the children that they are, or do they have a darker purpose, a more aggressive intent? Which is it, Mr Swift?"

"You," I hissed through the blood on my tongue, "will have to work it out for yourself."

He tugged my head up until it hurt, staring into our blue eyes, then, with a grunt, pushed me back and stepped away.

I tried calming our anger a little at a time with nice, rational placations, soothing over the fear with the thought that if killing was all he had in mind, we wouldn't have had a chance to notice. As I did, I carefully rubbed my fingers together in the palm of my hand, feeling the dirt between them, the heavy dark soil, with just a hint, delicate, and so hard to pin down with my city-attuned senses, of rich, active magic. I was no druid, I had no understanding of the lore of natural things; but perhaps, just possibly, there was a little strength to be drawn from here, if you could only look at it from the right point of view. Even in this place, strange and alien to us, there was the beauty that, to our eyes, made magic.

The silver-haired man said sharply, "I want to talk to them."

"To who?" I mumbled, probing my teeth with my tongue for any new looseness.

"Let's not waste time with definitions. I want to speak to them."

"You're an idiot," I said. "There's only me here. Do you think I've got an alien in my belly, do you think there's a Siamese twin attached to my shoulder that never had the chance to grow? You talk to me."

I half-expected him to hit me again. We almost relished the idea, ready for the fury that explodes with pain; enough, perhaps, just enough to give us the strength and passion to grasp the tiny fragment of elusive power in this place and use it to pop his chest open. To my surprise, though, he didn't hit me, but squatted down on his haunches in front of me, and said, "Let me tell you what I think."

I nodded, hypnotised by his gaze, taste of blood in my mouth.

"I'm a man of words, you see? I read, I study, I think, I train myself to think only in words, neat, linear structures, passages with correct punctuation that can define a train of reasoning, understanding – nothing left to chance. I am also a man of faith. At the end of the logical chain, when all knowledge that I have acquired – and the knowledge is significant – when the end of the chain runs out into an infinity of uncertain questions and doubts, I know that there is still an answer. You may object to calling it God, you probably find the term too vague – I understand that, it's fine. You think of a big man with a beard. I think of force. God is force. God is strength, certainty, movement, motion, direction, power, and he sits at the end of all things, and he will, sorcerer, condemn you. Not because you are a heretic – which, by the way, you are – not because your soul is necessarily so black or so tainted, not because you have killed or fought or stolen; all these sins can be purged in fire. He will condemn you, because you aspire to be like him, and have the arrogance not even to think of the consequences."

He seemed to expect some kind of response to this statement, so I said, nearly choking on the words, "You're going to burn me?" We added, "You can try," and I immediately bit my tongue so hard I could feel the pain in my ears.

He didn't show any sign of noticing our slip, just gave a dry, humourless chuckle. "Times have moved on. The good must be merciful, even if that mercy to the damned is merely in a quick dispatch."

"That's not much of a comfort."

"The problem is, times are not so simple as in the days of the Book. Utilitarianism, I think; we must choose the lesser of two evils. I take comfort, when I contemplate your evil enduring, in the thought that when the day of judgment comes, when we are all standing naked in front of the Lord, you will be damned and I will not. And in the mean time, I may, perhaps, do some good to the innocent of this life in setting you against another who is more foul even than your taint."

"Bakker." I didn't need to ask.

"Robert James Bakker," he agreed. He slapped his thighs and straightened with a sudden jovial expression. "Of course, if you were not in your current condition I would just let the two of you tear each other apart – sorcerer against sorcerer. But he is more powerful, I think, than you ever were, even though he chose you, Matthew Swift, to be his apprentice. I could take comfort in the fact that perhaps you could, for a time, weaken him with your attack, and that he, in killing you, had rid the world of one more sorcerer – but it doesn't solve the initial problem, does it? How do you defeat a man like Robert Bakker? A man surrounded by every kind of protection and ally, a man with powerful friends and powers of his own, a man whose enemies die, and they seem great until they fall. I find that under such circumstances, I am forced to deal with the better kind of devils, to defeat a worse. Am I making sense?"

I nodded.

"Which brings me to my only serious problem. I am more than prepared to let you live, for the moment, Mr Swift, so that you and Bakker can, I hope, destroy each other. But before I let you live, I need to know that you are not a greater threat, that the things which sustain you have not yet consumed all rational restraint. So, Matthew Swift" – he brushed invisible dirt off the black fold of his trousers – "let us talk about the blue electric angels."

We looked up into his eyes, and held his gaze, and I was happy to see an instant of doubt on his face. We said, "We are hard to kill, if you are thinking of trying. We persist, even if it will not be in this place."

He let out a satisfied breath, and murmured, "Well, it is nice to finally meet you."

"It's not like I went anywhere," I declared. "Even if you kill us, we will endure, we will find a way back; it is our nature, although I won't be too happy about it."

"That's remarkable!"

"What is?"

"The way you switch without even blinking. One second, monster from beyond the plane of flesh and blood; next second, angry little man, suddenly cut off from all that power he's used to throwing around. A seamless switch, not even dribbling on the way. Not normal for possession; something more subtle, yes?"

"We are the same," we said.

"The same what? Same flesh? Doesn't mean anything, haven't you seen any 1970s horror films?"

"We are Matthew Swift."

"However pretentious the man may have been in life, I'm sure he didn't use the plural pronoun."

"I am the blue electric angels," I explained, licking away the taste of salt and iron around the edges of my mouth. "It's really very simple. We are me and I am us."

"That doesn't sound simple at all."

"You have a limited imagination. I guessed as much."

His jaw tightened, but he didn't move. "I am curious, Mr Blue-Eyed Swift, how exactly you found yourself in this predicament."

"I'm assuming one of your men shot me," I replied. "It's all a bit blurred."

"I was thinking more of how you found yourself bonded to and controlled by . . ."

"There is nothing to control," we snapped.

". . . controlled by," he repeated firmly, "creatures as strange as the blue electric angels."

I said, "I doubt you'd understand."

"I'm not here to understand, I'm here to assess."

"That's not much of a comfort."

"Don't you want to buy some time, to see if you can get your senses round the magic of this place, see if you can coax your brain to the magic of leaves and sunlight rather than concrete and neon? I'm sure you must. Tell me."

I let out a long, shuddering breath that I hadn't realised was inside me. That seemed to take all the fight out of me, leave my chest empty, so I shook my head and muttered, "All right. All right; it goes something like this:"

* * *

First Interlude: The Sorcerer's Shadow

In which certain memories best left forgotten are duly remembered.

"When I was fourteen years old, the phones started talking to me. I dialled the wrong number one day – I was trying to get the local library, but instead I got a bank helpline. It said:

"'Welcome to telephone banking! To change your credit card details, please press one. To check your current account balance, press two. To dance in fire until the end of your days, please press three. Hi, this is Mara speaking; sorry, I'm out at the moment, but if you could leave your message after the beep, I'll be sure to get back to you when the shadows have swept down the wall. Thanks! Which service do you require, police, fire, ambulance or exorcist? To cancel a direct debit, please press the star key. To send your soul across the infinite void faster than the blink of the mind dreaming in the moonlight, please press hash now.' And so on.

"I would wait at the bus stop and the rats would come and look at me; I would run through the streets at night and the freedom of it, the exhilaration of it, nearly killed me. I forgot to eat, to drink, to sleep, grew drunk on the feeling in my bones, on the beauty of the lights around me, on the sounds of the city, on the senses of other creatures.

"When he found me, I weighed eight stone two, had just failed GCSEs, was on tranquillisers and on the verge of being consigned to a care home. He showed me kindness, took me away from my home, where my mother was trying to care for me – and my gran. She didn't say no when this wealthy, kindly man offered to take me under his wing; but only later did I realise it wasn't just his smile that had talked her into it. My gran told me always to trust the pigeons, and when I told him I didn't know what she meant, he just smiled, patted me on the shoulder and said it would be all right, I'd work it out one day. Magic isn't genetic, it's not something programmed in your DNA. But it does run in families – in the same way that you can say, these people are morose or these are funny or these have their own, unique turns of phrase. For example, my mum didn't like the city; but when we went outside to the country she became like I was when I first tasted that magic, glowing, alive with the feel of it, revelling in all its forms in her blood, strengthening her by mere presence. It wasn't a spell, it was something more than that, a link, a consciousness that here is something special, indescribable, infinitely rich. I learnt from her a relish for life; but for me, it was something to be found in the city; and that, nothing more, is what makes me a sorcerer.

"He said his name was Robert James Bakker, but I was to call him Bobby. I called him Mr Bakker though, like my mum said. He paid for me to retake my GCSEs and hired me a tutor, and I passed – not well, but well enough. He said that you had to understand the minds of others, their learning and their ideas, before you could excel them; that to be a good sorcerer, you had to be a good man first. The day I got my A-levels he took me out into the city and taught me my very first lesson. We walked through the empty arcade of Leadenhall Market, late at night, when the wind was cold off the river, and he taught me to *feel* the light on my skin, as if it was silk, how to tighten my fingers around it and pull it along like a cloak, drag it down to me away from the walls and ceilings until I was on fire with its brightness and everything else around me was smothered in dark, taught me to wear it inside me, as well as over me, a furious burning in the heart. I learnt how to summon the Beggar King, about the legends of the city – the Midnight Mayor, Fat Rat, the Seven Sisters, the dragon that guards the old London Wall, *Domine dirige nos*, the old rules and the new magics. He taught me everything I know, was teacher, sponsor, father, friend for nearly ten years. Rich, kind and powerful; things I had never seen or imagined in my childhood.

"Sorcerers don't have any textbooks, formal lessons, ritual incantations or spells like the magicians do. Magicians use the wisdom of others, gestures of power, words of binding to do their bidding – theirs is a precise, focused magic. Sorcerers bind a different kind of magic: ours is the power of seeing the power in the most ordinary thing, and binding it to our will; it is wild, free, beautiful and dangerous. Teaching control is the most vital lesson, one that is learned at various speeds. Some sorcerers submerge their natures entirely to the rhythms of the city, forget that they do not have wings or that their feet are in

Knightsbridge, because their mind is too busy following the route of the number-nine bus up Piccadilly at the same time that their eyes are lost in the senses of a rat somewhere in Enfield. Others establish control ruthlessly, minimise all that they do, everything tight, precise; they revel in what they can do only for themselves, everything for a neat, exacting purpose, rather than the richer enchantments known to some.

"Bakker said I could be whatever I wanted, that every sorcerer was unique to their own nature. I studied under him until I was twenty-four, but I could never have the control he had. He was, then, a middle-aged man, who didn't show a day of it: his personality – vibrant, powerful, passionate – was stamped all over his magic, in extravagant shows of force that you felt he could never contain, and yet which were always, in the most delicate manner possible, well within his control. I have never seen a more powerful, nor a more talented sorcerer; he could breathe the air off the river and, on its smell alone, run a mile. Perhaps that should have warned me. He was so full of the stuff of life, one day it had to burst.

"When I was twenty-four, he said I was fine, ready; that my life was my own and I could do what I wished. So I did. I travelled – to Bangkok, Beijing, Berlin, Paris, Rome, Madrid, New York; in every place I earned money by teaching English or serving as a cleaner or a kitchen dishwasher for a few months, just so I could experience the different magics of those places. In New York the air is so full of static you almost spark when you move; in Madrid the shadows are waiting at every corner to whisper their histories in your ear when you walk at night. In Berlin the power is clean, silken, like walking through an invisible, body-temperature waterfall in a dark cave; in Beijing the sense of it was a prickling heat on the skin, like the wind had been broken down into a thousand pieces, and each part carried some warmth from another place, and brushed against your skin, like a furry cat calling for your attention.

"It may not sound much of a life to you – travelling, with no real home, no constant friends as such. But for me it was a day-to-day revelation, which Bakker had taught me a sorcerer's life should be, even if it stood still. A sorcerer, he said, can walk down the same street, twice a day for the rest of his life, and should be able to spot something new about it every time. Relish what you see, what you have: sounds, sight, touch, smell, that's what keeps you a sorcerer, that's what lets you understand what magic really is. It took me some time to realise what he meant, but he was right. Whatever has happened to him now, I will always remember then – he was right.

"I will spare you the details of my doings. I was, as you have pointed out, not one of the most interesting sorcerers, I did not seek to change the world, and had no great crusade to fire me. I will jump ahead a little.

"I came back to London. Worked a little, lived a little; nothing extraordinary. Then, about two years ago, I got a phone call from Robert Bakker's office. He had had a stroke and was in hospital; he wanted to see me. I didn't understand, at first, how this strong, vibrant man could be a mortal. But everyone gets older, even if it's only in the flesh. I visited him, of course I did – anyone would have done the same. I was relieved to find his mind was still in one piece – he recognised me, spoke to me reasonably, lucidly, didn't seem to have any difficulty with the mundane, automatic skills that strokes sometimes kill, as simple as lifting a fork, or putting on a pair of trousers – all that, he remembered well enough. But there had been complications, the doctors weren't sure how serious, and all the best consultants were called in to offer placating sounds.

"Over the weeks, however, it grew evident how serious it was. He was paralysed from the waist down, and would not walk again.

"At first he laughed and said it was an excuse for the lazy lifestyle he'd always wanted. But the reality of paralysis is more than just being unable to move – it is a loss of dignity. He could not put on his own trousers any more without help, or go to the toilet, or stand in the shower, or climb stairs, or get out of the bath, or reach a book on the shelf, or reach a pot to cook a meal. I think it was the indignity that first started to turn him. I noticed it, in my visits to him, over the weeks at the hospital as he went into physiotherapy, a growing anger at the indignity of it all, the unfairness – he, who had never smoked, drunk to excess, travelled to dangerous places or even had any particularly reckless sexual adventures – still he was stuck in a wheelchair. He said he was getting old, that life was going to pass him by, and for the first time, he sounded angry.

"One evening, his office called me and said I needed to go to the hospital, urgently. I thought something terrible had happened to him; but when I arrived, he was sitting up in bed, quite composed, the phone in his hand. He said,

"'Matthew, I want to summon the angels.'

"I remember, because he said it so flatly, so calmly, that I could hardly believe my ears. I spluttered confused noises and eventually said something along the lines of 'Why?' and 'It's dangerous!' and other empty sounds.

"He said, 'The doctors tell me that I am dying. I have not had just one stroke, I am at risk of several, they said. They tell me that over the next few days, weeks, months, years, they can't be sure, I will have more minor strokes, one on the other, perhaps so small I don't even notice, perhaps large enough to leave me without feeling in my fingers, and that they will eventually eat away my brain, my mind, my memory, and my feelings until I am just a gibbering shell. I want to summon the angels.'

"'What good will they do?' I asked.

"'You've heard them, think about it,' he replied – he was never one for a straight answer, always liked you to work it out for yourself, said if you could understand by yourself why a thing was true, you would believe it more than just having it told to you by a teacher.

"'Why do you need me? Surely they're still there, in the dialling tone...'

"'I can't hear them.' He held up the receiver towards me and, for the first time, looked me straight in the eye. 'I want you to listen, tell me if they're there.'

"I took the receiver – I was trained not to disobey him; such things when you are a learning sorcerer are dangerous. I listened.

"He hadn't dialled any particular number, but with the angels you don't need to; an open line is what they always enjoyed. And eventually, through the dialling tone, I heard them.

"They started with just the *beeeeeep* of the tone. Then, when you listened, it was more than a *beeeeep* it was a voice, saying *beeeeee* at exactly the same pitch and tone as the dialling tone, but still a voice.

"It said, *beeeeee meeeeeee*...

"And then, when you realised that those were the words it was saying, it said more.

"Beeee meeeee beeeee freeeeee . . .

"And by increments, aware that they had an audience, the angels came, and they said at the tone of the telephones,

We be . . .

. . . to see . . .

set free . . .

We be light, we be life, we be fire!

We sing electric flame, we rumble underground wind, we dance heaven!

Come be me . . .

. . . and be free . . .

. . . we be blue electric angels . . .

"Bakker said, 'Can you hear them?'

"I said yes.

"'What do they say?'

"'What they always do.'

"'Tell me!'

"I told him; I confess, I was hypnotised by their sound. When the angels spoke, it was more than voices, it was with a presence that wormed its way into the mind and filled the senses with burning, fiery blueness. They whispered that they were the creatures of the wire, that their playground was the world, that they danced at the speed of light and rippled faster than sound, spread their wings across every wire, voice, mind, sense, sight in the world and when they had bounced from the Arctic to the Antarctic and back again through every telephone and computer and radio transmitter on earth, they would bounce into the radio waves in the sky, and spin away into space, circle the moon and then fly on, to see what sights they could see. They asked you to come be me, to be free – to let go of life and join them for ever, playing in the wires.

"It was a dangerous song – all sorcerers knew of the angels. They had a reputation, that of a young, reckless power that travelled as interference in the system, unexplained spots of static, moved too fast to catch, stop, or begin to understand. They had grown out from the wires only in recent years, but that shouldn't really surprise us. Where life is, there is always magic, and over the years we pour so much of ourselves, of our lives, into the phone lines – our hearts, dreams, desires, hopes, friends, enemies, hates and loves, tipped into the wire.

The angels started off as just a rogue piece of static but, over the years, fed on all that life being thrown at them – telephone conversations, radio broadcasts, internet, email – that unique magic altered them, made them grow into the form that you currently understand as blue electric angels.

"They relish life, rejoice in it; their whole lives are learning, understanding, a composite of other people's existences, an idea plucked from Jane merged into a word from Bob and a sigh from Joe; an entire personality can be formed from the throwaway bits of conversation we leave trapped in the wire. They are so proud! So bright and brilliant, the world's knowledge at their fingertips, the whole of humanity pouring itself into their soul. So beautiful, so bright, they delight in all that is new, feast and feed on it, for it was what made them. They are a child, and a god. All sorcerers love and fear them, for they are very much like the sorcerers are – feasting on all things that they see. Life is magic. And as I have said, too much life... too much of too much... mortals cannot sustain it.

"They are everywhere at once, thinly spread across the world like flurries of snow; but they can, sometimes, coalesce into one place for a special purpose. In that hospital, that strange night that had been like any other night, Bakker wanted to provoke such an event; he wanted to bring the angels together, and force them out of the phone.

"I asked why.

"He didn't smile, or sigh, or show any sign of emotion when he answered. He simply said, 'Because they are alive; because they will not die.'

"I wanted to know how he thought he could get them out of the phone lines that had spawned them.

"He just laughed and said he was sure that they, if he had judged their character right, would be all too willing to come, for the right incentive. He knew how I had first fallen into sorcery. He knew that as a child, I had loved to listen to the phones, and they had loved to talk to me.

"What then, I asked? When you have somehow dragged the angels out of the phone line, their natural place, what do you do then?

"'Life,' he said. 'Just life.'

"I only understood slowly. Even when he had explained it, I did not wish to comprehend. His plan was to draw the angels out of their natural territory, force them to take a human, physical form with his spells and, once they had achieved such a state, to steal that which made them alive.

"You must understand – the angels are created from the life that others leave behind in the phones: words thrown out into darkness, ideas left half unsaid. Their whole existence is speed and freedom and wild electric power and magic and life; they feed off humanity's forgotten thoughts. He said, 'Their blood is life, Matthew. Their souls are fire.'

"I finally – too slowly – understood. Bakker didn't just want to summon the angels. He wanted to *become* the angels, to be like them, no longer physical, restrained by the bonds of his own crippled body. He wanted to feast on their bright burning blood, become pure electricity and fire in human form, burning his way across the planet – a human consciousness in the form of the angels themselves. But he needed my help.

"I asked why.

"He said, 'I can't hear them. Things are different, I can't hear them. I need a sorcerer who can make them come out of the phone lines. I need your help.'

"I said no. I didn't even know why I said it; I was so appalled, I just spoke on instinct. I said that his plan would make him inhuman, a deity of blue light rather than a sorcerer, that I knew he must be frightened and in pain, but that what he proposed was nothing short of a bond with an electric devil.

"He wanted to know why I said no.

"I couldn't think of an answer. I couldn't say what I really thought – that the angels' whole nature was wild and reckless, and that in his flesh they would only be more so; that I did not trust him with that kind of power.

"We quarrelled. I think that part was well established after my death. I left there too angry to speak. I felt betrayed. As a child, I had put nothing but faith in Mr Bakker, who had come to my mum's front door and saved me from the nuthouse. I guess these childish things were suddenly going away.

"I walked. When I am angry, I often walk to calm myself, look at the river and let it flow through my mind, washing away the fury and dirt in my head. I walked along the river, but I don't really remember the route I took and had no clear objective.

"When it came, it was so fast, so sudden that I didn't even feel its attack. It came out of the pavement at my feet, arms first, claws that lacerated my ankles on their way up as it grew from the darkness around me. It was thinner then, paler, barely more than a shadow itself. I guess it has learnt as the years go by. I didn't have time to fight: its claws were in my chest, across my back, on my face. It hissed and spat, a breath of rotting teeth, its spit burning my skin where it touched, its movement cloaked in blackness.

"I will not describe particularly what happened there. I do not think I know much myself, the pain and fear of it was so great. The mind can't remember pain – the flesh won't bear it. But it remembers the fear. It remembers remembering agony.

"I knew that I was going to die, that with every pump of my heart, rapidly failing, blood was pouring out of me in regular, surging gouts. I call 'it' – the thing that attacked me – a 'he', since, though a creature of magic should not have a gender in the traditional boring human sense of which organ goes where, the face he wore was nonetheless an imitation of warped humanity, recognisable despite its contortions. He walked around me and whispered, 'So hungry, so hungry,' in a wheedling voice like a starved snake might have, and dipped his fingers in my blood and sighed in contentment at the taste, cupping his hand in the pools around me and lapping it up like a cat after milk. I crawled away from him as best I could, crying with the fear and pain of it, utterly helpless. He held my face and stared into my eyes, and said, 'Give me life!' I didn't understand then what he wanted; only later did I realise that he was trying to see what was in me as I died, trying to reach into my mind to follow my senses, see my thoughts and memories.

"But death wasn't so cooperative in coming quickly. He let me go with an angry hiss, knowing that I couldn't crawl far and that death was inevitable, and stalked the small concrete perimeter of the killing ground, looking around at it like a confused child in an art gallery, trying to work out what makes the paintings on the wall worth its attention. While he did this I had crawled to a telephone box. I didn't know who I thought I'd call – strangely, Bakker was the first number that had leapt to mind, although I didn't dial.

"I lifted the receiver. He saw, but only smiled with a mouth full of my blood, and didn't even bother to try and stop me.

"I heard the dialling tone and, as I lay there, the phone held to my ear, they came.

"And we said, *come be me . . .*

"So easy to die . . .

"And we said, *We be fire, we be light, we be life! We dance electric flame, we skim sense, we be the ocean and the burning and the sunrise and the sunset on the edge of the world, we chase moonlight and sunlight and we do not stop, we cannot be tamed, we be free!*

"And we said, *We be the singing in the wire, the whisper of the friend, the static on the line, our dance never begins and never ends, our voices be always heard, invisible silk in the ear, never feared, never alone, we be in every mind and every soul and every mind and every soul be we! Come be we and be free . . .*

"And I closed my eyes, held the phone to my lips, and with the angels in my ears, allowed myself to die.

"We caught my dying breath as it entered the phone and held on to it with all our strength. From the tip of the breath we pulled the warmth in the lungs, then the electricity in the nerves, the buzz in the muscles, the movement in the blood, the water in the skin, the colour in the hair, the strength in the bones; we pulled the dying embers of my thoughts, the expiring rhythm of my heart and, dragging me in by my last breath, we dissolved the sorcerer, and made me electric, melting away my original form to nothing more than blue sparks wriggling into the earth. We have always loved life.

"We have no need for time, in the wire. We were everywhere, everyone, everything; we knew all that we could want to know, and at every instant learnt something new, forgetting nothing. You spray out your ideas and your thoughts and your feelings and your knowledge so fast, every infinity there was something new to explore, an eternally growing world of first-time callers and last-call goodbyes, new papers on new subjects posted on new pages, new feelings towards a new lover whispered down an old line, new links from New York to London, Paris to Berlin, new paths to explore, new sights to see, new worlds to bathe in. There is never an instant in the wire that is not changing, alive; and together we danced in that world, in the richness of the life that others leave behind. You will call it two years that we danced together in the wire, splitting our thoughts to spread out across the face of the earth, pure energy, pure fire. We will not bother with such distinctions. Petty human tongues cannot describe our glory.

"When the spell came, we were entirely unprepared. At one moment we were riding a billion dollars through Switzerland, and sweeping through the radios of a NASA shuttle about to launch. The next, we were coming into one place, our thoughts becoming one, our senses becoming one; and I was there too, the scattered, formless substance of my nature dragged, with the angels, back into one collective piece. I realised this wasn't just some nightmare, some horrible reassertion of reality – it was a summoning. Someone was summoning us, and I was being dragged along with it.

"My presence disrupted the spell. Whoever called us back called only the angels, not me. My influence meant we did not appear where we should have; my mind took us to the place that I regard as home, and piece by piece, as we fell out of the phone like water off a leaf, the blue sparks of our existence formed a shape, a consciousness, a human form, and that form was me. Not how it should have been. We should have been summoned as gods. I should have died. Instead, you see us now as we are. Half-flesh. Human and angel for ever tangled into one soul, inextricable, mortal, eternal, us and I.

"And your world is terrible as well as beautiful. We are grateful to be me, to have my memories and thoughts and heart and mind; it keeps us from madness. How can you live in this place? How can humans endure it? It is so bright and loud; with each moment, every sense is overwhelmed: colours and noise and the feel of the air in our fingers, the smell of people, and the street and cars and vents and fans and animals and water and weather? How does it not overwhelm you, such endless existence all around you, always changing? We thought we understood life, we thought that we had seen everything that could be known, that our dance across the face of the earth had encompassed all of human being. But *sight*, and *sound*; or the simple act of feeling your own heart, knowing that somewhere inside you there's this fat red organ of lumpy muscle going *gu-dunk, gu-dunk, gu-dunk*; or tasting food, feeling it burn in the mouth or tingle on the teeth. This world of yours, a world of flesh, is the most amazing, frightening thing we have ever known. We delight in it! The joy of everything, of sense... had we but time or means, we would eat for ever for the wonder of the taste, play for ever in the child's playground, spend our lives listening to the stories on the stage or screen, devour every book in the library, smell every flower and bin. I have seen this world once before... now we see it again.

"How can you bear to understand that you will get old and lose this feeling, will die and wither and encounter nothing but dark? How can you bear it? Since we came here, we have been entirely fearful, snatched from our safe, comforting bliss of scattered feeling. But we would not die and leave this amazing place for any price. It is the closest thing to sacred we have ever seen.

"So, here I am. We were resurrected as one individual, brought back into life fused into a single form. There's no untangling that knot. True, you can shoot me – I die. But my consciousness is now tied up with ours; and if you have a phone, or a passing radio wave should happen to be overhead, we will crawl back into the wire, and still be me, and still be the blue electric angels. We would have it no other way."

* * *

I had finished speaking.

The man scratched at his chin, his nails making a harsh Velcro sound against his skin. He said, "Not entirely what I expected to hear."

"And you're a man of learning."

"I don't know whether it changes my opinion of you. Or, indeed, if it should."

"What did you think had happened?"

"Oh," he waved his hands. "You quarrelled with Bakker, doubtless over one of his Satanic schemes, walked away, faked your own death, went travelling, discovered some evil mystic art, bonded your soul to a devil for power, glory, et cetera; returned to wreak havoc and revenge... you get the idea?"

"You don't have much of an imagination, do you?"

He smiled tightly. "I don't know that your story is better than anything I imagined."

"Doesn't innocence help salve my soul?"

"Technically, you don't have a soul. You're a creature of other creatures, a compound of other people's lives."

"And in what way are you more than the flesh you are in and the memories that rule you?" we asked sharply. "Are you not who you are because experience makes you this way? Are we not the same?"

"I don't bleed blue blood."

"It's all about oxygen bonding," I retorted, glancing at Oda, who tilted her chin defiantly back at me, "and we saved Sinclair's life."

"You needed him," replied the man. "Besides, he is useful but obscene."

"He's long-winded. I don't see why that makes him obscene. We had his documents, his information. So do you really think that *need* is what made us do it? I don't go around killing random people, and I'm sure as hell not a fan of letting others die."

He sucked in a breath between his teeth. "Tell me," he said, "just this, honestly. If you thought a thing looked prettier in flames, would you really not set it alight?"

"Of course not," I said.

"I wasn't asking you."

"Oh, get a bloody sense of perspective."

He hit me, again. I thought we'd been doing quite well, so the shock and surprise of it, more than the pain, injured me, sent me recoiling back inside my shell. After a moment lying curled around our own unhappiness, we picked ourself up and glared at him.

He said, "You... blue electric angels... you are children with the power to kill, destroy and burn. You know nothing about life, its rules, norms, laws and understandings, and probably care less. Why should you not set the field on fire for the prettiness of its burning; why should you not kill wherever you go, simply because you can; why should you understand anything that the rest of humanity can?"

"Because I'm here," I growled.

"You are just one man," he retorted. "The angels are the sum of millions, billions, more than that; although before you start, I do appreciate that your relationship is complicated."

"We do not need to... to change anything. This life of yours is wonder enough without us setting it on fire."

He smiled, shoulders jerking as if a laugh was brewing, hijacked halfway up his throat. "You really are just a child, aren't you? A poor little bumbling power, crawling out of the nice safe confines of its telephone line. Utterly ignorant and totally confused. You must be going mad inside that good disguise of yours. But perhaps all you'll do is drool and gibber, when reality finally takes you down."

He paused and sucked in his breath. Overdramatically, I thought. Enjoying his power, perhaps, a bit too much. I felt the dirt between my fingers, the tiny heat of it. Not enough to do anything spectacular. But enough, maybe, to burn out something vital under his skin, before we died.

"I'll have to think about it," he said, with an unsympathetic face, and nodded at one of his henchmen. "Good night, angels, good night!"

We pinched that fragment of magic between our fingers, ready to slip it into the blood of anyone who dared to touch us. "You will be a shadow on the wall," we snarled. "A remnant of the night. You will fade, and your darkness will blend into the memories of the city and be forgotten, lost inside all the better things that happen around you."

Oda stepped towards me. Her hand went into a jacket pocket, her eyes meeting ours; and I hesitated. The grey-haired man leant down until his face was almost level with mine and whispered, "You have no idea who you're dealing with."

I grinned, and leant forward sharply, banging my head against his. Not hard, but it was contact I needed; just that moment of touching was enough. I let that morsel of power slide into his skin, a maggot of blue, burrowing down in an instant, seen out of the corner of the eye, and gone. Where our heads had banged, blood from my battered skin slid a thin red slide over his own. Some magics never change. Blood is one of them.

He blinked and recoiled, then slapped me, open-palmed. This time I didn't even bother to get up, but lay curled on the ground and said nothing. My blood on his hands; even better.

"We are the Order!" he snapped. "We watch you people all the time, we are everywhere! Can you begin to imagine our power?"

I laughed despite myself. "So powerful," I exclaimed through hysterical bursts of breath, "you can't even kill Bakker by yourself. You need to get us to do your work for you. We know you. We heard your voice inside our mind, when you whispered into the phone. You are an infestation in our skin, a worm in our flesh. You're part of us. Think about that next time you shoot us!"

He rubbed his head, a nervous gesture. Could he sense our magic, the tiniest curse, working through his body? Probably not. It was out of our hands. "Maybe I will," he said.

He nodded at Oda, who stepped up to me, pulled my head back with a quick gesture, and stuck something into my neck that filled my throat with oil and my head with the sickly blanket of darkness.

I woke and had never been more grateful to find myself uncomfortable. Everything ached, throbbed or stung; and it was bliss, simply because there was too much of it to be a dream. Nor, I suspected, was it anything resembling an afterlife. I was on a small, bare wooden floor in a small, bare room with rough plastered walls that had once been painted blue and were now a theme of faded and chipped. The room sported a plastic panel of flashing green lights that circled the head of Jesus Christ like fairy lights on a Christmas tree, while he looked on benevolently. There was one door, one window, and a smell of dust. It was also, very much, in the city. The smell of fumes hit immediately, and I heard the rumble of traffic, the screech of brakes on a bus; I was back in my home, alive.

I risked getting up on all fours, and looked round the room. By the door, fiddling with her rifle in the casual manner of someone accustomed to bullets, Oda said, "Hi."

"Hi," I replied, pulling myself into a sitting position and feeling around the inside of my mouth for any more loose teeth. There was blood on my shirt and face; I hadn't considered how quickly a vendetta, and prolonged magical confrontation, could eat through my wardrobe. We said, as reasonably as we could, "Why are you here?"

"Got to keep an eye on you," she said. "I'm not happy about it either, if you're wondering."

"You are – not afraid?"

"Afraid?" she echoed, raising one surprised eyebrow.

"Pissed off doesn't really cover it," I said. "We would kill you for what you did. And I want you to be impressed, by the way, at the fact that I'm not spontaneously combusting, because I promise, it's just two nerve endings and a snappy word away."

"The blue electric angels are much quicker to go around killing than the little sorcerer, aren't they? Or at least, much quicker to talk about it," she said, not bothering to look at me. "If you're going to throw up, there's a toilet next door."

"Why would I throw up?"

"It's a standard reaction to the drugs."

"What have you done?" we barked.

Perhaps the anger in our voice jerked her from her complacency. "Just to make you sleep for the trip," she said in a defensive tone. "We want you alive – for now."

"I'm not happy about this arrangement."

"And I am under orders to shoot you at the first sign of overly Satanic inclinations."

"What are those?" I asked, my genuine curiosity briefly overriding our fury.

"My remit is to use my own judgement to determine when the harm that you might do outweighs the necessary evil of using you against a worse danger. Or in order words, if you look like you're going to shape up to be a son of a bitch worse than Bakker, I pop two in your skull and three in your chest and make sure the phones are switched off."

"You're not making much of a case for my liking you," I said, flexing my fingers for that familiar crackle of electricity. There was a little, running through the walls only a few feet away, and a plug quite close to her feet from which I could snatch some power, if it became necessary.

"Well, there are a few things you can consider," she said, patting the barrel of her rifle with a gesture more motherly than threatening. "For a start, I can be immensely useful to you."

"How?"

"I can kill anyone who gets in your way," she explained, smiling hopefully, "so long, of course, as I deem them to be worthy of the death. And I know a very good dentist."

"I'm thinking that perhaps you're something of a breakaway cult."

"Cult?"

"References to God, damnation, dentistry, Satan, mixed with a violent tendency and samurai swords."

"We take all sorts. Those who believe are, naturally, those best equipped for our mission."

"And what, exactly, is your mission?"

She shrugged. "Ultimately, the complete obliteration of all magic on this earth, although right now we're dealing with priorities, and will settle for the obliteration of all actively malign and threatening magic on this earth, starting with Bakker."

"And progressing to me?" I asked, guessing the answer.

Her eyes flashed, stayed for a second on mine; then looked away. "We'll have to reassess our priorities when the time is right."

"Religion has got corporate-speak?"

She smiled, just for a moment. "We find it easier to mention 'issues' than talk about the advancing horde of the evil masses."

"And I'm currently not sending two hundred and forty standard mains volts into you for what reason?"

She ticked them off on her fingers. "One: you're inquisitive. Two: I know you need allies and we" – a grin – "are *very* good at what we do. Three: any second now you're going to wonder where your biker friend is and whether he's all right, and I'm going to give you an answer that's not entirely satisfactory from your point of view, yet really dead predictable. Four: there is still a part of you, Matthew Swift, that is human enough to give a damn, I think, about the entire killing thing in general. You didn't kill San Khay."

"What makes you so sure?"

"You wouldn't have had the guts," she replied. "The blue electric angels might have, but at the end of the day, you're still in there being a coward. Did I miss anything?"

I shook my head, feeling small. "No," I said. "I guess you didn't." With a sigh, "Where is Blackjack?"

"Is that his name?"

"It's Dave really."

"I see why he changed it."

"Really? I don't."

"Should you ever get into the world of online fantasy gaming, Mr Swift, you will find, to your surprise, that Bob the Master of Arcane and Mystic Arts is a rare creature, and that Gary the Sacred Warrior of Eternal Might doesn't buy so many potions of smiting when he goes shopping for his battle gear. You have no sense of style; your friend does."

"You have him?" I asked. "And he's not really a friend."

"Yes."

"Hurt him?"

"No."

"Going to?"

"Perhaps. Do you care?"

We thought about it. I knew the answer, though I couldn't find a reason for it. "Yes," I sighed. "What do you want me to do?"

"I want you to kill Bakker," she said with a bright, sucrose smile. "And I'm going to be there at every step, until you do."

"And if I do?" I asked wearily. "What then?"

She stretched, slinging the rifle casually over her shoulder. "I'm sure we'll work something out."

"Why?"

"Why what?"

"Why bother? What's your reason?"

"Did you miss the mission statement?"

"I think I understand what's going on with the Order. You're *The X-Files* meets the Jesuits meets the SAS, yes?"

She shrugged.

"What about you, Oda? Why are you the one standing there with the big sword, the nasty gun and the attitude?"

She thought about it for a moment, then looked me in the eye and said, "My brother is a murderer. He kills with magic. Is that enough, or shall I tell you of the light of God and the Truth of his Word?"

I shook my head. "No thank you. I think I've got the picture."

"Excellent!" she exclaimed. "So! Did you have a plan?"

The bathroom was chipped and brown, the white tiles filled in with old crumbling cement where they'd cracked, the floor warping with thin plastic sounds of distress, the sink too small, the tap too low. I washed as best I could, and in the kitchen found a small tray of ice in a freezer containing nothing else but fish fingers and suspicious tubs of home-made dripping. I wrapped the ice cubes in a tea towel stained with tabasco, sat down on the floor and tried my very best to relax.

Oda was packing a small arsenal of weapons into a sports bag, utterly uninterested in my self-pitying looks as I moved the ice around various ugly, swollen areas of bruising on my face. I hadn't been this hurt since I was fifteen and got into a fight at school; and that had ended by my accidentally sending fifty volts into the fist of my attacker, back when I hadn't understood why the squirrels brought me nuts in the winter, or why the local fox didn't run away when I found it digging through the bins.

I said, "The plan's simple."

"Well?"

"I intend to destroy the Tower."

"We're with you on that one; any bigger plans?"

"There were four people Sinclair identified as important in sustaining the Tower – San Khay, Guy Lee, Harris Simmons and . . ."

"Dana Mikeda, yes, I know."

"Sinclair thought that by targeting those four you could undermine the Tower itself. San Khay is . . . Amiltech is a wreck. They won't be able to provide proper security any more. Now I'm on to Guy Lee."

"One down, three to go. Sure, I get that."

"Oda?" I bit my lip. "There's something I need to make clear now. If the Order or you so much as touch Dana Mikeda, I will show you just how Satanically inclined I can be."

"I thought you might say that." She shrugged. "No promises, not that vows mean anything to you. We'll have to see how things play."

I grimaced and tried not to think about large quantities of electricity. "So," she said, with a thin smile, "Let's talk about Guy Lee."

Sinclair's files were thorough, but not nearly as useful as they had been for San Khay. For a start, Guy Lee was not a man of nice, predictable habit. He had no fixed address, no family, no real friends and no consistent lovers. Even his driver, shepherding him across town night after night, was changed on a frequent but unpredictable basis. Khay had offered to provide Lee with personal security; rumour went that Lee just laughed and said he was better off dealing with his own affairs. Certainly, he was a man with many minions, and his interests spread from Enfield to Croydon across the whole sweep of the city – brothels in Soho, beggars in Holborn, street cleaners in Moorgate, thugs in Dagenham and racketeers in Acton.

He walked a fine line between reward and punishment – those who openly crossed him tended to be discovered nailed to a tree on Hampstead Heath, or a remnant of their bloated flesh would be picked out of the water at the Thames Barrier; those who served him faithfully might acquire a penthouse suite overlooking the river at Putney, or a town house in Knightsbridge, and were driven in cars with tinted, bulletproof windows, and doors that closed with a thump so heavy they might have been weighted with gold. You did not take the charity of Lee for granted, and more than a few lieutenants had found themselves hung upside down by parts of their own internal anatomy for crossing Lee's will, his favour taken away as quickly as it had come.

Sinclair was a precise man who clearly disapproved of presenting things as fact when they were merely supposition. But as a best guess a marginal note in his file read: *Lee can summon for his needs at least 143 men and women from within his own adherents to any place at any time.*

Further down it added: *Amiltech can provide support.*

And last, scrawled in minute pencilled handwriting: *He summons monsters.*

I thought about the litterbug I'd run into on my first hour of reliving, and the craft and power that had gone into its creation.

All that Sinclair would say with certainty of Lee's personal activities was that his day began at sunset and finished around sunrise. All night he would not stop moving for more than an hour, inspecting his investments, making sure that the right enchantments were being cast to ensnare the appropriate MP or CEO, punishing those who did not appreciate his power, and paying visits to those families honoured by his good graces, like a royal prince shaking hands with a foreign dignitary before flying on to the next negotiation. Sinclair loathed the boundary that Lee crossed: he was one of the few in the city cocky enough to use magic to achieve mundane political ends, and his minions could be found lurking around the edges of a dozen government committees and corporate boards. Magic didn't change the scope of human ambition; just the means it used.

Outside his work, he didn't seem to pursue any special pleasures – certainly, he might demand a meal of such a quality, or a woman for his bed, or such and such a drug – but the delivery of each thing was given out as a test of abilities, or loyalty. Rumour was that he would deliberately sup at the house of a man he did not trust and, despite the fear of poison, would eat every last morsel, while his host quaked with the dread of failing to satisfy.

One last rumour, unsubstantiated but interesting, related to Lee's magical interests. In sum, the man was a magician – competent, no doubt, but a man who shaped the forces he controlled through learning, gesture, words – the traditional components of spells and spell-casting, rather than the less traditional arts such as sorcery. His magic was precise, neat, and highly competent. But a question arose over *where* he'd acquired these skills, since the forms taken by a lot of his magics were decidedly unwholesome. Enemies cursed by him were consumed from the inside out; those foolhardy enough to attack him tended to die choking on their own blood. There were even reports that some of his more unusual servants, as they moved around on their business, were never hotter nor colder than room temperature.

I didn't like to say necromancy. It's a messy art, not entirely without its uses but not for those with a weak stomach or who particularly care about personal hygiene. I could imagine Lee doing it.

"So your plan is . . ."

I foresaw Oda fast becoming even more of a pain.

"Allies. Khay was different, he was in the public eye. Lee is entirely below board; and this time, he'll know I'm after him. Allies. Help."

"You've got the Order."

"I wasn't about to call you an ally, as such."

"Get used to the idea."

"Whites."

"Who are the Whites?"

"The Long White City Clan."

"What are they?"

I smiled and stretched, getting up to put the remnants of my ice pack in the sink. "Artists."

When I asked the Beggar King how to find the Whites, his answer had been short and to the point: the writing is on the wall.

"So what does that mean?" snapped Oda.

"Oda, has it ever occurred to you that if in the good old days ladies with bad skin and big hair drew mystic pentagrams and pointed stars on the walls with bits of old chalk, then the invention of spray-paint would only have enhanced this tendency?"

That evening, we found the first one sprayed onto the local launderette's closed shutters in bold white and black: a frog with a huge snout and long, bulbous fingers. With one hand it stroked its beard, while the other pointed a curling finger towards the bus stop. On its head was a big top hat with the price still in it, $1.41, and in its mouth a fat, smoking cigar.

We followed the curved finger to the bus stop, Oda's sports bag clanking with its weight of weaponry. When the 141 bus came, we rode it till we came to a rectangular, railed-in area of grass beneath huge plane trees floodlit in bright green, blue and purple. Oda snapped, "There!", and we hurried to get off.

What she'd seen was a picture of a small girl with angel wings. It was painted on the side of a Unitarian chapel, beneath a dredge of less artful efforts making statements like **DaN iS gAy!** and *C4D 4ever.* The girl's face was turned up, studying a large red balloon drifting upwards towards the shiny aluminium venting funnels of a patisserie next door; one small painted white hand reached up in vain for the trailing string.

Oda said, "Well?"

"Angel," I replied, trying to sound more confident than I felt.

We took the first bus to the Angel. Outside the underground station we looked around for a few minutes, until I spotted a small black-and-white rat, painted below an ATM by the Bank of Scotland offices. It wore a long scarf, carried a suitcase and a bunch of rosemary wrapped in paper like it was a bouquet of roses; and its long black nose was twitching towards the south.

We followed the nose of the rat down to Rosebery Avenue, where we found a mock ATM painted in a walled-up window; from its money dispenser there emerged a huge mechanical arm, clutching in its claws a child. She was almost the image of the little angel-winged girl who'd lost her balloon, and held her hands to her mouth in a gesture of surprise.

The arm was gesturing towards Farringdon Road, so we walked down that wide, dull artery of traffic, until the yellow brick walls of a railway line grew up on one side and Oda said, "Swift."

She was pointing at a hoarding covered with posters advertising bands, albums, low-budget films and desperate struggling magazines. In one corner was a small stencilled image of a train, forever looping in on itself, round and round until it swallowed its own tail, the carriages blending into each other.

Oda, who'd said almost nothing all evening, now asked, "Where does it want us to go?"

I groaned. "Circle line."

"Circle line where?"

"Where isn't the important part."

"What does that mean?"

"Come on," I said. "We need to buy a few things."

I'd bought a book of sudoku, a biro, a packet of chewing gum and a small trashy romantic novel, placing them all with loving care in a single plastic shopping bag. At the local pub, I was now trying to convince the girl behind the bar that she wanted to serve me coffee, not beer, before Oda's patience snapped.

"What are you doing?" Oda demanded, indicating the bag.

"Sacrifices." I was secretly pleased that she'd asked before I'd been obliged to tell her, and felt determined to make her suffer for her curiosity.

"Sacrifices for what? Why aren't we taking the Circle line and finding the Whites?"

"We've got to wait," I replied.

"Why?"

"For the last train."

"*Why?*"

"Because that's what the symbol means. It's not just the Circle line; it's the train that swallows itself again, travelling round and round forever, no stations, no stops – it's not just 'Go take the Circle line.' It's much more complicated. Sacrifices." I waved the bag with the sudoku book.

"You are deliberately being cryptic," she exclaimed. "Why?"

"Because I don't like you."

"On my word your friend's life hangs. And yours," she added, eyes narrowing.

"So you tell us," we said. "It must frighten you, not being entirely sure what we will do next."

"I'm not afraid of you," she retorted, her voice cold and level. "You are a dead nothing, whatever forces you've made bargains with."

"That's not the point," I said in my gentlest, most placating tone. "You are afraid of not being certain."

"No."

"If you say so."

"You know nothing," she added vehemently.

"I know that I want a coffee, and that beer would be a bad idea, all things considered."

"Why? What's so important about catching the last train?"

"I'd much rather let you work that out for yourself," I said, and resumed trying to order coffee.

At 11.45 p.m. Oda and I walked down towards Farringdon station. The last train of the evening was written up on the board for six minutes past midnight, in blue marker pen. There weren't many people waiting on the platform. Some late-night theatregoers lingered, in their pearls and smart suits, at a distance from a group of girls whose feet ached from having got lost hereabouts in the wrong kind of shoes. At the opposite end of the platform, pushed into a brick alcove by their passion, a couple of men soaked in sweat and hormones were engaged in the longest, loudest kiss we'd ever seen. I tried not to stare. We were fascinated.

A Metropolitan line train came, heading towards Baker Street, where, selfishly, it had decided to terminate; the girls got on it anyway, as did the theatregoers in their silk scarves. A Hammersmith and City line train didn't do much better, giving up the ghost at Edgware Road, but that was clearly far enough for the two men, who, to the surprise of the polite Arab-looking couple sitting in the carriage amid piles of free daily newspapers strewn across the floor, resumed where they'd left off.

The indicator cleared itself of all but one more train – on the westbound Circle line, its destination picked out in bright orange dots. A group of young men and women ran onto the platform, giggling with the adrenalin of their own having-nearly-missed, until one of the girls, dressed almost entirely in cold pink skin and bra strap, was sick behind one of the benches. Oda scowled and looked away. The girl's friends clustered around her, patting her, soothing, stroking her hair, and dabbing at the remnants of bile around her mouth until with a final heave she was empty, and sat down on the bench and started to cry. We felt a sudden burning in our face at the sight of it, which we could not understand or control, and it was only Oda's cold expression that stopped us from sharing the girl's distress.

At 12.09 a.m. precisely, the Circle line train rattled and wheezed into the station. Oda stood up quickly, slinging her bag onto her shoulder; but I caught her arm, pulling her back down. She said, "But the..."

"No. Not this one. The *last* train."

"This is the..."

"Trust me."

She hesitated, then reluctantly sat back down. The girls and boys staggered onto the train, which with a clunk and a beeping of door alarms slammed its carriages shut and, engine whirring with a rising pitch, rattled its way out of the station. It passed the graffiti on the opposite wall: long, incomprehensible names made entirely of angles, and doodles in green paint. By a board showing you where to go for trains to Luton, someone had drawn a pair of closed black-and-white eyes, each eyelash ending in a long Egyptian curve.

After a moment Oda said, "You've got a plan, sorcerer?"

I nodded as, above us, the indicator board swept itself clean with a single orange asterisk, and didn't display any more messages. I stood up, and walked down the platform past signs for

"Sensational!!!"

Bollywood Romance – a Love Story for Our Time!

"The Most Amazing Thing I've Ever Seen!!" – News of the World

"Astonishing!" – Time Out

and further down.-.-.

The new voice of now! – **Love and Lost** – *a heart-breaking album to inspire a generation.*

When I reached the end of the platform, I pushed back the swinging *"Danger! Do not cross!"* sign, ducked past the array of mirrors to show the parked train driver the platform's length, and followed the narrowing, dirty concrete slope of the platform down towards the ballast and electric spice of the line. I could taste the thick, smoky dirt of the tunnel on the end of my tongue, the dryness of it in the air; I could feel the buzz of thousands of volts in the track beside me, feel the cold wind of the last train's passage still being pumped through the tunnel, fading into the heavy heat of the motionless underground. With my back pressed against the rough, black wall bursting with coils of cabling that hummed even through their once-coloured plastic sheaths, I slipped down onto the narrow remainder of the platform's edge, into the darkness.

Oda stared at me from the light of the platform itself with undisguised surprise and distaste. "What are you doing?"

"Oda," I said, "when Hunger came looking for us at Bond Street station, do you really think he would have left you alive? Do you honestly believe he would not have drunk your blood as well, just to see if it tasted the same as the sweat on your skin as you died? Trust me. Please." I held out a hand to her. Scowling, she pushed past the *"Danger!"* sign, picking her way down until she squatted next to me. She was straining, I noticed, to avoid the bulky snake of cables locked into the wall, even as her eyes swerved uneasily to the electric rail. In that darkness, we had no space, and we could feel the heat of her proximity on our skin, a strange, living warmth in the stale gloom of the tunnel's edge. We stared at her, curious and unashamed, until, glancing up, she saw our eyes on her and quickly looked away, muttering, "Jesu preserve us."

"What's the matter?" I asked.

"I can see them in the dark."

"What?"

"Your eyes. Like a cat's – they reflect blue."

"It was an almost perfect resurrection," we hazarded.

She spat into the dark. Her spit fizzed off the live rail.

I said, "I can't help . . . it's not . . . sorry."

She glanced up again, then away before I could see anything but the question in her face. "What are we doing here, exactly?"

"Waiting for the guard to inspect the platform."

She only grunted in response, and we felt the heat of her breath tickle our skin again, like the brush of dying sparks.

We didn't have to wait long. The guard came, muttering into his radio, a few minutes after the last train had left. He walked briskly along the platform's edge, picking up bits of litter with a prong on the end of a plastic stick, opened up the vending machine, took the day's coins and filled it with tomorrow's old, overpriced chocolate and cans of drink. That took us nearly ten minutes of sitting, huddled in the darkness at the edge of the platform, trying to limit the sound of our own breaths.

When he finished, he turned the lights down, so that the entire place was washed with a low pinkish-orange neon glow rising up from behind the benches, reflecting strangely off the glass panels of the advertising boards. I heard the clattering of the iron gate at the front of the station being drawn shut. At my side Oda whispered, "Enough?"

I nodded.

She scrambled back up the platform, hastily moving away from me and self-consciously brushing the dirt off her clothes. I looked up at the dead indicator board and said, "We just have to wait now."

"Wait for what?" she groaned.

"You wanted to be part of this so badly you had to attack me and kidnap a man," I said, surprised at how calm I sounded. "Now you just watch and learn."

I sat down on a bench, wrapping my dirty coat around me against the cold and sudden stillness of the place, and waited. Oda paced, jaw set in a tight, angry line. I tried to judge the minutes by the length of her walk – four progressions back and forth seemed to equal roughly a minute. My eyes felt heavy, my skin hot and tired, my hair dirty and my stomach full of lead. I let my head hang down, although we stayed on edge, ears more alert even as our eyelids fell, and drifted. We heard the drip of a water pipe and the distant rumble of a bus somewhere overhead. Our senses drifted without thinking into those of a mouse scuttling along by the electrified rail, sniffing out discarded food. We enjoyed the sensitivity of its nose, twitching it and feeling our entire face change shape slightly with that movement, and the sensitivity of our whiskers as they picked up on the reverberation of Oda's walking, like each footstep was the last hum of a ringing bell left in the air.

"Sorcerer!"

Her voice frightened the mouse, so I let its mind go and quickly looked up. Oda's face was a garish pinky-orange in the light of the platform, and her eyes were turned up towards the indicator board. In large orange letters, it read:

"1) Circle line via KingsX – 2 mins"

And nothing more.

For a moment we both looked at it, then Oda said, "Is this a spell of yours?"

"No."

"Then what is it?"

"It's the last train," I explained gently. "The *real* last train. It's... like the Beggar King, or the Bag Lady."

"This means nothing," she snapped, and the anger meant there was fear too – fear of magic in general, or the train itself; I couldn't be sure.

I struggled with the words. "Some ideas are more than just random moments of good inspiration. Some ideas become real whether you mean them or not."

"So what... *idea* is it that's due here in two minutes?"

"The train that doesn't ever stop travelling," I said. "That goes round and round the Circle line forever."

A cold wind on my face, from the end of the tunnel, a smell of dirty deep underground. We breathed it in, deeply.

"That's absurd."

"For a woman who has dedicated her life to the eradication of mystic forces, you have a very limited comprehension of what you're dealing with." A distant growing *te-dum, te-dum, te-dum*. The hairs on my scalp twitched with the coldness rising up and tickling my skin; the track itself gave a creak of added strain. I got to my feet, picking up my small plastic bag of sudoku, biro and chewing gum.

"And this train..." she said, struggling to keep the fear out of her voice, "this will take us to the Whites?"

"The Whites should already know we're coming," I said.

"How?"

I pointed across the other side of the platform. By the board telling you how to get a train to Luton, the pair of painted-on black-and-white Egyptian eyes, with their long curves and deep, stylised quality, were now open. Their black pupils and grey-flecked irises stared right at us.

Oda followed my gaze. She stammered, "It's not a trick of the mind."

"No."

"Is what you do always like this, sorcerer?"

"No. But if it was, life would be perfection," we said. We walked towards the edge of the platform, toes peeking over the edge of the yellow *"Do Not Cross"* line. In the tunnel at the other end of the station, a pair of dull white lights appeared, like the eyes of a hunting cat, glowing bigger and bigger out of the darkness. As they emerged, so did the dim light of a driver's compartment, empty except for a black shadow of no definable features. Growing with the sound of the rattling, hissing, spitting wheels as they threw up fat blue sparks across the ballast of the track and with the shrieking of brakes like the final breath of a dying banshee, the last train pulled up onto the platform of Farringdon station, and opened its doors.

The last train had once been white, but its paintwork was stained off-grey with neglect and age, and its surface scratched and tainted with brown bubbling rust. Its windows were almost impossible to see through, they were so scratched and criss-crossed with messages scoured into them. The doors, when they opened, did so with a scrape like fingernails down a blackboard, as rust edged over rust. Looking into the dim yellow glow of the carriages, I saw no passengers, just a slatted floor stained black by trodden-in chewing gum, and scattered with the remnants of old newspapers that drifted like feathers in a breeze. The seat covers were so thin, you could see the stuffing beneath, where it hadn't already spilled out; the glass on the emergency alarm was cracked and looked like it might fall out of its holder at any moment; and the fabric straps hanging from the support poles in the ceiling swayed gently by themselves after the train had stopped. At either end of the carriage the windows were open wide, and the place hummed with ventilation rising from behind the battered seats.

Oda said, "This is what I think they meant by Satanic inclination."

"You haven't even given it a go," I said. "Think of how small the human race would be if people didn't give such inclinings a chance."

I stepped cautiously up into the carriage, and when nothing happened, I turned and faced her, still standing uncertainly on the platform. "You trusted me at Bond Street," I said, holding out my hand. "Trust me now."

"Is it . . . necessary?" she asked.

"Yes."

She took my hand; she stepped up into the carriage. Almost immediately, the doors started to wail, a high-pitched, shrilling, too-loud sound that made me wince away, as with a heavy, final bang, they slammed shut. The train jerked sharply, and started to move. I wrapped my hand into one of the fabric loops drooping down from the ceiling and said, "I have a confession."

"What?" she asked, as the train slowly picked up speed with a low whine.

"I've never taken the last train before."

"Why not?"

"It's easy to get lost."

She grunted, then nearly lost her footing as with another jerk, the train accelerated more sharply, the warm glow of the platform vanishing as we hit the tunnel. She dropped her bag and wrapped her hands quickly round a pole in the middle of the carriage, pressing herself against it for support as we picked up speed. The wind from the open window at the far end of the carriage tore past us and away as we ploughed into the darkness, pulling at hair and clothes until my coat snapped like a flag in a gale. I saw the pale red and yellow shades of the dirty cabling outside the window draw apart as tracks joined, split, widened; then saw the cables disappear entirely, the light from inside the carriage falling on, as far as I could tell, nothing at all, no texture outside, not even the curve of a black wall, just blackness itself. The lights flickered in the ceiling and for a moment, in each intermittent flash, the carriage wasn't empty, but I was standing pressed in shoulder-to-shoulder with a hundred grey faces, featureless, with perhaps the hint of a hat here or the suggestion of a baby's buggy there, blocking up the doorway, pressed in so tight that for that moment I could barely breathe and the heat of it burnt down to my bones, before the lights shuddered again and the carriage was cold and empty, the wind driving at our faces like each particle held microscopic knives, and a grudge to make it worse.

Oda screamed over the roar, "Do you have any idea what you're doing?"

"Give it a minute!" I shouted back.

A flash of light outside, and for a second I saw the walls of Kings Cross St Pancras underground station – but only a second, and we made no attempt to stop; the entire length of the platform was gone by in the time it took to draw a breath. Newspapers billowed around my knees, old crunched-up drinks cans and hamburger packets rolled down the carriage as we picked up yet more speed, and when I tried to lift my foot, the chewing gum glooped and tugged my ankle back down, so only with a great physical wrench could I get free of its hold.

When the stop came, it came so fast and so hard that it threw me to the floor, and tossed Oda hard against the cracked glass panel dividing a row of seats from the door space. I picked myself up onto my knees, ancient black gum clinging to my palms, and looked round. We were still moving, I realised; I could feel the hum of the engines through the floor and hear the high-pitched whine of the ventilation and the electric belly of the train pushing power into the wheels, but it was no longer the heady drive of our first acceleration. Now, with the lights steady and low, the carriage was no longer empty.

Shadows, semi-transparent forms, filled every seat and every corner of the carriage. A grey, faceless woman rocked a silent grey sleeping baby; a grey, faceless man bopped to his silent music, its thin grey wires flapping around his head as he moved. A man in a bowler hat made way for an old woman with a walking stick; a family with big touristlike bags on wheels shuffled deeper into the carriage as a woman struggled to position a 'cello against the far wall. They weren't ghosts – ghosts have faces, expressions, sounds, reasons – these were utterly silent, anonymous, forgettable faces that had been forgotten, their features melted into each other to leave nothing but a blank shadow. I looked out of the window and saw only the glowing straight lines of railway tracks, dozens of them, hundreds, on either side, stretching away in parallel, polished steel glowing on the top, black rusted metal beneath, spread out on either side of us like lanes on a motorway, as far as the eye could see before they faded into the inevitable darkness.

Oda crawled up painfully from where she'd fallen, shaking her head when I offered her a hand, and whispered, "What is this?"

"The train needs passengers," I replied, turning to let a shadow of a man in a baggy jacket with a prominent beard push by me towards the carriage door, where he grabbed a fabric handle with fingers no thicker than mist, swaying gently with the quiet, steady rhythm of the train, *te-dum. Te-dum. Te-dum.*

"Are they . . . alive?"

"In a sense. They go everywhere in the underground, all the time, forever; they're part of it, like its memory."

"That doesn't sound alive to me."

"They are like us," we said. "They are what comes when you put so much life into one place. They are everywhere and nowhere, they came into existence when the first people gasped at the wonder of this new way of travelling, and marvelled at it, and they will only die when the last train closes its doors, and no one remembers that there ever was a railway underground. That is to say, not for a very long time. We are the same."

"*Wonderful*," she hissed between her teeth.

I grinned. "Not even slightly afraid?" I asked.

She glared.

I opened up my bag of goodies and pulled out the sudoku book. All heads turned in the carriage; dozens of empty eyes fixed on us. I waited until I was sure I had their attention, then, still kneeling down, I put it on the floor of the carriage. I laid the biro on top of it, the romantic novel next to it, unwrapped the chewing gum package so the top button of white gum was visible, and stepped back. The shadows drifted towards us, the shape of a fat lady in a big dress rising up from her seat, the image of a girl with a heavy rucksack moving down towards us, the ghostlike form of an old bent man. They huddled towards the pile, reaching out for it. As they advanced I pushed Oda gently back, until we were both pressed into the doorway. The shadows grew thicker and thicker around the sacrificed goods on the carriage floor, flooding in; and still more came, until there were at least two dozen figures occupying barely a square foot between them, their forms blending into a dark, opaque mass. The books, biro and gum became obscured by a churning mass of almost-solid-looking shapes, from which the occasional ghostly head or shadow arm would emerge, before sinking back into the mêlée.

When the shadows emerged again, pulling themselves clear, each drifted back to where they'd been without a sound or a backward look. Where they had congregated, there was nothing left on the floor but a scrap of chewing gum wrapper, and a torn page of a sudoku book, all the numbers filled in with neat blue biro.

Oda opened her mouth to speak, and the train jerked, nearly sending us flying again. She clung on to a handle and shouted over the roar of the accelerating engine, "What happened there?"

"It's a sacrifice," I yelled back as we began to sway and bounce along the tracks. "You sacrifice what they most desire!"

"A sudoku book?"

"Something anonymous, occupying, something to do so you don't have to look at the rest of the train – yes, a sudoku book and a trashy novel! That's what you do on the underground!"

Another wrench as we built up speed. For a moment, as we rounded a corner, I could see the other carriages curving away for ever into the darkness, before the line straightened again and they vanished. Sparks flew up from the wheels and flashed across the windows; the lights in the carriage faltered and one or two burst, with a pop and a puff of smoke. The rising and falling darkness raised and banished the shadow figures, so that one second the carriage was full, the next empty, with each dimming of the lights. Outside, for a second, another train rushed by, with a roar and a scream and the *thumpthumpthumpthump* of air trapped and pounded by the passage of so much metal – I saw a man reading a newspaper, a woman doing her knitting – before the image of the train was snatched away from us again and there was just the darkness and the reflection of our own faces in the scratched glass. We laughed out loud as the sparks splashing up from the wheels rose up around the windows in a blinding backwards waterfall, filling the darkness with electric pops that made the carriage burn with whiteness and the air hum with electricity, obscuring our view and rising up so high and so bright that we had to turn our eyes away and squeeze them shut against their radiance.

The sparks drifted down with the tone of the engine as we began another sharp deceleration. The shock of it knocked me sideways, banging into Oda as her grip slipped from the handle. I caught her instinctively as she staggered across the carriage with the declining movement of the train, and held her tightly by the arm while the sheet of fire outside our window faded, and the lights became dull and normal, the shadows receded down to nothing and, once again, outside I saw the flash of dirt-covered cabling.

Then came a dimly lit platform: neglected concrete and old beige tiles. We came to a halt and, clunking, the carriage doors opened. I stepped out into the cold air of the platform; Oda picked up her sports bag and, with an unsteady step, followed me. Behind us, the carriage doors slammed shut, and the train rattled away.

I looked around for a sign, and saw one: Aldwych.

I laughed. Oda said, "I'm glad you found that funny."

"Live a little," I replied. "Welcome to Aldwych station."

"I've never heard of Aldwych station."

"It's a closed station. It used to be on the Piccadilly line."

"Then how did we get here?"

"Are you really going to ask such inane questions all the time? Mystic bloody forces; just accept them and cope!"

There was a polite cough from the other end of the platform. Oda's hand flew to her bag. I said, "Hello."

There were three of them, a man and two women. They stood in the entrance to the platform, underneath an old-fashioned sign of a black metal hand with an outstretched finger, below which was the word "*Exit*". They had guns. They weren't smiling. "Evening," said one of the women, stepping forward. "Were you wanting to see us?"

They took Oda's bag. That made her angry but at least she coped without shouting. They took my satchel. I said nothing, and wished I had deeper pockets.

Then they blindfolded us and, with a hand on our arm, took us walking. By the gentle rumbling through my feet and the hot, heavy nature of the air, we didn't go above ground. Besides, our senses were tingling, picking up a low, familiar buzz, a texture to the air between our fingers that seemed... enticing, and which grew with every passing second.

We walked, I estimated, for nearly ten minutes. At one point the smell of the sewers – congealed fat and diluted waste – hit my senses; at another I walked in the company of the rats, watching through their eyes as they scuttled in the dark ten paces behind us, until one of the people escorting us heard the pattering of their claws, and shooed them away with a violent shout in their case, and a clip across the back of the head in mine – not painful nor particularly threatening, but a warning enough that they guessed why the rats were so interested. Our footsteps echoed, and the air grew thicker. So did the taste of magic in that place, a heavy texture as if the breeze passing through my fingers when I moved were liquid, not gas, and as if the floor were covered with treacle, which clung to my feet when I moved.

As we walked, I heard the opening and shutting of several heavy metal doors or gates, and the clicking of many locks. The overall trend seemed level – what few steps up we took were counteracted by a similar number leading back down, so that I imagined we couldn't be much higher than the Piccadilly line itself by the time we reached our destination. When we arrived, we knew the place at once, familiar to us even from the outside, and I had to struggle not to laugh.

The place where they took off our blindfolds was close, gloomy, made of concrete – concrete walls, floor, ceiling, once a uniform pale beige, now inclining to grey – and full of giant, silent old pieces of machinery. There were banks and banks of it, cables drooping from the monoliths of their bulk, wires sagging and exposed, bulbs off and rust beginning to creep onto the exposed circuit boards inside their slotted structures. But still you could see these were, undeniably, the remnants of a telephone exchange. We could sense, even now, the humming of the place, the clatter of its underground workings – though, by the look of it, many years had passed since the place had been put to its original use.

What had been put to use, however, were the floors, walls and even parts of the ceiling, which were vividly covered with paint. Swirls of colour, messages in orange, blue, purple, pink, images of watching eyes, scampering rats, elves in fancy clothes, creatures fictional and real and some who walked the fine line in between, caricatures of politicians, images of images done in mock-graffito style – here a Rembrandt, reproduced with all the characters playing poker rather than watching the potatoes boil, there a Monet where all the faces were reproduced as beady-eyed ferrets jostling each other in their frilly dresses – if there was any space at all, someone had filled it with paint. The floors glowed with it, the ceiling dripped it, the walls ran with it. The place looked like a psychedelic nightmare, an LSD trip gone wrong, down in the remnants of the Kingsway Telephone Exchange.

They took us into a room whose walls were variations on a theme of purple – purple tower blocks melting into violet flowers that curled around maroon caterpillars squirming their way around lavender bushes that themselves melted into tower blocks again, whose lights described little faces peering out from the rectangular frames of their windows. A heavy iron door, with the words "Committee Room" in old-fashioned lettering, was slammed behind us, and locked. At the far end of the room, someone had left an old mattress stained a suspicious brown, and a bucket.

Oda said, "Is this part of your plan, sorcerer?"

I sat down – not on the mattress – yawned and said, "It's fine for now."

"In what way is this 'fine'?"

"You're not dead, I'm not dead, they haven't killed us, we haven't killed them, it's fine," I replied. "If I was a White being pursued by the Tower for nonconformity and antsiness, I'd be iffy about strangers too. I suggest you get a bit of sleep and try not to worry."

"I won't sleep in this place," she answered, pacing across the room and scowling.

"Why not?"

"It's horrific."

I stared at her in surprise. "Why?"

"They've painted enchantments into the walls, sorcerer! How can you sleep, knowing that?"

I looked round the room at the swirling landscape. "We think it's beautiful," we said. "Tire yourself out if you must; I'm going to sleep."

With that I pulled my coat up around my shoulders, tucked my knees into my chest, rolled onto my side, closed my eyes, and was quickly asleep. My dreams were all purple.

They woke us – there was no way to tell when: day, night, we had nothing to go on – and took us down the corridors, past a reinforced iron door and into a room with a large round table and a single suspended light. A woman was seated there with her red-booted feet up on the table, examining her nails. Her hair was black, and heavy quantities of make-up made her eyelashes seem to stretch on for ever; the corners of her eyes were painted with the long curving lines I'd seen in the Egyptian eyes at Farringdon station. Her lips were black, her skin was pale, her nails were painted bright blue and her clothes were all leather, studs and chains. She said, not looking up as we entered, "I haven't got much time, so let's get it over with."

Oda's bag of weapons stood in the corner, opened and rummaged; at the sight of such disdain for her equipment, Oda's face darkened.

"OK," I said, sitting down where indicated by one of the people who'd brought us here. "Briefly – I'm a sorcerer, and this lady here represents a truly vile and unimaginative group of idiots who may prove useful. I've got a grudge against the Tower; I was responsible for the campaign against Amiltech, although not for Khay's death; Dudley Sinclair recruited me to an alliance of people cooperating against the Tower, including bikers, warlocks, fortune-tellers and bag ladies; the Beggar King told me how to find you; I'm told that you and Guy Lee are locked in a bitter and losing battle. Would you like my help, and will you help me?"

The woman flicked the end of one of her nails and didn't look at me. "I'll think about it," she said. "Thanks for asking."

She nodded airily at the wall, and our guards pulled us back up by the elbows and led us from the room, back to our purple prison.

With the door locked again, Oda stared at me in horror. "What was that?" she asked, in a voice too calm to be what it seemed.

I sat back down in my corner. "Personally, I thought it went rather well."

More meaningless time.

No one had told me that vengeance could be so boring.

They fed us sandwiches – spam and stale bread, with tea in chipped mugs. We ate, curious to see if spam was as bad as I remembered it, and were satisfied to find that it was. Oda ate nothing; so, just to make sure, we ate hers.

Oda started doing push-ups in a corner.

"What the hell are you doing?"

"I have to stay fit," she replied.

"For what?"

She glared at me. When she'd done fifty push-ups, she switched, and did fifty sit-ups. I felt tired just watching her.

When there had been what I guessed was a whole no-night and a long no-day, Oda said, "You know, if I don't make regular calls, they start cutting bits off the biker, Blackjack."

I groaned and stood up from my corner. "Right!" I snapped. "*Fine.* Everyone's expecting this so why don't I just bloody get on with it?"

"Bored?" she asked, raising one cocky eyebrow.

I glared, marched up to the iron door and hammered on it. "You talk to me right now!" I shouted. "Or I swear I will fry everything in bloody sight and lots of stuff besides!"

When there was no answer, I gave them a count of thirty seconds, then stood back. "Right," I muttered. I pressed my ear against the door, half-closed my eyes, and started murmuring the guiding, meaningless sounds of an opening spell, whispering imploring noises into the iron, coaxing the touch of my breath all the way down to the lock, stroking it with my fingertips like you might caress a frightened kitten, wishing I had my set of blank keys from my satchel to make life easier. Purple paint bubbled and hissed on the walls; the tower blocks swayed, the lavender bushes whispered in the wind, little faces of office lights blinked uneasily at us from the surface of the walls; until, eventually, with a reluctant snap, the lock came open.

I pushed the door back. There was no one in the long, gloomy corridor, but also no rats I could hijack for a little scouting. There was, however, a *lot* of electricity around. I said to Oda, "If I ask you to keep out of my way, you'll just make a hollow laughing sound, am I right?"

"You give me more credit for humour than I deserve," she replied. I wasn't entirely surprised.

I held up my fingers and started dragging the electricity out of the walls, wrapping it round my hand, my wrists, wreathing it up my arms and around my neck like a scarf, letting it drape down my back in a mass of angry worms of lightning, feeling it wriggle across my chest and make my hair stand on end. When I had enough of it in my grasp that my blood ached with the pressure of it, and my eyes stung from the closeness of its heat to my face, I started marching down the corridor. Oda followed at a tactful distance. As we walked, the paintings very gently turned to watch us.

I chuckled.

"What's so funny?"

"They're watching," I said.

"Who's watching?"

"The Whites."

"Why?"

"I'm not entirely sure. Come on. This way."

"How do you know?"

"We know this place from the inside, from the old days."

"What do you mean?"

"It used to be a telephone exchange. We would come and play here, when the lines weren't so busy. Remember – trust me!"

"You try, one day," she retorted. I grinned and kept walking.

When we ran into the first guard, he had a fireman's axe in one hand, took one look at us, and ran straight for us. I threw a handful of electricity on instinct, and that knocked him back, but, to our surprise, didn't do anything more. He charged again, mouth open and face twisted with rage – it occurred to me that, for an angry running man, he made almost no sound. So I lowered my hands and waited, while the electricity popped angrily between my fingers. Oda leapt forward to push me aside, but at the last instant, when the axe was an inch from striking, the man stopped, wobbled, and shattered into a thousand spatters of paint, which quickly wiggled their way into the concrete. "Illusions," I said.

"You seem to be enjoying yourself," she replied, self-consciously flicking bubbles of paint off the back of her hand.

"I think I understand what's going on."

"Perhaps you can explain it to me."

"I think the whole thing is a bloody inane test."

"A test?"

"To see if we're really any use whatsoever."

"'Use'?" she echoed with disdain.

"Are you just going to repeat select parts of what I say?"

"I just wish to remove any hint of cryptic mystery you're attempting to push."

I sighed. "In the good old days you said, 'Hello, I'm a sorcerer and this is what I want' and people bloody listened. But these days…I guess Bakker has given the profession a bad name."

I relaxed, turning my fingers towards the floor, and slowly let the electricity on my skin make its way to earth, tickling its way down my legs, across my feet and into the concrete.

"If I understand you, is that wise?" she asked, watching the last sparks die.

"Bollocks if I'm going to play their games," I replied. "We have too much we need to do." I raised my head and shouted down the corridor, "All right, you've had your fun, you've seen what we're up to. Now either you cut this crap right now or I'll bring the bloody street down on your head, and don't think I'm not in the mood."

"Can you do that?" asked Oda quietly.

I dropped my voice again. "Oda, even if I was inclined to tell you the extent of my abilities, do you really think now is the time for an academic exploration of the subject?"

"You were saying?" she asked, lifting her eyebrows and smiling a sickly smile.

"Oh, right, yes." I raised my voice again. "I mean it! We talk right now or everything goes fucking mythic. Right *now*!"

From the far end of the corridor a petulant voice said, "Oh, all right, sorcerer, you've made your point. Jesus, it's not like we wanted the sermon on the fucking mount."

I grinned at Oda. "Now, that wasn't so hard, was it?"

We ended up back in the room with the round table. She said her name was Vera and she was, she coldly informed us, the mostly properly elected head of the Long White City Clan, and proud of it.

"What's a mostly properly elected head?" I asked.

"It's generally accepted that if there was an election, I'd win," she answered, with a dazzling tight smile. "So I figure – why bother?" She sat down, stretching out a pair of legs clad in more tight leather than it seemed circulation could bear, and said casually, "So, you really are a sorcerer. I wasn't sure."

"You could have bloody asked," I said. "No one these days seems interested in just *asking*."

"I thought it'd be more telling to see what you did on your own initiative," she replied. "And I figured... if you were out to get us we would have been got quicker. Sorry about the sandwiches. Would you like something better?"

"Not hungry," said Oda, in a voice like icebergs creaking in a high sea.

"I wouldn't mind," I answered. "But I would like to know – why the theatrics?"

"We have to be careful; the Clan is under siege. Guy Lee has promised to destroy every trace of us, and is throwing around a lot of money and a lot of threats."

"So you lock up anyone who comes to say hello?"

"Until we can find out some more information about them. For example, in the day and a half we've had you here..."

"Day and a half?" echoed Oda incredulously.

"Yes." Statement, matter-of-fact; this was not a woman used to remorse or even polite social embarrassments. "I've learnt that you" – one long, pointed finger uncurled luxuriously in my direction – "are almost certainly Matthew Swift, sorcerer, ex-corpse, formerly a cleaner for Lambeth Borough Council and..."

"You were a cleaner in Lambeth?"

"I needed the money," I said.

"You cleaned?" Oda couldn't have looked more surprised if she'd been told that I'd built the pyramids in my spare time.

"...and the chosen and favoured apprentice of Robert James Bakker," Vera concluded with an irritated exhalation, her moment of revelation spoilt.

"That's all true enough," I admitted. "Although again – you need only have asked."

"Can't be too certain."

"How did you find out?"

"It wasn't too hard; sorcerer, living and not in a mental home, ostensibly not working for the Tower, grudge against Bakker. Amiltech in pieces, Khay dead, no one to blame and a rumour going round that Bakker's apprentice is back, with a serious grudge against the master. Just needed to match up some photos and sweet-talk a few filing clerks, to get the proof."

I shrugged; there didn't seem much use denying it.

"Heard you were dead."

I shrugged again.

"Good recovery," she added, eyeing me up for a reaction.

"Thanks." I didn't feel like offering her anything more.

A moment while she waited; it passed, she moved on. "As for you" – another finger uncurled at Oda – "I have no idea who you are or what you want, and that bothers me."

Oda tilted her chin proudly and said, "You cross me and mine, and you die."

"Don't give her any credit for humour," I agreed quickly. "She really does believe all that."

"Quaint. Who are you?"

Oda glanced at me. I said, "Give her the bad news."

"I belong to the Order."

"Never heard of you."

Oda smiled thinly. "That's how good we are."

Vera hesitated, then a slow, nasty smile spread across her face. "I see."

"We can help you destroy Bakker."

"Charming of you. Where's the catch?"

"I need to make a phone call," said Oda flatly.

"Tough," retorted Vera, eyes flashing.

"Please let her make the phone call," I said wearily, "she'll be insufferable until she does."

"Why should I?"

"Because she's a member of the Order, an evil group of unimaginative people who are holding an acquaintance of mine hostage against my good behaviour, and I'd like him to survive long enough to join you and to join me in helping bring down Bakker and all his works. How does that sound?"

"What kind of sorcerer are you?" chuckled Vera, doing her best to look unimpressed.

"A reasonable one. I know that I can't fight Lee alone, not now he knows I'm coming; I know that I need your help. Will you help us?"

To my surprise, Vera grinned. "When you put it like that, sorcerer, we may have grounds to talk."

*

Oda got her phone call, and I got a tour of the Kingsway Telephone Exchange.

"It's built to survive a nuclear attack," explained Vera as we wandered through the bland, tight tunnels. "Nuclear attack didn't happen so they used it as a telephone exchange. You could come down here at seven in the morning and go out nine hours later; and in winter it'd still be dark, the entire day gone, poof, just like that. Time loses its meaning away from the sunlight."

"What are you doing down here?" I asked as we drifted through the endless corridors of psychedelic paint. "Why's the Clan here?"

"We used to be in White City – that's where our name came from. Then they demolished our home in order to build this new shopping mall, and by then, Guy Lee had decided we were a pain. Harris Simmons has fifteen million invested in the shopping mall – tell you something? Fingers in every pie. The Clan picks up lost magicians – kids who don't understand that the things they draw are coming alive, voodoo artists possessed by the spirits, enchanters who can't control their own creations – we look after our own, make sure that the word doesn't get out about what we do, keep the authorities out of our hair."

"What makes you better than Lee?" I asked.

"In the grand scheme, I suppose not much. Our members will still steal, bewitch, bedazzle and charm when they need to, in order to profit or survive. We have a lot of strays to look after; you mustn't be surprised that some of them bite. Prostitutes who are not afraid of a cantrip for temporary beauty, thieves who sometimes find that it is useful to be more than just a metaphorical shadow – these things happen, you live with it. But we don't nail people to trees if they break our rules. And we don't rape the women who don't obey us when we order them to cast a spell. And we don't torture the fortune-tellers who refuse to give us money, and we don't experiment on the plucked-out eyes of the seers to see if we can leech away any of their sight, and we don't poison beggars with heroin so we can ride their trip without the drugs in our blood, or sacrifice human flesh to the spirits of a place for their good favour, or cast impenetrable glamours enriched with the blood of children to make our whores seem more beautiful, even the pig-ugly ones. And we don't like to talk with the dead. They tell you things that are sometimes best not heard. Is that what you wanted to hear, sorcerer?"

"I was hoping for something in shining armour, but thanks for the run-down," I said.

"You're welcome. So, Lee doesn't like us. He thinks we're treading on his toes. He wants things from us."

"What sort of things?"

"Money. Services. Snitching. We've got a lot of contacts and he doesn't like rivals. And he's tough – there's an army out there who'll follow him, and more just waiting at the Tower to do his word. He likes to have control. Whites don't like to be controlled. It's only going to get shittier. Although, with Amiltech kinda fucked . . ."

"It'll recover," I sighed. "Sure, it's bad, it looks bad, but Amiltech will always recover while the Tower's around."

"Even though San Khay is dead?" she asked quickly.

I rolled my eyes. "I didn't kill him. Let's get this sorted right here, right now. I didn't kill him."

"Pity," she sighed. "Why not? I would have."

"Someone else got there first."

She waited.

I said nothing more.

She shrugged. "Fine. OK. So Amiltech are fucked for now – that's a good thing. What can you do for me?"

"I can help you against Lee."

"How?"

"I can get you some help."

"Warlocks, bikers and religious psycho-bitches? Thanks; I'd rather take my chances."

"The Beggar King too."

"And you of course!" Mocking doubt bit acid into her voice. "Our own pet sorcerer, hand-trained by the man sitting at the top of the Tower."

"Bakker is my enemy too."

"Yeah. I heard he might be. Why can you get me all this help, when no one's given a fuck until now?"

I considered the reasons, ticked them off on my fingers. "One: I'm a sorcerer, and I'm told that right now, that's a bit of a novelty. Two:

Sinclair has already laid the groundwork for this, I'm just finishing it off. Three: I was Bakker's apprentice. His chosen pupil, surrogate brat kid, spoilt adopted fucking son. You're scared of him? Be scared of me too. Four..."

We hesitated.

"Four?"

I thought about the telephone exchange, looked into the bright knife-edge of Vera's gaze, bit back our words. "Never mind about four," I said quickly. "It's not important, yet."

She grunted, half-shook her head. "OK. Whatever. There's something else I need to ask you, though."

"Ask, then."

"You heard how so many sorcerers died? About Awan, Akute, Patel..."

I nodded.

"Good. Then you'll know the basics. A creature that can't be killed, that delights in the death of its enemies, that kills Bakker's enemies, that can't be stopped and..."

"I stopped it. Ask Oda. I held it back."

"How?"

"It was just temporary, a spell – but it came looking for us, and didn't succeed. Not this time."

"You know about this creature? Can you kill it?" She spoke quickly, eager – afraid. "Kill it and you'll have a bargain."

She knew about Hunger.

Better – she knew enough about it to be afraid.

That, I could respect.

"I think I can kill it," I said. "But I need to see Bakker first."

"Well, that's a problem, since I'm imagining you're not his favourite person right now and the guy's as hard to find as El bloody Dorado."

"You misunderstand. I think, to kill it, I'll have to kill him."

"Why?"

I lowered my voice. "You keep a secret?"

"No," she replied. "Not unless it's fucking monumentally important."

"This one could be. This could be the key to everything, the answer to the question you didn't know to ask."

She shrugged. "Hit me; no promises."

"The shadow, and Bakker?"

"Yeah?"

"I think they might be the same thing."

She opened her mouth to protest, then hesitated, face shuttering down, blanking off all emotion. "Oh," she said finally, a long slow sound. "Shit. You got proof?"

"I've got . . . a lot of circumstance."

"Who else knows – suspects – whatever?"

"No one that I know of. Although I guess the Beggar King will have it figured out, and if there's any sorcerers still left alive, not hiding or mad, they'll have guessed. But they'll be afraid."

"What makes you so sure of this?"

I thought about it, licking my lips, remembering the taste of blood. "The people who are attacked. The nature of the attacks and the creature – hungry, longing for life that it can't have, a shadow. Something Bakker's sister said; he wanted her to summon some creatures, voices in the wire, he thought they would keep him alive. 'Make me a shadow on the wall'. It attacked her and let her live – why? And lastly . . ."

"Lastly?" she asked, sharp, when I hesitated.

"I've seen the creature's face. It has his face, withered and pale, but still his face. The shadow is related to Bakker – I don't quite know how, but I'm almost convinced of it. I think that if you stop Bakker, you stop the shadow. Chicken and egg."

She drew in a long breath. "Yeah. Right. OK. Let's say I'm running with this for a moment. But to kill Bakker you're going to have to eliminate his security: Guy Lee, maybe a few others – Dana Mikeda, almost certainly. To do that, you risk drawing the attention of this shadow. You're also going to have a problem with Mikeda."

I looked up sharply and saw her eyes fixed, intelligent and bright, on my face. "It'll be fine," I said.

"She was your apprentice," she said mildly. "I hear that sorcerers get quite attached to their apprentices."

"It's complicated."

"I bet it is."

"I'll deal with it," I said, harsher than I'd meant.

"I hope you do. You're going to have to anyway. Were you and Elizabeth Bakker...?" I didn't answer the lilting question in her voice. She added, "Probably not important."

"No," I said sharply. "Not to you."

Her smile lurked for a second; a moment of cruelty, verging on laughter. "All right, Mr Matthew Swift," she said finally. "I think it's fair to say that you have got our attention. What exactly do you want to do?"

I sagged, unable to hide the sudden relief. "It's very simple. I need to eliminate Guy Lee and his underworld army, and I need help to do it."

"I don't trust that girl you're with."

"Neither do I. You ought to know that she won't be your friend, when this is over."

She raised her eyebrows. "Have you brought me trouble?"

"I'm sorry. I had no choice."

"No choice? In what?"

"I need people to help me against Lee. I'm willing to pay as high a price as need be."

Her jaw tightened. "I see. Sorcerers."

"What does that mean?"

"You are usually so high on your own power that you forget the other bastards in your way. You say things like 'necessary sacrifice' or 'needful losses', because you have to be the fucking hero." She rolled her eyes in exasperation. "Bloody sorcerers."

"You're leaping to conclusions," I said mildly.

Her eyes flashed. "It's how Bakker began," she said. "Things are *necessary*." I said nothing.

"You've got some way of beating Lee without getting my people killed?"

"Does he know you're here?" I gestured at the paint-encrusted walls. "I mean, down here, in the Exchange?"

"No. Perhaps. No."

"I imagine it's a secret you like to keep well."

"Very," she said. "Why?"

I looked down the long, splotched corridor. "Nuclear bunker?" I asked.

She nodded.

"That could come in handy."

The doors were painted green, were thick and made of iron, and clanked, with solid locks. The walls between each room were half a foot thick, the fire notices thirty years old, the ventilation system chugging and clogged with the thick dirt that drifts down eventually on all things in the city, turning even white marble foggy black. There were a lot of doors; they at least had been well maintained. There were miles of dipping and winding tunnel, slowly sloping upwards, their gradients almost imperceptible. Signs had been painted onto the occasional wall with an arrow pointing towards their destination – Chancery Lane – High Holborn – Lincoln's Inn – Aldwych. As we walked I could feel the rattling of the Piccadilly line in the walls beside us. Vera said, "There used to be other trains too."

"Which ones?"

"The Post Office ran trains between its depots. The government always had something being moved about down here. The markets – they'd bring meat to Smithfield in subterranean trucks. Some of the lines never went above ground. You can't say that about many trains in the city. But it's different now. People forget about the things underground."

I thought about the spirit I'd spoken with in Camden, guardian of the old railway line, and the empty magical circle that I'd intended for Khay. Perhaps, I thought, it might still have its use.

When I emerged, up a hooked ladder embedded in a concrete wall stained with flaking rust, it was to one side of Lincoln's Inn, in a shaft full of the roar of sucked-in wind and heavy machinery. For a moment I thought it might be daybreak; but the clock on Holborn tube station left no room for doubt. Time moved differently underground. It was a drizzling, overcast evening, with the thin London rain and thick London clouds that never quite do their stuff, but constantly threaten.

Vera left me there. She said she didn't like to be seen above ground, and didn't offer to shake my hand goodbye.

Oda was standing outside Holborn station, her bag of weaponry slung over her shoulder, mobile phone in her hand. The big stone-built blocks of Kingsway and the wide, blank slabs of High Holborn's offices met in a medley of traffic lights, bright corporate signs, and crowding pedestrians jostling for space while the bendy buses hogged the middle of the road.

"Well?" I said, blinking as my eyes adjusted to the grey, monochrome evening outside after the glaring bulbs and sinking shadows of underground.

"They cut off a couple of the biker's fingers," she replied briskly, folding the phone up and slipping it into her pocket.

"They *what*?"

"That's the last time you call me humourless," she said with a smile as welcoming as the open jaw of a shrieking bat. "Are the Whites going to help?"

"Yes."

"What exactly can they do?"

"They can stay exactly where they are," I replied with forced brightness. "And with any luck, that should be enough. Now, I need you to do me a favour."

"A favour?" The word sounded dirty in her mouth.

"Yes. I need you to call your pissy bastard friends and tell them to let Blackjack go."

"Why?"

I ticked the reasons off on my fingers, just like she'd ticked them off on hers. "One: it's *nice*. Two: you don't need to hold anyone hostage to get me fighting the Tower; that'll happen anyway. Three: we need the bikers as allies and Blackjack is the only man I know of who can conveniently find them, and perhaps get a message to the warlocks in Birmingham as well. Four: I've cursed the head of your Order – right now he'll think it's flu and soon he'll realise that it's not, and I'm not going to uncurse him until you people stop playing silly buggers – how does all that sound to you?"

She thought hard about it; then said, without any change in expression, "When we are away from this place and these people, I will kill you, sorcerer."

"That," I replied, "would be what the corporate consultants call 'unproductive'. Make the phone call – I'm sure we'll have plenty to talk about."

I was beginning to feel better.

*

I waited in a café on Kingsway, drinking overpriced coffee with some kind of foul-tasting syrup in it, while Oda paced in the street outside and talked and talked into her phone. By the looks of things, she was having one hell of an argument. When she'd been talking for half an hour, I tried as casually as possible to move further into the recesses of the shop, away from the windows, just in case she was serious about shooting me.

I wondered what form my curse on the head of the Order had taken while I was gone, how deeply it had burrowed into his flesh, how far the worm of blue maggot magic had feasted on the heat of his blood. He'd had our blood on his hands, by the time we'd finished our conversation – such proximity to our blood, we hoped, could only make the passage of our spell more deadly and swift.

When Oda eventually finished on the phone she stomped into the café, face glowing with anger, sat down on the sofa in the alcove opposite me, threw her bag down on the floor, reached into her jacket pocket and surreptitiously pulled out a gun. It lay under the table in her grasp, pointed vaguely at me – but in such a small space, accuracy of aim didn't matter. Though our heart skipped faster at the thought of it there, I struggled to keep my face calm, a smile half in place against impending disaster.

She said through gritted teeth, "What have you done?"

"Are you planning on using that?" I asked, nodding down at the thing under the table.

"I have orders to shoot you as soon as you've reversed your spell."

"Thank you for your honesty at least, but you're going to have trouble there."

"Why?"

"I'm not going to reverse it, and you're not making much of a case for me trying."

"What did you do to our leader?"

"He had our blood on his hands," we snapped. "You should have known that our blood is potent. Am I going to have a conversation with your boss or not?"

"I knew you couldn't be trusted."

"Of course you did. But the fact is, you kidnapped *me* and my friend, and did a lot of shouting and hitting in the mean time; and really I'm only" – I considered the choice of words – "evening up the balance sheet?"

For a moment she looked pained, small, almost childish, but then the mask was back on. "He'll talk to you by phone."

"He'll see me in bloody person," I said, "and without his damned armoured bodyguard, thanking you kindly."

"Impossible. You'll kill him."

"Oda" – I struggled to keep the anger out of my voice – "I have done nothing to harm you. I have told you the truth. You didn't need to try and hurt me to get my attention – I was willing to help. I still am."

She said nothing.

"Are you going to shoot me?" I asked, forcing a smile onto my face. "It's more of a test of faith, really, shooting someone and getting caught for it, rather than dying in a heroic bloodbath. If you die in the act, you become a martyr, you get nothing but glory or at the worst, unanswered questions – your motives remain entirely your own. If you get caught, alive, you'll have to take responsibility, explain why, answer all the world's questions and I bet, I just bet that the Order won't bother to bail you out when the police come asking, 'So, Oda, why are you armed to the teeth and why did you shoot that utterly harmless Mr Swift?' They'll call you insane and lock you up and you'll never have the glory or the thanks or the innocence that dying in the attempt might, in its own twisted way, have given you."

"Sorcerer?"

"Um?"

"I will kill you – maybe not now, maybe not in the eyes of men, but I promise, I will kill you."

"Good!" I said brightly. "Then I look forward to our meeting. I'm sure you can work something out."

I left her in the café. It was a risk, but it had to be done.

I thought about how I'd feel with Blackjack's blood on my hands. I hardly knew the man, had little reason to trust him, and nothing more between us than a common enemy. I wanted no responsibility for the man's welfare; but the obligation had been given to me anyway. If he died, it would be my fault.

And if he died, we knew with absolute certainty that we would not stop until we had destroyed the Order, washed away our guilt with their blood. Another enemy on the list, and one we were happy to oblige.

But I want . . .

. . . we feel . . .

come be me

and be free

but I

and we

but I AM

. . . and we be . . . we be . . .

I bit my lip until it bled, and until my thoughts were nothing but the grey wash of the early evening street, filling with the gently pattering rain.

We met in a place and at a time of my choosing: 10.30 a.m. at Stansted Airport. There were a lot of reasons; for a start, Stansted Airport is my least disliked of all the airports ringing London, not as packed and confusing as the heaving mass at Gatwick, or as clinically airless as Heathrow; not as isolated and battered as Luton, not as small as City, which sat in the middle of a disused wharf, surrounded by housing and old patches of neglected concrete, and didn't even have the good grace to be at the *end* of a railway line. I liked Stansted because its roof was high and clear, letting in white morning sunshine, because the train service left Liverpool Street on time, was fast, clean and, as express services went, relatively cheap; most of all I liked it because in every corner and on every wall, coffee shop booth and behind every door there was a CCTV camera, and because the police were everywhere, and always suspicious. Even outside the technical limits of the city, the air in the airport hummed with its own slick, fast, silvery-shimmered power.

We met by the security checkpoint leading to international soil, where the travellers of the day queued in bored, neat lines to have their baggage scanned and their passports swiped. He arrived alone – at least, he walked up to me alone, although there were plenty of suspects for an entourage – and we were shocked at how ill he looked already. Fat blue veins bulged on his hands and face, their colour visible even through the thick pigment of his skin; his eyes looked sunken, his hair more bedraggled. His expression was no longer one of triumph but cold, determined hate; his walk was uneven and when he raised his hands they trembled, the fingers convulsing in little bursts, like the nerves wanted to exercise themselves without permission from the brain. He walked up to me, stopped a metre away, looked me straight in the eye and said, "You have become a liability already, Mr Swift."

"So shoot me!" I said.

"Don't tempt fate."

"I wasn't tempting fate, I was asking you," I replied. "I'm sure that all these lovely gentlemen with the guns" – I gestured round the court at the security guards patting down the passengers as they passed through the endless rows of metal detectors – "would be only too happy to testify the case."

"You want the biker freed – we can do that."

"It's not just my personal pissed-off mood," I retorted. "I need Blackjack."

"Why?"

"To convince the rest of his gang to join the Whites; to stir up a few allies against Lee."

"The Whites – Oda told me of your plan."

"And I'm sure that when you're done with the Tower you'll be turning your attention to them," I sighed, "but right now, you need them, and you still bloody need me – more than ever, by the looks of things."

"You did this," he snarled, eyes flashing dully in the folds of his diseased skin.

"Yes. If you'd just talked to me politely, we could have avoided this entire situation."

"I am willing to die for my faith," he declared, edging a step closer. "What makes you think that this curse of yours will change my mind about you?"

"Nothing at all," I said. "You hate me and I hate you, end of story. But you need me, and I may just bloody well end up needing you and all your pig-stupid moronic cultist followers. So. I'll lift the curse when I know that Blackjack is free. And you'll still help me even though you don't have a hostage against me, because you still need me against Bakker. And I won't do anything against you because I still might need you to help against him. And when this whole thing is over we'll do a tally list of who hurt who the more. And if it doesn't come out even, we can fight it out till doomsday, what do you say?"

"What... *help*..." he spat the word, "do you need?"

"Men with weapons," I replied. "Everyone you have available, in the Kingsway Exchange by midnight tomorrow, ready to fight it out with Guy Lee."

"In the Exchange? Why there?"

"Because that's where Guy is going to attack."

"You're sure of this?"

"Not yet. But if you give me a few more hours, I will be."

"You're... luring him into a trap?" suggested the man weakly. "How? Why will he attack?"

"He'll be ordered to from above," I replied. "Do you really want the quibbling details, or will you just help me?"

"Undo what you've done," he said.

"Your word pretty please on a plate."

"I will help you in this."

"Your word pretty please on the Bible."

A flicker of anger around his eyes, just for a second; but then he raised one shaking hand and said in a clear, precise voice, "I swear before God. Until the Tower is defeated and Bakker is dead, if you do not harm mine, we will do nothing to harm yours. We will support and help each other against this... greater... evil. Before God I swear."

I grinned. "Good. I'm glad that one is sorted."

I spoke to Blackjack on the phone before I undid the curse, just to make sure. He sounded tired, but alive, and promised that he had all his fingers intact. I asked him to find allies. When he'd heard the details, eventually, he said yes, and hung up briskly without another sound.

In the men's bathroom, I put my hand on the priest's forehead and slowly, shivering as it wormed its unfamiliar presence back into my skin, drew the curse out of his flesh, the sliver of blue magic trickling across my fingers and melting back into my skin.

The man said, "Is that it?"

"Yes. You'll recover soon enough. Plenty of bedrest."

"I do not understand how you managed to cause me harm. You were defenceless."

"Prayer," I replied cheerfully, washing my hands clean in the basin. "Prayer and a soul soaked in positive karma." I glanced at him in the mirror, to find his expression not so much angry any more as curious. "And I am a sorcerer. Magic is just... a point of view. We don't know your name."

His eyes flashed up to mine, met them in the mirror; then he looked away. "Names give power."

"You know that I'm Matthew Swift. I'm assuming you're ex-directory – secret cultists tend to be – so you might as well tell me."

"Anton Chaigneau."

"French?"

"My mother was from the Congo. My father was from whatever Satanic pit spawns such creatures." He was rubbing his forehead where I'd pulled the curse out, head on one side, a look of discomfort in his eyes.

I said, watching him, forcing myself to sound disinterested, "You've come a long way."

"The Order is good to those who adhere to it," he insisted. "They are kind."

"You're not in charge?"

"I am a servant of the Order, I bring their will..."

"Who's in charge?"

He shook his head. "Is there anything else I can indulge you with, sorcerer?"

"Who did Oda's brother kill?"

His face became stone for a moment, then widened out again into a tight grimace. "She told you?"

"Yes."

"Did she tell you that her brother was a witch doctor?"

"She implied it."

"Did she tell you that when he first discovered his magic, he tried to help the family, heal others and use his craft for goodness? Did she tell you that the power of it tainted him, corrupted him, as such power always does, and that he swore he could only do the best by creating things of such evil as, I think, will never leave her dreams?"

"Again, it was implied."

He met my eyes and said, utterly flat, "He killed her two little sisters, and tried to kill her. He said it was a necessary sacrifice to summon creatures of knowledge, spirits. He said that nothing else would do but the blood of kin, and apologised and wept but said it was the *necessary* thing. Oda was fourteen at the time – her sisters were nine and eleven. She escaped, and didn't speak for three years after. Her brother was killed by the local police when he refused to surrender himself, but not before his arts had burnt Oda's family home, and everything she possessed, to the ground. The Order loves her. We will be a better family than any formed of kin. What do you do that's 'necessary', Mr Swift?"

"Necessary?" We tried the word a few times, rolling it around our tongue and lips. "We work with you, Mr Chaigneau. Only because it is necessary. I hope to be seeing your men armed and ready for battle by tomorrow night; in the mean time, I wish you a speedy and successful recovery. Good day to you, Mr Chaigneau."

I turned and walked away, and to my relief, no one tried to stop me. On the train, my hands were shaking. I had never played such games before; no degree of magical inclination can teach you the character skills necessary for cloak-and-dagger dealing; never before, however bad things had got, had I felt that my life was in danger. At least, not while I was technically alive, last time, and living it.

After lunch, I went back to University College Hospital.

Sinclair was still sleeping a sleep that was too close to death for our taste, and Charlie was still on the door.

"Did you visit her?" he asked, slipping into the room as I looked down at Sinclair's sickbed and listened to the puff of his machines.

"What?"

"Elizabeth Bakker. Did you visit her?"

"Yes." I wrenched my gaze from Sinclair and forced myself to meet Charlie's ever so slightly feral gaze. "I saw her."

"Did you kill Khay?"

"No."

"But... he is dead," said Charlie, in the strained voice of a clever man trying to work out something obvious.

"I didn't kill him ... I need to ask you a question."

"OK. What do you want to know?"

"Two things. First – I'm mustering allies in the old Kingsway Exchange. We're going to fight Guy Lee."

He laughed. "Perhaps Harris Simmons will invest in the coffin-making market today and make a huge profit tomorrow?"

"I mean it."

The humour faded from his face. "Lee has an army of paid and bought troops at his command. And those are just the ones whose breath still condenses in cold winter air."

"He can't get support from Amiltech."

"He doesn't need support from Amiltech!"

"I'm raising allies against him. I can't go it solo, not now. I was wondering if you had any friends who might be interested in joining?"

"Friends?" He didn't understand for a moment; then he let out a long breath and drew his shoulders back. "I see."

"This is our best chance to break Lee's monopoly on power in the underworld," I murmured, studying his face for any kind of reaction. "The Whites are willing to cooperate, the bikers, perhaps the beggars . . ."

"You want to see if any of my kind will help?"

"It'd be useful."

"Lee doesn't bother us. He *employs* us, most of my kin – most others simply spit at the thought of what we are, unclean."

"Employs to spy, to cheat, to steal, to kill . . ."

"We have to survive."

"This is what Sinclair would want," I said gently. "This is what he was trying to achieve. I'm just finishing the job."

His face tightened for a moment in uncertainty, then relaxed. He nodded slowly, fingers loose at his side.

"Second thing," I said. "You were the closest to Sinclair . . ."

"*Am* the closest to Sinclair," he insisted. "He's not dead."

"I apologise – are the closest to Sinclair. That gives you a certain something when it comes to this question."

"Well?"

"Of all those people Sinclair gathered together to fight against the Tower – the warlocks, bikers, fortune-tellers, religious nutters, mad old women and me – who do you think is most likely to have betrayed us to Bakker? Who do you think told them where to shoot the night Sinclair was hurt?"

His eyes went instinctively to the slumbering form of the big old man, then back; and they were hard and certain. "The woman. Oda."

"Why?"

"I know nothing really about her. Ignorance might mean there is something to hide."

"What if it's not Oda?"

"You know something?" he asked quickly.

"I know something more than I did," I replied. "Although it didn't make me happy to find out. Who would be next on the list?"

He thought about it long and hard. Then, "The biker. Blackjack."

His answer caught me by surprise, but I tried not to show it. "Why the biker?"

"His smell, when we were attacked."

"His *smell*?"

"Yes." Charlie's eyes flashed up to mine, daring me to disagree. I raised my hands and shook my head defensively. His mouth twitched in triumph.

"All right," I said. "What did he smell of?"

"Nothing."

"Nothing?"

"When the first bullets started hitting," said Charlie, "I could smell the fear on you, the sweat on the warlock, the terror on the fortune-teller, the blood on the hurt men, but on him – on the biker – there was nothing. His skin did not perspire."

"I see."

"You do not believe?" he demanded, fingers tightening.

"I believe you," I said hastily. "I just don't know what to make of it."

"Why do you ask now?"

"I'm getting allies together against Lee, just like Sinclair tried to get allies together against the Tower…"

He was nodding already. "You think one of them might betray you."

"It's possible."

"What will you do if they do?"

I thought about it, then smiled. "Absolutely nothing," I replied. "At least, for the moment. Nothing at all."

It took nearly thirty-six hours for the first emissaries to arrive. The bikers sent messages out to Birmingham, Manchester, Edinburgh, Glasgow, all the cities frightened of being next hit by the Tower. The Whites sent whispers through the tunnels of the city; the Order cleaned its guns, the beggars skulked and the skies turned. Among so many people, so much preparation, someone would, sooner or later, say something stupid. Sooner or later, Lee would hear of Sinclair's plans. That was just fine by me.

Necessary things.

They assembled at the My Old Dutch pancake house at suppertime, around a table booked for eight, although we weren't sure how many would arrive.

The My Old Dutch served massive plates covered with batter, covered in turn with almost anything imaginable. Chicken, ham, bacon, egg, cheese, tomato, salad, chocolate, coconut, cream, lemon, sugar, honey, syrup, treacle – ask, and it would be delivered. I sat with my back to the wall, head away from the window next to Vera and ordered the most sugary, exotic-sounding dish we could find. Vera ordered tap water and a Caesar salad, and flinched at the prices. She wasn't used to daylight; she especially wasn't used to being seen through glass.

Oda and Anton Chaigneau arrived together; slipping in behind them came their bodyguards in the guise of an amorous courting couple. Outside, a pair of badly disguised traffic wardens each tried to hide their gun under their bulky black jacket and reflective vest. Neither Oda nor Anton looked happy; but they both sat, and both ordered very dull, very vegetarian salads. His face didn't bulge as it had at Stansted airport, his hands didn't tremble; nonetheless he didn't grace me with so much as a nod of acknowledgement, but sat, when not eating, with his hands folded and his face immovable.

The small talk was not extensive. There were séances with livelier chatter. Oda glared suspiciously at Vera; Vera glared suspiciously at her. I ate pancakes.

"I don't like having armed men eat in the same place as me," Vera offered at last.

"I don't like your manner of dress, your soul, your duplicity or you," replied Chaigneau. "But that is besides the point."

Vera made an indignant snorting noise.

I said, through a particularly rich bite of coconut, cream and hot chocolate sauce, "What has our religious nut friend here upset is the two men at the back of the restaurant with the tattoos running across every inch of their skin and the rich purple glow of embedded power emanating from their flesh – although it is ironic that someone that insensitive actually noticed them. Are you going to be civil or do I have to bang heads together?"

Vera simply grunted and ordered more water.

I was settling into my second pancake when the two shapeshifters arrived. I could tell by a number of things what they were: by the emanation of slippery, unstable deep brown magic crawling off their skins like oil off a puddle of water, by the flash of yellow in their eyes when they turned their heads quickly round the restaurant, looking for the table, but most of all, by the old man's sandals they wore over their neatly socked feet, which, while being in appalling taste, left room for the shape of their toes to change. I waved at them, and they, sniffing cautiously, drifted over to our table.

"We're looking for Mr Swift," said one.

"And what do you do?" asked Vera. "Write fortunes on the back of cigarette packets?"

"We bite," replied the woman coldly. "Among other things."

"Have a pancake," I said, waving my fork in cheerless welcome. "I'm Matthew Swift. I'm guessing a nice young man with a pair of stylish whiskers called Charlie sent you?"

They sat down carefully, eyeing up the table. "There are . . . those who do not like . . . anything," said the woman at last, pretending to scan the menu as she spoke. "We're committing to nothing."

"Sure thing," I said with a shrug. "Welcome to the pack."

The last to come was the biker, and he certainly wasn't alone. He came with two others, one of whom could have been three men. When he turned sideways he just about managed to fit through the door, and when he sat down, the chair, creaking and moaning, just about managed to support his weight. It wasn't that he was fat – not in the traditional saggy-belly, drooping-chin sense of fat. He was pure and simple *big*: his thighs bulged in their black leather trousers, his shoulders strained the edges of his studded, extra-large black jacket, his chest threatened to burst through his black T-shirt, his beard ruptured off his face like curling smoke from a volcano, his hands were the size of the plate from which Vera ate her salad, his fingers were thick and raw, his every breath was like the rising and falling of a glassmaker's bellows, his expressions stretched from ear to ear and twitched over the end of his expansive Roman nose. I had never seen such a man – and more, there was a slippery power about him, more than just the bulk of his presence, a flash of orange and golden fire on the senses, visible out of the corner of the eye, impossible to pin down. He smelt of dirt and car oil and the road, and uncontrolled, risky power. He looked at us and said, "Fucking hell. Who hit you lot with a fucking haddock and hung you out to dry?"

Behind him, Blackjack said, "I don't think they're really looking for love."

"Hello, Dave," I murmured at Blackjack.

"Hello, sorcerer. Hello, bastard pig priest and your bitch consort slut of a minion," said Blackjack, nodding at Chaigneau and Oda. He sank himself onto a chair next to me with an expression of polite goodwill on his face. Then to me, "Hear you got into trouble."

"It's fine."

"Yeah? How fine?"

"Chocolate pancake with cream fine," I answered. "It's not going to be civil; but there are people here, aren't there?"

"Oh, it's going to be another massive fuck-up," murmured the third arrival. I looked again, and recognised him.

"Survived, then?" I asked.

The warlock was still dressed to the nines in what I could only politely call "ethnic dress", although by English standards he looked as ethnic as mushy peas. He grunted. "Got the old gang back together? A little talk, a little chat, a little sniper fire through the window at night?" he asked. He helped himself to a fingerful of hot chocolate sauce still in its pot, licking his digit clean with a loud slurping noise. "You know, I really hoped it was you who fucking got done at Sinclair's place."

"How did you survive?" asked Oda incredulously. Then, only a little quieter, "Why *you*?"

"Psycho-bitch," sneered the warlock, "there are gods watching over me older than the furry fucking mammoths."

"This is going to be hilarious," sighed Blackjack.

"Is this it?" asked Vera incredulously through a slurp of thick pink milkshake. "The best that Sinclair and Swift could muster – a bickering pack of badly dressed drones?"

"I'm a fucking warlock!" he retorted. "Master of mystic fucking arts!"

"*He's* a sorcerer," she replied, indicating me, "and I'm told that means he could like, totally pop your eyes out of your skull with a thought. Doesn't stop him looking like a starving pigeon, does it?"

"Thank you," I muttered, snatching the hot chocolate sauce away from the warlock's dabbling fingers. "I'm glad we're all getting on so well. Sit down, warlock, no one's going to get shot here."

"You sure of that?" he replied.

"This is a public space. Besides, too many people have brought far too many reinforcements. It'd be a bloodbath and if anyone here is planning on shooting us" – my gaze moved round the table – "they sure as hell wouldn't get out of it alive."

"There are always car bombs," said Chaigneau with a bright, white smile. "Guy Lee is renowned for his flexibility in these matters."

The big biker said, "You think you can park anything round here without it getting done? Traffic wardens would have it in thirty seconds. 'Sides, Guy Lee isn't going to kill us in the pancake house, because, talking straight, us being here is one big fucking joke. Are we going to do any introductions?"

"I'm Matthew," I replied.

"Halfburn," said the biker, neck bulging in what might have been a nod. "Although if we're going to be real friendly about this, you can call me Leslie."

"Leslie?"

He met my eyes full on, and his gaze was the colour of burnt tar on a night-time road. "Yeah," he said. "You got something to add?"

"No."

"Good. This is Blackjack," jerking his chin at Blackjack, "and the guy in the skirt," indicating the warlock, "goes by the online chatroom name of Mighty Magician 1572, and his real name's Martin."

"Hello, Martin," I said, nodding at the warlock, who grunted.

Halfburn grinned, leant forward so his saucepan-sized fists rested heavily on the table, looked round until he had every gaze fixed on his face, and said, "So – is there anything other than fucking pancakes to eat in this dive?"

There have been alliances before, within the magical community. Magicians and all their subspecies come in every shape and size, faith, creed, sex, colour and political inclining. This naturally leads to affiliations, groupings, clans of like-minded individuals with similar buttons to be pressed. Sometimes, even these pig-headed bickering clans can agree on a common cause. Back in the Dark Ages they agreed to fight a couple of faerie hordes, although myths and records for those times are blended. In the Renaissance, rumours leaked of epic battles with demon spawn crawling out from their caves, and alliances of alchemists in the cities swapping intelligence with the last hiding druids cowering in the countryside on where the necromancers were hunting for their dead. In the 1800s there were stories that one of the very earliest urban magicians, among the first to taste power in the machines and smoke and bricks of the city, rather than the older sources of magic, created an alliance of beggars and aristocrats, to further the study of this new wonder together. Stories also tell that the magician in question died impaled on the end of an enchanted rapier thrust through his chest by one of his erstwhile allies; but, again, records and myth tend to blur into each other.

The last alliance of its sort that I knew of came in 1973, when a sorcerer by the name of Terry Woods went out of control and started hurling his magic across the city streets with all the delicacy of an angry gorilla throwing coconuts at startled monkeys. It took the lives of seven wizards and a sorceress called Lucinda to stop him, and the alliance afterwards remained until the last of its members died in the late 1990s, again the victim of unpleasant circumstances. Become too involved in these kinds of battle, and sooner or later, circumstances will become unpleasant.

Our own alliance, made in the pancake house on High Holborn, was very simple, and in many ways carried on the traditions of the past. For a start, none of us liked each other. No one trusted anyone else either. But that was fine. I was perfectly happy to let them bicker; the more they argued, the more the chances were Guy Lee would hear of all that was happening. And with the subtlety of a hand grenade in an oil refinery, he would try and stop it. And that, like all good stories where fear is the theme, should be enough to make an alliance real.

Necessary things.

It helped that we didn't like them either.

At 7.30 p.m., I looked up from my examination of the bottom of my third milkshake and said over the bickering, "Have you heard of the shadow?"

Silence settled over the table.

"I call it Hunger," I explained. "It describes what it is: pure hunger, lust, without control or restraint. It resembles a man. His teeth are yellow, his eyes watery blue. His skin is the colour of wet tofu, and on his back he wears a coat stained with blood. My blood, but let's not split hairs on this. His hair is a thin straggle of nothing; when he leaps, the darkness bends with him. When he stalks you in the night, you can see nothing, touch nothing, but you will know he is coming for you by the bending of your shadows. He kills Bakker's enemies. His fingers are claws that tear through flesh and bone like they were parting a silk curtain. He runs his tongue over hands soaked in blood, smells the sweat on your skin as you die, looks into your eyes, so close that all you can taste is the rotten stench of his breath. He says, 'Give me life.' He is not Bakker. He destroys all that Bakker wishes destroyed, but would not kill Bakker's sister. Would burn her, send her mad, curse her for not giving Bakker the thing that he desired. Sorcerers are dead. Seers are dead. A prophet who saw his own end ran and could not run far enough. He is not Bakker. He is not human. How long until he comes for you?"

At 7.45 p.m., Vera proposed the final agreement, and all agreed.

She proposed a blood oath.

Some magics never change.

I was quietly opposed to it, but my position wasn't one where I could say so. Any show of dissent after so long arguing would destroy a day of work. So it was done.

The warlock, the bikers, the Order, the Whites, the weremen and I: over pancakes, milkshakes and beer we swore to help each other until we had destroyed the Tower; and because some things never change, I pulled my penknife from my bag, a napkin from the pile underneath the ketchup bottles, very carefully cut the top of my thumb, and swore on my blood.

So did everyone else, letting a few drops fall onto the napkin, where it spread into the whiteness and merged with everyone else's blood in a thickening scarlet stain. When we were done, I burnt the napkin in the flame from a cigarette lighter, spilling the ashes into the empty bottom of a coffee cup. Then, when no one was looking, I tipped the ashes of our blood oath, along with several cigarette stubs, into my jacket pocket, just to be on the safe side.

I did not go to the tunnels that night. Nor did Oda insist on following me when I started walking. Perhaps she'd been warned off, perhaps learnt tact; I didn't care which, so long as I could be alone.

We walked, without direction, through Covent Garden, feeding off the tingling sparks of magic in the air, feeling it dance across our skin like physical illumination. We wandered through Leicester Square, past Piccadilly Circus, stared up at the endless moving lights and sat on the steps of the statue of Eros, until we felt that any more saturation would make our skin start to glow. We wandered down to St James's Park, and through the palatial back streets near by: grand offices, old red-brick mansions, high-walled royal palaces, densely hidden mews and the occasional sly, cobbled lane. Shop windows selling bespoke leather spats and cigars. We watched the late-night tourists baiting the guards outside Buckingham Palace while the traffic roared around it, lingered in the maze of fumes and subways and lights and grand hotels of Victoria, wandered through the station and listened to the last trains of the evening chug away towards obscure destinations with improbable names – Tattenham Corner, St Martin's Heron, Epsom, Sutton, Carshalton Beeches.

When we were finally calm, our mind soothed by drifting down the silver flashing rails of the lines along with the dozing commuters and sleepy lights of the trains, and lulled by their regular rhythm, we left Victoria station, and wandered back onto the streets. Outside a domed Catholic cathedral that could have been transported from the streets of Rome, hiding in a plaza that burst out between the local launderette and a cobbler's shop, we found a telephone box.

I dialled the number from memory, and waited.

The number was disconnected.

I swore and tried some others. Two more were disconnected, and one was a XXX video store in Soho whose assistant introduced herself with a silky voice and the words, "Hey hon, looking for something special?"

In desperation, I tried one last number. The phone rang. A voice said, "You're through to KSP reception, how may I help you?"

"I'd like to speak to Robert Bakker."

"I'm sorry, we have no one of that name..."

"But you know where to find him. Please. It's very important."

"I'm sorry, but..."

"My name is Matthew Swift."

After a while, a voice said, "Please hold."

The phone started playing the remnants of Beethoven's 3rd Symphony on a xylophone. I endured the pain and waited.

Fifty pence later, a new, bored, woman's voice said, "Hi, you're through to reception, how may I help?"

My heart rattled at the speed of a train, my mind scuddered along endless silver tracks; but my voice, strengthened by all that buzzing life in one place, was steady. Just like he'd taught me. Forget you are afraid, he'd said. In a place like this, when you step out into the road you could be run down, when you turn a corner you could be knifed, when you come home you could die from a short circuit in the mains, or eat a curry poisoned with badly cooked cat meat and in somewhere this big, and this busy, you will never know what hit you. Forget you are afraid – there is too much worth living to just hide behind your own uncertainties.

I said, "Hi, I'd like to put in a call to Mr Robert Bakker."

"Mr Bakker is busy at the moment..."

"He'll want to talk to me; please, it's very important."

"May I ask who's calling?"

"My name is Matthew Swift. Please – tell him."

"If you will hold the line..."

"I'll hold."

I held for another 70p and almost half a movement of xylophone Beethoven. I began to understand the power of tinned telephone music – it gave me something else to get angry about, to marvel at, instead of letting my thoughts dwell on what I was doing.

The woman's voice came back. "Mr Swift?"

"Yes?"

"Mr Bakker would like to know if there's a number he can call you back on."

"Miss?" I answered in my sweetest, gentlest voice.

"Mr Swift?"

"I want you to call Mr Bakker back and tell him that, as well he knows, my body was never found and that this should tell him something about the urgency of my call. Please tell him those exact words."

"Uh, Mr Swift . . ."

"Please, miss," I said nicely. "If that doesn't get him to the phone, I'll go away; I promise."

"I'll be right back, Mr Swift."

Vivaldi was the next composer, murdered by someone on a harmonica. Thirty pence later the woman's voice was back.

"Mr Swift?"

"Still here."

"I'm transferring you now."

"Thank you."

A beep. A long silence. A sigh of distant breath. I found I couldn't speak. After ten trips of my shuddering heart he said, in that familiar, rich voice, "Matthew?"

"Mr Bakker, sir," I stumbled, tongue tangling over the automatic, familiar words, feeling like a fifteen-year-old boy again, about to be prescribed tranquillisers.

"Matthew! My God!" Nothing but surprise; no anger, fear, just marvelling wonder, tinged with an odd flavour of almost laughter – perhaps delight. "I heard you were . . . there was a funeral!"

"Yes. I wasn't."

"Clearly, clearly. My God. God. But where are you? I must see you at once!"

Panic was beginning to make my skin burn; whatever I'd been expecting, this was not it. "I don't think that would be a good idea," I said.

"Matthew! Are you all right?"

"Fine."

"I must see you! You must tell me everything – they said you were dead!"

"They were pretty much right."

"What's happened to you? My God . . ."

"I'm fine," I said. "I'm fine. I'm staying with some friends."

"Well you must come round, at once! We have to talk!"

"No, thank you."

"Why not?" Again, hurt, almost fatherly pain in his voice – whatever I had expected, it was not this, nothing like this, and for a moment, just a moment, I almost said yes. Then we shuddered in fear and turned our face away from the receiver. His voice came, tinny and small, through the phone in our hand. "Matthew? Are you there? Matthew!"

My teacher, Mr Bakker, who came and knocked on my mum's front door when I was just a kid, voice full of worry and concern.

Give me life, the shadow had said.

And if you gave him a tropical disease, starved him for a month, fed him on nothing but darkness and fear, then Hunger's face was Bakker's.

I could taste the blood in my mouth again.

"Make me a shadow on the wall," I said, leaning my head against the cold of the glass. "Mr Bakker? A shadow on the wall."

"What's happened? Tell me what's happened! Matthew . . ."

I slammed the phone down on the hook, turned, and ran from that place into the dark, spreading my mind into the wings of the pigeons and the claws of the rats and the honking of the cars and the spinning of the wheels and the drifting of the dust until I forgot that I was running and forgot from what it was I ran.

I did not notice myself sleep, and my dreams flowed like the river.

I woke huddled in a corner underneath Battersea Bridge, brought awake by the sniffing of a dog at the hem of my coat, out for its early-morning run with its well-exercised owner. I smelt of river mud and cement dust; and my legs, when I tried to stand, burned. I had no idea where I'd gone or what I'd seen or done. Although perhaps if we wished . . .

. . . we see . . .

. . . we were . . .

so free

Couldn't remember.

Didn't want to remember.

I picked up my few possessions and went to find a shower.

At midday, I found Oda sitting by herself on a bench overlooking the river, outside the white palatial mass of Somerset House, a strange building of stately, many-paned windows, massive stonework, pedimented roofs, and dignified statues surveying its spacious courtyards. It held within its walls a museum, a university, part of a tax office and more besides; a place as confused as the streets compressed around it.

"Where've you been?" she asked as I sat down.

"Went wandering."

"At a time like this?"

"Needed to sort out a few things." She grunted in reply. I glanced up at her, raising my eyebrows, and said, "Worried?"

"You've got us all together – for now – are you going to bail now?"

"I'm staying," I answered.

"And you've made an alliance, sworn on blood – well done. Congratulations. Happy for you. What next? Pitched battle with Guy Lee, blood in the streets and so on?"

"No."

"You've got a plan," she groaned. "Naturally."

"It'd be nice to just deal with Lee on his own."

"Not going to happen," she said sharply. "Not now San Khay is dead."

"There've been battles before; but they have to be done quietly."

"A quiet magical battle," she said with a scowl. "That must be interesting. What do you do – poke each other with your pointy hats?"

"We've already got the perfect location."

She stared at me, understanding. If anything, her expression of dismay deepened. "The Exchange?" she murmured.

"Yes."

"You're seriously going to try and get Guy Lee down there?"

"Yes."

"And what makes you think he'll be even halfway inclined to do what you want?"

"Because we're going to be betrayed. Someone's going to leave the back door open, knock out a few guards, turn off a few alarms and when we're not looking, poof, Lee is going to sneak right on in there and execute the perfect, self-contained massacre."

She was on her feet. "You are expecting the people in the tunnels to die?"

"I didn't say that," I replied. "I said I'm expecting us to be betrayed."

"Why?"

"Because we were at Sinclair's house. Because you know, like I do, that the Tower has contacts everywhere. Because no matter how powerful and important an alliance like this one might seem, it will also look like the number-one opportunity to wipe out the leaders of all those pockets of resistance that Lee has been fussing over for all these years. Someone's going to tell Lee where we are and what's going on. Might even be you."

"Me?" she echoed incredulously.

"Yes."

"You think that I would..."

"You've made your feelings towards me and mine very clear," I replied sharply, "I'm sure the idea of wiping us all out at a go doesn't entirely upset you."

"I don't just... it's not..." For a moment, just a moment, there was something in her eyes, a flicker across her face; but it passed, and the mask was there, harder than I'd ever seen it. She swept up her bag and stalked past me, without a sound, without a look. Just for a moment, I felt almost sorry for her.

I met Vera that afternoon outside the local library. She was smoking, with every sign of enjoying it; when I approached, she huffed a cloud in my direction and said, "Have a fag."

We coughed and recoiled from the stench, from the idea of it, of black tar drifting in our breath. I mumbled, "Thanks, no."

"Feeling pleased with yourself?"

"Should I?"

"Got an alliance, haven't you?"

"It wasn't too hard."

"It'll end in blood."

"I know."

"And you think it wasn't too hard? It hasn't even fucking begun."

I said, "Sinclair laid the groundwork. I'm just here for Lee, then for Bakker."

"And you knew the biker, and the warlock, and the Order, and at the end of the day . . ."

"Yes?"

". . . you were Bakker's apprentice."

"Is that it?"

"Yes."

"Does it matter?"

She sucked a long cloud of smoke into her mouth, then puffed it out between her teeth. "Yes," she said, rolling the cigarette between her fingers. "People want to see if the sorcerers can be redeemed. They're curious about you – an investment, you might say."

"Is *that* it?"

"Don't you want to be redeemed?" she asked quickly.

"I haven't done anything wrong to be redeemed."

"Yes, but what you are, your buddies who like to play with the artificial forces of nature; all horribly gone wrong with the Tower, hasn't it?"

"This is revenge," we snapped. "There's nothing more to it."

"Fine," she said, her voice too light. "Sure. Whatever. What was it you were wanting to chat about?"

"I'm looking for a traitor."

Her eyes flashed. "There's a traitor?"

"Almost certainly."

"The Order?"

"Perhaps."

"How do you know there's a traitor? Everyone swore on blood . . ."

"That's not the point," I replied. "Besides, a blood oath doesn't *stop* you breaking your vow, it simply makes life difficult once you have, and even spells like that can be broken. Redeemed, I think you'd say."

"Then who's the traitor?"

"I have no idea."

"You have no idea, yet you're certain that there's a traitor?"

"There's got to be!" I said brightly. "All those disparate groups of unlikely people working together, all those busy little people with the big ears who suddenly are ordered to go and hide in the tunnels and prepare for a battle – there's got to be someone in their numbers who will betray us. Sinclair *was* gunned down in his room, we *did* run into the night, the shadow *did* follow us. Ergo – traitor."

"This is something you've already considered." Not a question.

"Yes."

"You want... what? To go around trying to read minds? Shouldn't the good guys in any heroic battle desist from such tactics?"

"On the contrary," I said, "we need someone to betray us. We just need to make sure we know what they're saying when they do it. Need to make them come to us, need to make Guy Lee think it's important enough to make a stupid move. Take a risk. Come out into the open."

"And you look like a guy with a plan," she sighed. "Well, thanks shit."

"You know you have to fight Lee eventually. Why not now, when everyone is still – sort of – on your side?"

"You're a real bastard, sorcerer. You're going to let that many people die, to have your revenge?"

I hesitated, licked dry lips. "Necessary things," I replied at last. "If... there are greater evils than... there are... Bakker will... it will never stop, Vera? Do you understand that? It will never stop. We have to make it stop, and we have to do it now. If not like this... then how?"

She sucked in a long lungful of smoke, then blew it out between the thin jut of her lips into my face. I coughed, she smiled. "OK," she said at last. "So we're gonna be fucking betrayed. Whatever. Lee is going to know of us; he's going to try and stop us before we can stop him. I get it. You want him to do something stupid. The question is – how stupid do you think stupid can get?"

I shrugged, not really understanding the question.

Her smile widened to a grin, turned nasty. She said, "Matthew Swift – how would you like to meet Mr Guy Lee?"

Oddly enough, she meant it for real.

We went to a club in Soho. It was in a basement and smelt of hot breath compressed into a tiny space, and sweat, and spilt alcohol, and testosterone. The floor was sticky with dried beer splashed across its grey lino surface, the ceiling was low and made lower still by the revolving lights, and the shaking speakers pounding out drumbeats with the rhythm and resonance of a racing heart; and when we saw the dancing, we didn't know whether to crawl away and cry at the thought of such a hollow, graceless thing, or to stare for ever, hungry to learn. The scent of that place was burning wet heat on our tongue, the sound of it buzzing whispers in our mind, the desire and appetite of it so overwhelming that we didn't even have to try to hear it; but the feeling of it forced its way into our brain, demanding that we look and be amazed.

Vera looked completely at home. As she trailed through the crowd, myself in tow, men and the odd woman reached out for her and here she'd trail her fingers through there, and press her hips to the waist of some stranger, and even, when an especially tall man with hair spiky from gently melting gel grabbed her round the middle, kissed him, until he let her go and moved on to the next woman to walk across his path. We stared, enthralled, until I forced my eyes away and stared at the floor until my head ached, trying to paste its greyness across my thoughts to keep out the pounding assault on the senses.

We found a corner of black leather sofas underneath a dull red lamp. Vera bought cocktails, strange bluish things in tall elegant clear glasses that were the coldest things in that place. She sat down with her shoulder pressed right into ours and said, "Not your kind of place?"

We took a cautious sip, recoiling at first at the cocktail's bitter taste, then relaxing as it heated our throat all the way down to the belly with an oddly pleasant sensation of burning. "Different," I said. "Why are we here?"

"I want you to meet someone."

"Who?"

"Guy Lee."

We felt our stomach tighten. "Lee's here?"

"He will be this evening."

"This is . . . his place?"

"No, it's run by a man called McGrangham; he pays protection money to Lee, and Lee leaves him alone, except for when he occasionally sends some of his men here, to learn how things are done. But that's not the point. McGrangham also pays money to the Neon Court."

I nodded slowly, running my finger round the top of the wide cocktail glass. If the Tower made the mafia look polite, then the Neon Court made those members of the mafia locked away for ever gibbering at the back of the asylum look like fluffy teddy bears. It wasn't a case of punishment and reward; you crossed the Neon Court, you died, pure, quick, simple. The only redeeming feature of the place was that it had only a few very special interests, and never messed with you unless you were stupid enough to mess with it first. And like all the best mafia families, once you were in, you never, ever got out again.

"OK," I said, "I get it. Neutral territory. No one makes a move in this place without getting a knife in the back. Sure. Why's Lee here?"

"There's a pit."

"A pit?"

"I'm sure you've heard of them."

"Only by reputation and the occasional coroner's report," I declared, trying to contain our rising anger.

"Good," she said, unflustered. "There's a lot of things going down here," she added, waving casually around the room. "Trade, sport, knowledge, games – you know how it is. Lee sends his bully dogs here to learn how to fight. And Lee likes to fight."

"I don't see how this will help us."

"Know thine enemy. And . . ." She let out a long breath. "If you're gonna fuck with me and mine, sorcerer, I'm gonna fuck with you and yours."

"I guessed that much; I don't suppose you can go into specifics."

"You want Lee to come after us? You want it now?"

"Yes."

"Then how do you think he'll feel if he knows, *knows* that the Whites have allied themselves with Bakker's fucking apprentice?"

I took a slow, careful slurp of cocktail, smaller than I pretended. "It's dangerous," I said at last, "what you're trying to pull."

She grinned, stretched like a black leather cat. "Sure," she said. "It's the right place, the right time. I'm guessing Lee will know Matthew Swift is alive. I'm guessing he'll recognise you, tonight. And if he tells his boss – and he'll have to tell his boss – I'm guessing Bakker will order

Lee to do something a little bit stupid. How much does Bakker want you back, Mr Swift?"

I shrugged.

"Mr Swift?"

As casual as a fly creeping down the side of a cream-covered bowl.

"Vera, mostly properly elected White?" I replied, staring into the depths of my glass.

"Mr Swift, how long have your eyes been blue?"

I smiled. I felt old, tired, too big for my skin.

"Bakker will want you back, won't he, Matthew Swift?"

"Yes."

"He'll want Lee to find you. Bring you in. Alive?"

"Perhaps."

"He'll know you're working with us, he'll know it's a bad idea. But you don't argue with Robert Bakker and live. So let's remind Guy Lee of that. Let's show him how alive you are. Let's make him do something stupid."

"This doesn't seem like a world-beater of an idea," I said.

"Necessary things," she replied.

It was a pit. Very much according to the traditional definition of the word. It lay beneath the club, down deep spiralling stairs where the-*boomboomboom* of the disco music faded under the sound of the ventilation hum, behind thick metal doors and metal-faced doormen; and when you finally got down there, you stepped into a room plastered with enchantments. They were painted across the walls-in black swirls, ran across the floor with yellow road-marking thickness; the air was oppressive with them, so dense they almost crushed the gestures of incantation beneath them, made the casting of the-lightest spells tantamount to lifting a heavy weight, or to speaking underwater.

That was the observers' platform.

The pit itself lay beneath, with high black concrete walls and fierce uplighting, its floor also black, and covered with sawdust. We stood among the observers, hundreds strong, from everywhere and dressed in every way, men and women and wizards and people who had no sense of magic at all but could smell the hidden blood waiting to be spilt below. They roared and cheered and screamed with delight as a lurching demon, all bound up in chains, its skin formed from the slimy fat that congealed in the sewers, its eyes burning with blue paraffin flame, lashed and lunged at a group of three men dressed in all kinds of strange armour – shields welded from broken car doors, spears made from torn aerials sharpened to a point – who with every stab got a shriek of pleasure from the crowd, while the demon dripped bleach for blood from the tears in its warping, wobbling skin.

I knew such things existed.

Mankind has always loved its blood sports, and with magic there was an infinite variety of ways to draw fresh, exciting blood.

The smell and the sight of it nearly overwhelmed us. We struggled to control it, keep it out, shocked by the depravity, the sickness, the blackness pouring out of every wall, the bloodshot delight in the eyes of every viewer, the pain in the creatures as they suffered and died; life corrupted, twisted. It horrified us, that all these people seemed to wish to do with life was seek its end; it appalled us that any gift so great could be so easily disregarded, as if they had grown bored with ordinary living and needed to seek out this new thrill to make up for the mundanities of existence. And very quietly, on the edge of the screams and the shouts and the stench of rotting magic, was an excitement and a thrill that threatened to blanket out all sense and leave us howling like the rest.

"We can't stay here," we whispered.

"Why not?" asked Vera.

"It is... compelling," we said.

She looked at us for a long moment, then muttered, "Shit, sorcerer, you'd better not go bang. Come on."

She dragged me by the sleeve through the crowd, to where two men stood by a locked metal door, and moved to block her way. "McGrangham," she snapped. "I'm here to see McGrangham."

"He's busy."

"I want to place a really big bet; and he might want to think about doing the same."

McGrangham's office was soundproof and looked down on the pit. But it didn't block out the power of that place, and we pressed our head against the glass and trembled to keep it from filling our senses with its presence.

McGrangham himself was a short man with dark hair and a big moustache, who lolled behind a desk counting crumpled banknotes and wore a mildly amused expression. "You're telling me," he said in an accent full of rolling rs and thick, weighted vowels, "that johnno here," nodding at me, "is a fucking sorcerer?"

"Yes," said Vera.

"The man's a mess! Christ!"

"Guy Lee," she snapped. "Guy Lee comes here to see the fights. I want you to arrange an introduction, on neutral territory, underneath the Neon Court's eye. I don't want anything flash; just prod Mr Swift and Mr Lee in each other's direction. There will be payment for your time."

"I give money to Lee, girl," snapped McGrangham. "Why the hell would I deal with the Whites anyway?"

Vera could act the mostly properly elected head of the Whites when she wanted to; she exuded it from every pore, a dangerous, rich charisma that hinted, below the surface, at something more. "Things are going to change," she snapped. "Bakker is going to tell Lee to do something stupid. Lee is going to obey. He, and everything about him, will be destroyed. Now I know you get your protection from the Neon Court, but you still need customers. You still need goods, trades, deals, money. Lee is going to lose all these things, and the Whites are going to get them. You seriously want to fuck around with the next big thing?"

McGrangham stared long and hard at us. "I heard Matthew Swift was dead," he said at last.

"Imagine people's surprise," I growled.

"Lee's got a pit bull down there tonight. A girl who thinks that kinky is the same thing as confidence, and confidence is the same thing as strength. He's going to be watching her. She's going to do great things. He's not going to talk to any old corpse."

"So?" snapped Vera.

"If this guy is a fucking sorcerer" – a fat red finger stabbed in my direction – "there's one great way to get Lee's attention."

Two pairs of eyes turned to look at me. I said through gritted teeth, "I don't have time for this."

"Kinky, huh?" asked Vera.

"You wanna get Lee's attention? Wanna let him know oh-so-kindly that your whacked-out sorcerer isn't dead? Wanna make a profit on a game?" There was a sparkle in McGrangham's eye; he could smell money a mile off, was already thinking about a big, bright, treachery-filled future full of booze, blood and wealth. Eyeing us up, studying, thinking of the best way to make more profit from our flesh.

Vera's eyes had the same glow, for a different cause.

"OK," she said, "I'm listening."

"Take down Lee's pit dog," McGrangham proposed. "He'll be interested then. Hell – he might even have a conversation with you before he uses your skin for wallpaper."

I had to wait almost four hours for my turn – into the small hours of the morning – and the crowd at the edge of the pit simply grew bigger. We waited outside in the cold of the street, but now that we were sensitive to its presence, aware of what was going on beneath us, we could feel the fire of every roar and the shuddering of every hit rise up through our body like the rumble of a train beneath the tarmac.

I had never fought in a pit.

It was a thing for either the desperate, or the insane. Those with nothing to lose, or those who believed that they could never fall. A man who had fought and failed was thrown out of the front door, and told to make it to the end of the street before calling an ambulance. They didn't want the police to investigate. He made it halfway to the end, and collapsed in a puddle of blood, skin and bile. I dragged him to the end of the street by his armpits, and dialled 999 from the nearest call box, skulking in the shadows to watch as the paramedics came and went, glancing into the darkness of this Soho street with the weary faces of men who knew enough not to ask, had seen enough to no longer care to know.

Vera came to fetch me, when it was time.

The "kinky pit dog" of Lee's was a woman who called herself Inferno. You can't be Dave the biker, Bob the master of mystic arts. *X-Men* had seen to that. She was roared into the pit with a friendly clamour of familiarity, and posed, hands on hips, chin thrust out, wearing as scant a mixture of leather and hooked chain as I had ever seen, every part of her bulging and gleaming like it would at any second explode from the thin patches of clothing that held it in place. She was armed with a whip, wore purple contact lenses to disguise the colour of her eyes, and had dyed her hair pure black. There was nothing sensuous in her, I decided, nothing particularly sexy – the costume was intended to be something that a fantasy hero might have worn, but it just looked ridiculous and childish. I skulked by the door that Vera had pushed me through into the pit, ashamed and foolish at what had to be done.

Above the ring, to one side of McGrangham's office, was a window of reflective black glass.

I tried to imagine Guy Lee standing behind it. Wondered if he was leaning forward, watching my face, trying to see why I was so familiar.

I would remind him.

When the horn went for the battle to start, she slashed her whip a few times up and down through the air, just to make her point, and grinned with pure white teeth as the end of her rope wound and curled by itself, the end lifting off the ground and wriggling towards me like a snake, defying gravity and the laws of physics while it lashed across the empty air between us, searching for a way to bite. This part was a performance, we realised, designed to raise the crowd's blood as they saw the intricacies of her art. It was also, in terms of pure and simple combat magic, an immensely stupid thing to do, and in that instant our respect for her hit absolute bottom.

In the pit, the crushing weight of the spells that suppressed magic upstairs was less. We watched her snarl and hiss and her whip wriggle and worm its way through the air, straining to reach us, growing at its base as it writhed its way in our direction; and we considered the tools at our disposal. I didn't want to expose yet what I was capable of, nor did I feel particularly inclined to indulge the crowd with any sort of performance. So I waited, until, with a scream of attack, she hurled the tip of the whip towards me and it grew, convulsing through the air towards my throat. Patiently we watched it fly towards us, then stepped aside with the speed of the electricity in our blood and grabbed the end of it just before the tip, squeezing down on it like a zookeeper pressing down on the jaws of a snake. We shook it once, hard, sending a ripple flying back through the stretched-out rope that jerked the handle from her grasp.

Without her power sustaining it, the whip held in my hand became a lifeless thing of twine and leather. I let it drop to the floor. She spat and hissed like a feral animal and brought her hands together in the opening gestures of a spell I recognised, lips shaping traditional words of invocation. I wasn't sure how far I wanted the onlookers to realise my capabilities, so raised my hands and roughly mimicked her gestures, twisting my fingers in familiar, half-hearted forms of magical gesture, and moving my lips in a silent whisper. The sounds of magic came to me instinctively, slipping onto my tongue – not merely words, but the whisper of tyres through a thick puddle on a lonely street, the sound of wings beating in an empty sky, the snap of a door slamming in the dark – these were the new sounds of urban magic.

I dragged my hands through the air, feeling its particles thicken around my fingers as it congealed at my command. My ears popped, sensing the pressure decline around my head, and the wall of controlled air in my hands became thick enough to be almost visible. Moisture condensed around it as I exhaled, billowing out of its heart as I compressed more and more into that fistful of contained wind.

She finished her spell almost without me noticing and with a shriek sent it my way; the shriek became a roar in the air between us; the roar filled with the sounds of traffic – cars, wheels, exhaust, rattling engines, the smell of diesel, unleaded petrol, engine oil, tar, burnt rubber. For a moment, I saw, about to impact, the shadow of a hundred vehicles heading towards me, carrying with them the sounds of screeching brakes and the pressure of bending air, all of it thrown out of her throat. It was not the world's most dangerous spell, but it looked good and I did not want to cause myself any more harm than had already befallen me; so, in old-fashioned style, I threw myself out of its way. The crowd on the observers' platform upstairs roared its disappointment at such a mundane tactic, and started stamping, a regular growing *boom boom boom* like the heartbeat sound of the disco drum upstairs. I picked myself up and, by now thoroughly irritated, let my spell go.

The wall of rapidly decompressing pressure I threw at the woman called Inferno picked her up, threw her backwards three feet across the room, slammed her against the wall and, at the pinch of my finger and thumb, held her there, writhing and slapping her fists furiously against the black concrete, screaming amplified and deepened indignities through the thick wind that held her in place.

The booming of the audience continued. I waited. I was happy to wait, ten, twenty seconds, let those who were smart enough to see, or perhaps simply not-stupid enough to care, that this was something more than a cheap spell.

Let Lee watch my face, see the blueness in our eyes.

I waited, holding her trapped there in my spell for nearly twenty seconds until the horn finally went to end the combat, at which point I dropped her. Feeling oddly unclean with my victory, I went to sit down on the cold floor in my corner of the pit, hugging my knees to my chin, while Inferno, face inflamed an appropriate colour for her name, was dragged off screaming defiance to the walls.

We were surprised that we felt no sense of triumph, only a sick hollowness, as if our stomach was empty but had no sense of gnawing hunger to match.

The Master of Ceremonies announced in a bright, overly cheerful voice, "Ladies and gentlemen, five minutes please while we prepare for a new champion! Drinks are available upstairs and if any of *you* brave contestants want to try your hand..."

I tuned out the noise, huddled myself in my coat and tried to ignore the staring eyes and the sick swirls of expectation around me like tendrils of smog on a murky evening. Vera stood at one end of the observers' stands and, through the long, dark shadows that the uplights drew across her eyes, I saw not a glimmer of a smile.

"Oi, you!"

The voice came from a staff member in a T-shirt which bulged around muscles so highly exercised I was amazed there was any room left for bone. With an imperious gesture, he summoned me into the preparation room behind the pit.

Sitting on a rough wooden bench in that grey concrete room, wearing stylish black and drinking from a bottle of mineral water, was Guy Lee.

He looked me over and grunted. "Scrawny bastard, aren't you?"

I said nothing.

"You're Swift, yes?"

I nodded.

"What the fuck do you think you're playing at here, Swift?"

I put my head on one side and examined his face. He looked middle-aged, but that could simply have been the passage of many events, rather than much time. His nose was crooked and a long-healed scar ran across it; his skin was worn and dry and tanned, and he was clean-shaven. His hair hinted at grey peeking out at its roots, although through the defining clinginess of his black shirt and trousers he looked as well-built and hale as any man of twenty. He sat with his elbows on his knees, leaning forwards, like a boxer between bouts, and his fists were big and meaty, with signs of scarring across the back of his left hand, badly healed; his feet were set wide apart, legs tense like at any moment he might uncoil like a spring.

There was something very wrong with the entire picture.

We leant forward, peering, trying to work out what it was.

"You want to lose those fucking eyes?" asked Lee, glaring up at us. "I told Robert I'd have them for him on a plate."

We said, "There is . . . no magic about you."

"You just wait and see," he replied. "Just because I can't get you here, doesn't mean I won't have you out there," jerking his chin up towards the street. "You bastard – you think we weren't expecting you after you killed Khay?"

We murmured, "We think we understand."

Outside, a horn bellowed, three times, a summoning to the pit. Lee stood up, slapping his hands together briskly. "You know how many sorcerers I've killed?" he said.

"One," I answered. "Although you claim six."

He grinned, but there was unease in his defiance. I felt a moment of gratitude to Sinclair and his excellent files. "Looking to double it soon."

With that, he strode out into the pit to the roar of a sycophantic crowd.

I followed slowly, surprised. I didn't understand what he expected to achieve by this gesture, here, where the Neon Court was watching and the spells were thick on the walls. He couldn't kill me in McGrangham's, nor could I kill him while the wards were written up on the walls and the crowd looked on. Others would intervene, and this was, after all, neutral territory.

Perhaps it was the arrogance of someone who couldn't understand the possibility that they might lose.

I followed after him, and the crowd screamed and roared to see us beneath them with sick glee. I moved away to the other side of the pit, and watched him as he shook his fists at the ceiling and grinned and lapped up the applause of those people. They knew who he was; knew when to scream and clap.

I found myself wondering, with a genuine sense of scientific process, how I could go about killing Lee, although that was not, I realised, the exercise for the evening.

The horn blasted and Lee, without even pausing for the echo to die away, turned, opened his mouth and puffed in my direction. His breath rolled out in big, black, billowing clouds that stank of carbon and sulphur and filled the pit in a second with its polluted smog, blinding me. Automatically, I dropped to my knees and sent a random blast of force through the smoke, spinning it backwards towards what I hoped was its source in an eddying of black fumes. I didn't know if it did any good, but heard it smash into the wall on the other side of the pit a moment later and, in that instant, Lee emerged from the darkness, brought his hands together in two clenched fists, and pulled them apart. Where his fingers touched his wrists, he drew from them, pulling them out of the skin itself, although there was no blood, two long white daggers made of bone.

The crowd roared its appreciation as he flourished the blades. I could not tell whether they failed to recognise cheap necromancy when they saw it, or if they simply didn't care. He slashed the blades a few times through the air in smooth, careful movements; and where they moved, they trailed red sparks.

Slowly, grinning like an ape, he advanced towards me, bone-blades first.

I backed away, moving at the same speed as his walk to keep him apart from me, until my fingers brushed the concrete wall at my back. His grin widened. I shook my head in response at him, and pressed my fingers into the concrete. It bent like cold butter, slowly easing away under my pressure until my fingertips, buried in it up to the wrist, brushed the iron edge of a foundation support. I wrenched, sending chilling power down to my fingertips as I did, and with a heave and a shudder that made my arms ache and my head throb, dragged a length of twisted hard iron out of the wall itself. The concrete behind me melted back into its place like water filling a wound; I had no interest in keeping it as anything other than what it was, now that I was armed.

The audience screamed its applause as I tested the weight of my weapon, turning it a few times in the air and feeling it swish in my grasp. It was approximately two feet long – a very short staff by the tradition of any wizard.

Lee's confident face became, for a moment, something else entirely. With a roar, he threw himself at me.

I have little experience of fighting hand-to-hand. But we were fast, and the dance – the dance at least we were used to. We jumped onto our toes and leapt away from the first slash of his bone knife, feeling the twisting in the air as it passed by us, ducked our back beneath the high swipe of his second attack, spun to the side of his next onrush, and rolled past his stumbling feet and landed a kick on his shin as we did. The air burnt with our passage, we were on fire with the blood and stench and brightness and hunger of the place, we loved this dance! We realised almost for the first time that the weight of our my flesh and bone was not just a burden to be borne from sense to sense; it was a living tool. We could feel the movement of every muscle and nerve, the booming of every capillary under our skin and they obeyed, our body obeyed as we caught a slash on the end of our weapon and lashed the longer tip of the iron up until it clipped his elbow and knocked his arm back hard, and we were already away by the time he knew what had happened, marvelling as our arms went up and our feet went back and our head went down and our stomach went in all at once, everything corresponding to the dance, everything, for a moment, completely alive. And for a moment, we couldn't hear the shouting of the crowd, or their stamping feet, or the cat calls or the cheers or the screams or our own breath; for a moment, we were nothing more than the brilliance of that room, the minds of those people, the life dancing on the knife's edge, nothing but the dance, and the freedom of it.

Just like we were before . . .

. . . come be me and be free . . .

but I am . . .

And just for a moment, as we spun away beneath Guy Lee's blades, we were entirely ourself, and we burnt with blue fire across the air as we passed.

I do not know what happened in that place, that night. I am frightened by the things I cannot remember.

What I do recall was the sounding of the horn and hands pulling me back, someone shouting, "Enough, enough!"

And there was Lee, his bone daggers broken at his side, his arms slashed and bruised from the impact of my weapon's edge, his nose bleeding a slow, thick blood,

but no magic

and how silent the audience was.

Absolute stillness.

Just the settling of hot air like snow on stone.

I pulled myself free of the arms that held me and dropped my iron weapon. Its tip was bloody, and so were my hands.

but no life

The wards were blazing up the walls, lit up with Lee's blood. They crushed me like the great fat belly of a woolly bear, pushed my fingers to the earth, stopping this going any further.

It had already gone far enough.

blood on fire

and empty, utterly drained, I turned and walked away from that place.

Outside in the cold air, Vera took me by the arm and said, "And now we need to get you to safety."

"Why?"

"Lee is going to come after you now with everything he's got – nothing will stop him."

"What did I do to him?" I asked. "We just . . . I don't . . . I didn't . . ."

She looked up at me, surprised, and said, "You were on fire, Matthew Swift. Your skin was on fire."

I looked down at myself, half-expecting to see blistered and withered flesh, but my hands looked fine in the cold, pale neon light. "Will he attack the Exchange?" I stuttered as she pulled me down the narrow, sleeping road.

"After that, nothing short of a total annihilation of you and yours will serve," she replied grimly. "Honour – prestige – they matter. Forget Bakker, that's nothing now. Fear is just the perception of a threat, sorcerer, and I think you altered a few perceptions tonight."

"Did I . . . ?" I began, and then decided I didn't want to know.

"Come on," she muttered. "Time to get you home."

A thought struck me. I grabbed her by the shoulder, harder than I'd meant – she pulled back quickly, face opening in an expression of surprise. "Lee," I stuttered, "Lee is dead."

"Let's not get carried away . . ." she began.

"No, I mean . . . right now. Right now as we're talking. That wasn't Guy Lee down there. His flesh has no warmth, he gave off no scent of magic."

"Are you fucking kidding? He pulled bloody knives out of his wrists!"

"Life is magic," I insisted, shaking her by the shoulders. "*Life* is magic, there is no separating the two. Where there is life, there will be magic; the one generates the other. He has no magic. At least, not of his own – he leeches it from the air, feeds on its use by others, but he, *he* gives off no scent of it. Life is magic. He has no life. Guy Lee is a walking corpse."

She pulled herself free with a sharp wrench. "Bollocks," she muttered. "Bollocks!"

"We saw it!" we shouted, and she flinched back from us, fear in her face, clear now, easy to read. I felt ashamed. "I saw it," I said. "I'm sorry. Sorry. I . . . I'm sorry."

Slowly she relaxed, and patted me half-heartedly on the shoulder. "You're very screwed, sorcerer."

"I know."

"Yeah," she muttered. "But who can tell? Maybe it'll be in a good way."

We slept on the floor of the Kingsway Exchange, in a room packed with other sleeping forms, pressed in shoulder to shoulder, snoring and breathing and warming each other in the darkness, the light wavering through the empty, glassless window of the room, in the concrete corridor outside. I wondered what would have happened if there had been a nuclear war, and people had tried to live down in these tunnels, without time, colour and space. Vera said that all the Whites were coming in, that they'd been warned not to walk alone at night, that Lee would want his revenge.

And Bakker would want his apprentice back.

Guy Lee, a man of no magic. I ran scenarios through my head, twisted spells around, considered the powers that might have, could have, would have stopped Lee's heart but still sustained him. Or perhaps it wasn't Lee at all who I'd fought; perhaps something else inhabiting his flesh, mimicking life. He wasn't any sort of traditional, boring, hollow-eyed, pale-skinned zombie; his movements were fluid, his face healthy, his skin tanned. Not death in the traditional vampiric way; simply an absence of life, as if his body had been frozen at a single moment.

I couldn't sleep.

Shortly after dawn – I had expected it to still be night – I climbed out of the Kingsway tunnels, and went to find a phone box.

I called the Tower, and this time, when I asked for him, I was put straight through to Bakker. He didn't sound like he'd been asleep.

"Matthew? Are you all right?"

"Fine."

"I've been hearing rumours. If you want to talk..."

"Guy Lee isn't alive. He has no magic about him, no spark of life. He's cold."

"Matthew, I don't know what you've been doing..."

"Necromancy – the magic of the dead. I want to know... what you did to him."

"What *I* did to him?"

"You fear dying, Mr Bakker," I said to the voice in the phone, "you are so afraid. If his non-life, his frozen existence could offer you the solution to your problem, wouldn't you have taken it? I have racked my imagination, all the things you taught me, and I can't think of a single power, magician or enchanted tome which could do the things to Lee that I think must have been done – only you. You'd do it, I think, and not look back."

A sigh, tired and old, down the phone. I watched the sunlight thicken on the pavement and crawl over the tops of the grand old houses surrounding Lincoln's Inn. "He told me you attacked him, you went to a pit?"

"Yes."

"I thought I had taught you better."

I shrugged, then realised the absurdity of the gesture. "I will undo whatever it is you've done, Mr Bakker."

"Matthew?" His voice had a darker, lilting edge of polite, poison-edged enquiry.

"Mr Bakker?"

"Lee tells me that when you fought, you burnt blue. Your skin was on fire with flames the colour of your new eyes, and the rumour goes..."

"Yes?"

"...the rumour goes that the voices in the telephone stopped talking, when you came back, that the angels suddenly stopped singing their blue songs."

I said nothing.

"Matthew?"

Nothing.

"What have you done, Matthew?" he whispered. "What did you think you could do?"

"Mr Bakker?"

"Yes?"

"Did you bring us back?"

Now he was silent on the other end of the line. A breath, a slow exhalation transmitted in zeros and ones to our ears. "My God," he murmured.

"Did you bring us back?" we repeated.

"It's true!" Not a confession: surprise, horror, perhaps a hint of delight in his voice.

"Mr Bakker?" we said.

"Matthew Swift, what deal did you make? What did you think you could *do*?!"

"We are coming for you," we said. "We will not stop."

We slammed the phone down onto the hook, and walked until we were me again, breathing furious, angry, frightened breaths, and the dawn light was starting to bring some warmth to the streets of the city.

In the Kingsway Exchange, for the whole of a non-day and a non-night, they prepared. The Whites painted every wall, sprayed every inch of glass, every door and every frame with their winding images, and when there was no more space left in the tunnels, they climbed up onto the streets and drew their creatures and their words onto the walls of the university library, and the Starbucks, and the closed shutters of the newsagents, and the pillars of the stations.

Below ground, the delegation of a dozen or so warlocks moved from room to room and blessed them in the names of the spirits from whom they drew their special powers: Harrow, Lord of the Alleyways; the Seven Sisters, Ladies of the Boundaries; Ravenscourt, Master of Scuttling Creatures; and of course, our personal favourite spirit to invoke – Upney, Grey Lord of Tar. Theirs was a borrowed magic of other powers; high priests in the service of skulking city shadows.

The Order kept themselves to themselves, but the street kids under the Whites' protection, scampering from room to room with wide, marvelling eyes, whispered of enough weaponry to fight a war, and I believed them. I didn't like to ask what the shapeshifters did, and they didn't offer to tell. We all knew Lee would come. He would find us. Nothing would stop him now.

Blackjack found me, eventually, sitting with my back against an old, abandoned stack of telephone connectors, standing like an overgrown tombstone of dead wires and slots and metal frames and broken bulbs. Its presence comforted us, reminded us, in a strange small way, of our life before now, when we'd been on the other side of those wires, looking out.

He sat down next to me, considered his words, then said what I think he'd been intent on saying all along. "You look like a piece of rotting road kill."

"Thanks."

"Why the long face?"

"We don't like waiting. Sitting around waiting for them to attack; we want to be outside, looking, exploring."

"You're talking in plurals again."

"What?"

"'We'," he explained with an embarrassed expression.

"Sorry."

He leant back nonchalantly against the bank of forgotten equipment, its edges flecked with rust, and pulled a small whisky flask out of his pocket. He downed a slurp and offered it to me. I took it and we risked a cautious gulp of the stuff; an acquired taste, we decided, although it grew in charm as it sunk deeper into our stomach. "So," he said finally, in a strained voice that was leading to something more.

I waited.

"I got told I owe you for getting me away from the nutters with the guns."

"The . . ."

"The Order."

"Right. Yes."

"Nice stunt; how'd you pull it?"

"I cursed the leader of the Order – Chaigneau – with a long and withering death," I said. "He saw my point of view."

"Bastard's going to kill you, Matthew Swift," he said brightly. "Just in case you hadn't figured it out."

"I know."

"Although, if you need help when push comes to shove . . ."

"Thanks. I appreciate the offer."

He gave me a long, sideways glance. "That means 'no', doesn't it?"

"What?"

"You like working alone."

"I . . . have nothing here," I said, struggling to find the right words, caught off guard. "The people I trusted or thought I could trust either can't be, or are gone. Vanished, dead. Or those who may live I put at risk by my presence – people will get hurt around us. Given those circumstances, wouldn't you rather work alone?"

"Don't get me wrong; I get the whole lone rider vibe," he said, raising his hands in defence. "But I'm just saying: it'll put you in the scrapyard twenty years earlier than might've been."

"We think . . . that we are grateful for your concern," we stumbled. "Thank you."

"That's a fucking weird thing you've got going there," he grunted, turning away and half shaking his head, hand going towards the whisky flask again.

"What is?"

"For Christ's sake, Matthew, this is a fucking telephone exchange! Do you think no one noticed when suddenly *poof*, the voices in the wire went missing? Do you know how many nerds in basements were watching those rogue pieces of frequency, the bursts of inexplicable interference in the system? One second there's a semi-demonic power whispering out of the telephone to anyone with half the senses to hear it, and the next second it's just gone! And there you are, walking around with bright blue eyes and a bewildered crap expression and, you know, it doesn't take a million brain cells to work it out. That's what's so fucking weird, the way you can't work out if you're even bloody human any more."

I looked away, ashamed. We mumbled, "We . . . meant no harm."

"Jesus Christ," he muttered.

We looked up sharply, trying to read his voice, his words. His eyes were fixed on an opposite bank of dead machinery as, with shaky fingers, he unscrewed the top of his whisky flask. "We also have nothing here, except what I remember, and that's largely gone. We did not mean for any of this to happen; we hope you will understand."

"This is a new one," he groaned.

"What is?"

"Me talking to a bloody mystic power no less, disguised as a guy with a face like a soggy sandbag." Clumsily he touched his forehead with a couple of fingers and smiled. "Nice to meet you, blue bloody electric bloody angels. How you doing?"

We looked him straight in the eye and said, "Things have been better."

"I bet they bloody have." He waved the whisky flask at us again; we shook our head.

"Was that Matthew or the angels saying no?" he asked. "Just in case one of you's teetotal."

"We are the same," we said. "The distinction is merely one of presentation and form. To us . . . all things are new. Humans and the things they do. We were made by them . . . but had never *experienced* them before. As for me . . . I just want to get on with it. When we blaze, when we fight, when we rejoice, then I am all us, for that is all we are. When I am . . . afraid . . . we do not understand, do not like these things. We are me. It is . . . frightening, having to be me." I caught his expression, somewhere trapped between genuinely bemused and hopefully open. I shrugged. "And I'm not teetotal. Thank you. I'd just like to keep a clear head."

"Things are very weird," said Blackjack.

"There," we said, "we also agree."

We waited in those tunnels for another two days before it happened. By the time it did, I almost believed that it wasn't going to, that Lee had got his head screwed back on right, that Bakker wouldn't order it, that they wouldn't come. No one said it; but we had begun to think it even after the first night. It was hard to tell whether I felt disappointment or hope when Vera woke me up with a shake in the dark and murmured, "Come. Now."

I followed her through tunnels lined with sleeping bags below still-damp paint, stepping over the hunched forms of snoozing weremen, the curled-up shapes of slumbering warlocks and around the heavy black, weapon-laden bags of the Order, until we dropped down a narrow flight of grey concrete stairs, illuminated by a single light that sat in the wall like a squid clinging to the side of a sunken ship. The shadows here were almost thick enough to swirl like fog, and at the bottom, by a heavy, shut iron door, there lay a body, almost floating in a puddle of its own accumulated blood.

Holding up an electric lamp to see more clearly, Vera said in a hushed voice, "The door leads down to the Post Office tunnels. Trains used to go through there to the sorting offices. It's not marked on the map."

I said nothing and squatted down on the steps just above the body. Repulsed and fascinated, we reached out without thinking, even as our stomach turned, and carefully prodded the side of the broken man. His skin was still warm through the remnants of his clothes, and as we pushed his body over we saw that something had torn open his belly, dragged out a handful of intestines and wrapped them round the man's middle a few times, like a badly knitted belt. We tasted bile in our throat and felt a physical convulsion through our body as our heart skipped a beat, and stood up quickly, backing a few steps and suddenly not sure what to do with the blood on our fingers, running them over the wall to try and wipe it off.

"Is it Bakker?" hissed Vera. "Are they here? Is it Lee?"

"They're coming," I answered. "But it's not Bakker."

I snatched the lantern from out of her hands and held it close to myself, sweeping it from side to side in front of me; as the bright light moved around my feet, my shadow, stretching out behind me, did not move with it, but simply grew longer and thinner, like a rubber band being drawn towards breaking point. We felt a laugh grow in our throat, shrill and frightened, and I bit down hard to contain it, so the sound that came out was more like a whimper.

"What is it?" Vera could see how the light didn't bend the shadows at our feet, and was smart enough to be scared.

"Something much, much worse," I declared, handing the lantern back to her. "Wake everyone up. Don't let anyone go around in groups of less than five, or without a strong light. Tell them that Lee's coming."

To the best of my knowledge, this is what happened in the Kingsway Exchange; but in such chaos, even with the best of intentions, it is hard to tell.

Guy Lee had an army at his command. It wasn't a big army, nor was it well disciplined; but when the individual soldiers of the said army can blend their skin to the colour of concrete or burst bubbles of burning hydrogen in the pipes above your head or scream with the roar of the exploding fuel tank on the back of a bus in billows of black fumes, size doesn't matter. They'd been paid, bribed, threatened, blackmailed, cajoled, promised, and coaxed into working for Lee, and when the survivors were questioned they all whispered that somewhere, behind it all, they knew what Lee was. Not just a man with a will: a servant of the Tower. And those who disobeyed the Tower did not live to regret their mistake for more than a few days of blood loss and pain.

They entered the old, forgotten Post Office train tunnels at the Mount Pleasant sorting office, a truly unpleasant collection of tin roofs and grey walls that sat beside heavy fuming traffic at the junction of Rosebery Avenue and Farringdon Road. They slipped down through the darkness, their way lit up by the witches who coaxed the mould around the leaking pipes to fluoresce into vibrant light and guide the travellers on their way to the Exchange. They didn't know how Lee had known where to go. They said there was a traitor somewhere within the Whites. It could have been anyone.

The watchman on the Post Office tunnel was called Yixiao, a White from Brixton who specialised in inscribing his spells in towering green letters on the brick cuttings of railway lines, and in his youth had been part of a gang who labelled themselves **MORTON BOYZ** in big black letters across the wheelie bins of their local estates. That was before Yixiao had discovered, to his surprise, that the crows he drew in the daytime flapped their way across the white walls of-the tower blocks at night, squawking the words *"caw caw"* in squiggly small black letters from their beaks across the paint on the walls, before sunrise forced them to land again across the garage doors where they'd first been painted. In the tunnels behind the big iron doors that he guarded, he'd painted on the encrusted walls, their surface finely textured with layers of solid dirt built up over the years, the images of his coal-coloured crows, who patrolled up and down the corridor every night to see who might be coming in the dark, and shrieked with silent letters their warnings across the concrete walls, for Yixiao's hearing only.

Doubtless he had seen the advancing troops of Lee's army as they marched down the forgotten tunnels, and was doubtless on his way to sound the alarm when he'd met his untimely end, claws scratching at his eyes, tearing straight through his cheeks to reveal the teeth inside, ripping out his belly and playing with its contents like a child fascinated by a new toy – had I known that this would be how he'd die? Perhaps. One more thing about which it was best not to think.

However Yixiao had died, Vera had always speculated that they would come through the Post Office tunnels, and whatever she thought of my role in letting the man meet his end, she said nothing about it as she started to sound the alarm. The problem was that Guy Lee didn't just come up from the tunnels – he came in through the underground, from the ventilation shafts, and from the street, and all at once.

This, more than anything, is why I still do not, to this day, fully know the secrets of the dead of the Kingsway Telephone Exchange. Did some die that day who didn't need to? Did the Order aim every shot at enemies, or were a few friends caught in the fire? Did the were-men fight their own, did the Whites stand or run?

Sometimes, it is better for the historian to wait until their subjects really are dead and gone, just in case no one wants to hear the truth.

This, then, is what I saw.

I don't know where I was when I felt the first shudder of the first explosion. The concrete surfaces blended into each other, the endless colours and paintings just one long bad hallucination trip. The shock of the blasts sent shimmers of concrete dust down from the ceiling; it hummed through the exposed pipes and tangled wires that ran across the roof, with a high-pitched ringing note, like the striking of a distant church bell that lingered even after the thud through the air had faded. I knew where I was meant to be – finding Lee and dispatching him before he could hurt us – but as the corridors filled with running bodies and shapes and shouting people pushing and shoving and racing with eyes wild and a scent of the animal about them, I followed my own shadow, let it guide me as it twisted across the floor in front of my footsteps.

Just because you can use magic, that doesn't mean it's always the best tool for the job. Guy Lee understood this and had put explosive charges on the sealed-off metal doorways down to the tunnels beneath the street, blasting them in with a cacophony that set the car alarms wailing, along with the burglar alarms of all the lawyers' chambers and the local university buildings that were now howling into the dark. Then, just to make his point, he started pumping in tear gas through the ventilation shafts. I noticed it first as a puff of white drifting vapour trickling out from a crack in the ceiling, and an odd smell that couldn't be defined by the nose so much as the stomach, where it burnt its way to the centre of the body's mass, gripped its tight, sticky hot fingers around my middle, and twisted.

I dropped to my hands and knees instinctively as the vapour started to fill the corridor, and tried to find an appropriate spell, fingers scrabbling on the cold, dry floor for a handful of warm, solid magic to throw up around me, blasting the thicker plumes of white gas away. Before I could do so, a hand fell on my shoulder and another grabbed at the back of my head, pulling me up even as the first dribbles of bile started pouring down from my mouth and nose. Something hot, rubber and heavy was pulled down over my eyes and mouth, and then tightened at the back of my head, and a hand pushed me back against the painted wall as the clouds of impenetrable smoke billowed around us, gushing out of the ceiling like a waterfall on the edge of freezing. I blinked through the condensation-dripping lenses of the mask that had been pulled down over my nose and eyes and saw the dark eyes of Oda blink back at me through the black, nozzle-like thing over her own face. She was trying to speak, but the words were nothing more than a muffled *mmmwhhh* through the layers of plastic between us and the infected air. She was silenced by another series of short booms that I felt as much as heard, like the sensation of a lift suddenly stopping in mid-descent, all the parts of the air moving too quickly around us in different directions.

Oda hefted a rifle that looked like it hadn't been manufactured so much as carved out of some primal black void, and tugged at my sleeve. I shook my head and pulled away, trying to find my shadow on the floor through the smoke, and when I couldn't, I crawled over to a wall, holding up the lamp to see my own shape cast on the concrete. For a moment, just a moment, the shadow that I cast, thick and black against the close brightness of the lantern, looked up, looked straight *at* me, flexed its fingers into a clawlike spread, and opened its wings.

The lights went out in the tunnels, spitting into nothing on the ceiling and on the walls by the doors. My shadow was suddenly gone, melted into a rising backdrop of blackness, and only my lantern was alight in that place. Oda looked at me and despite the mask, her face, her entire body language, was an open question. I looked around but saw nothing but stretching, rectangular, contained blackness in either direction, until at one end I also saw the movement of torchlight struggling to break through the billows of gas and smoke, and heard distant muffled bangs and tasted the scent of magic. In that darkness we did not want to chase our shadow, regardless of what it might be up to; not yet. So we pulled at Oda's sleeve and ran towards that light.

The torchlight splitting the gloom of the corridor belonged to the bikers; and it wasn't torchlight, but firelight, oily orange, dripping off the ends of flaming rags that each one twirled at arm's length. For all their fire, spitting red droplets onto the floor, the ignited rags didn't seem to be getting any shorter as the bikers swung them into darkened and empty rooms of endless stained paint and broken machines, which looked more and more like electronic tombs as we hurried through the dark. The bikers all wore helmets – some painted with white angels, or a skull and crossbones, or a spider stretched out in all its furry detail, or a dart heading towards a bullseye, or other such symbols of identification – and all wore goggles and had a scarf over their nose and mouth; implausibly, this seemed protection enough for them as they moved slowly, confidently, through the tunnels. They swung crowbars, lengths of chain, even the odd spanner at the end of their leather-covered arms.

They didn't run, but their walk was . . . odd. A subtle shifting of perspective, perhaps, a magic so fleeting and hard to define that all we could say of its nature was that in one step we were by a white door with the words "Storage B08" written on it, and two steps later we were at the end of the corridor and looking back to see at least thirty steps behind, the door that only a moment ago we'd glanced at. Chicken or egg – what moved us more? Us walking, or the world moving beneath us? Perhaps the bikers, at least, knew the answer.

We found a small hall that I imagined had once been used as a canteen by the telecom workers; and there we also found the mercenaries. At first, we didn't recognise them for what they were, and the whole crowd of us stood uncertainly in the doorway, staring at these men dressed in gas masks and black, wondering if they were part of the Order or not. In that moment of uncertainty, it was they who recognised us as adversaries – and they threw themselves at us with alarming speed. I guessed they were mercenaries by the markings on their skin – in many ways like San Khay's, swirls of power and magic embedded in their flesh. But unlike San Khay, this wasn't just a tattoo – the mercenaries had carved their magic into their skin with knives, and each of them wore precisely the same symbols of strength across their flesh as their brothers.

The fight in that hall was a confusion of shadows and black-clad bodies caught in the unsteady light of flames. I saw the bikers slash through the air with their crowbars, and as they did, the gashed air poured out fire from where it was torn. I saw the mercenaries leave the surface of the floor and dance a few paces across the ceiling before dropping, nails-first, towards the eyes of their nearest enemies; I saw bikers hurl their lengths of chain, which ignited with the colour of boiling oil, flying and coiling like living things and following the enemy through every twist and dive like a writhing Chinese dragon. When the bikers screamed, their voices were the roar of an engine firing; when they spun, the air whipped around them like they moved at eighty miles an hour; and when their blood dripped onto the floor – perhaps it was the light – it had the look of engine oil.

Watching the mêlée, I moved my fingers through the air in search of subtler powers that might let me help my allies and harm my enemies, without doing both to each in that confined space. Oda, however, had little patience to see what we might do, and stepped briskly past us, dropping her rifle and pulling instead, from a sheath across her back, a sword.

The likely effect of a sword in that place was ugly, especially when wielded by a faceless figure in a gas mask. When Oda stepped into that fight, she moved the blade like it was a ribbon in her hand; and slowly the horror dawned on us, the realisation, that for Oda as she stepped neatly round each flailing figure and ducked each tattooed swipe from a mercenary's knife, she was dancing, and as with all good dances, she was enjoying it: each swish of the blade through another person's flesh, and every turn of her foot to meet some oncoming attack, and every flicker of shadow, and every movement of her arms – she relished it.

And for a distracted moment, we watched her, horrified, delighted. Then a voice whispered in our ear out of the darkness, *"Hello, Matthew's fire."* We spun round, unleashing a fistful of crackling electricity from the wires overhead into the space where the words had come from; but there was nothing there except shadows moving across the wall. I saw one dance away towards the end of the corridor; it wasn't moving right; its shape was too defined for all that darkness. I grabbed two fistfuls of electricity from the ceiling and ran, racing after it down the corridor, snatching the lamp in one burning blue hand and holding it up to light my way. At the end of the corridor I reached a set of heavy, shut iron doors. I hesitated, then put down my lamp, let the electricity out of my fingers, and pressed my ear to the door. The metal felt oddly warm to the touch, and through it, very faintly I could hear the *clink clink clink* of machinery, and feel the hum of a growing electric current.

Realisation hit; I was halfway up the corridor and throwing myself face first towards the concrete floor, hands over my head, willing the concrete to open up beneath me and encase me in its hold, feeling it warp obediently to the shape of my body as I fell, when the vaultlike doorway exploded. My ears probably popped, it was hard to tell behind the overwhelming punch dealt straight to the eardrum by the force of that bang. I felt the tips of my hair curl up in indignity at the heat that rushed over them, the pressure and force of it racing across my back, raising hot bloody blisters through my clothes, which smoked on the edge of flame.

I didn't bother to see who was coming through the hole behind me, but staggered up, crawled a few paces towards the opening of the corridor, then pulled myself round the corner and slumped against the wall while waiting for the static to fade from my eyes. I heard shouting behind me and tasted sickly bright magic, smelt the stench of the sewers, right at the back of my throat; and instantly had a name for the people coming up that corridor. And didn't want to think about it.

Deep Night Downers. A clan not unlike the Whites – a collection of like-minded magically inclined individuals – a conglomeration of magicians who understood that the city you saw in daylight, and on the surface, was only a lie, an illusion sustained by all the things going on underneath, and at night – the lorries delivering food to the shops between 1 a.m. and 5 a.m., and the men cleaning the congealed fat from the sewers, painting lines onto the roads when all the traffic had stopped, changing the bulbs in the street lamps, checking the rails in the underground, fixing the water pipes when no one was awake to want something to drink, and listening for the wires under the streets – the Downers understood that all these things had to happen for the city to survive, and they drew their power from it, a slick, invisible, pulsing presence of magic, that was almost imperceptible by daylight and became most powerful at 3 a.m., flooding the streets with its subtle, silvery glow.

Sitting raggedly round the corner from where they were slowly advancing up the corridor, I reached a dusty hand towards the ceiling. I let my thoughts tangle up in the mess of wires and piping running through it until I felt I had a good strong grip, then wrenched the whole lot down and spun it across the corridor until it formed a spider's-web-like mesh of metal and sparking electric wire across the tunnel between them and me. It wouldn't hold them for long, I knew; but I didn't feel the need to stay there for long – at this time of night, and in this place, I didn't want to take on Downers single-handedly, when their magic was strongest and they felt that the city, the *true* city of necessary pulsing daily functions, was most alive.

I moved to get up, and run away, but before I could move, something cold splatted onto the top of my head, like the first drop of a rainstorm. I looked up. On the ceiling, someone had painted a spaceship racing towards a series of bright blue and green ringed planets – something that might have been appropriate in a 1960s comic book; and underneath, in large stylish letters, the caption: *"CAPTAIN ZOG SAVES THE DAY!!!"* As art went, I could see its merit, in a retro way; but now, watching them, I saw something a good deal better as, silently, the big blue and green planets started to revolve across the ceiling.

On the wall opposite me, a figure of huge, bulging muscles, heaving chest and impossibly small waist, picked out in thick blue paint with yellow shiny buckles, stirred. Its fingers flexed. On the wall next to me, a tiger drawn in neon pink and lime-green stripes twitched its bright purple whiskers, its red eyes narrowing. Above it, a flock of jet-black doves flew up onto the ceiling and down the other side on the wall, before doing a complete circle, rippling across the surface of the floor. A single bright blue eye set on a bed of trolley wheels blinked at me with an eyelid of sparkling scarlet paint, then rolled from side to side on its gently turning wheels. A pair of cyclists made entirely out of human ears started peddling with their tiny ear-feet, cruising across the bottom of the opposite wall, and then up onto the ceiling, and doing a quick orbit of a rotating blue planet before descending again.

I stood up slowly, as footsteps in the corridor behind me grew louder; the roar of a chainsaw suggested that the Downers had come equipped for the obstructions I had thrown up in their way. But we were unconcerned, and our face split into a slow grin as, his arms dripping blue paint, Captain Zog stretched across the length of the wall, and reached *out*. First came yellow-gloved fingers, then a cautious yellow toe, then a bright blue kneecap – tiny and knobbly, far too small to support the bulk of his frame – then the blue hulk of his chest. His face came last of all, stretching behind him as a few residuals of paint clung to the wall, before peeling away from the rest of his dripping form with a few colourful pops. Next to me, the ruby-red nose of the tiger protruded from the wall, then a hint of pink neon stripe; a spider the size of my hand, bright emerald green and completely smooth except for where black brushstrokes picked out a hint of fur, scuttled across my leg, leaving pinprick stains of bright green points across my trousers. On the ceiling, a pointed spaceship sprayed a fine grey paint from its exhaust vent, that settled in a mist on the floor; the craft spun out of the wall and back, then twisted once more into the air and accelerated away again, amid silence except for the *dripdrip dripdrip* of paint falling in its wake.

I jumped as the tiger brushed affectionately against my legs, leaving a long streak of muddled pink across my trousers. Its feet made a flat *splash, splash* sound on the concrete, as it padded towards the corridor from which I'd just come running. Then Captain Zog and all the tiny scurrying creatures of the walls – painted butterflies with the mandibles of soldier ants, children with faces longer than the bodies that carried them, and tubby black and yellow bees walking on two legs and carrying carving knives with every limb, with three black fingers to support each dribbling blade – all the monsters of the Exchange marched in silence apart from the running of wet paint, straight towards the corridor where the Downers were. As they went, they flowed in and out of the wall and each other, and, where their features were human enough to read, every face wore a single intent.

"Hello, Matthew's fire!"

I spun round, but saw nothing in the glow of my lantern but dancing darkness and running colours. I half-closed my eyes, and listened.

A brush of cold across my shoulder . . .

. . . smell of sewage

ripple of magic in my ear

taste of salt
bile
blood
silk
. . . hello Matthew's fire . . .
. . . we be . . .
fire
light
life
fire
stop
we be
enough
so brightly burning
make me
be free
STOP
. . .
Thank you.
Better.
"Hello, little sorcerer."

I lashed out at the whisper of cold in my ear and, for a second, my hand closed around something like fabric-woven ice, a bite of frost that went straight to the bone, then up the wrist, a slither of silk under my skin, malleable, bending to the touch. I opened my eyes as it slipped from my fingers, and saw a tendril of darkness vanishing into the wall and rippling away, and for a moment, just a moment, I thought that perhaps, I could beat him after all.

I picked up my lantern and ran between the heaving masses of living paint, closing my ears to the Downers behind me as the first screams began, before they were choked off by a mouthful of paint.

Dark tunnels lose meaning after a while; I had had no idea how many there were in the Exchange – it takes being lost to give you a true sense of proportion. I didn't care where I was going, and it was only instinct that made me obey when I heard, through the darkness, a voice shout, "Swift, get down!"

I threw myself flat on basic principle, since the voice hadn't sounded too threatening, merely urgent, and saw a burst of fire at the end of the corridor, and felt the mechanical snaps of bullets biting overhead, striking something that made a dull thumping noise on each impact. When the firing stopped, I looked up and behind me, to see the body of a woman, dressed in very little indeed, torn apart by the impact of the bullets. I recognised her; when she went out in those clothes, her name had been Inferno. I tasted bile.

Hands pulled me behind a short line of men armed with rifles. With them was Chaigneau; he held a short, heavy mace, inscribed with scratched words in Latin that in the gloom I couldn't decipher. He glared at me and said, "What are you doing here, sorcerer?"

I staggered away from him, dragging my lantern with me, and ran on into the dark.

"What do you think you're playing at?" his voice echoed behind me.

Gunshots in the dark.

A taste of magic blooming and dying all around me, we felt...we smelt...sickly black spots of pain bursting behind our eyeballs, we felt...trickles of red agony down the back of our spine and I knew, even if we were too afraid to acknowledge it, that this was what a sorcerer felt near to too much death.

We came to a corridor of bodies. Warlocks and witches and wizards, their flesh burnt half away to reveal carbonised bone, the walls scorched black, all the paint long since bubbled away by the force of magical fire, wires and pipes shattered from the ceiling, and, when we risked pulling off the gas mask to sniff the air, the smell of roast skin.

We put the gas mask back on, the smell of rubber better than the stench of all that, and the limited vision afforded by its goggles a blessing, rather than a disadvantage. We put one foot between the bent arm of a woman whose face had been burnt away to a hollow shell, and the scorched body of a man whose eyes were, mercifully, turned away from us as we advanced. At the end of the corridor the shadows crawled across the wall, roiling despite the steadiness of our lamp. We made it almost halfway down before we spotted a robe of exotic, tasteless colours and knew who was wearing it, and knew that he was dead. We had nothing we could call affection for the warlock, but stopped and pressed our head against the wall and trembled and felt our flesh burn for many minutes before the realisation came that all this fear and sickness made no difference. We had to keep walking regardless, turning our head away from the sight of the bodies and trying to make the exercise a mechanical one, flinching nonetheless when our toe prodded the remnants of some dead magician.

At the end of that corridor was a metal door, rusted crispy brown. The bolt had been twisted out of shape, by what power I didn't know, and the thing stood ajar, inviting. Like an idiot, I nudged it further open, and ducking under the low top, stepped down the cold staircase beyond it.

The room I came into was too big for me to see anything but its nearest edges, the ceiling lost in darkness, and the walls stretching out in long perspectives. The floor full of telephone servers. They stood like the dead black trunks of some haunted forest, gleaming with the occasional hint of circuit-board green and solder silver when they caught the lamplight, stretching on in neat rows as far as I could see. I picked my way carefully down the nearest aisle, not daring to call any more light than I already had, for fear of who else might be looking. My footsteps were flat, dull and impossibly loud in that still room; the air was heavy, like it hadn't been disturbed for years; as I moved, puffs of white dust swirled up beneath my feet.

It took me almost five minutes of padding through that empty, dead place, between the straight lines of the telephone servers, before I found another set of footprints. They had been made by a pair of man's shoes, business wear rather than trainers. I turned and followed the line of their walking, feeling like a counter in a game of snakes and ladders, who might at any moment step on a snake and find myself back where I'd started. The tracks were, however, fairly easy to follow. They led between the endless rows of servers to a junction resembling any other, except that here there was another bubble of light, just like the one I carried. It lit up a hunched shadow dressed in black, wearing a pair of large man's business shoes, hunched over what I realised were my own footprints.

The figure looked up as my pool of light merged with his own from where I stood some metres away. His face twitched into an expression of surprise, followed by curving contempt. "Sorcerer," said Lee. "I thought you'd wind up down here. Prophetic powers couldn't have done a better job."

"Bugger prophetic powers," I replied, putting the lantern down and scanning the thick, still darkness around us. "You and I both know, I think, what's got me down here. Tall guy, wears my coat, bad complexion, essence of living darkness – seen him anywhere?"

"And here I was thinking you and I were about to enter the history books," he said, straightening up, and brushing dust off his knees. "But all along, you aren't really interested in me, are you? I don't think you give a damn about the things I've done, or that Khay did, or even about the Whites and the warlocks and all the other cretins I've killed to get here. You're far too busy to care. Am I right?"

"No, but nice try," I said.

He shrugged. "Do you know what the difference is between a soldier and a murderer, Mr Swift?"

"I haven't given it much thought."

"Intent. Whatever I do, I always intend. It keeps me in control. I have an anger, a beast... but control. You cannot imagine. But you – did you even think about all those bodies lying in your way? I think you kill and don't even have the knowledge of what you're doing, or why. Useless fucking moron."

"You know, you're right."

"Of course."

"No, not about everything – but you're right that I'm not here for you. You are just a dot on my way to something more important. A door that has to be opened, a minor tick on the list before getting to the major, and the fact that you're a murderer, a rapist, a thief, a coward and a corpse only makes it easier to do what I was always intending all along. So let's get this whole thing over with so that Hunger can come and take his fill."

"Get what over?" Lee grinned, and gestured expansively. "Robert wants you alive, Mr Swift, and alive is what I intend to give him."

A shadow in the darkness behind him. I reached instinctively out for that warm tingle of magic on my fingers. Then a shadow to my left, and my right and, when I dared to glance backwards, a shadow behind me, faces, figures emerging from the gloom. Guy Lee opened up his hands, whose cupped hollow started filling with a thick black smog;

and he was grinning, utterly unafraid, as men and women emerged around us from the gloom. As they stepped into the pool of light, I saw the flash of a brightly coloured robe and the remains of the warlock's face, empty, devoid of life.

I turned to Lee as the dead of the corridor I'd come down from, their bodies still dripping the last of their blood from their open wounds, filed into a circle around me. "Zombies," we said, with open scorn in our voice. "How 1960s."

"Not zombies. Zombies are too crude. These are . . ." Lee searched for the right word ". . . uniquely empowered."

My gaze swerved back to the eyes of the warlock. They were not entirely empty, not quite; and his mouth, as it hung open, showed a piece of paper, the white just showing behind his teeth. Life, fuelled by words, shoved down his throat as he died; a spell in paper somewhere inside his chest, rumbling around the remains of his stomach.

"We won't hesitate to kill them twice," we said as the last of the bodies from the corridor stepped into the circle closing around us.

"Hard to kill dead things," said Lee.

"You should know," we answered, full of immediate purpose. "We set them free."

And we reached out, grabbed a fistful of heat from the lantern on the floor, cupped it in the palms of our hands, and blew a tiny piece of life into them. The heat bloomed into blue flames between our fingers, rolled out across our hands and arms, billowed around us like a cloak as, with a wrench and a shove, we sent it spilling out between the dead monolith servers. It rolled across the floor and up the walls in a flash of bright blue fire that for a second illuminated the whole stretching expansive dome of the place, burning away every shadow and inch of skin that it touched, boiling the solder in its frames to bubbling, spitting silver bubbles and sweet smoke, blinding out every inch of darkness

except for

just a moment

caught in the flames . . .

I saw him, fingers outstretched to catch the surge of blue fire, chin tilted up and eyes wide as if trying to breathe my flames, face open and in an expression of absolute delight as the blue light seared around him.

Just for a moment, with the shadows that hid him burnt back and away, I saw Hunger through the fire.

Then it went out.

Darkness all around.

I was on the floor, eyes running. I couldn't see through Oda's gas mask, the inside was steamed up and the outside cracked with heat. I tugged it off and instantly smelt the solder smoke and dead flesh, but no tear gas, not this far down. There was no sign of Lee. I scrambled on all fours across the floor until I found the warlock, lying on his back, blood now soaked through every inch of his clothes. I yanked his twitching jaw open while an arm hanging on by a thread of tendon tried to lift itself up and gouge at my eyes, I dug through the dry hollow of his mouth past his snapping teeth until I found the tip of the piece of paper and carefully, so as not to tear it, pulled it out through his open jaw. The black words written on it in spidery ink were almost illegible with saliva and blood. I saw:

live for
black burnt
fire command
be free

I tore the paper into pieces and threw them away before looking down at the warlock who lay, entirely still, face empty, life utterly gone.

We felt movement behind us, and turned instinctively, snatching a fistful of light up through the air and hurling it at the shape of Guy Lee as he dropped down from on top of a server frame. He staggered back for a moment, throwing his hands up to cover his eyes as the whiteness flared off my fingers; but still he kept coming towards me. A foot staggering forward connected with our side, and we fell back, moving with the pain to try and avoid it, sprawling across the bloody remnants of the warlock. Then Lee's hands were on the back of our head, pulling it up, an arm going round across our throat and squeezing with an almighty strength that we could only hope was unnatural. There was no breath from his mouth although it was an inch from our ear. With a shudder of horror we realised that he was going to break our neck before we suffocated, even though waves of static darkness were already flashing up and down in front of our vision like the confused black curtain of the final act.

His voice hissed without bothering to exhale, the sound little more than a whisper from the dead air already in his throat. "Robert wants you alive, he says. Bring Swift to me; don't hurt him more than you must, keep him alive. But you know and I know" – a tug across our neck sent numbness through our limbs – "that of all the people in the world who Robert hates more than any other, he hates you, Matthew Swift, sorcerer, apprentice who betrayed his master. Even if Robert doesn't know it himself. So what I have to ask is – why does Robert want you alive? What is it in your blue flames and unlikely resurrection that makes him so excited, seems to give him so much life, just in *thinking* of it? Because whatever it is, I want it for *me*. It can set me free!"

We tightened our fingers around his arm where he held us, and brought blue burning to our skin, then pushed it down towards his flesh in a wave of searing heat until we could feel the bursting of his skin through his sleeve – even so he didn't scream, but dug his teeth into the back of my neck hard enough to draw blood and pulled his arm harder across my throat. I whimpered, but we reached up behind ourself until our fingers touched his head and tilted his face up until our fingers brushed his teeth, pushing his jaw open and reaching down inside his mouth. He bit and I felt blood spill across my knuckles but we kept digging, ignoring the pain even as my world grew faint until, at the very back of his throat, past his teeth and the ridged palate of his mouth, into the soft tissues of the windpipe, our fingers touched a slim piece of paper, and pulled.

Now he screamed, and in that act gave us space to tighten our grip inside his mouth and pull the paper, and keep pulling, falling forward even as his grip relaxed, tumbling head over heel but keeping hold of that paper, and it kept coming, rolled up in a tight tube, half a metre of it, a metre unravelling in my hands, with words illegible from blood and spit on both sides in tiny, tiny lines running from edge to edge; a metre and a half of bloody, stained inky paper that I pulled up from the back of his throat. It flopped around me like wet bandaging, rotten in places, stained with what chemicals I didn't want to know; and as the end came out of Guy Lee's mouth, he collapsed backwards, face empty, colour gone, eyes lifeless, and twitched no more.

I fell onto my back next to him, letting the endless sprawl of paper fall at my side. There, without further ado, it hissed at the edges, blackened, curled and crumbled to ash. I lay and wheezed while we brushed our hands unconsciously against our side, trying to rub off the spit and blood and ink and feel of his teeth on our skin, and the touch on us of the paper and its black magic. I was too numb even to cry.

I knew now what Sinclair hadn't known: that Guy Lee was animated by a metre and a half of crabbed written commands made up of ink and paper. He had been kept alive by magic alone, unable to feel, whether emotion or touch, unless it was so inscribed on the paper in his chest. Not quite a zombie; perhaps just... uniquely empowered. Empowered enough to crave life and wonder what was in our blood that could give it.

There was a dull slapping noise in the darkness. After a while I realised it was clapping. I sat up, taking my time about dangerous things like breathing, and looked into the darkness. A darker patch of shadow stood just outside the circle of lamplight, white hands visible only because they moved, beating out a regular applause.

I staggered up and retreated closer to the lantern, keeping my eyes fixed on that shadow. The clapping stopped. A voice said, "Was that Matthew, or Matthew's fire, that cried? I really couldn't tell."

"Didn't cry," I rejoined. "You wouldn't understand."

The swirl of darkness drifted nearer, acquired a face, withered and white and pale and smiling and indescribably, sickly, *his*. "Well," he said, "perhaps it's all the same now."

He knelt down by the body of Guy Lee, and scooped up a handful of black papery ash. Smiling at me, watching my reaction, he ate it. Then scooped up another handful, and another, and another, until the ash of the paper was just a thin black stain on the floor, and ate them all down. He stood up with a sigh and a shudder and tilted his head upwards, as if sniffing the air.

"The taste of life... is this it?" he asked, licking black flakes off his lips with a grey tongue.

"No," I said.

"I've tried water, food, fire, blood, flesh, skin, hair, bone, organ, breath – I've tasted them all. I was wondering where he hid his life; it was something hard to fathom, or perceive," prodding Lee with a toe, "but now I've tasted it, it seems... unsatisfying. A drop of water on my thirst, a corner filled in my stomach, but my appetite still... desiring. Still hungry."

"I don't think you'd like me," I said. "My diet is unhealthy."

"It's not your blood I desire," whispered Hunger, moving closer to me, sticking a cautious toe into the light. He drew it back quickly, like a swimmer testing water, surprised to find it so cold. "Just your fire."

"Can I offer a theory?"

The figure of Hunger gestured dismissively.

"I'm going to suggest that Robert James Bakker sent you here."

"'Sent'? Do you think you can apply your little ideas to me?"

"Perhaps 'sent' was a mistake," I conceded, rubbing my burning throat. "Maybe . . . influenced your desire to come here. You do desire, don't you? Deep down you want more than you can ever say. You don't know entirely what it is you want, but you want it now. Perhaps it's not just your inclination for blood and ash that's got you here; maybe it's his?"

For a moment, Hunger almost looked confused. Then he shook his head. "No," he whispered. "A human can't . . . a creature of blood and skin and senses . . . wouldn't understand."

"We do."

A grin of sharp grey teeth. "Yes," he whispered. "But you aren't human any more. Is that why you couldn't cry, little sorcerer? Won't you burn out your lovely blue eyes?"

"I'm a little confused," I said, crawling back onto my feet and straightening my back to face him.

"Shall I be the one to give you enlightenment, or do you simply not want to understand?"

"We understand," we said, opening our fingers at our side, stretching them out to catch the feeling of that place, one last time, pulling in the blue fire ready to burn. "But it doesn't mean we have to feel sorry for you."

He opened his fingers, a second before we could – he'd seen the attack coming and he loved it, opened his mouth and breathed in the magic around us, sucked it down like air. He raised his arms, and all the darkness moved up with him, stretching arms across the ceiling, drawing out the length of his form behind him in a wing of blackness; and from his fingers came nothing but dark, was nothing but dark, a living burning fire of it rushing forth and popping out the light of the lantern, swimming towards me in a tide that sucked the colour from the servers, the light from the wires, the heat from the frames, and left nothing but dry grey frost in its wake.

We saw all this and, for a moment, it made perfect sense to us, and we didn't need a sorcerer's tricks to match this darkness, just the fire inside that made us bright.

We opened our fingers, and let it blaze. The blue fire burst across our flesh and rippled up our arms, rolled over our face and set our hair blazing, we breathed in and it rushed up through our nose and down our throat, filling our lungs and stomach and passing across them into the blood, setting the arteries under our skin exploding with bright blueness, filling the blood vessels in our eyes with its flame until all we saw was the blue of it; we let the fire run through our clothes and spread out from our fingers and it didn't burn, that wasn't what was needed; it simply blazed. We put all our strength, our anger, our fears, our senses into it and pushed the flames out of us in a blue rippling wall of power that slammed into the tide of darkness, like two glaciers made of silk charging into each other, a silent swish of force that nearly sent us off our feet, and for a moment

just a moment

Hunger was afraid.

Then the fire started to burn. There was no controlling it, not once it was locked into opposition with that wall of moving shadows. It started at the edges, where it rippled against the encroaching tide of blackness, solder starting to smoke and boil, plastic beginning to drip and melt, frames glowing an eerie purple as the redness of the metal was lost somewhere behind the blueness of our perceptions. We could feel the rising heat start to run across our skin and the pain of it start up in our blood, but we kept burning

my blood

because to stop was to let that darkness suffocate us, tear us in two, and in its own strange way the burning was beautiful

my blood burning

and we didn't mind the pain because it was sense, a pounding demand for attention, a physical awareness that was interesting as much in its intensity as its symptoms – what was it about the rising redness of our skin and the smoking of our clothes and the bleeding of our ears that caused this thing we thought of as pain, *what about this sense was not in itself amazing* my blood on fire my skin burning *my* pain and I want…

in itself beautiful?

For a moment

just a moment

I forgot that I was Matthew Swift. And I looked up through my blue eyes and saw the creature that I called Hunger, and recognised in it a power not entirely unlike myself, and I was nothing more than a creature of the wires. We were me, and I was the blue electric angel, and nothing more, and nothing less.

Through the walls of competing power, I met Hunger's pale, drained eyes, and saw him blink.

The spells broke – his and ours, they snapped almost simultaneously. The tide of darkness rolled back in on itself then broke forward, slamming into the wall of fire we had raised against its progress and in that instant neither of us could control the scale of magic that we'd thrown against each other, nothing could keep it controlled or in that place. The shock of the two spells meeting, tearing, breaking loose, picked us up off our feet and threw us backwards; it illuminated the entire room, every distant wall, and its endless cobweb of trailing dead cable, with a flash of light so blue and so bright that when we closed our eyes all we could see on the back of our eyelids was the dazzling glare of a clean winter sky. The combined, uncontrolled magic ripped through the body of Guy Lee and burnt it down to dust in a second, tore apart every inch of the reanimated paper servants he had summoned down from the stairway, and sent cracks splintering through the roof above. It smashed through every dead, dark server tower, splintering the circuitry and twisting every joint of every frame so that they fell like crooked dominos, tangling in each other in a mess of concrete dust, broken metal and twisted plastic, blocking out every path around on every side and filling the place with the toppling trunks of corkscrewed dead machines. In the streets above, the LSE university shuddered, glass cracking in every old window frame, dust trickling down from the bricks. Car alarms started to wail, the leaves trembled in the trees, the roads, some said, seemed to shudder under their own weight.

Then nothing.

We fell somewhere in the dark as it settled quietly back over that place. We curled in around the pain throughout our whole body, shook with it, screamed with it until I...

...because it was my pain...

forced control, crawled, with dust filling my nose and throat, blood wetting my lips, a relentless pulsing at the end of every nerve, forced myself to lie flat on my back in the nearest patch of open space. I breathed through the pain as it rolled over my system, while we contorted our mouth and tried to shout or scream or cry through the worst of it; any sound or sight or sense to distract us from the fear and the horror of it. I tried to think about it medically, assess the whirling of my vision and sickness in my stomach, patted the back of my head and felt blood, ran my hands down my side and felt an uneven lump around my ribs, twitched my legs and felt an ankle twisted at the wrong angle, not a pretty picture, I imagined; and managed to get a laugh through our overwhelming desire to scream. That was good, it was a start, better.

We heard a gentle *click, click, click* in the darkness. Blinded with all the lights gone, I tried to crawl away from it, while a shower of mortar dust filtered down from the ceiling and something creaked in the darkness. I got a few yards before I found my way blocked by some twisted metal remnants, scorching hot, and turned, tried to find enough strength to summon a little light – a flash within my fingers, burning bright neon, but gone too fast – to see my imminent demise, before it occurred to me, despite our terror, that in the dark, Hunger made no sound as he walked.

A single match flared in the darkness. It illuminated rounded shadows and grainy textures, then the end of a cigarette, before it went out. The shadow behind that tiny red glow squatted down next to me and said gruffly, "Cigarette?"

I shook my head.

"Now," said the beard behind the glow, "I want to offer a few thoughts for you to consider right now."

I said nothing.

"You see, I figure, here you are – kinda looking like a watermelon after a nasty accident, thinking, 'Shit, I've just blown up half of the Kingsway Exchange in an uncontrolled magical explosion that really I should have stopped before it went mental; and I wonder if the primal force of darkness and shadow that I keep on forgetting to mention to people is going to come back?' And I figure that this is the prime opportunity for me to impart a few pearls of wisdom that I, in my extensive travels, have gleaned about life."

He drew a long puff from his cigarette, then blew it sideways and away. "Now, being Beggar King," he said, "I see things. People don't see me, in fact they go out of their way not to see, quite deliberately avert their eyes, but I see things. I know that when you were a kid, getting older, you'd give a few pennies to the kids on the street and I liked that, I respect that, you know? Sure, nine out of ten might be pushing drugs and you might have just bought that one last fix they need, but that every tenth penny you give – hell, it might just keep someone alive. Now, a callous person would say, 'Don't be so dramatic, they're not going to die, and besides, you're just supporting a useless burden on society, encouraging them, not helping, and, hell, you're only in it for your own ego.' But as I look at it, you can die a whole number of ways that don't involve your skin. Death of the soul. Death of the spirit. Death of youth – sure, it's kinda tied into the death of the flesh, but I reason, you waste away before your time, still alive, still ticking over, but you might as well be bed-bound for all the strength you have left in your bones, and there's no way twenty pence in a coffee cup will buy you that bed for the night. Getting old before your time with none of the perks of age.

"As for the ego thing – no point thinking you're good and fluffy inside if you don't keep up the habit on occasion. You seriously gonna tell me you're a compassionate bastard and not meet the beggar's eyes and feel sorrow? But I figure, hell! You're a good sorcerer, you understand this whole cycle of life crap, you get the fact that when you die, it's just one set of thoughts snuffing out and that somewhere else there's six and a half billion other buggers whose minds will tick along just as bright, just as clear, just as loud, just as alive, because that's what sorcery is, right? That's why you put the pennies in the cup, because when you're dead and gone and your thoughts are silent and you are nothing but shadow on the wall, someone will think of you who you forgot, and their thoughts will be richer for it. Am I right?"

I didn't answer, didn't move, didn't know if I could do either.

"Then there's this whole vendetta thing you've got going. Now, that seems strange to me." Another long, thoughtful puff. "You'd let people die so you can kill Lee. Granted, the guy is already dead, if you'll excuse the pun – sometimes I astound myself at my own bad taste – but you're willing to let others die just so you can pin him down so you can pin down Bakker so you can pin down this shadow and for what? The greater good? There's a lot of shit done for the greater good, sorcerer. When the lady with the swish coat and the expensive shoes doesn't give the beggar a pound on the street, it's because she's giving ten to a charity and sure, that's the greater good. Sure, of course it is. It's giving more, probably to be used better. But it isn't compassion. To look away from someone in pain because you know that your e-account is paying monthly contributions to the 'greater good'; to walk on by while all those people suffer and die because you've got a cause and a *big* sense of perspective... says something about the soul. Compassion. And that" – he flicked the end of the cigarette at me in the dark – "is the first thing that died in Robert James Bakker."

He drew another breath, tossed the butt away, ground his heel into it and sighed. "I guess you'll want a few reassurances. I don't pretend to be the good guy, that whole moral crap is for someone with a bigger beard; but this is basic survival instinct stuff, yeah? You've rattled your shadowy friend. That's what you're hoping to hear, isn't it? Now, the thing I find myself wanting to know is what your lady friend will ask when she comes to rescue you any minute now" – a glimmer of light somewhere in the shadow, the sound of footsteps on metal, and not from his hard-heeled boots. The Beggar King's teeth flashed white in the dark, although I couldn't see where the light came from that reflected on them. "Like, are the blue electric angels any better than the shadow? What'd you think?"

He leant down so his ear was a few inches from my mouth. "Go on," he said brightly. "Just between you and me, seriously, tell me why your lady friend shouldn't kill you like all those other faceless people who are dead upstairs. Go on. Give me a clue."

I thought about it, felt the hot, smelly breath of the Beggar King on my face. "Because..." I said, then realised what I'd been about to say was stupid, and tried again. "Because... because we *are* me." I saw reflected in his eyes a dull glow, moving through the dark, and heard the sound of falling debris somewhere in the distance. "And I won't forget," I said.

The Beggar King straightened up and grinned. "Good!" he said. "Well, fair dos, good luck to you, enjoy, don't be a stranger and all that so on and so forth; glad, all things considered, that it was you, not Lee who made it through after all – unhygienic, all that paper, a mess – be seeing you!"

He started to retreat into the darkness. I called out as best I could, which wasn't good at all, "What if I don't want this?"

"Want what?" his voice drifted back through the darkness.

"To be . . . me."

A laugh, fading as he did. "Then you're kinda stuffed, sorcerer!"

The *click, click, click* of his heels faded into nothing. A new sound replaced them, a scrabbling of fingers over broken machines, and a voice, rising up in the dark.

"Sorcerer! Swift!"

I recognised it, and tried to call out. "Oda!"

She heard me eventually, and the gentle bubble of dull torchlight swept over my feet, then found the rest of me, a spot of brightness scrambling unevenly out of the dark. Oda slipped clumsily down the side of a fallen bank of servers to where I lay. Her clothes were stained with dust and blood, but by the relative ease of the way she moved, very little of that blood could have been hers. She knelt by me and ran the torchlight in a businesslike manner over the length of me. Clearly I didn't make a good impression. Professional fingers felt around the back of my head and turned my face this way and that, digging into me in search of injuries with a strength almost as bad as the injuries themselves, whatever they were.

"What happened to you?" she asked.

I coughed dust in answer.

"Head hurt?"

I nodded.

"How many fingers am I holding up?"

"Three."

"Know what day it is?"

I thought about it. "No," I said, surprised to find it was the case. "Not really."

"Can you walk?"

"Perhaps."

"Any demonic magic you've got useful right now?"

I laughed through the dryness of my throat, and regretted it as the movement of my lungs sent pain racing all the way to my elbows. "Nothing," I whispered. "Nothing."

She hesitated, her face draining of all feeling, becoming suddenly cold. She looked suddenly stiff by my side, eyes fixed on mine, mouth hard. Fear wriggled into my belly and started doing the cancan all across my stomach wall. She didn't move, didn't speak.

I croaked, "You still..." The words became tangled behind my trembling tongue. "You still – need me."

No answer; her hands didn't move, her face didn't change.

"Not yet," I whispered. "Please. Not yet."

Her eyes darkened, then a half-smile flitted across her face. "Maybe not," she answered. "A conversation for another time."

I grabbed her wrist as she started to stand, and to my surprise, she didn't try to pull free. "What about... everything else? What about the Whites?"

"Lee is dead, isn't he?" she said, sounding surprised. "Half his goons just died with paper in their mouths – isn't that a sign? What does anything else matter?"

"It matters to me," I rasped.

There was a look in her eyes, taken aback; but the mask was so finely drawn and so expert, it was down in a second over whatever she felt. She said, "Come on. Let's get you out of here," and put an arm under my shoulder and, a bit at a time, and with surprising gentleness, helped me to my feet.

Part 3: The Madness of Angels

In which things must end.

Hospitals. Life suspended. Not our favourite place.

Oda told no one where we went, and I did not, in honesty, even know that the place existed – a private ward somewhere south of the river, where the nurses were all old, loud, and, by implication, far too experienced to tolerate any sort of strop or independent thinking from their patients. They fed us boiled vegetables and slices of overcooked meat, until Oda, to my surprise, brought us ice cream, which we ate by the tub.

The attending doctor, a small, infinitely cheerful woman who introduced herself with "Hi, I'm Dr Seah – hey, who beat you up? *Jesus*," and who wore a long stethoscope that went almost down to her waist, informed me that I had a nasty cut to the back of my head but no need for stitches, several cracked ribs that necessitated my staying still while the world moved around me, a twisted ankle and various lacerations, burns and bruises, some on the inside, that only time and a good diet could heal. We were furious at the vulnerability of our own body, but we scattered wards as best we could around the bed, threatening to walk out, healed or otherwise unless they were left untouched by the cleaners, and, despite ourself, we obeyed the doctor's orders, and stayed in bed. From our room we could see the sun rise, and watch the shadows bend to long, luminous angles as it set in the west, and the regular cycle of days and nights had never seemed more reassuring than it did then. Of Hunger, we saw and felt nothing. Perhaps we had frightened him more than we thought; we didn't know and didn't want to.

The only person I saw in that time confined was Oda. She would arrive every day at 11 a.m. precisely with a new pile of books and some new secret food smuggled in past the wary eye of the nurse and the cheerfully unfussed eye of the doctor ("You know, I figure . . . fuck it!'), and sit by my bed saying not a word unless I spoke first, until exactly 6.30 p.m., at which point she'd stand up and say, "There's a guard downstairs who'll watch you," and pull on her coat.

"Shouldn't it be 'look after me'?"

"What?"

"Shouldn't the guard be looking after me, rather than just watching me? Watching makes it sound like I'm a prisoner, instead of the valiant injured."

"In that case, he'll do both," she said, and without further comment, swept out of the room, leaving me alone with the radio headphones and the latest three-for-two book offers from the bookshop down by the riverside market.

Days passed and they were, I realised, little better than the passing of days when I had been underground. Down in the Exchange, though time had been a sunless, timeless series of patiently ticking events, at least underground the non-today and non-tomorrow had kept me occupied. In the hospital, the day was well enough defined by the rising and setting of the sun outside my window, but there were no events to make yesterday any different from today, or tomorrow any better than the day after.

To keep ourself busy we read books, tuning down our worries and fears into the strange, artificial reaction of feelings in the face of ink and paper, until we forgot that we were doing anything so mechanical as reading; the things we saw simply *were*, rather than being a conglomeration of syllables. Thus, drifting through the best of the three-for-two offers, we managed for a while to forget the passing of time.

I don't know what day it was when Oda came in, her bag of books slung under one arm and a paper bag of bread rolls and salami hidden in her jacket pocket, and I asked, "Who knows I'm here?"

"Me, Chaigneau, the men guarding you."

"Just the Order? What about Vera?"

"What about her?"

"Shouldn't she know?"

"The Whites are alive. Guy is dead. Half the people he employed have expired with bits of paper in their throats; everyone's up in arms against what's left of his men. They had to hire a lorry to get the bodies out to Essex for a burial." She saw my face and her eyes narrowed. "You look like a wet tissue. Isn't that what you wanted? Lee dead, his army broken?"

"A lorry of bodies?"

"Get used to the idea. Sacrifices have to be made. Besides, they were mostly the other side."

"I didn't mean for... I didn't think that..."

"No, you didn't think that, did you?" she said, slicing open a bread roll with a penknife and loading it with folded salami. "But it's fine. You didn't think about it and it happened and it's a good thing it happened and frankly we should all be pleased that it did. So go on and pretend you're guilty that people died if you must, but do it somewhere else, please? It was necessary."

She handed me a roll with an imperious tilt of an eyebrow. I took it automatically and rubbed the thin white flour on its top between my fingers for a moment, then licked my fingers clean again before taking a careful bite. Oda watched all this and, for almost the first time since she'd sat vigil by my side, spoke without being spoken to.

"Tell me about the paper."

I mumbled incoherent throwaway noises through a mouthful of salami and chewed more slowly.

"How does paper keep someone alive?"

There was a neediness to her voice; so, resignedly, I swallowed, put the rest of the roll to one side, folded my arms and said, "What do you want to know?"

"Paper. Explain to me about the paper."

"It's nothing too special."

"Then it won't tax you too much to tell me about it."

"There is a history of... people trying to stay alive under unusual circumstances. In the good, old-fashioned days, magicians would pluck out their own heart and encase it in a lead chest dropped at the bottom of a well where no one could ever find it, thus gaining a degree of invulnerability – hard to kill someone when you can't stop their heart beating. Problem with that, of course, is that if you become too hard to kill, too invulnerable, then all the other bugger need do is cut off your arms, head and legs, scatter them in twenty different places, chained to a rock, and there you are, still alive, head on a spike in Newcastle, scrabbling arms chained to a wall in Cardiff, and heart still beating, senses still functioning, still alive, still not dead; just in pain. You can be too safe, you see – and what's the point of being alive unless there is a progress, a journey, and somewhere, at some point, an end? What else other than that motivation makes us really *live*, the sense that this is a chance we must use, and now? Think of the laziness of immortality – so easy to say 'tomorrow' for ever."

"I was hoping for a technical explanation; thank you anyway."

"I'm telling it to you as . . ."

"As what?"

"As it was told to me."

She grunted, but said nothing more.

I wiped my mouth with my sleeve and tried again. "Necromancers go other ways – traditional magics that will never lose their validity, I fear – blood of the newborn babe, or even better, placentas, transplants from blessed vessels of Godly might, vampirism, reanimation, possession and so on and so forth. The modern medical era has made it easier; you'd be amazed how useful the MRI scanner has been to necromancers. But it is a messy business, unhygienic, usually defined by bad complexions, spots and rapid hair loss; and besides, it causes a lot of attention and provides little gain. Dead is dead is dead; even if it's walking and talking, the flesh decays – nothing yet, that I know of, can stop time."

"You know a lot about this."

"I was well taught."

"Bakker?"

"Yes. Why do you think he hasn't tried any of these things? He is desperate to stay alive, determined to survive at any cost – but he understands that life, real life, is much more than just survival in dead bones. He wants to live in every way. He wouldn't try necromancy."

"But Lee did?"

"Sort of. A different kind of ripping out of the heart, you might say. The magician writes on a piece of paper certain incantations, a few spells of a kind that usually are old enough and vague enough, that have been through endless mistranslations, to carry *consequences*, and to that adds a few compulsions. To the servants of the magician, usually there's a clause in there to obey and serve, to never wither until he commands, to feel no pain unless in failure. But when a magician does it to himself, swallows that paper with those enchantments, the words are usually . . . aspirations."

"Aspirations?"

"Things like, 'I am a good man', or 'I will never age' or 'My favourite colour is blue' or 'I will be for ever powerful' or 'I will not sleep' or . . ."

"Why?"

"Because you die when you eat the paper," I explained, surprised at the sharpness of her voice. "You choke on it, you have to swallow it whole and it kills you, invariably; it's part of the deal. That's why it's magic – at that instant, the paper absorbs your death, your . . . well, I suppose, life – it absorbs your dying breath and that gives *it* life, the words on the paper define who you are from that instant onwards; define everything about you. You're not technically dead, because there's still your life inside your body. But unlike a heart in a box you can die if the paper is removed; the spell is broken, it is a guarantee against extreme eternal agony, and at the same time . . ."

"A form of invulnerability?"

"Close."

"But . . . when you fought Guy Lee, you hurt him?"

"No. I hurt his flesh – he felt nothing. There was no pain in him until I actually pulled the paper out of his throat; the spell probably went with an 'I will feel no pain' clause – it's fairly standard."

"What happened when you pulled it out?"

"Imagine having a metre and a half of rolled-up paper stuffed down your throat and suddenly becoming aware of it," I answered. "Then guess."

She nodded slowly, eyes elsewhere. Finally she said, "What about . . . the others. The dead with the paper . . ."

"A basic command. I'm guessing that the warlock I met wasn't dead when Lee found him, merely dying, and that Lee pushed a simple spell of obedience down his throat when he died, catching his last breath in its snare, trapping it in his lungs. Not alive, not dead, just . . . bound. The magic of a dying breath is a powerful thing."

"Even today?"

"Even today. Christ," I muttered, "what do you think? Life *is* magic!

Where there is life there is magic! Sure, the magic is in the city, in the street, in the neon lamp and the coughing pigeon and the stray cat and the sewers and the cars and the smell of dirt; that's something new – but life really hasn't changed so much. Certain things – blood, skin, breath, words, paper, ink – will always have their own very special power, one which I don't think will ever really change."

She thought about it, then nodded again. In a voice that wasn't entirely there, her eyes fixed on some distant, other place, she said, "Is that why Bakker wants you alive?"

"What makes you think..."

"I found one of Lee's men. I asked him things."

"You..."

"I asked him things," she repeated firmly, eyes flashing bright and angry towards me. "That's all. He said they were under orders not to harm the sorcerer."

I shrugged.

"You don't seem surprised."

"Not really."

"Why?"

"Oda, you know why Bakker and I argued."

"He wanted you to help him summon the blue electric angels and you said no."

"He wanted me to summon us, so that he could feed off our power, off our life, use it to sustain him. He wanted to force us from the telephone, get us into the world of flesh where we would be vulnerable so he could steal our essence – we are creatures of left-over life, creations of surplus feeling whispered into electric energy – to his eyes, we are the answer to his problem. He desires life and we are all that he desires. And here we are, trapped in this skin, vulnerable, just like he always wanted."

"I see."

"Would you betray us?"

"Me?"

"It is always a fear."

She made no answer.

"We... do not know who we should trust. When we were in the blue, there was no need for 'friend'. We were all the same, our thoughts burnt off each other with static fire, we were one, never alone. Here, things are different."

"My breaking heart," retorted Oda with a scowl.

I glared and snatched up the rest of my salami roll, biting into it-to hide my anger. Not hiding it very well, clearly, since Oda sat up straighter and said, "I didn't mean that..." She hesitated, then made a grunting sound, relaxing. "Chaigneau hates you," she said finally.

"It's mutual."

"You embarrassed him."

"It's something I'm good at."

"It's more than that – you tainted him. He's now been touched by magic."

"So? He's a killer of magicians, a paladin of narrow-minded insanity; surely it's good to know his enemy?"

"He doesn't believe you've really lifted the curse you put on him."

"Why not?"

"He won't say."

"Is this another of his paranoid irrationalities coming through?"

"Did you undo what you did to him?" she asked sharply.

I met her eyes, unafraid of her cold glare. "Yes."

Another hesitation – perhaps something more too? "If you live," she said finally, "if you meet Bakker and have your revenge, if you kill him – what will you do then?"

"I don't know." I thought about it. "Clearly Chaigneau will try to kill me, the instant all this is over. So either you and I become implacable enemies, or I run away to another city and learn French or something."

"He'll find you."

"Then you and I become enemies," I answered. "And if I survive that..." There was nothing on her face to answer the hopeful enquiry in my voice, so I just said, "If I survive your Order, then... I don't know. My CV isn't great; and, besides, there's this two-year gap where I vanished, which employers will assume was spent in prison. I don't have any money that isn't obtained by the use of a spell; I don't have a home; I don't even know what's happened to my friends. I just... I don't know. Maybe I'll pack up and go. Head out to some other place and start again. Go back to being eighteen with just my qualifications and a week's work experience, wipe everything else clean, say I had cancer or something. Maybe be someone else, get a false name, try discretion and tact for a change. It could be an adventure."

"What about them?"

"Them?"

She tapped the side of her head conspiratorially and said, "Them with the blue eyes."

We thought about it, and grinned. "We will find joy in all life, anywhere. To be whoever we want to be . . . nothing but joy."

"Doesn't sound joyous to me," said Oda.

"That's because you don't like living without certainties," I replied. "You're just afraid."

"I am not!"

"It's nothing to be embarrassed about. Fear is the art of being alive – without fear there's no bravery, no heroism, no . . ."

"Shut up," she exclaimed.

I raised my hands defensively. "Sorry – I'm sorry. Is there anything else to eat?"

We lost patience before I was due to be discharged; in the middle of the night I got up, wrote Oda a brief and reasonably polite note, gathered up what few clothes we could find, and slipped out of the hospital, into the empty streets. Cold air on our face and hard pavement under our feet was a bliss we could not describe.

I spent the next day replenishing my stock – I found a new cardboard ad offering the services of "***PLAYFUL SEXY CHICK!!!!***" and scribbled my symbols of magic onto its back with a biro, sliding it into the ATM to withdraw enough money for my day of shopping. I bought new clothes and replenished my supply of tools for the trade – then went to the dry-cleaners and sat and waited while they struggled to remove the endless swirls of paint, dust, smoke, dirt and blood from the fabric of my coat and the surface of my bag. The result looked like a faded clown's costume that had once been dyed beige, but the fabric felt warm and dense, a weight without which I would have felt naked. For lunch I had a curry at the local tandoori house, dipping poppadoms into every chutney and spice. We were determined to find out what even the fiery red one was like, having avoided it in my previous life, and found that there were indeed flavours that could make our teeth burn. In the afternoon I booked myself into a hotel, and that evening, I went out for a drink.

I met her by the bar of a small jazz café near Hyde Park. She said her name was Felicity, and that it was nice of me to try, but she wasn't really interested. I told her I just wanted to have a conversation and she answered that that was what everyone said, that men were all the same. But she didn't say no when I bought her a drink; and we talked about the weather, the price of tickets on the underground, the embarrassment of our current politicians and all their useless prancing for the media, and what was on television, until at last I felt human again, and when it was time to say goodbye, we kissed and promised never to see each other again.

When I dreamt that night, I didn't wake up with the taste of paper in my mouth, and that, I concluded, could only be a good sign.

The next day I bought a mobile phone – the first I'd ever bought in my life – and rang the hospital where I'd been staying until they put me through to Dr Seah, who after a lot of umming and aaahing and "Have you been in a fight yet?" agreed to ring Oda and give her my number.

Oda rang me no more than ten minutes later. She was not a happy person.

"You bastard! I'll kill you if you ever do that again!"

"Hello to you too."

"Where the hell did you think you were going, what did you think you were doing, you can't just . . ."

"I needed some air."

"You needed two days of air without telling me? Just walking off into the dark like you were . . . what if something had happened?!"

"Please don't try concern; you're much better at indignation."

"If you *ever* pull something like that again . . ."

"Oh please, like the sniper rifle isn't gleaming through the window already," I said. "I'm calling now, aren't I?"

"You're a selfish pig, sorcerer. A lying, selfish pig."

"I just thought I'd let you know I'm OK."

A calmer edge entered her voice. "I've got something to tell you."

"Is it abusive?"

"Sinclair woke up."

"You're sure?"

"Yes."

"Where is he?"

"I don't know – they moved him the second he gained consciousness."

"Who's 'they'?"

"His assistant."

"Charlie?"

"If that's his name."

"You know where?"

"I just said I didn't."

"Right – got any way to contact him?"

"No."

"Then how do you know he woke up?"

"Because he's not in the morgue and he's not in the hospital, what do you think?"

"All right, thanks. I'll try and find him." I hung up quickly, before she could shout any more.

I spent the day with the pigeons, on a bench in Trafalgar Square, my bag of belongings huddled to my chest in case someone thought of taking them, and a pile of breadcrumbs at my feet. I let the pigeons congregate around me, listening to their thoughts, too brief and insubstantial to be anything other than a glimpse of yellow sound or sight. Eventually a local warden came up to me and said, "Sir, we ask people not to feed the pigeons," with such an expression of civic determination that I pretended not to understand English. Instead, I lisped my way through various "eh?" sounds until, having exhausted his two words of French and three of Spanish, he concluded that, since I was neither nationality, I wasn't worth the bother.

Though the pigeons' thoughts were too fleeting to give me anything really coherent, I lingered in their minds, drifting with them over the rooftops, until a tingling on the edge of my senses warned me that my own body was starting to get pins and needles. London from above only emphasised how dense, furious and busy it was; with the height of the houses obscuring the streets, all you could see was building on building, stretching as far as the pigeon's sight could perceive, way beyond Alexandra Palace on its hilltop to the north, and then beyond that by quite a way, and south as far as the Downs, whose slopes were obscured by sprawling suburbs. At ground level, it was harder to remember that only a few metres away was another street running parallel, and another and another, each filled with as many people as those you could see. Doubtless they had the same sense of significance as I felt when I went about my day, all of them walking at the Londoner's brisk speed to their own Very Important Meeting Thank You. It was only the pigeons overhead who understood the scale of the city.

The rats were more useful. Their brains were sharper, and as I sat by the dumpsters behind a restaurant in Chinatown, letting them flock around me and nibble at the chocolate I'd bought for their delight, their noses picked out scents that the pigeon brain was simply too harried to consider. A flash of strong, unusual scent – creatures that were sometimes rats and sometimes foxes and sometimes neither. I dabbled my senses in the rats' memories, felt the claws flex at my fingers and a pelt of dark, greasy fur on my back, remembered how it was to sense the width of the tunnel with the twitching of my whiskers and to smell the tantalising poison of the rat-catcher being laid down three floors above me.

In the evening, I sat by the Regent's Canal, near Caledonian Road, with a hamburger in a box and waited in the drizzle for the foxes. They came along the towpath, limping in the twilight from badly healed injuries or scampering with uncertain fearfulness out of their holes, and nuzzled at the hamburger with their curious black noses, sniffing through the stench of their own matted fur for a scent of something interesting.

I stroked them behind the ears, and through that contact borrowed their senses, searching their brief memories for a recollection of something out of place. A flash of an unfamilar smell, the sound of unusual movements, the image of a creature that resembled a fox but wasn't quite of the right mould. Weremen left all sorts of interesting scents across the city, to which the animals were perhaps more sensitive than even the average alert magician. I took the sensations gleaned from the rats, the foxes and the pigeons, who along with the beggars and the dustbin men probably see and know more than anyone else in the city, and followed the wavering smells they'd detected, to where the strongest sense of something out of place seemed to combine; the smell led north, to the wide, tree-shaded streets of Muswell Hill.

To most of the population of London, Muswell Hill is simply a name. An interesting name – unlike many, there is no easy guess at how it arose. Certainly there's a hill, but was there a Mr Muswell who named it, or was it simply well mussed? It has none of the easy recognition of Bishopsgate or Aldersgate – the gates for bishops and aldermen, in their times – nor of Westminster nor Kings Cross – each with a physical feature to give it a name. More, it was hemmed in by places that had tube stations, whose very presence on the underground map made recognition a hundred times easier – Wood Green, Finsbury Park, Crouch End – so that Muswell Hill tended to exist in relation to somewhere else.

The scents and memories I had gleaned from the animals weren't enough to pin down the wereman's location to one particular house, not least since the red-bricked, heavy doorways of every street seemed identical, and the long, curved avenues made it hard to judge which way was north or south.

From the overall impression got from the pigeons, foxes and rats, I focused on a block of four streets. These encased a series of terraced Edwardian houses, whose windows featured rectangles of stained glass set above the larger panes, to give an impression of traditional gentility rendered on a reasonable budget.

The glances of the foxes and the swoops of the pigeons gave me no clue as to street number, and there were too many houses for me to start knocking on doors. But after wandering for a while I found a flat green telephone switchbox tucked into a corner of one road; and with much banging, and levering with the end of my penknife, I finally coaxed the cover off it, to reveal the circuits inside. I pulled out my newly purchased mobile phone and, from my paint-splatted satchel, a thread. I tied the thread round the phone at one end, and round a single wire in the telephone box at the other, turned on my phone, spread out my coat under me and sat down to wait.

In a while, my phone started to talk.

"Hello, love, uni treating you OK? Hum. Hum. Yes, Dad's here too..."

"I just want you to talk to me! Is that so much to ask? Just talk and..."

"Three pizzas with the mushroom topping and the...no, the mushroom...yes and the...no, crispy crust..."

"Look, I was really sorry to hear about..."

"Tomorrow evening? Yeah, great, what shall I wear?"

As my phone caught the signals travelling through the wire, the sound of it was strangely therapeutic, like a medley of lullabies being sung just for me. I sat on the pavement and waited for something to happen; in the mean time it calmed us down, made us feel stronger for it. This was, after all, where we had come from – bits of life transformed into electrical signals and sent round the planet, all those sighs and laughs and shouts and thoughts and feelings transmitted in electrical bursts until eventually, as these things must, they had become too much for just one signal to contain and had, in their own way, come alive, become us. Perhaps, now we were no longer in the telephone wires, it would all happen again. Maybe even now, a new blue electric angel was starting to grow, fed by all that surplus life in the system, and would eventually become like us, and start to feel alive.

We felt somehow happy at the thought. It seemed like an appropriate development, the right thing. Circle of life doing its revolving thing, all over again, just like it probably should. It made sense.

"Sweet and sour pork, special fried rice...yeah...yeah...black bean sauce..."

"I was in! I was in all bloody day and you people couldn't just wait for the bell to stop ringing to see if I'd answer the door...you try without hot water!"

"OK, can you see the button in the left-hand corner? Now I want you to click on it just once...look, you rang *me*, do you want this document to print or not?"

"Please press one to top up. Please press two for customer services. Please press three if you wish for payplan details. Please press the hash key for the flight of angels. Please press the star key to hear the options again..."

I shifted my weight, and wished I'd brought a coffee.

"Yeah, hi. No, we don't know. Yeah. No, we're going to keep him here a bit. No. I heard. Yeah."

I sat up.

"Don't, for Christ's sake. Not even the sorcerer, he might . . ."

Clutching my phone, I pressed the call key. "Hi, Charlie?"

There was a grunt on the other end of the line and a tinkling of something falling. Then, a voice trying not to shout but not quite making it: "Who the hell is this?"

"The sorcerer, remember me? Swift?"

"Swift? How the hell did you . . ."

"Magic." I managed to bite off the "duh" sound before it could escape my lips, but only just.

"Right. Yeah. Of course."

"We need to talk."

"I'm . . . I'm on the phone."

"Yes, I noticed that. And hello whoever's at the other end of the line, sorry for interrupting."

A woman's voice, confused but otherwise friendly enough: "It's fine."

"Is there going to be a problem?"

Charlie's voice: "Where are you?"

"Muswell Hill."

"What are you doing there?"

"Looking for you and doing, I think, a very good job of it too. We *really* should talk."

They'd put him on a bed too small for him in a room too small for anyone, dominated by a large wardrobe and with a stool by the bed. The curtains were closed and, as I entered the room, Charlie warned, "No light." I fumbled my way to the stool in the orange glow seeping past Charlie's outline in the doorway, and sat down next to Sinclair's bed.

Charlie said from the door, "I heard Lee is dead."

"Yes. Was all along, really."

"I heard the Whites killed many of their enemies."

"Yes. Although some of them were dead already too."

"My friends helped you."

"Yes."

"Some of them died." It wasn't a question, but still surprised me.

"Yes," I said. "I'm sorry."

"They knew what they were doing. Everyone who went to the Exchange knew what they were doing – even Lee."

I looked up at the tone of his voice. Charlie added, "Do or die. That's how sorcerers are – there's no middle ground. You fight or you die."

"That's not true," I said.

A voice wheezed from the bed next to me, audible only because of its strangeness, "Yes it is."

I looked down at Sinclair. His eyes reflected dark puddles in the orange glow from the doorway, and his breathing was slow and laboured. His skin looked a strange, sickly yellow, his eyes protruded, and his chin had been badly shaved. He raised a hand towards Charlie, but I couldn't read the gesture – dismissal, warning, greeting, hard to tell. Whatever it was, Charlie didn't move, although his jaw grew tight.

Sinclair smiled a grim smile at me and added, "Sorcerers . . . burn too brightly. Their magic is life: their life and the lives around them. When you fight with the purest powers of blazing life, all you can do is fight . . . or die." He coughed and feebly gestured again at Charlie, who reached past me to the top of the wardrobe and took down a bottle of water, tenderly lifting the old man's head to help him drink.

When Sinclair was done he flopped back, eyes staring up at the ceiling as if turning his head was too much effort, and said, "I think I am meant to thank you, sorcerer."

I didn't answer.

"Candid as ever," he said. "Good, of course. Khay is dead, Lee is dead . . ."

"Was dead, all along."

"He dabbled in necromancy."

"He wrote the essence of his life on a sheet of paper and swallowed it whole," I answered. "That's how dead he was."

"Really?" Sinclair let out a disappointed breath that rattled through his throat like it was made of loose marbles. "An absence in the files. And now . . ."

"I want to find Harris Simmons."

"He'll run."

"Why?"

"He's a poor magician. He depends on other people's enchantments – Lee was always the toughest, and you made an alliance that... crudely, I suppose... 'killed him good'." There was a tone of harsh mockery in his voice. "Simmons knows he can't stand up against that. He's always been a coward."

"Where will he go?"

A half-shrug, followed by another burst of wheezing.

"The Tower won't be destroyed until the money stops; Simmons provides the money."

"The Tower is already crippled; why waste the time? You've killed the security, the soldiers..."

"I want Bakker to know," I said. "I want him to know that I'm coming. I want him to know that there'll be nothing left. All of it, gone."

"Revenge," rasped Sinclair. "Of course, of course... revenge is perhaps a mundane motive, but when it leads us to excel, perhaps... perhaps useful. Listen to me. Come close. Listen."

I leant closer. "The woman – Oda – there is something about her you must know."

"I know she's part of the Order."

A glint of surprise, then a smile. "Good, good. Yes, I am glad. Good. She hates with such fire, she despises you all. All magicians. She is their killer. Do you understand me? Their killer, their assassin, the lady of the knives, that's what they call her. They think I don't know, but in the Order... there are also concerned citizens."

"Charlie was telling me about concerned citizens."

"Good; it is good you know. They will send her after you, she will try to kill you."

"I know."

"Do *not* trust her. She hates with such fire..."

"I know. I won't. You have... contacts... in the Order?"

"Contacts? Yes, yes, I suppose I do. It is a tool, sorcerer, a useful entity: gather up the hate, the anger, put them in one place, use them..."

"A tool?"

"Use them to . . . to eliminate creatures as dangerous as they are; and they have such hatred, such passion . . ."

"Chaigneau wouldn't tell me who was in charge of the Order."

For a moment his eyes turned to me with an effort; his hands trembled. "Anton Chaigneau? He doesn't even tell people his name."

"I cursed him."

"You cursed Chaigneau? How?"

"He had my blood on his hands. There are some magics that don't ever change."

Sinclair's eyes went to Charlie. "Charlie, dear boy . . . Charlie . . . leave us."

"Mr Sinclair . . ." began Charlie, starting forward.

"Leave us, Charlie. I'll call when I need you."

Charlie reluctantly moved away from the door; I listened as he plodded downstairs. Sinclair gestured me closer still, until my ear was only a little way from his mouth and I could feel the strained tickle of his breath. "I mis-spoke when I said, before, that you were a poor sorcerer."

"I don't remember . . ."

"I said you were not powerful, before you became what you are, Mr Swift. I said you were merely average."

"Doesn't matter."

"I mis-spoke. You are . . . were . . . perhaps . . . afraid of what you could be, what you could do. That is why you argued with Bakker. You were afraid. He wanted you to give power, so much power, the blood of angels in his veins – you said, Mr Swift, you said – some magics don't ever change. You were afraid of that power. That isn't weakness, it is intelligence. To feel so alive, have the heartbeat of a city under your shoes – fear it. Fear what you may do. It is human. For misjudging you, I apologise. And perhaps for misjudging *you*, I apologise."

"You know about us?"

"Dear boy, it is my business."

"I accept your apology. *We* accept your apology."

"You are . . . smart . . ." he said hesitantly. "Yes, smart. You hide it well, perhaps; but you know when a power shouldn't be used." His eyes gleamed in the dull light. "You said some magic didn't change.

Charlie told me what you did, told me about your blood burning blue, told me that... and I know. Should not have lived, they said, fire in the blood. Isn't that your story? We be light, we be life, we be fire? Such creatures that revel in such living, should not be afraid... Ask me."

"Why does Oda hate magicians?"

"Her brother was one. She killed him."

"Why?"

"No one knows. They say he turned bad, went mad with his power. I do not entirely believe it. I think they lie, and so does she. It is a question that you do not ask."

"Why did you ask the Order to come to the house in Marylebone, the night we were attacked? Knowing what they are – it was a risk."

"A risk? To expose so many magicians to such hate, yes, well, I suppose... a risk."

"Why?"

"I think you may guess."

"Chaigneau didn't know who was in charge of the Order – he said he followed orders, and so does Oda."

Sinclair's smile widened.

"Mr Sinclair," I said, struggling to keep some patience in my voice, "are you the head of the Order?"

"No, dear boy, no! Just *a* head. One of many. Best not to know how many there are, or who they are, or where they are; dangerous, dangerous indeed. No. A head, Mr Swift, *a* head."

"You use them?"

"A tool. If you know who those are who hate magic with such fire that they would burn the world to be rid of it, you can tame them, use them, direct them, yes? Yes, and when you need them, perhaps you can give them that magic that they long to destroy, point them at a target and say, 'There is the sorcerer' or 'There is the shadow' or 'There is the demon' or 'There is the angel', yes? And they will strike, and it will not go back to me."

"They have decided to kill me," I pointed out reasonably. "That has me a little concerned."

"Chaigneau will follow orders."

"How ironic."

"Oda won't," he whispered. "Once she has her target, she will not stop. I can tell them to stop – difficult, perhaps, but then you can always say, 'He is a lesser evil. Let him be damned in his own time.' There are ways to spin these things. Oda will not stop."

"If you knew that, why did you introduce me to her in the first place?"

Sinclair grinned, then flinched at the pain even of that, and gave a grunting sound. "Because you are Robert Bakker's apprentice," he wheezed, pressing his fat fingers into his chest like he was trying to massage the pain from his bones. "Because you are the blue electric angels. And if he were to take your power, to catch you and work out how to steal that life that keeps your eyes blue . . . well . . . well . . . imagine."

"So you'd have me killed?" I said, forcing my voice to stay low. "Like that?"

"I would have anyone killed whom I deemed a risk," he replied, voice rising in stern reproach. "And you always will be a risk. But, I think, you will always be smart, and smart enough to be afraid. And perhaps that will be enough."

"We have something else we need to ask."

"Go on?"

"Did you summon us? Did you bring me back?"

"No, Mr Swift. I would like to see Bakker gone, but to bring the blue electric angels into this world? No. A risk – indeed, a terrible risk. Such a deed would have required a sorcerer's skills. I would suggest, in fact, that if anyone did summon you, it would have been Bakker trying to bring the angels into being, or, perhaps, his more sensitive apprentice, Dana Mikeda." He let out a long, easier breath. "You will have to fight her, sorcerer. That's how it is in these things. Neither of you, I think, can just walk away."

"Dana Mikeda is my problem."

"No," he murmured. "Not any more. She serves Bakker now. He took her hand when they held your funeral with the empty coffin, and he said he was her friend, her new teacher; now she serves him utterly. He helped her when you were gone; she's his apprentice now, not yours. And I would not like to think what he may have taught her; no, indeed. You may, in fact, save some time by directing Oda her way.

You could eliminate two threats in a single stroke – the woman who . . ."

"No."

"The Order hopes you will destroy each other; Bakker and Swift. Why should these two not do the same?"

"No," I repeated.

"I can send the Order word, command them to . . ."

"Our blood is in your veins," we insisted. "Some magics never change. Leave Dana Mikeda to me."

His voice didn't alter, nor did his light smile; but there was that edge there, that danger. "Kindly don't threaten me, blue electric angels. You are so far lost in this world that the lightest push could send you toppling over the edge into madness. Save your anger for someone else."

I swallowed. "There is one last thing I need to know."

"Go on."

"The night we were attacked, the first night I met you . . ."

"Yes?"

"Who attacked us?"

"At a guess, San Khay's men."

"And who sent the litterbug to attack me on my first night?"

"Those kinds of magic . . . Guy Lee."

"How did Guy Lee know where I was?"

"I would suggest," he said carefully, picking every word out like a piece of stuck apple from between his teeth, "that the house you were living in was sold on after your death to a woman who works for a company called KSP. KSP stands for Kenrick, Simmons and Powell and is the company run by Harris Simmons. I suggest that, since you clearly returned to a place of comfort in your old home, she phoned Simmons on the night of your resurrection and warned him that a naked, confused-looking man had just crawled out of the telephone lines and that perhaps someone should investigate. Lee would have been the one to send the litterbug; Khay would have been the man following on foot. You see – the Tower doesn't like loose ends."

I thought about the business card stolen from a wallet in my old home that I'd seen on the first night of my new life; Laura Linbard, Business Associate, KSP. I said, "I . . . I had friends, before this. I haven't dared . . . it seemed risky to . . ."

"Until the Tower is gone," replied Sinclair flatly, "everyone you knew or valued is being watched. Bakker will know by now that you are . . . perhaps shall we say . . . more than you once appeared. He'll have worked out why the phones went silent the night you returned; he isn't a fool. He will do anything he can to find you and if that means killing the people you once knew, he will. That's the Tower, Mr Swift, that's why you should really be fighting rather than from any motive of revenge; and when this is over that's what I will tell people you died for – a good, heroic cause, rather than your loosely defined sense of injured personal pride. My advice, if you'll take it – and please, consider it well intended – is to forget everything you were and everything you think you can continue to be; to stop imagining that things can go back to normal when Bakker is dead, and accept. You are not Matthew Swift any more."

I nodded. "Mr Sinclair," I murmured, "I feel I must tell you something."

"Of course, of course."

"There are times when I can believe that you are right." I met his eyes, and he didn't look away. "There are times when there isn't *us* in our skin, when there isn't the fusion of miscellaneous life and thought that is what we have become, Swift and angel mixed up into one great roiling cauldron. There's just me, just fire in the blood, just vengeance and anger and pure blazing blue life. I let the angels be all that I am, let them do what they want and . . . do you know why, in the telephone lines, we would tell those who wished to listen, 'come be we, and be free'?"

"Enlighten me."

"When we are the angels, we do not care about the thoughts of men, or their laws, or their ideas, or their conceptions of morality. We are beyond that, above that, free from these petty fictions by which you live your days – laws, rules, duties, responsibilities. We are pure fire and light and life, and nothing can contain us or bind us, and nothing can make us die. That is what it is to be free. That's why I *let* them be me." I straightened up, shook my head. "That's it. That's all that I wanted to tell you."

"A curious choice of conversational matter," he said with a half-laugh. "Are you telling me in the hope that I will . . . maybe reconsider my orders; perhaps, even, permit your demise? A strange hope, for a creature who blazes without thought for lesser species in its path. Perhaps you're just telling me for the sake of telling someone. It must be lonely, yes indeed, of course it must, inside your life. Not quite anything at all. Not quite human, not quite angel. Come be we and be free – and you're stuck as both, and neither. Indeed, difficulties, naturally. I am tired."

"Tired? Is that it?"

"For now," he replied, waving absently towards the door. "Charlie!" He hardly raised his voice and Charlie was there. I stood up, acknowledging my dismissal, and noted his slow, shuddering breaths.

"Mr Sinclair?"

"Yes?"

"Who do you think betrayed us the night you were shot? How did they know we were there?"

"A pertinent question, indeed, yes. I would say Oda – but no, it isn't her style. Perhaps the warlock . . ."

"He's dead. He died fighting Lee. Lee stuffed paper down his throat to catch his dying breath."

"Indeed." Sinclair showed not a tremor. "I trust the fortune-teller, she has too much history to be a convincing suspect; and the wizard died. The Bag Lady, well, she is . . ."

"I know about the Bag Lady."

"Well, then," said Sinclair mildly, "you are starting to run short of suspects, aren't you, Mr Swift?"

I nodded and forced a smile. "Thank you, Mr Sinclair. I hope you recover soon."

"I will, Mr Swift, I assure you, I will. It's all in the blood."

I glanced at his face, but his eyes were shut and his expression that of a sleeping child, innocently relaxed as if it had always been that way. I let Charlie show me out, and wandered off in search of a bus.

This is the history of Harris Simmons.

He was born Harry Simon in a small town just outside Colchester, a fact that he didn't like other people knowing – to the tune of one dead teacher, a mysteriously vanished family member with a Swiss bank account, and an arson attack at the local County Records Office.

At the age of twenty-two, Harry Simon disappeared from his job at the local estate agency and Harris Simmons materialised in London with a degree in Econometrics from the London School of Economics, a perfect new pinstriped suit, a big briefcase, an accent that could have been polished on velvet and three months' work experience with HSBC in Boston. Perhaps it was simply a bad year for PricewaterhouseCoopers in terms of intake – or perhaps they respected the kind of man capable of forging such credentials, as a useful asset to the team on his own basic merits. Whatever the reason, potential employers found it hard to say no to such a confident and self-possessed young gentleman, and Harris Simmons was soon earning more per bonus than his entire family had earned in twenty years of taxi-driving and bar service down at the pub. Sinclair ascribed no great moral evil to the fact that Simmons no longer supported his family – once he was so much more than just Harry Simon, he didn't look back; and that, it was grudgingly admitted, was probably the only way to survive, with such an ambitious agenda.

At twenty-five, Harris Simmons became the youngest, best-paid executive inside the Golden Mile, that area of EC postcodes in the centre of London where between Monday and Friday you cannot move for sharp suits, and which on Saturday and Sunday lies as still as the morgue. Somewhere around this point, he was also introduced to the supernatural, and on the realisation that it was possible to manipulate markets by something as easy as cursing a German steel company on the Wednesday, having invested in their competitors on the Tuesday, he took to it with the slick ease of a man bred to such devices. At the age of twenty-six, a few months before I abruptly found myself dead beside the river, Harris Simmons was approached by Mr San Khay on behalf of a budding new finance and investment company largely owned by Mr Robert Bakker, and asked if he would like to be a partner. When he demanded what this company had going for it that made it worth his highly expensive time, the answer was simple. Market manipulation was a profitable business and at this company they knew the value of a good goblin in the files. Thus, Kenrick, Simmons and Powell was born, and quickly swept into the FTSE 100 and onto the markets with Simmons's hand at the rudder. Indeed, its success was so astounding and its predictions so true and accurate, as it followed market fluctuations, that several discreet investigations were launched within its first year, in an attempt to determine whether it might be influencing events to its own advantage. But no conclusive evidence was found, and even the concerned citizens, of whom Sinclair was one, had difficulty understanding how such a new company could have such astounding success.

The profits from KSP did as profits do – fed more profits, and more, cycling back forever into the system that created them, largely for the sake of yet more profit. When that profit was simply too absurdly large to invest, and after the taxman had been sent away with the sneaky suspicion that he hadn't taken his fill, the rest – millions a month – was siphoned off into the organisation loosely known as the Tower. Some went on simple personal pleasures – the wine, girls and general luxury of a particular lifestyle. Some went to Lee, to fund his bribery and blackmail throughout the lower magicial communities in the city; some was sent to other cities to establish more links for the Tower. And a large part went on what was simply known in the records as "Operations".

It took Sinclair eighteen months to get an inventory of the needs of Operations, and the result explained to a large extent why so much was sucked into it each year. The silver teeth of dead prophets, the finger bones of ancient sorcerers, the blood of mythic beasts filtered through a sieve of frozen mercury, the jade-encrusted skull of a deceased necromancer, the still-beating heart of a newborn child whose mother's womb was cursed by the hand of a voodoo witch – these things all cost money, particularly in the quantities in which Bakker, Khay, Simmons and Lee were acquiring them. For Lee, a regular supply of corpses and high-quality paper seemed a priority; for Khay, his tattoos were hardly cheap; for Simmons, endless trinkets of magical enchantment were wanted, to compensate for what was by nature a weak magical inclination.

To Bakker went all the rest. I recognised some of the ingredients and could guess at their purpose. There were only so many reasons why tens of thousands of pounds could have been spent on phone lines, modems, servers and intercept technology, only so many excuses to purchase shards of stone dug up from the first Roman ruin found underneath the city's streets; only certain spells that could possibly require blue laser light reflected off a fairy's aluminium wing – it was easy enough to recognise the ingredients of summonings and enchantments in Bakker's wish-list, and to guess at their purpose. And it was all paid for by KSP, and Harris Simmons.

Did we need to find him?

Perhaps.

What would we do if we found him?

A problem for another time. Best not to think about it now.

I started by making a few phone calls.

"Good morning, KSP reception, how may I help you?"

"Hi, I'm calling on behalf of Amiltech Securities, I'm hoping I could make an appointment to see Mr Simmons."

"Mr . . ."

"Harris Simmons, yes, sorry, you must have a lot in the business."

"I'm sorry, sir, but Mr Simmons' schedule is entirely full . . ."

"I'm willing to be very, very persistent."

"Amiltech, was it?"

"Yes."

"Can I take your name?"

"Adam Rieley."

"Just a moment."

The moment lasted five minutes of what sounded like the nose-pipe rendition of "Greensleeves"; it felt like five years. When she came back, I was so close to falling off the end of my hotel bed in dismay and irritation that I nearly did just that from surprise.

"Mr Rieley?"

"Still here."

"I'm very sorry, but Mr Simmons is out of the country right now on business and won't be back for several weeks. If you'd like to contact him, I suggest you send an email to his secretary – would you like the address?"

"Any idea where he's gone?"

"No, Mr Rieley, sorry."

She didn't sound very sorry, but I couldn't really blame her. "Thank you very much, ma'am, you've been most helpful."

"Sorry I couldn't be of . . ."

"It's fine. Thank you." I hung up and went in search of my satchel.

Harris Simmons lived in that elusive part of London to the north of Marylebone station that doesn't quite know what it's trying to be, and ends up being a bit of everything – old, new, rich, poor, sprawled and compressed all at once, so that the most expensive fish and chip shops in the world can find themselves between a council estate, with its police witness-appeal signs, and a walled-off, high-gated mansion. In the midnight-dimmed shops between the area's quiet mews and its wide thoroughfares, parmesan cheeses the size of chubby babies were displayed, and Italian and Greek flags drooped from windows here and there. From the pubs a polite buzz of thick-carpeted gentility rolled out from half-open doors and warmly lit interiors.

The house I was looking for, directed by Sinclair's immaculate notes, sat behind a high wall fronting onto a broad avenue that rose up from the end of the Westway towards the long bank of hills that encased north London, whose names – Gospel Oak, Hampstead Heath, Primrose Hill – promised leafy parks, and steep streets furnished with coffee shops.

There was an electric intercom on the gate; I buzzed it and waited. There was no answer. There was nothing so crude as a keyhole, and shards of broken bottles were cemented onto the top of the brick wall. I walked round the block until I found a cul-de-sac that led to the rear wall of the house. Here there was a smaller gate, also with an electronic buzzer, and a CCTV camera peering down at it. When I approached, a single bright light flicked on automatically next to the gate. I dragged the light and warmth out of it and curled them into the palm of my hand, immersing the gateway area in darkness again, except for the trapped glow between my fingers. Once again, I tried the electric buzzer, and got no answer. I ran my finger over the wood of the gateway, feeling the polished sheen on the black paint, until a faint, cool buzz beneath my fingers murmured tantalising hints of electricity not too far away. In place of a keyhole, Simmons had substituted an electromagnetic lock. I pressed my hand against the door and pulled gently at the electricity in the lock. It sparked into my fingers with an angry pop, burning a small hole through the wood of the gate; then wriggled its way into the earth at my feet as I chucked it aside. The gate swung open.

Inside the high walls, there was no light; so I let some of the trapped white glow from the outside lamp slip from my fingers. It rolled across heavy flagstones, over shallow curving walls planted out with blooming purple and yellow bulbs; it swept round the trunk, and tangled in the leaves of a weeping willow; and displaced the shadows around a hulking concrete-pretending-to-be-stone griffin which crouched outside the back patio doors, its black eyes staring angrily at the garden gate, its tongue licking the air in front of its-nose. A dry yellow and brown crust had settled over part of it, like skeletal moss, and on either side of it was a low wooden bench looking onto a scorched area of brick that had the dismal semblance of somewhere you held barbecues. I found the whole tableau – the well-maintained garden, the bright flowering bulbs, the civilised layout of the place – slightly unsettling. It would be all too easy to imagine Simmons, the illustrious middle-class wealthy host, serving sausages to the congregation at the local Anglican church on a Sunday, while a wife (who he didn't have) chatted nicely to the vicar. As a semblance of what normality was meant to be, we found it disturbing. Uninspiring.

I scurried past the frozen griffin as quickly as possible and went to the back patio door. The lights were all out in the house, and a burglar alarm clung to the second-floor wall above the sloping roof of what looked like a dining room, glassed round on three sides with windows onto the garden. Throwing the last of my light ahead of me in a buzzing sphere of white neon, I felt the surface of the back door until I found the keyhole – at last, a keyhole! I rummaged in my bag for the set of blank keys I'd bought almost on my first day of new life, fumbling through them until one fell into my fingers that looked of the right make. Having put it into the lock, I was pleased at how quickly it assumed the appropriate shape – far easier to unlock things using tools, I was reminded, than when it was just you, murmuring gentle placations by yourself. I twisted, and opened the door.

The alarm immediately sounded – but not in the angry, distressed manner of a security system faced with an intruder; merely the low warning bell of a timer counting down to an emergency. I hurried down the corridor until I found the controller for the alarm – a keypad set into the wall. A numeric keypad was the last thing I really wanted, since the kind of magics that can predict the numbers embedded in a circuit tend to require preparation, consideration and a lot of time in execution, being of a subtler nature than the usual fistfuls of power magicians like to throw around. I found myself wishing I had the kind of equipment that all spies seemed to be assigned in prime-time BBC drama – number-breakers, silenced pistols, safe-cracking devices, fingerprint scanners or even a plastic sonic bloody screwdriver. In the event, I fell back on guesswork. Hoping for the best, I rubbed my hands together, feeling the friction build up between them. When the resulting warmth began to buzz, I caught it in the palm of my hand, feeling the hairs stand up all the way along my arm from the static around my fingers, and slammed my palm as hard as I could into the keypad. The static jumped from my fingers into the piece of machinery, which gave a loud electric pop, and fell silent.

A wisp of embarrassed black smoke curled out from under the panel. The alarm stopped wailing. Feeling pleased with myself, I felt my way down the corridor until I found a light switch. Turning it on, I saw that the corridor was bare, apart from the alarm keypad and a small wooden table below it. Not a painting, not a book, not a mouldy tax demand; not a thing. I walked into what I guessed, by the empty brick fireplace, was the living room; and there, too, was nothing. The shelves were bare, the walls bare, and only the faintest indent in the cream-coloured carpet remained to suggest that a scrap of furniture had ever sat on it. The bedroom showed the same rough outline of a bed that had once been present, and the odd faded patch on the wall where a picture had hung; but other than those hints, there was nothing to suggest that the house was anything other than a hollow frame. The cupboards in the kitchen were bare and spotlessly white; the bathroom smelt of bleach. Only when I went upstairs did I find anything – the one object left in the house.

It sat on the floor of what had probably been the master bedroom, a spacious, irregularly shaped area with a window onto a west-facing balcony. It was propped up on the floor by its own open shape, by the sturdiness of its expensive, thick paper. On the side facing the door someone had written in familiar handwriting: *For Matthew*.

I sat down with it on the floor of an alcove away from the windows, wary of deceit. It read:

My dear Matthew,

If you truly wish to continue with this course of events, I cannot prevent you. But I hope you will at least give me the opportunity to speak with you and talk about why you have returned so full of the determination to be my enemy, when I have never meant anything but the best towards you. If you would be interested, I am attending this event and hope you receive this note in time to join me.

With ever the best regards,

Robert

P.S. Out of concern for his safety, I have removed Mr Simmons from the country and hope you will respect his innocence in anything that may lie between us enough to not endanger him as you did M.s Lee and Mr Khay by your actions.

Between the pages of the note was a small piece of yellow paper. I read it, folded it back up, put it in my pocket and, leaving the note behind, went downstairs.

What did I feel? A mixture of anger and disappointment, certainly; nothing else could explain the tension in my back and the sudden ache in my eyes. Curious, maybe? And perhaps, somewhere at the back of my mind, perhaps just a moment of uncertainty, perhaps if you stopped and thought, perhaps just . . .

Keep moving, that was the rule. Stop and think too long and you might never move again.

Simmons's house had clearly been emptied out by someone who understood that it wasn't enough for *you* to vanish – your life had to disappear too. Not just physical absence was needed, but an absence of any property or other evidence that might give your tracker a sense of how you thought, what you thought and where it might have led you. More to the point, someone had taken immense trouble to remove all personal traces that might be turned to a more magical form of pursuit.

On the other hand, not for nothing had I spent nine months as a cleaner for Lambeth Borough Council.

I tried the bathroom. The shower was immaculate, the bath glowed with polished white pristine hygiene. If it was possible for a toilet to smell of lemons, his managed it – even the ventilation shaft had been dusted to shining silver perfection.

Some things, however, never change. I squatted underneath the sink and, grunting at the stiffness of the stainless steel bit, unscrewed the bottom of the waste pipe. As I pulled the part free, a splash of turgid, smelly water spilled out. A pool of water lay at the bottom of the pipe-end, but it too smelt of bleach, and the edges were largely free of the thick, muddy dirt you might usually find. I ran a finger round the rubber seal at the top, and came away with a layer of slime. I slid my nail under the seal and pulled it away from the metal of the pipe and, as I did, something so thin it was almost imperceptible moved, catching the light for a moment. I peered closer, the smell of the pipe enough to make my eyes water, and turned the pipe until the thing flashed again with a dull, dark gleam. Pinching it between thumb and forefinger, I lifted it away. It was short, might once have been almost blond, was stained with dirt and withered from the bleach, but was, despite it all, still very much a single human hair.

That was all I needed.

Back at my hotel, I washed the hair under the hot water tap until it glowed a dull browny-yellow; and, with the tweezers from my penknife, I put it carefully by itself in the middle of the soap bowl. I then put the soap bowl down in the middle of the bedroom floor and went in search of the ingredients for the spell that I needed. I pulled the telephone out of the wall and the telephone wire out of the telephone, and wrapped the wire a few times round the soap bowl to create my protective circle. I bought a packet of ten blank CDs from the local general store and took the top one for my mirror, idly spinning it round on my finger as I considered what power might be most useful.

I settled on a minor spirit, who I felt might be equipped to my purpose and, sitting cross-legged in front of my little bowl with its single human hair, smashed the topmost CD on the table end, took the largest piece from the remnants and with the sharpened point drew a doorway in the air in front of me. Then, in my most commanding voice, I invoked the demon of the lonely night, of the travellers on the midnight train, the lord of the lost parking space, by all the names I could think of, including the shrieking noise of brakes, made at the back of the throat, to call him forth, and by the red light of the "STOP" traffic light that I twined between my fingers and poured into the shard of broken CD until it glowed the colour of newly spilled blood.

The doorway I'd drawn in the air shimmered, wobbled like a mirage. I felt a breath of warmth from it on my face, heard a sound like the swish of tyres through a puddle in an empty road, and the distant rattle of a train heard far off, when the wind is in the right direction. I looked up to the doorway as it started to leach from the colour of the red traffic signal down to an emerald green and just as I thought I saw a figure take shape inside it, there was a knock on my bedroom door.

The bubble of colour winked out in front of me. I swore, the noise snapping out of earshot in an instant, scrambled up and hurried to the door. I left the chain on, and opened it an inch. There was no one outside.

Realisation struck. I turned, raising the shard of broken CD in front of me, but he was already there, emerging out of the darkness in the centre of the room and right in front of me, the fingers of one hand twining round my throat while the other smacked my head back against the door hard enough to knock it shut behind me with a loud *bang*. His eyes were the amber of traffic lights, his breath the swish of traffic passing on a wet night; his skin had the colour of old chewing gum. A dry warmth rolled off it as he tilted my head back, pressed his fingers into my throat and hissed, over a tongue the shade of uncooked chicken, "A devotee of the lonely traveller, or a fool?"

"Shouldn't you have come through the *other* doorway?" I croaked.

His eyes glowed. His clothes were shifting black shadows that, as he adjusted his weight, parted for a moment to reveal nothing but dull orange neon glow underneath, as if his whole body was little more than a collection of trapped lights compressed behind the darkness of his coat. "I am the lord of the lonely traveller, I am the last passenger on the train, I am the shadow when you close the garden gate, the stranger in the dark, the..."

"As far as I'm aware," I said sharply, "I summoned you knowing all this, spirit. So, please" – I closed one hand around his wrist and with the other I levelled the gleaming shard of broken CD against his throat – "give it a break."

A smile. His teeth weren't even solid, but lumps of pale, half-chewed bubble gum that formed sticky fibres between his thin blue lips. A wisp of breath that rattled like train wheels across shining new rails, a creak in his bones as he shifted his weight like the sound of a rusted gate banging in the wind. "You threaten me?"

"Ah, well, this isn't any ordinary bit of broken plastic," I said quickly. "This is a piece of broken *reflective* plastic." I held it up quickly before he could shy away, pressing it in front of his eyes. There was a flash of orange-pink neon so bright and so sharp it hurt as it went into my head, and burst the light bulb in the middle of the room with its force. From the creature's lips came a wail like the horn of a lorry just before it's about to crash. He curled back, instantly cowed, crouching animal-like and raising his hands to shield himself from the sight in the broken shard. His whimpers were the nagging sound of a distant car alarm in the night. If there was one thing this spirit could not abide, it was his own reflection, showing him for what he was – nothing at all. You cannot be the lord of the lonely travellers and be in the company of your own reflection.

He whispered in a voice like a pigeon's feather on the wind, "What do you wish, master?" He squatted by the end of the bed. Through the loose shadowy folds of his huge coat, the dull glow of orange-pink neon poured out of any opening like the shimmer of lamplight under a doorway – bright enough in the dark to see everything in black and white, except for the light itself, which shone with chemical colours.

I crouched down in front of him. As spirits went, I could feel a certain sympathy for this one, a reluctant affinity for the magics that had spawned it. They were much the same powers that had created the Bag Lady, the Beggar King and, perhaps to an extent, the angels of the wire, the forgotten lives left in the telephone. Where there was life, there was magic, and even in the lonely tread of the commuter, and the fearful breath of the traveller by himself in an unknown place, there was a very special kind of life; and from that life, there was the spirit.

"I'm looking for someone."

"Does he travel alone?"

"Who doesn't?" I answered with a smile.

His eyes glanced up to me, and in the dark they glowed with the dull red illumination of a traffic light. "You know me," he whispered. "I hear your footstep in my belly; you have offered me your prayers."

"Everyone has offered you a prayer at some point or another. When they're alone, in the dark, even the SAS probably jump at the sound of a stranger, or the unexplained door slamming in the empty house, or the tinkling of glass somewhere near by; and when they do, their thoughts are with you."

His lips curled in what might have been a smile, but came out a sticky, gummy sneer. "Who do you wish to find?"

"The man who owns that hair," I said, pointing at the soap dish in the middle of the floor.

The lord of the lonely traveller – whose name could only be pronounced properly in the shriek of brakes or the last rumble of the train engine before it's turned off at the final stop, but who was known to everyone through the swish of distant traffic in the rain, or the sigh of a breath condensing in a lonely night – leant forward, eyes narrowing as he studied the hair. He pinched it between two fingertips, then licked it slowly, and carefully, his saliva hanging off it in a thick yellowish goo. His eyes half closed, and he whispered, "A traveller, so many travellers . . ."

"Where is he?"

"He runs, his footstep is sweet, a *tumtetumtetumtetumte* . . . he is chased! So afraid of the dark, and a man who used not to fear; but now he runs, he runs from the monster in the night."

"Where does he run to?"

"He is praying."

"To you?"

"They all pray to me, when they are alone and afraid," he whispered, eyes flashing. "Even those who think they are brave."

"What does he say?"

His tongue rippled across the thin blue edge of his lips, and he let out a sigh of contentment, shoulders relaxing to let more neon light spill through his clothes. "The monster is close, his feet on the tarmac and it sings to the time of his rhythm . . . he prays for life; so sorry, so sorry, he says, so sorry that it went like this, forgive me in the night, forgive me the past, forgive me time and forgive me . . . forgive me . . . oh, his fear is so bright! He fears the blue-eyes!"

"None of this is helping me," I declared. "I'd be happier with points on a compass or GPS coordinates, please."

"He fears you," whispered the creature, curious as he studied me. "He fears the blue-eyes, and prays . . . so sorry . . . so sorry . . ."

"Where?!" I shouted.

"On the sea. He is at sea."

"A boat?"

"Salt and endless dark falling, and the smell of petrol from the engine towers pumping out heat into the cold wind."

"A ferry?"

"Would you like to hear his prayer, blue-eyes?"

"Why, what does he say?"

"He says . . . we be light, we be life, we be fire! We sing electric flame, we rumble underground wind, we dance heaven! Come be we and be free! Forgive me, forgive me, forgive me and have mercy in the night, make me a shadow on the wall but do not let him eat my heart, forgive me . . ."

"He prays to the blue electric angels?" we said, incredulous.

"And to me," he murmured.

"And he's on a boat?"

"Crossing the seas. Oh" – a look of sadness moved across the creature's face – "but he's not alone. How sad, how sad not to be alone on a night of such cold winds and hidden thoughts . . ."

"Who is with him?"

"It runs silently across the water's edge . . ."

"Enough of this crap!" I raised the reflective edge of the plastic in warning. "Here's me, sorcerer, pissed off and blue-eyed and not in the mood; so you tell me who is with him like you had a grasp of concise necessity; otherwise I'll bind you to a bloody hall of bloody mirrors!"

"He doesn't have a name that I can hear."

"Give me your best shot at a description."

The creature thought about it, tilting its head up towards the roof to find inspiration, while cracks of pinkish light crawled up round the edge of its neck, running through its skin. "The one who travels with him . . . he is hungry," he said. "He is so very, very hungry." A quizzical tone entered his voice. "He knows I'm here. He wonders why I watch, since he does not travel alone. He reaches out and says, what are you? Why have you come? He smiles. He says, I see blue fire in your strings, and stretches a wing and . . ."

"Leave!" I shouted.

"So hungry . . ."

"Leave right now! Piss off, be dismissed, get your arse banished out of here, *get out!*"

A tightening of shadows around the edge of the creature's face? A sunken quality to the eyes, a twisting of the pinkish light around its limbs? I wasn't about to take the risk. I picked up my stack of blank CDs, and threw them at the spirit. The orange-neon glow split and reflected off the spinning disks as they fell around it, and the lord of the lonely travellers screamed with the sound of a plane crashing from the sky, of brakes snapping on a speeding bike, of the emergency cord being pulled on the train. It raised its arms above its face while cracks of burning light spread through its skin and blazed the colour of sodium street lamps, so bright I couldn't look, so loud the windows shook, and, its face a mask of surprise and light, it shattered into drifting pinkish shadows that skittered across the wall, oozed out under the door, and were gone.

I grabbed up my belongings, and left that hotel without looking back; and didn't sleep until the comfort of daybreak.

In the afternoon I phoned Charlie. He said Sinclair was sleeping and wasn't about to be woken. I said I thought Simmons had left the country and was on a ferry. He said he'd look into it. I didn't mention the shadow. Nor did I mention the folded piece of yellow paper and the note *For Matthew* that I'd found at Simmons's house. I didn't see any need to let him know.

The yellow piece of paper advertised a play; and at this play, I assumed, would be Bakker. I took only one precaution before going: I went to Bond Street to find a jeweller.

His name was Mr Izor, he was American, but, he assured me, despite this he still had perfect taste. We wondered whether something as subjective as taste could be "perfect", but decided not to ask further and let our eyes drift over the sparkling mass of diamonds, gold and silver watches, necklaces, rings, earrings and miscellaneous pins that were on display in a dozen cases around the plush, red-carpeted room. Even the door handles looked like they were gold, but Mr Izor assured us when he saw our stare, "Oh, Jesus, no; manager's way too cheap."

I told him what I wanted. He said, "OK, different, who's the lucky girl? Or is it a lucky guy?"

I said, "I want it to sacrifice to the spirits of the wishing-water in the direst of emergencies; but should I ever meet the lucky girl or the lucky guy, I'll be sure to come back to your shop for advice."

"Don't go with the diamonds; tasteless, totally common."

"I'll keep it in mind."

"Guys like silver."

"Thanks. What about my current needs?"

He found it for me, eventually. It was about the size of a two-pound coin and cost a figure that made me shudder. Sums that large, I decided, shouldn't be paid using a credit card, let alone one that wasn't real. For the first time since my resurrection, I felt a pang of guilt at my lifestyle, and the credit card/prostitute ad that I was using to steal the things I now loosely called my belongings. The attraction of a home to call my own was suddenly a hunger, like the need for fish and chips when hungry and having just smelt vinegar. It stuck in my mind and in my belly, a sense of emptiness.

I bought the thing anyway. We told ourself that our need outweighed the damage, if any, to the jeweller's business. We told ourself that all the way to the theatre.

The show was by Waterloo Bridge.

I bought a ticket for £10 from the returns queue and was assigned a seat in a box-like black theatre, two floors up beside a large red button with the alluring notice "THIS BUTTON DOES NOTHING" stuck up next to it, a label that troubled and confused us throughout almost the entire performance. I was wedged into a seat between a polite couple from Cambridge wearing a business suit and pearls respectively, and a pair of old ladies in huge padded jackets who didn't once meet my eye and looked disapproving at every irreligious reference in the play, of which there were plenty. The play was full of torture and swearing and stories, in roughly even measures, creating a strange mixture as it floated from physical violence to battles of grammatical wit to renditions of things that should have been for children, if you took out some of the decapitation; so that by the interval we were thoroughly befuddled, and strangely entranced. We bought a chocolate ice cream then, despite the pain it caused me to pay so much for it, because it seemed to be the *thing that was done*, and because our stay in hospital had taught us that ice cream was a thing never to be refused, in any weather. Then we stood out on the balcony and watched the reflection of the tourist cruisers' lights on the river, the buses on the bridge, the tracery of little blue lamps in the trees along the bank, and listened to the comments of other people with their ice creams on the terrace below.

"Well . . ."

". . . yes . . ."

"I think *he's* awfully good, don't you?"

"Well . . ."

An audience of disconcerted people, I decided – they didn't know if what they were seeing was good, bad, clever, inane, witty or crude, and this was, I decided, probably a good thing. They could walk away after the second half and not know what to think, and for that, they would probably think about it all the more.

The bell rang for the second half. I filed back in and resisted the temptation to press the big red button, until my fingers itched with desire. There was a buzz on the air, a tingling all of its own quality, a thick swish of bronze potential, elusive, edgy, aware, as the play resumed and all those minds concentrated on a small space with three shouting men in it, a focus and a magic so absorbing that we almost didn't notice ourself being sucked in, becoming part of that state of crackling hot thought that filled the theatre.

Just an edge, just a moment, a blink of green awareness, a flash of a thought not entirely directed on the play?

Hard to tell.

The play's hero, although it wasn't a term that could really be applied, murdered his brother for killing by stories, and was eventually shot for his pains. A nicer outcome didn't seem . . . *right*, although we couldn't say why. The bad cop turned out to be not such a bad cop; though, again, "bad" left no space for the imagination. We decided that the best thing was not to try to guess, and to be unsettled. It was, strangely, a sensation we enjoyed, although we could not understand why we should be elated by such unease and uncertainty about the last three hours' experience, as if it was the adrenalin rush of fear.

When the lights went up and the applause faded down, the lady to my left said, "Well!"

The man to my right said, "Interesting."

The tubby woman in the row in front of me said, "Oh, *he* was really very good!"

I picked up my coat and bag and joined the long shuffle of a large audience trying to get through a small door to fresher air. As we walked past the big red button, our hand reached out instinctively and, as fast as only the spark can fly, we pressed it.

Nothing happened.

My face turned red and, head bowed, we sidled away, feeling all the more bemused.

I felt no desire to wait and see if anyone might approach me in that place – after such a sleepless night, I wasn't in the mood for games or deceits. Besides, there was a safety in the crowd; I doubted Bakker would be interested in harming me in front of so many people, assuming he could spot me at all.

A flash of awareness, a bright spark of familiarity among the buzz of voices.

"Yes, obviously a use of religious imagery . . ."

". . . very interesting . . ."

". . . what have we seen *him* in?"

"Come be and be . . ."

I turned on the stairs and nearly walked into a lady with curly white hair wearing more padded silk than it seemed plausible that her small, bony frame could support without tottering or getting a rash. I apologised and kept moving with the flow of the crowd down the stairs. At the bar in the halfway foyer I paused while waiters swept away used plastic cups and champagne glasses, and scanned the crowd; but the density of people I had counted on to protect me also obscured anything that might be familiar. I kept walking. On the ground floor, a sign said, "If your bag is bigger than this" – a square the size of a small suitcase – "you MUST leave it at the cloakroom." I patted my satchel, roughly twice the size indicated, which had stayed next to me all the time, and felt a thrill of guilty, criminal pleasure.

I let out a long breath and tried to clear my head. The difficulty I had in focusing on anything other than stories and images and happy green pigs – another theme of the play – hinted at a further reason why Bakker's note had suggested the theatre; it was hard to sense any power in that place, that didn't flash in the crowd itself with a transient glow. A trick, perhaps, to lure us to a place where we, more than ever I would have been before, risked becoming lost in a stranger spell?

"Mr Swift?"

The voice came from behind me, and our immediate instinct was to throw our bag at it and worry afterwards about what spell could follow. However, the owner of the voice looked too bemused and unarmed to merit the black eye that our jerking elbow desired to give, being a young woman wearing the heavy, slightly embarrassing T-shirt of a theatre stewardess. She said again, "Mr Swift?"

"Yes?" I stuttered, surprised to find I hadn't answered already.

"Your uncle asked if you could help him."

"My . . .?"

"With the wheelchair."

"Right. Yes. Of course. Where is he?"

"He's attending the sponsors' drinks."

"Sponsors . . ."

"Mr Swift?"

"Yes?"

"Are you all right?"

"Yes. Fine. I didn't realise he was such a patron of the arts."

"He said to tell you not to mind the crowd. He was very insistent I said so."

"I'm sure he was. Could you show me the way?"

The sponsors' drinks were in a bar with almost no windows, and a lurid decor of mirrors, uncomfortable furniture and odd angles. Men in black and white served champagne, and nibbly things made from tiny slices of fish and puffs of pastry. The theatre clearly needed a lot of sponsors to fund its plays, and some of the rich and the cultured had spilled out onto the landing. There, they sipped their drinks and indulged in banter about how *he* had actually slept with *her* back when *they* were running the theatre, and the only reason *they* put on such old-fashioned plays was because of the influence of *them*.

In the face of so many people's importance, we felt small – and so, rebellious. We were pleased that our coat was scruffy, stained with faded paint, that our satchel was soaked through with ink marks and that our hair was badly combed; we were grateful for the looks of uncertainty and unease in the face of our charity-shop trousers and thrown-away trainers; and I was glad, just a bit, to see how one or two of the more discerning theatregoers flinched away from the blueness of our eyes.

In one corner a cluster of champagne-quaffing men and women were gathered round a shape. I went towards it, knowing instinctively what was behind that wall of silk and linen. As I approached, I heard the voice, still rich and wry like it had been when I was a boy, with that humorous air of putting on a performance and loving it, the attention and the buzz of being admired, that showmanship he'd always relished, back before he was in the wheelchair: "Tell me if you spot an anonymous, we can ask if they're in it for the drinks as well."

I leaned past the nearest member of the crowd, and looked down.

It was a new wheelchair; odd, perhaps, that this should be the first thing I spotted. Perhaps other realisations were also there in my unconscious, but too afraid to come out and make themselves known – whatever the explanation, that's what I saw first. It was a stylish thing, all light titanium and smooth edges, tailor-made to his shape, unlike the crude hospital wheelchair I'd last seen him in; he wore it like a model might wear a pair of glasses, as if at any moment he might leap out of it to a cry of "Why, Mr Bakker, you're beautiful!", and amaze the audience with his agility and strength. It didn't look like a tool for dealing with his paralysis, nor the thing in which he would almost certainly die, but just a piece of metal clothing, or some family-inherited piece of furniture that he'd sat in as a lively child.

We were surprised at how relaxed and friendly he looked: a rich old gentleman who loved the theatre and wanted to spread that love.

Despite my memories of how he once was, throughout years and years of acquaintance, the sense we'd had of him when he'd called to us in the telephone and begged us to come and give him some of our strength had been of a withered, hulking thing, a black spot of consciousness just beyond our reach, who we had shied away from as he extended his thoughts into our domain. But here, we were astonished to see his smile, even brighter than the sense of his magic that we had tasted in the past.

He noticed me the moment I saw him. He kept on talking, eyes darting to my face, and then away, smile still in place, chatting to a lady in gold earrings and a shimmering dress to match, about the tragic trend towards revivals rather than original art in the West End, and whether the dumplings in Chinatown were to be trusted. To our surprise, we found ourself getting interested, curious to hear his opinions as he talked on about theatre and music and food – things that I'd always meant to learn about, but had never had the time.

It was only at a natural pause in the conversation – and it was quite clearly a full stop imposed politely at the end of a theme – that he looked us straight in the eye and said, "Hello, Matthew. I'm glad you could make it."

"Hello, Mr Bakker."

"I don't think you know anyone here, yes?" The smile, still bright, a little laugh as he looked round at the people gathered around his chair and, God help us, they laughed too, feeding off his presence and character as if he was weaving an enchantment even then – and perhaps he was. There was a gentle tracery of power about him, subtle and hard to distinguish – but they laughed when he laughed, even though they did not know who I was or why I looked afraid.

"No. I don't think we've met." We sounded empty. We didn't know what we were meant to put into the words.

"I may be rude, then, and skip the introductions; good manners are important but when there's this many people the names tend to just blend into one unless you know who you're talking to. Everyone, this is Matthew – my nephew, in a way."

"'In a way'?" said one lady in a voice that could have resonated glass, and now I noticed the little tape recorders in odd pockets, hints and clues that this night was about more than the drinks and that everyone was on display. Another reason, perhaps, to feel safe in the crowd? I couldn't imagine Bakker doing anything in front of the press – however, I still didn't feel inclined to sample the champagne.

"A sort of godson, nephew, surrogate cousin relationship," explained Bakker airily. "I knew Matthew when he was just a spotty kid, didn't I?"

"Yes. You did."

"Do you like the theatre?" asked the same woman, favouring me with a glance like two hot needles in the eye.

"What we've seen, very much, although it is a little frightening. I never really got into it in the old days."

"Frightening?"

"You let yourself fall into a spell, willingly," we explained. "You know that it is there and you allow yourself to be deceived. It is a powerful magic that can enchant someone who is knowingly aware of the illusion."

"The magic of theatre!" chuckled a man through a monstrous fly-trap of a moustache.

"Even bad plays?" asked the woman.

"We don't really know how to judge."

"Matthew," said Bakker quickly, "would you like something to drink?"

We met his eyes squarely. "No. Thank you."

"To eat? I think there're vol-au-vents of some kind."

"No."

"Well, please yourself," he said with a shrug. "Forgive me, all – Matthew, could you wheel me in the direction of the bathroom, please?"

I did wheel him in the direction of a bathroom, but took him no further than the foyer outside. We were still in comfortable proximity to the buzzing noise of sociability, but far enough away so that the conversation was merely a pitch and yaw of polite sound, rather than distracting words and sentiments to be understood. He put on the brakes of his chair and smiled at me, gesturing at a staircase with an inviting hand. I sat down on one of the steps so that my face was level with his, leaning my elbows on my knees and bending in towards them to create a small target, huddling like a child, like I'd sat in front of him all those years before.

He didn't speak, just sat in the chair and studied me head to foot, the smile not fading as he raised and lowered his head, quite clearly observing my clothes, my face, my eyes, my expression, reading everything about me and taking it all in, without a glimpse of feeling either way. We let him look and waited, patiently.

Finally he said, "You look well."

I grunted, unimpressed.

"You probably need a haircut," he added.

I resisted the temptation to run my fingers through my hair at his glance, but only just.

"Your coat – it's not quite the old one, is it?"

I shook my head.

"But still enchanted. A delicate, subtle whiff, yes? Anonymity, the beige jacket of anyone in the crowd. Not quite invisibility – but close enough."

"It's been to the cleaners a bit."

"It's a good coat. A sorcerer should always have a good coat, with deep pockets and proper waterproofing. Only an idiot wastes their time trying magically to ward against the rain – getting soggy socks is important."

"Why?" I said, knowing the answer from the olden days but still wanting to ask.

"So that when you get home you can take them off and put them up in front of the fire and let your clothes steam, while drinking a hot cup of tea and feeling your skin dry out of all its wrinkles."

"That's important?"

"Of course it is," he said with a tight smile. "It is a reminder that we are part of our own flesh, not a blazing magical fire in the sky. Or a signal in a wire."

We smiled and looked down, studying our hands, stretching them to feel the tension in our skin. We said, "How long have you known?"

"Known what?"

"About us."

"I don't know that I do know, yet. I hear rumours, of course. From the seers who I have in the basement listening all the time for the voices of the powers whose blood is formed of surplus strands of life, I hear it reported that at such a time, on such a night, the voices of the blue electric angels buzzing in the telephones winked out, vanished like they'd never been there. I hear that San Khay's body was found among the corpses of rats, and that on a none-too-special evening at McGrangham's pit, a stranger with bright blue eyes, whom no one recognised, fought against Guy Lee and won, and that when he did, his skin burnt with blue fire. This, I think, is what computer nerds call *data*, rather than *information*. Trickles of digital fact, just waiting to be interpreted into the bigger picture."

"What do you want to know?"

"You're asking me?"

"Yes," we said, surprised to find how calm we sounded.

"I want to know . . . if there's anything of my apprentice left alive."

"What?"

"I would like to know if you've hurt Matthew."

"You want *what*?" I squeaked. "To know if *I'm hurt*?"

"He was my apprentice," replied Bakker calmly. "I wish to be assured of his well-being."

"It's me! It's bloody me! Short of having been fucking murdered two years back, do I look like I've been hurt?"

A hesitation on Bakker's face, a twitch of doubt; then a polite smile. "For all I know you are nothing but a demonic parasite infecting his skin, using his memories to pretend to be human. Since what I know of the angels is an entity hungry for life, experience and sense, blazing its presence across the world with a bright fury, such an occurrence is not impossible. Matthew could be dead, and you could be nothing but a replica of him, a crude imitation that doesn't know what it means to be alive, really *alive*."

"You patronising, hypocritical, miserable bastard."

For a moment, the smile widened. "That sounds, at least, like the apprentice I knew."

"Whatever I say, you're going to see nothing but the angels, aren't you?"

"Why?"

"Perhaps because we are what you *want* to see."

"Why should that be? You think I'm pleased at what's happened to my apprentice? Glad to discover the kid I taught is now possessed by the spirit of telephone interference?"

"We think that you are dying, Mr Bakker," we said simply. "We think that you've been dying all these years, and you're terrified of it; and we think that when you tried to coax us out of the wire all those years ago, you wanted us for more than just a dance in the fire. Why don't you swallow a piece of paper, like Lee did?"

"Necromancy is such a clumsy way to survive – I told you that, almost the first week."

"I take it then that drinking the blood of the black-mass-baptised babe is out of the question too?"

"My God, what do you make of me?"

"Hungry," I said, rubbing my eyes to wipe away the fatigue. "So hungry."

"What does that mean?"

"Don't you know?"

"Matthew!" He raised his arms in an expansive, open gesture. "I'm the one trying to understand! Am I next? Is that what all this is leading up to?"

"My God, haven't you seen it? Look at the Tower!"

"This is about the Tower?"

"Haven't you noticed the bodies, the threats, the extortion, the death, the battles, the . . ."

"This is about the organisation that *I* created which, for the very first time, brought together under one roof all magicians, witches, warlocks, voodoo practitioners and . . . and bloody enchantresses of ancient and mystic lore, united at last, regardless of race, faith, creed, colour, gender, social status or wealth, to protect all magic-users in the city from the bias and bigotry of . . ."

"It's a monster! It gobbles up the best of the magicians and spits out the bones in a voodoo way! You really think employing a man whose guards carry guns under their armpits, or a dead necromancer with a sheet of paper down his throat, was going to create a friendly public image? You think it was nice of Lee to wage war against the Whites, or charming of Khay to guard a warehouse full of human organs that were most definitely not for the transplant business? The Tower is a unified organisation – a massive one – and the thing that unites it is fear! Of you! Of your servants and your power and your ambition and your . . ."

"How *dare* you judge me? I'd like to say that you were my apprentice and thus should have learnt some respect; but you're not even that! A blue-eyed demon crawled out of the telephone lines into the skin of someone I used to know – and you speak like this to me?"

Our voices had grown too loud. People were looking towards us, their conversation turning to a low buzz, while curious hearers tried not to be seen snooping. Bakker scowled and put his fingertips together in front of his nose; took in a long breath. Quieter, struggling to control his anger, he said, "You are correct; I have wanted to meet the angels for some time now; but I do not know what purpose you think I had in mind. I wished to study them, to learn about them, to understand what kind of a creature the angels are, nothing more."

"Hungry," we muttered, feeling tired and drained. "Hungry."

"Should have had a vol-au-vent then."

"The last time we met," I said, "you said you wanted to summon the angels; you wanted to bring them out of the phone lines into this world. You said you couldn't hear them any more, that you needed the help of another sorcerer to make the spell work. I asked why you wanted them out of their natural realm, and you said, 'Because they are alive; because they will not die.' I asked what you wanted. You said, 'Life. Just life.' Did it ever occur to you that there was a reason we didn't want you to hear us when we played in the wire? Did the thought cross your mind that perhaps the reason you couldn't hear us any more was because we didn't want you to? Did you think we were unaware of your attempts to summon us, to pull us out of the wires even before you approached me and asked for my help? What made you think you could just snatch us from our home and bind us to your desires? And Mr Bakker, give me credit for a little imagination. You don't want to *study* us; it was quite clear what your aims were. When you taught me you said that the angels were too dangerous to be listened to; that they preached freedom from all restraint, all laws, that they had no conception of responsibility, duty, need or even basic moral principles; that they were *free* in the purest, most unbound sense. You don't summon creatures like that to *study* them. You summon them if you've got their song in your head, if you think that perhaps, the freedom that they enjoyed could be yours. Power and fire and light and movement in a simple, cure-all spell."

"Well," he replied softly, fingers tight around the arms of his chair, knuckles sticking up through the skin like at any moment they might pop out, "that part at least sounds like my mistaken apprentice."

"We kept away from you," we said, "because even then we could sense that there was something about you that did not conform to our sense of what we should be, and what we are. It poured off you then and you stink of it now."

"And what, tell me," he half-growled, fighting to keep his voice civil and his face fixed in the polite smile of good company, "is that?"

"Hunger," we replied. "You do not simply want to study us, you were *hungry* for it, a starving creature desperately scrabbling for life – but not your life. Ours. You had passed the point where you made a distinction between what others had and what you desired for yourself. We sensed your intent, and I know it."

He half-lowered his head, tucking in his chin and nodding to himself in silence for a moment. Then he looked up sharply and said, perfectly level, "I'm sorry."

"You are?"

"I'm sorry for the bad opinion you have of me. I do not know how you have reached this, but I am sorry for your . . ."

"How I've reached it?! I reached it at roughly the same point the first set of claws severed a long list of my arteries! I reached it about the time my blood pressure dropped so low I started to go blind. I reached it at approximately the same moment that the shadow – *your* bloody shadow – pressed its fingers into my face, stared into my eyes and whispered through *my* blood on *its* teeth, 'Give me life!' Try that and see how it alters your long-held opinions in a very short time!"

A tremor of confusion on his face. "What?"

"When I walk out of here, do you know the first thing I'm going to do?"

"No."

"I'm going to find an underground station and sleep in it behind the biggest protective ward I can raise with a travelcard and a good spell until sunrise, so that the creature that you sent after me last time we met has a hard time killing me this time round too!"

"Matthew, what creature? What happened?!"

His voice was pained, shrill, tense. But I didn't know whether it was from the effort of lying – something I felt sure he could do perfectly well – or a genuine sound of need and upset. And just then, for an instant, we felt a hint of uncertainty, and almost pitied him. But this was what we were here for, what we wanted to know.

"It's a shadow," we said. "He has your face."

"I don't understand."

"He comes up out of the paving stones, wherever there's a thick enough patch of darkness. He killed Patel, Awan, Khan, Akute..."

"A creature? A summoned creature?"

"He has your face, this shadow," I repeated gently, studying his eyes for any hint of a reaction that wasn't a trembling uncertainty, tainted with fear. "The night we argued, he attacked me when I was alone, by the river. I'd never seen anything move so fast. He just appeared, *bang*, right behind me, and he had won before I even had a chance to raise a spell. Now that we are here, he is less certain in what he does. It seems he doesn't just want to kill; rather, he is interested in what makes us alive. 'Hello, Matthew's fire,' he says; and we are sure that if he wished to kill us he could have done so. But instead he toys, watches, studies, tries to work out what makes us what we are. We can hold him off for a while. But in the end, we doubt there is a way to kill *just* him, and for what he did to me, and what he wants with us, we *will* kill him."

"You... think this creature is connected to me. That's why you've done all this?"

"Yes."

"Why, because... because it looks a bit like me?" His voice was rising again, I could hear the tight edge in it as he struggled to keep it under control.

"Yes. And because it kills your enemies..."

"My enemies? I have no enemies!"

"The sorcerers who said 'No' to the Tower?"

"Do you really think I'd kill someone just because they couldn't see a good thing when it happened to them? Do you really think I'd hurt *you*?"

I hesitated and for the first time that evening, reluctantly let myself think about it, the certainty draining away like blood from a corpse. "I don't know," I answered finally. "I really don't."

"So on a hunch you're attacking my friends?"

"I have . . . seen evidence."

"Evidence? What kind of evidence?"

"Concerned citizens . . ."

"You're being used."

"Dead was dead was dead," I replied. "No getting round that very personal fact."

"And you blame me?"

"Yes."

"Why? Because we argued?!"

"Yes."

"I don't believe that my Matthew would be so stupid. But perhaps with the consciousness of an entity that is incapable of grasping more than its own flightiness . . ."

"This is my battle."

"You're just using the angels?"

"No."

"Then how does it work?"

"We are also angry."

"Why?"

"We . . . we . . ."

He looked at me and drummed his fingers impatiently on the armrest of his chair as we struggled to find the answer. "Well?" he spat finally. "You . . . *things* of little surplus electricity, you odd remnants of feeling, confused signals, what's your anger about? You've been given a gift beyond the wildest comprehension – you are alive! You've been called out of the wires where you were nothing more than a conglomeration of sense, and been given your very own, pre-packaged body, memories, experiences and learning that is probably the only thing that stopped you going mad at the first realisation of sight, sound and senses all for yourself. You have all your power and you have the pleasure of being really *alive* with it, in perfect, three-dimensional, physically stable sorcerer form! Why should you be angry at such a thing?"

"We . . . are not . . . we are glad to have seen this world, to understand at last what it is that the thoughts in our signal meant when they described 'yellow' or 'pink', to hear sounds as more than a flash of mathematics across our wings when we were travelling in the telephones. But we are not ourself any more. We were free. This world leaves you no capacity for what we were, and... in coming here, we have gained perceptions and... instincts... that we could never before conceive of. But we have lost everything. *Everything*. We were the blue electric angels, we could be in a thousand places at once and still be whole, we could bounce off the moon for sport and skim the sum total of the world's knowledge in an instant, ride the signal from America to Zimbabwe without even travelling, the world moving around us, we flew on radio waves three times round the earth and knew every inch of atmosphere that we touched as we went by. We were gods. Now we are just... *mortal*."

He nodded slowly. "I see. You really are just a child in this place, aren't you?"

We didn't answer.

"A child with a lot of power," he added, in a reproving voice. "There's an irony there."

"How so?"

"When I asked Matthew to help me summon you, he refused. Now that he is you and you are him – a complicated relationship, I'll grant you – surely *he* can see the irony."

"The thought had crossed my mind."

"Well? Now you know what the angels are like, do you still begrudge me my desire to know them better?"

I thought about it. "Yes," I said.

"Why?!" He nearly laughed on the word.

"I think... it boils down to intent."

"That isn't an argument the judge would respect."

"You're going to sue me?"

"Don't be so shallow."

"I don't have a permanent address to send the order to."

"You vanished for two years!"

"And now you know where I was."

"No, not entirely."

"I think you can guess."

"Guess at what? You say you were *killed* – now that is something I find hard to get my head round, not least since I taught you so well never to dabble with necromancy; and you don't look like a man suffering from the skin complaints of the average animated corpse."

"I'm not particularly inclined to tell you the details, to be honest."

"Then you're not really giving me a chance, are you?"

"A chance?"

"Are you here for any better reason?"

"I don't know."

"Do you know why you're here at all?"

"You invited me."

"Yes – because you were my apprentice. What's your reason?"

"I think . . . I wanted to be absolutely sure."

"About what?"

"Whether you were as I remembered."

"And am I?"

"I don't know."

"You seem confused."

"It's very complicated. Can I . . . I just want to ask something. I think it might be why I came, in fact."

"Ask away."

"Do you really not know that the shadow has your face?"

He met our eyes squarely. "Matthew – or whatever you'd like to be called now – I have no idea what you are talking about."

We tried to read some sort of truth in him and, for a second, I desperately, desperately wanted to believe it, to say I was sorry and that I'd never do it again and I hoped he could understand and forgive me and we could explain everything and it would all go back to how it was and . . .

. . . never going to be how it was . . .

wouldn't that mean Lee and Khay were dead for nothing?

. . . a lorry of bodies . . .

we simply didn't know.

I stood up quickly. "Sorry," I said, not knowing why. "I'm sorry." I stepped round him quickly and headed for the stairs.

"Matthew, wait!" He struggled to turn the chair in that small space. "Matthew!"

"Matthew?"

The voice came from the doorway of the bar. Its owner held a champagne glass in one hand, and a handbag in the other, its small chain hooked in at her elbow. The bag was the same silvery colour as her dress, and her shoes gave her an extra few inches of height that she didn't really need. The dress clung to every inch of her like a libidinous friend, revealing that, along with a haircut that had removed all but a short skullcap of red-tinted dark brown hair, she'd lost a lot of weight since I'd seen her last, rounding down in some areas and out in others. She held herself with the same good posture, and had the same relaxed dignity in the curve of her arms and openness of her eyes. But when she looked at me in that moment, as well as weight loss, there was something about Dana Mikeda that meant I hardly recognised her.

I looked from her, to Bakker, to her again, and then, drawn by a nervous tic when I had looked at Bakker, again to him. He stared at me with pain, uncertainty, even a touch of fear on his face, sitting at the top of the stairs on the very edge of his chair, leaning towards me as if at any second he'd leap up and run after me, but unable to do so. It took a moment to realise what was so wrong with that picture – nothing in how he looked or the way he sat, but in the environment around him as, opening one arm out towards me as if trying to call me home, he cast no shadow.

I turned and ran.

I had run once before two years ago, on a cold night quite like this, along the same river, after speaking to the same man. I tried in vain to remember if there'd been a dark reflection around him then, or if the light had just tripped off him like it forgot to notice how he blocked it. My memories were too easily movable – if I wanted, I could paint that image of him in the wheelchair on the night I'd died with no shadow at all, or with a big black shape of himself looming halfway up the back wall. There was simply no way to tell, as my imagination worked overtime, desperately trying to find gaps and plug them, in everything I thought and believed.

I walked as quickly as I could without being called "Thief!" or knocking into the pedestrians still turning out of the theatres, restaurants and concerts along the bank by the river, just like I had two years ago – but this time, I knew what was coming, and watched the image of my own shadow moving under my feet, waiting for it to turn. I was halfway to Hungerford Bridge, the pedestrian walkways bolted onto the original railway bridge lit up like snowy knives, my shadow splintered into a dozen pale blue fractures in front of me from the lights in the trees by the riverside, when a bit at a time, like the hands coming together on a clock face, my shattered shadow started to come together into one pool of me-shaped blackness, and bend *towards* the light.

That was when I started to run for real. I slung my satchel as securely as I could across my shoulder and turned into the crowd, keeping close to the silvery rail at the edge of the bridge, snatching up some of the cold from it into my fingertips as I ran, breathing the river air as deep as I could; there was power by the river, an intense, old magic that the druids had been drawing on back in the days when wizards had burnt the colour of forest fires and summoned ivy from the paving stones, instead of barbed wire. I breathed it in as deep as I could as I ran, felt its cold seep down into my lungs and into my blood, pushing away some of the heat and pain from my underexercised legs and filling me with a sense of giddy lightness and strength, so that for a moment I knew, *knew* that I could run the length of the marathon, and if I did my skin would be cold and my mouth wouldn't be dry. My feet slapped with a dull, metallic shudder as I ran, and we savoured our own confidence as we dodged round late-night tourists on their way from eating deep-fried oysters in Chinatown or heading to a grand hotel on the Strand. We were moving with the satisfaction of a mathematician on the edge of solving some mysterious problem, knowing that it can be done, and done that night.

At the end of the bridge I took the steps down onto the Embankment. I was fearful of how empty the greeny-yellow brick tunnel looked towards Charing Cross station, how easily we might be ambushed in that space, and drawn by the crowd moving towards the station entrance. In the street, with its sandwich bars, cobblers' shops and dirty news-stands, the sense of the power was different, that we swept up in our fingertips like seaside breeze tickling the palm of our hand. It gave off none of the sense-numbing, consuming balm of the river, but had a lower, hotter sensation to it, through which we could feel the rumbling of trains beneath us and sense, as our legs hit their stride, the pulse of the city. We ran with the rhythm of that road, the commuter's rhythm, the pace of life you only get around railway stations; that puts the step of every mother, father and child into a regular *tum tum tum tum* leaving no room to pause and consider which way to go or how to get there, but pushes you on towards your destination with no messing or hesitation, thank you. For a moment, I understood a bit more of the bikers' magic, that fed off these rhythms embedded in the city's life and was most potent between 5 p.m. and 7.30 p.m. when the entire population seemed to be travelling, like the changing of the tide; even now, at this hour of the night, I could taste some of its potency lingering on the air.

I ran up the street, catching the smell of the last sandwich in the bar, spilt beer, the whiff of curry powder from the open door of the tandoori, urine from the door of some lawyer's firm, rubbish being thrown out from behind the back of an Italian restaurant, and sweat mixed with disco music from the basement window of a gym beneath the station, and still my shadow refused to move with the bending of the light.

At Charing Cross station I dodged past the waiting taxis and paused for a moment at the central spike of sludgy-brown stone that, so legend had it, marked the traditionally central point of the city. Legend or not, the thing burnt in my senses in all its spiky, multi-layered tastelessness. I stood in front of it and half-closed my eyes, and for a moment, in that place, I could feel every pigeon like they were hairs on my head, blowing in the wind, and taste every rat like their claws were the serrated edges of my own teeth. It was the same sensation I'd felt at the very top of the Royal Mile in Edinburgh, or at the Arc de Triomphe in Paris, or standing in Temple Bar in Dublin; whether or not the place really was the geographical centre, it was still a hub, magical north on the compass. As such, its power sent a tingle through my skin; and for a moment I knew exactly what it was to be the woman remembering the first kiss of her ex-boyfriend on the number 9 bus, or the train driver leaning on his handle underground, or the child eating chips and watching the departures board in the station, or the sleepy passenger in the plane overhead, looking down at the city beneath him as they circled in to land.

For a moment, I considered diving into that sense, just like so many sorcerers had before me, letting go of their own skins and their own feelings and immersing themselves in the city. Wherever I'd gone, I had been told that it was the most dangerous thing of all for two sorcerers to fight in the very centre of a city, at its heart, where it was so easy to forget why you were there, and just sink yourself into the endless magic available in that place. You'd think you were using the magic to your own ends, until you were found days, sometimes months, later, wandering through the city's streets with the absolute certainty that you were the 91 bus to Crouch End. There was nowhere better in the city to become lost.

Come be we and be free!

We jerked our eyes open but didn't move; our thoughts were still tangled in the swirling of dirty newspapers caught in the wake of a passing lorry; in the almost inaudible ticking of the traffic lights; in the slamming of shutters over the supermarket windows of the...

Come be me!

So easy to become lost...

...just sink into the city...

Hello, Matthew's fire!

We snatched at our satchel to make sure it was still securely there and ran, no longer bothering to see where we were going or whether the cars would stop when we crossed the road; no need to ask or look – we felt the brakes pressing into our flesh, although when we had last checked our arms weren't made of tyre rubber. We heard the echo of our footsteps from the drains underneath where we were nibbling on dropped chow mein in a cardboard box; we saw ourself running past the side of St Martin in-the-Fields, looking down from our nest in the high gutter of the tall white houses with the big shuttered windows and the poor insulation in the roof that helped keep us warm when it rained – we knew we were running, by all these signs.

We ran towards Trafalgar Square, through the traffic and down the steps into the wide, pedestrianised area around Nelson's Column and the big stone lions crouched on their pedestals. Pigeons scattered towards the Arab Emirates Bank, and Admiralty Arch, embedded with figures of imperial triumph and heaving bosom, and framing a vista of the Mall and Buckingham Palace. Distances changed perspective in the centre of London: only close to did Nelson's Column seem to tower up for ever, whereas from a few hundred yards away it seemed scarcely higher than the rooftops around it. From its broad, stepped base, in equal measure I could feel the buzzing, gaudy excitement of Leicester Square, and taste the sedate, patient, weighty magic of St James's Park, even though in my imagination they had always seemed far apart.

Perhaps because our senses were fired up with fear, again, at Nelson's Column, we felt that focus of magical energy waiting for our attention, sitting at our feet with a big friendly expression and an open maw full of sense, inviting us to forget that we ran or what it was we fled, but to be instead the beggar sitting by the ATM and the actor taking his final bow in the theatre, or even just the hotness in the theatre lights shining down on the stage; whatever we wanted to be, a part of the city.

I ran my fingers across the smooth side of one of the lions and down the rougher edge of the pollution-crunched stone, centring myself with the reality of those textures beneath my hand.

I am . . .

we are

Or perhaps . . .

we am me

Already free, already me. Don't need to fall tonight.

Catching my breath, I turned and ran on, up towards the imposing pillared entrance of the National Gallery and its modern, glassy extension, ducking into the small passage between the two and bounding up the steps while in the other direction, skater kids rattled down the ramps and leapt over the shallow steps the other way, spinning their boards and making grunting sounds whether or not their manoeuvre had worked.

Leicester Square, even at this time of the night, hadn't stopped; the doors to the cinemas were still opened wide, though the park with its guardian Charlie Chaplin statue was chained up tight, with the lights of a funfair extinguished. I slowed to a walk and struggled to get my breath; then headed past the Swiss Centre with its terrible clock of musical bells and automated figures, whose tastelessness was, nevertheless, an attraction in itself, being tacky enough to embody the spirit of the whole area. I hurried past ticket touts and music shops, and vendors of woolly hats, umbrellas and plaster models of the Houses of Parliament, until I reached Piccadilly Circus. Traffic whooshed up Shaftesbury Avenue, or slogged resentfully the other way. I slowed to an amble, and paused by the sculpted horses exploding out of their fountain on one side of Piccadilly Circus. Running my fingers through the water, I watched the reflection on a hundred pennies at the bottom, as they caught the lights from the flashing billboards overhead, reflecting from red to blue to gold to green to burning white as the messages rolled in their metres-high illuminated font. I dug in my bag until I found the jeweller's little purple box from Bond Street, then took out the single gold coin, heavy and cool in my palm. If you didn't know it was gold you might have thought it was just a tacky plastic badge painted a certain colour; but there was no doubting the weight, or the texture of the metal. I closed my eyes, gripped it until my fingers hurt, and made a wish. Then, still holding it in my clenched fist, I stuck my arm into the water up to the elbow joint, and let the coin go.

I felt the movement in the air and turned instinctively, knowing what it would be; I had felt the air change like that once before, and I had dismissed it and died – the same mistake would not happen twice.

Hunger was still only halfway out of the paving stones and rising, emerging out of the shadow of a lamp-post in a thin, pale line, his shape only half there, coat billowing in and out of shadowy existence around him. His claws, however, were real and solid and black enough as I raised my arms and caught him by the wrists even as he slashed down towards my face with his curved fingertips. His arms were ghostlike; I could see the traffic barrier behind them, and through his chest a rickshaw man pedalling his latest fare towards Soho, as Hunger rose into the air and I turned to face him.

I hissed, "Do you really want to fight here? In this place, with so many lights and people and so much *power*? Do you really think this is wise?"

"You forget," he replied, and his breath was like the cold blast of air when a train is about to arrive at an underground platform. "They will never see me, nor know who I was, when I drink your fire!"

He twisted his arms in my grip; my hands had no difficulty encircling his wrists, they were so thin. But as he twisted, his fingers stretched down to brush my skin, and his black claws gouged through my clothes and into my arms. There was no sudden shock of pain; he dug the tips of his black fingers into my skin with the slow inexorability of a knife cutting into cold butter: a laborious work of strength but one that he would do, breaking the skin, the capillaries, the muscle, the tips of his fingers brushing bone and . . .

I think I must have called out as my blood rose under his hands, seeping out and staining my jacket an odd dark purple in that reflective, changing neon light, because he smiled and whispered, "I do not care for the rules of your kind; that is what it means to be free, yes? You drove me back too many times, little sorcerer and his blue flames!"

But even though his strength was unstoppable, and I could feel the dull pain starting to throb up my elbows and into my chest as his grip tightened and tightened and I struggled to hold on to his wrists in turn, he still wasn't all there. He didn't have feet, merely a trailing-off of coat into the shadow of the lamp-post, as if he was a seal halfway out of water; and his chest was still an incoherent grey smear across the air, not real or solid at all.

I said through gritted teeth, "Make a wish?"

"To feast richly," he replied. "Always, to feast!"

"Probably have to invest more than a ten pence, then."

For a moment, he didn't understand. Then a glint of comprehension entered the sunken, half-there, half-gone eyes. His glance darted up to the horses rearing behind me in their fountain, then to my face, then to the wet sleeve beneath his grasp, turning pinkish red with my blood. His hand was too thin, I realised, too insubstantial even to notice that the thing it held was damp. We grinned triumphantly and exclaimed, "We know now that you are weak!" and with every ounce of strength we had, with every flux of power and magic we could find, digging our toes so hard into the soles of our shoes that the pavement hummed beneath us, we clenched our fingers around the ghosts of his wrists, and turned. We heaved him to one side and threw him straight towards the fountain, twisting ourself head first towards the water line and dragging him along with us. As he was pulled towards it, he stretched. His legs melted into a grey blur within the shadow of the lamp-post, then elongated like elastic pulled taut. We plunged his head into the water, which burst into steam as he touched it, boiled and bubbled around us while he thrashed, his fingers instantly coming free from my arms and lashing up towards my face. But he was blind while his head was driven down as far as I could push it, towards the floodlight lamp that burnt towards the horses rearing overhead. I snarled, "Make a wish, and let there be light!"

And the stretching shadows of the lamp-post thinned, paled, fled. The floodlights scorching upwards at the horses took on the colour of an angry equatorial sun; the neon lights above Piccadilly Circus spat sparks and grew brighter and brighter, until I had to close my eyes against them; and still the intensity of it grew through my eyelids as every car lamp, brake light, street light, shop light and reflective surface lit like a newly born sun, burning away every shadow and hint of darkness so that for a second, in the middle of the night, it was daytime.

The cold slippery head beneath my hands vanished. It disappeared so suddenly that I staggered and nearly fell forward into the icy bubbling water of the fountain. I heard a sharp electric pop nearby, then quickly dragged my hands out of the water as beneath its surface the floodlights brightened so that the horses' eyes above me seemed mad, and then snuffed out, the burning wires of the lamps withering into scorched black worms. I heard a snap and a crack like lightning on a hot, rainless summer's day, and the skid of traffic as the headlamps of vehicles all around, heated to bursting by the intensity of light pouring out of them, burst. Above the junction of Regent Street and Shaftesbury Avenue the neon lights grew too bright to look at and exploded, showering the street below with hot sparks and light, hurling out fragments of glass. As a final, apologetic encore, the street lamps snuffed out, plunging the Circus into panic-struck darkness.

I sat on the rim of the fountain's basin as Piccadilly Circus exploded into chaos. As the lights around them popped out into nothing, the pedestrians went quickly from yelping with surprise, to getting on their mobiles and telling their friends and family in rushed, excited voices, that they'd just seen the most amazing thing. The more enterprising of them rushed to take photos with maximum exposure, or film the still-glowing lamps of Piccadilly in contrast to the dead lights of Haymarket, hoping to flog their images to the London *Evening Standard*. The traffic came to a standstill, after one 38 bus driver, seeing his lights explode, had swerved across Shaftesbury Avenue so that his front wheels had skidded up onto the pavement. With his bus being eighteen metres long, all other traffic had been stopped in both directions. Some drivers trapped by the bus blared their horns; others, seeing that order wasn't about to be restored, got out to buy coffee and a doughnut from the nearby twenty-four-hour store, paying by torchlight. As with the best curiosities in London, the crowd gathered in half the time it took the police to arrive, congregating to see the strange thing of the lights *not* being on, and to speculate on what it was that could have blown so many bulbs at once. The police cars eventually managed to crawl their way through via the back streets of Soho, the sirens being audible several minutes before the cars became visible, preceded by several officers in yellow fluorescent jackets, who'd despaired and climbed out to try and make sense of the situation on foot.

As all this went on, I sat and rolled up my shirtsleeves. Four perfect crescent moons had been incised on the underside of each forearm, and all were bleeding copiously. I was tempted to wash the injuries with water from the fountain, but it seemed inappropriate to the magic of that place to use wishing water for cleaning wounds. Instead, I drew out a penny from my pocket, offered up a thought of thanks to whatever spirit of urban magic had blessed the waters of that place with the wish-maker's mark, and dropped the coin into the water, watching it sink. In the darkness of the Circus I couldn't see my gold coin, and half suspected there wouldn't be anything left to see.

I crossed over the road and went to the all-night pharmacy. There I bought a roll of bandages and some disinfectant liquid that stung so badly we almost ran outside again in search of water. Sitting in a passport photo booth for privacy, we wrapped up our bleeding arms in rolls of bandage too thick to be covered by the remnants of our shirtsleeves. With just our coat protecting the bandages from the queries of the police as they struggled to organise the traffic, we went home.

When we woke in the morning, our arms were still bleeding; in fact the bandages were soaked through. It was a bad start to what, we thought, should have been a day of relative triumph.

By mid-morning, with no sign of clotting, we checked out of our hotel and went in search of a doctor.

At the hospital south of the river, Dr Seah studied our bloody arms and said, "Uh-huh. OK. You know, they train us to be like, you know, all sympathetic and comforting and shit? But looking at this . . . you're kinda totally fucked."

"What's wrong?"

"Haemophilia?" she suggested in a pained voice.

"It's not very likely."

"It didn't seem very likely, seeing as how you were here last week and didn't bleed out. Know what, just for kicks, shall I call an ambulance?"

We raised our bloody arms to the light and studied the blood still trickling into the crooks of our elbows. "It may not be enough," we replied. "Perhaps a taxi would be better."

Weakness. Human weakness, frail, pale, failing. How could we be ourself, trapped in dying flesh?

Time to take charge of myself. Be practical, businesslike; keep a level head in a situation of growing tension, keep the voice steady, the eyes locked, the chin down and the shoulders back. If you start to sound afraid, start to look afraid, you'll be scared before you know it.

Dr Seah ordered a taxi. We climbed in the back, our hands starting to shake, and I gave an address. The driver said, "You sure you don't need a doctor? You don't look . . ."

"There's a doctor friend at this address."

"OK, if you're sure."

He took me to where I wanted to go: Chalfont Street Market, flanked on one side by the reflective grey glass of Euston station, and on the other by the red bricks of the British Library as it tried to blend in with the fairy tale castle towers and arched windows of St Pancras station. I got out, thanked him, paid with what little money I had left, and staggered enough up the road to make him think that I was serious about continuing on it. When the taxi was gone, I turned back the way I'd come and, feeling the tremble in our knees as we walked

to fear is not to be free

we are . . .

. . . I am . . .

come be me . . .

I walked, I *made us* walk, because I knew what it was like to be this weak and we had no conception of it, round the corner to the boarded-up, broken windows of the Elizabeth Garrett Anderson Hospital for Women. Its tea-coloured walls were cut off from the public street by high chipboard hoardings, plastered over with ads for concerts, magazines and, in the odd place here or there, the scrawling graffiti of the Whites, the snouts of their crawling black-and-white crocodiles pointing towards the Kingsway Exchange. Round the corner, towards the main doors overhung by a drooping green entrance sign welcoming you to the hospital, were notices warning "danger" and "keep out" and "no children". The doors themselves were covered over with corrugated iron, and padlocked; on them someone had painted the face of a white-skinned nurse, with eyes shut, and over that someone else had added in big black letters, "**WERE HAV WE VOICES??**". I knocked, but the corrugated iron just banged loudly against the empty door frames behind, while broken glass crunched under my feet like thick snow.

I kicked at the iron barrier, and shouted, "Hey!" up at the hospital's broken windows, but my voice was snatched away by the passing of a bus, crawling round the traffic lights away from Euston station.

Losing our patience, we reached into the satchel for our skeleton keys, and fumbled at the padlock with slippery, bloodstained fingers. At length we found the right key, coaxed it into shape, turned, and opened the lock. We pulled the chain off the door, and dragged it back, the heavy metal squeaking and scratching painfully across the pavement, before ducking through one of the broken glass door panels.

Inside, traceries of overcast daylight seeped in around plywood panels boarding up the window panes. Though the corridors were bare, they were full of broken glass, water dripping from shattered pipes, and rotting pieces of splintered wood, all suggesting nonetheless what this place had once been. The tiled floor was discoloured from years of floods and droughts and more floods, staining it with moulds and interesting tufts of vivid green moss that gave the place a cold, sharp smell of decay. At a crack in the wall I pulled a few purple buddleia flowers off their stem, and crunched them in my palm to a handful, before slipping it into the frontmost pocket of my satchel. Buddleia grew in London wherever buildings were left neglected; they sprouted through every wall by every railway cutting and out of every derelict site, spreading roots into the stone itself. As such, buddleia flowers had their own special properties within any urban magician's inventory; wherever they were found, they weren't to be ignored.

With the last fragment of purple in my bag, I chose a left turning at whim, and splashed my way through puddles of stagnant water stained with clouds of chemical whiteness. I found a flight of stairs, with half the tiles missing from their treads, and the scarred concrete showing underneath. It led past a wall supported by scaffolding; on the first floor was another empty, airless corridor.

I called out, "Hello?"

My voice was eaten up so quickly by the dead silence of that place, I half-wondered if I'd called at all.

At random I turned right, then left. I was about to climb the next flight, when behind me in the corridor I heard a click. I turned. A woman stood there in a nurse's uniform. Her face was the same near-perfect white of the graffiti image on the iron door downstairs, her hat the same old-fashioned, almost theatrical blue of the painted nurse's cap. Her expression was one of immense seriousness.

"And who are you?" she asked in a prim voice.

Her hair was silvery-grey. A nurse's watch hung from her apron; she wore black tights and black sensible shoes, had skinny legs, and old hands, folded neatly in front of her.

When we didn't answer, she repeated, "Well, come, come now, I haven't got all day."

"Swift," I stuttered. "My name's Swift."

"Well, Mr Swift, can I help you?"

"I'm looking for the hospital."

"As you can judge for yourself," she said, voice not changing, expression not wavering, arms not moving, eyes looking down at me across the length of her nose even though she had to be half a foot shorter than I was, "this is a hospital."

"Yes. Sorry, yes. I can see."

"If you can see, why did you ask?"

"I . . . need help."

"That is why most people come to a hospital. What exactly appears to be the problem?"

I rolled up a coat sleeve to reveal one of the blood-bandages. Her lips thinned. She made a little *ummm* noise, tutted, then barked, "Very well, come this way, chop chop." Turning on one heel, she set off down the corridor. I struggled to keep up, striding as fast as I could without breaking into a run. "I suppose you have tried the regular services; there is a waiting list, yes?"

"Yes."

"And? Please don't waste my time with the usual inadequate excuses, Mr Swift. 'I just happened to be playing with the bones of the dead' or 'It just so fell out that I accidentally summoned the spirit of a thousand shards of falling glass' or other feeble tales. I really don't care how the injury was inflicted, I simply need the full information to make a good diagnosis."

She turned into a room as mouldy and dark as the others; but unlike them, it was possessed of a large wooden cupboard with another padlock across its doors, and a dentist's chair set in the middle, with a bright lamp lit up above it. Although the lamp had no electrical lead, it grew brighter as the nurse approached it. She waved me to the chair, and as I sat down she added another "Well?! What happened?"

"Honestly – I was attacked by the living shadow of a sorcerer, a creature of darkness and hunger that longs to drink my blood and which I managed to defeat by the use of a wish-spell and a lot of burning light. It dug its nails into my arms; and now they won't stop bleeding."

"Interesting," she said in a voice of a woman who couldn't care less. She reached into her apron and pulled out a pair of glasses that she rested at the end of her nose, and a pair of very sharp-looking scissors. "But nothing special. I don't suppose you killed this living essence of darkness?"

"I doubt it."

"Wouldn't that have been the most sensible reaction?" she said, peering at me over the tops of her glasses straight down the sharp tip of her nose as I lay on the chair.

"It's a shadow," I replied. "It dies when the man that casts it dies."

"How terribly tedious," she intoned. "You know, sometimes, I don't know why I bother – they all come back here eventually."

She started snipping neatly at the bandages around my arms, and when they came away, tutted at the bloody half-moon indents in my skin. "Yes, well . . ."

"I . . . do not know what it is I should offer you for your help," I said as we turned our head away and half-closed our eyes against the sight of our own blood.

"Offer me?" A shrill note of indignation entered her voice. "Young man, there are three things that make Britain great. The first is our inability at playing sports."

"How does that make Britain great?"

"Despite the certainty of loss, we try anyway with the absolute conviction that this year will be the one, regardless of all evidence to the contrary!"

I raised my eyebrows, but that simply meant I could see my own blood more clearly, so looked away and said nothing.

"The second," she went on, "is the BBC. It may be erratic, tabloid, under-funded and unreliable, but without the World Service, obscure Dickens adaptations, the *Today* programme and *Doctor Who*, I honestly believe that the cultural and communal capacity of this country would have declined to the level of the apeman, largely owing to the advent of the mobile phone!"

"Oh," I said, feeling that something was expected. "Oh" was enough.

"And lastly, we have the NHS!"

"This is an NHS service?" I asked incredulously.

"I didn't say that; I merely pointed out that the NHS makes Britain great. Now lie still."

I lay still and tried not to flinch as her fingers probed the tender flesh on both my arms. She tutted again.

On a whim I asked, "What about the Beatles?"

"What about them?"

"Do they make Britain great?"

"Don't play silly buggers in my hospital, thank you."

"Sorry."

After a while she said, "Did you collect some buddleia?"

"Yes. Was that OK?"

"There's plenty around, why should I care?"

"But . . . you asked."

"A nurse is supposed to put the patient at ease during unpleasant procedures, in order to facilitate a calm and quick medical process."

"You haven't done anything too unpleasant . . ." I began, then hesitated.

"The word you caught your tongue up on was 'yet'," she said with a small-toothed grin. "I'm glad you thought it through before making a rash utterance."

"This is a reassuring medical procedure?"

"You survived – badly – being attacked by a living shadow, essence of darkness," she said. "A little honesty isn't going to hurt. Not as much as the medicine."

"Do you enjoy what you do?"

"It's a living."

"How?"

She pulled a key out of her pocket and undid the heavy padlock on the cupboard. Inside, the shelves were in shadow. "You're scared of doctors," she said briskly to the clinking of jars. "You're frightened by medicine. It's fine. You've also had a couple of splintered ribs, a twisted ankle, a lot of bruising and been clinically dead sometime in the last two years. So I can understand your point of view."

"How do you know all that?"

"I read your palm, do you really want to know?" she retorted in an uninterested voice. Turning, she revealed a large glass kitchen jar containing some sort of dark, sludgy goo. "Crushed rat's skull, desalinated Thames water, ground dried moss scraped from the base of a leaking pipe in Kings Cross station, a pinch of mortar dust and a vestige of unleaded petrol drawn from the top of a puddle of torrential August rain; ground together, microwaved for ten minutes and filtered with the light from a photographer's lamp for three days and three nights – sound all right to you?"

"For what?"

She tutted again at my impertinence. "Mr – Swift, wasn't it? Mr Swift, did you bother to consider some of the medical implications of being injured by a creature of pure darkness *before* you rashly engaged it in mortal combat? I doubt it. Young people never do. You all think you're immortal. Lie still." She popped the top off with the hiss-snap of escaping pressure, and from one of her pockets, which I was beginning to suspect were not nearly big enough for all the things that she seemed to fit in them with perfect ease, pulled out a small wooden spatula. She scooped a large dollop of the slippery, shining dark gunk from the jar, took a grip of my right wrist, pulling my arm straight with a hand like an iron clamp, and started smearing the stuff across my wounds with the casual air of a grandmother icing a birthday cake.

The effect was like eating hot Vietnamese curry: for the first few strokes of the spatula, there was no sensation beyond that of thick soap bubbles moving on the skin, or of sticky flour being washed off the fingertips. Only when the mind had been fooled into thinking that it wouldn't be so bad did the burning hit. It started as a dull itch, quickly rising to an intense, fiery pulse that went right down to the bone and shot up past the elbow joint and into the shoulder blade; my fingers burnt and my neck cramped. We jerked at the shock of it, but her grip was unrelenting, and her face showed no sign of humour as she muttered, "Don't be a baby."

"It hurts!" we whimpered, mostly for the relief of having breath in our mouth and sound in our ears; any sort of sense to distract us.

"And it'll be over soon," she said. "If it was really that bad I'd have thought about giving you an anaesthetic; but you know how it is with budget cutbacks these days." On our skin the dark substance started to mix with our blood, in brownish-black whorls the colour of treacle. "You'll get a little dizziness," she added, "but please try and control any latent sorcerous urges you might have to incinerate my hospital. Despite its infinite patience, the NHS isn't that understanding, and we have to serve everyone equally."

We squeezed our eyes shut and bit our lip until we could taste blood. It wasn't dizziness; not quite. It was . . . more of a loosening of thoughts, a disintegration of the straight, neat lines of thoughts-with-words, of structured reasonings and human sounds, splitting down, as our mind inflated like a hot-air balloon, into its component parts, like the dream-state just before sleeping or wakening when it seems perfectly logical for the goldfish not to like to peel its own potatoes on the bus. I thought of my thoughts, those conscious processes and pains, as thoughts-with-words, as understandings and rationales within the constraints of language; but in that state, our thoughts were nothing of the sort, they were . . .

hello hello? yeah hi i'm looking for jeff yeah jeff the guy with the no I can't hang up will you just listen he's

mum died on thursday. yeah next week its

three poppadoms no three. three. well if they said that

look move the thing to tuesday, i've gotta go and

help me! he's in the house and he's coming for me and oh god oh god if you

yeah miss you too

hello?

hello?

HELLO?

We opened our eyes. We grabbed the nurse's arm as she reached across with another dollop of gunge, and hissed, "When did you last make a phone call?"

"Mr Swift, is this entirely . . ."

"Your name was Jean but then your father died. He was a doctor. You cried down the phone and said help me, help me, please, but she was in Paris, she couldn't come in time, there weren't any tickets, it was Christmas she said baby, it'll be OK, it'll be OK, and you found the costume and you knew about magic you knew what made it tick, you told your friend on the phone that you were going to make it work and he said, what are you doing, what do you think you're talking about and you said goodbye. Sorry I have to leave you goodbye. I'll always think of you and then you hung up. You haven't picked up a phone since. You fell silent, you don't want to know, nothing that isn't in front of you, no one that isn't there, no voices, no distance, no responsibilities, just this, just goodbye Alex, I'll sometimes think of you, but don't think of me, goodbye."

Jean pulled her wrist carefully free of our fingers and met our eyes without flinching. "Fascinating," she murmured at last. "You know, you really should have informed me that you were sharing your consciousness with the stranded memory of the telephone wires, it qualifies as relevant medical history." Her voice was level, her hand was shaking.

"We know you," we whispered.

"Do you?"

"We know what you said."

"How?"

"It's . . ."

somewhere in flying thoughts

blue memories of what we are of

hello!

you there?

anyone there?

hello?

gotta go, darling, gotta go now

don't hang up

bye

good night, sweet dreams!

hello? i'm looking for this number it's for this guy

hello?

"We are the thoughts you left behind," we murmured. "We-are . . . the feelings in your voice, even if he didn't hear. We are . . ."

"Responding interestingly to what should really just be dizziness," she said briskly. "Does your blood usually turn blue and wriggle like maggots in the presence of oxygen?"

We glanced at the trickling blue sparks crawling across our skin where the medicine had met our blood, and I felt suddenly sick, the world a spinning vague thing seen through a heat haze, tinnitus in my ears and my head aching, no longer a hot-air balloon but stuffed with lead, dragging me down with the sound of

hello!

anyone there?

never had a chance to say...

look i know this shouldn't be done by phone but i want you to know that

looking for someone is there

operator?

hello? Hello? HELLO?

"Help me!" I blurted through gritted teeth. "Please, help me!"

"Well now, that all depends on the problem," said the nurse in a voice of infinite patience.

"I can't remember! I can't remember what... what I was before! I can't remember being me!"

"You'd be wanting a shrink more than a nurse," she explained, and she had got her composure back, in an instant switched back into professional, businesslike mode. "I can give you a referral." Then, quieter, sharp little words to be spoken and forgotten again, "You still want the bleeding to stop?"

"Don't know, don't know..."

"I don't want to cast a shadow on your evening, but it's that or a slow and anaemic death, which, may I add, will do nothing for your complexion..." The smile gleamed, not exactly cruel, but neither bursting with compassion. She leant in close and murmured, "... unless that's a tempting thing?"

I hesitated.

We said, "No."

And we were surprised that we had spoken, surprised to hear ourself sound so confident, so sure of it, surprised that I hadn't spoken sooner or more certainly.

"You sure? I mean, if you want the shrink..."

"No. We want... no. Please. Help us."

"Help us, or help me?"

"We are the same."

"You sure?" she asked nicely. "Only it seems to me that one of you has blue blood, and one of you has red, and one of you knows about the things that were in the phone line and one of you, probably the clinically dead one, has a better grounding in the personal ego – not that I want to speculate beyond my training, you understand. You may share the same skin and the same voice, but I'm really not entirely sure that you're working on the same track."

We thought...

But then *I* thought...

"I... am sorry," I said.

"We're sorry," we added.

"I... please, forgive me, I... spoke..." I mumbled.

"We did not think that... we are..." we explained.

"Other arm," she said, switching the iron grip from one wrist to the other. "This time, try not to drip electric blue sparks everywhere, please? It's really not my place to judge my patients."

"Why not?" we asked. "Would you treat a murderer?" I added.

"Yes," she said flatly. "If he was ill."

"Why?"

"Medical oath, vows of service, duty, legal reasons, NHS policy, all that."

"But *why*?"

"You should know. One of you."

"Which one?" I asked, smiling despite myself and the pain in my head or on my skin. "It's not how it is," we grunted with a wince.

She paused, staring down at us, black splotch running down the edge of the wooden spatula in her hand. "Life is magic," she replied. "That's all there is to it. You're losing it, aren't you, sorcerer? You can't keep control."

"Yes," I said. "I mean . . . no."

"Which one?"

"That depends on whether the question was rhetorical."

"Oh, a wisecracker as well as magically confused." She shrugged. "Oh, well."

"That's it, 'Oh, well'?"

"Not my place to . . ."

". . . to judge, I know."

"I'm going to finish up here, and bandage it." She beamed. "Change them every twelve hours for the next three days, then you might consider going with plasters. Men in bandages feel so righteous it's almost unbearable. Not having period pains every month gives them a whole superiority complex, but when they're in bandages they just want to be loved."

"Are you talking about me, or is this a general piece of medical observation?"

"I suspect you wouldn't complain to my supervisor, if you didn't like my attitude," she replied.

"Who is your supervisor?"

"Oh . . ." She waved the wooden stick with airy abandon, splattering gobbets of sticky black goo around the room. "Higher powers would give them too much ego, demigods brings in this whole religious aspect, spirits seems a bit Peter Pan-esque, so we'll just go with..."

"Mystical forces?"

"Smart button."

"Thank you."

"Feel better now? Less gyrating black spots, fewer screaming voices and uncontrollable magical memories?"

"A bit, yes, thank you."

"All part of the service," she said. "Now – I'm going to get bandages. Please don't evaporate into your constituent parts before I get back."

"I'll do my best," I replied, and, to our surprise, we meant it.

She got bandages. She let the black slime settle on our arms, and set into a thin crust, before brushing it off briskly with a rough cloth that tugged and strained against the cuts on our skin until we thought they'd bleed all over again just from the sheer vigour with which she cleaned. However, as we looked again at ourself, we saw in the half-moon marks left by Hunger's attack no sign of more bleeding, and the beginning of thick, dark scars instead. Such a sight had never seemed more of a relief, or more natural to us.

She bandaged up our arms with prompt efficiency, then patted us on the shoulder and said, "All right, show up the next patient."

"There's another patient?" we asked.

"Cursed with severe acne," she replied.

"Is that a threat or the patient's condition?"

"Would you like to find out? Bugger off, will you; I'm working to a tight schedule, and haven't you heard that there's not enough doctors per patient in this country?"

And that was it. She didn't seem inclined to talk to us any more. With a shrug we picked up the satchel, and walked to the doorway.

In it, we turned, saw her putting the jar of medicine back in the cupboard and said without thinking, "Can I ask something?"

She didn't answer, didn't move, didn't flinch.

"If we become... all that this body is, if we become..."

"Me?" she said, not glancing up. "I mean in the metaphorical sense – if you plural become you singular, rather than actually growing breasts, should you accidentally find yourself thinking like a human, feeling like a human, instead of like a medically unsound mess of crossed wires . . ."

". . . will we be so bad?"

She hesitated, then turned, looked straight at us and said, "Life is magic. Magic is *not* life. You'll be fine. Now bugger off before I call security."

"Thank you," we said.

"Thank you too," she replied, but she didn't sound like she meant it.

I sat on the bus heading south from the derelict hospital, my bandaged arms hidden inside my coat, and resisted the temptation to roll up my sleeves so that everyone could see, and I could feel righteously injured, like a wounded soldier walking with pride.

I resisted.

Or possibly we resisted.

The distinction was becoming harder to make. Or rather, it had always been hard to make – we had always been me – but lately we were not so sure if we were any more than a useful set of memories, magics and ideas that I accessed at whim. Or was I nothing more than a strange recollection of Matthew Swift that we thought was ourself, but who had in fact died some two years before? We knew that Matthew Swift had died, his dying breath entering the phones and spinning into our domain. We knew that we had decades of memory and experience and thoughts and feeling and that, more and more, these guided us, shaped who we were in the world and what we did and how we behaved. Or so it seemed, as we came to understand *why* the strange, singular sorcerer that had been Swift had done what he did; but we did not know if this signified more than just memory.

We are me, we are Matthew Swift.

And I am the blue electric angels.

Did the distinction really matter?

It's very simple, Mr Swift. Can you keep control?

I don't understand.

And in the end, so what if I was, technically, dead? I felt pretty damned alive: I felt the breaths I drew tickle the inside of my lungs,

I felt the beating of my heart in my veins, I felt fear and sorrow and happiness and pain and uncertainty and dread and hope and all the other good and bad tick boxes of humanity that, no matter how bad bad might be, at least proved that the depth of feeling and emotion I could experience now were as I remembered experiencing them. Was that not enough? If we were me and we could experience such pangs, did that not make us alive, or human? The technicalities of whether we were genuinely human seemed increasingly irrelevant, since we felt, more and more, that we were the oh-so-human I. The blip that perhaps Matthew Swift had died with no way of coming back and that possibly the blue electric angels were nothing but the gods of lost voices in the wire increasingly did not concern us.

Did not concern me.

We will not bother with such distinctions.

I sat on the bus and looked at the world through my blue eyes and felt the ache in my burning arms and knew that I could understand every language spoken on the top deck of that vehicle as we rattled down Gower Street; knew also that inside me was the capacity to blaze burning blue fire so fast and so bright and so far that it could, for an instant, eclipse the sun, and this felt . . . natural.

Life is magic.

I knew, without having to ask, what she meant. Life was not the magic of spells or enchantments or sorcery; or, it was, but that was not the point. Life *created* magic as an accidental by-product, it wasn't, definite article, absolute statement, A = B, *magic*. Life was magic in a more mundane sense of the word; the act of living being magic all of its own.

This was something we instinctively understood – it simply hadn't occurred to us that it might need explaining.

I went south, towards Holborn.

Vera and Charlie met me in a small sandwich shop made of linoleum; it was round the back of Drury Lane and advertised itself as *Tasty Cafe* in big blue letters above a squeaking door with a bell on it that clunked more than it rang. We sat at a small orange plastic table, while around us large men in fluorescent jackets from a local building site drank tea and ate dried-out ham sandwiches.

Vera looked tired but alert; Charlie was his usual implacable self.

She said to me, not unpleasantly, "You buggered off something royal in the Exchange, bastard."

"I'm sorry. I was hurt."

"They told me."

"Who they?"

"The bloody fucking Order, thanks a million for getting them involved, by the way."

"Is there a problem?" demanded Charlie.

She glared at him. "No sooner have we smashed the massed undead army of Lee to a thousand itty pieces, wereman, than we've got a group of religious nutters sitting on our doorstep who know exactly where we live and what our tricks are."

"They're causing trouble?" I asked.

"Not yet."

"Then is there a problem?" I hazarded, uncertain of where her anger was coming from or what she wanted.

Her hand tightened round her cup of coffee until the knuckles were white. "When there is, are you going to come and make it all better, sorcerer?" Her voice dripped acid. We felt oddly ashamed.

"Oda didn't tell me how many died."

"Plenty."

"But are . . . did it . . ."

"Did it make a difference?"

"Yes."

"Perhaps. With Lee dead, with his men beat . . . there's only so much power that you can have at the end of a gun. First you've gotta fear it, and perhaps . . . that's changing." Her grip relaxed, her shoulders rolled forward. She looked drained; we wondered if she'd slept. "What's next?" she asked.

"Harris Simmons."

"Do you know something new?" said Charlie.

"Perhaps. I think he's on the run."

"How does that help?" asked Vera.

"He's being followed. Bakker knows that I'm looking for him, cleared out the house and left a message for me."

"You didn't mention a message." Charlie looked reproachful, edgy.

"It was personal."

"I thought we'd gone past that."

"Oh, get real," snapped Vera. "You blind?"

"If they know you're looking for him, things will not be so simple," pointed out Charlie reasonably.

"Thank you for the profound insight," groaned Vera. "What do you want, sorcerer?"

"Your help."

"Again?"

"I think we can bring down the Tower."

"What, exploding concrete, or in a more organisational sense?"

"Harris Simmons can lead us to Bakker."

"Doesn't seem very likely," murmured Vera.

"Bakker is hard to find; he keeps moving all the time," added Charlie. "Especially now that Khay and Lee are dead – he'll be alerted to the danger, won't stay more than one night in one place until you're..."

"Deader than a decapitated zombie!" shrilled Vera. "Deader than old Marley's ghost, deader than a tombstone on Mars, deader than..."

"Thank you, we understand the image," we said. "Besides, 'dead' isn't quite the full story, as far as Bakker is most likely concerned."

"Is he a zombie too?" hazarded Vera.

"He is not," said Charlie firmly, as if Vera's question was a foolish thing asked by a child to annoy. "But he is dying."

"And he was very interested in talking to us before," we added. "So I think that, given this information, a few risks might be worth taking."

"What kind of *risks*?" Vera's eyes were instantly narrow.

"I think Harris Simmons is going to be a trap," I replied. "It makes sense; he knows I'm coming, on the run, being tracked by a shadow..."

"...a shadow?" Charlie's voice was hard.

"Are you an important person?" Vera asked Charlie quizzically. "Sorcerer, why is the wereman here?"

"He's an important person," I sighed. "Please be nice to each other, I still need your help."

"Just our help? Not the biker, the Order, the warlocks, the..."

"You're the two I trust."

"Thanks," said Vera with a grunt. "Touched, but a little surprised, since we hardly know each other."

"All right, put it another way. You," nodding at Vera, "have too much to lose, and have lost too much already; and you," nodding at Charlie, "come with good credentials and an honest face, when it hasn't got whiskers. Therefore, I'm talking to you both."

"What about Oda?" asked Vera. "You seem quite pally with the psycho-bitch."

"I trust her utterly," I replied, surprised to find that it was true, "but only up to the point where she no longer needs me. Which, if what I suggest can be made to work, could be quite soon."

Soon was three days.

I spent each night at a different hotel, not least because in every case my relentless casting of wards around the bed, and the mess this left, didn't please the management.

In those three days, Charlie called by twice. The first time he provided £100 and a note from Sinclair that read simply, "Try legality, and best wishes," as well as a change of clothes and a first-aid kit for the scabbing nail marks on my arms. The second time, he came by with a pair of shoes.

After I'd looked at them, I said, "You're joking." We added, "Are you sure it'll work?"

"These things don't just grow on trees," he replied.

"The image is ridiculous enough already," I retorted. "Besides, what if someone takes the shoes?"

"There is another option."

"Which is?"

"Surgery." We turned pale. "They can slice your skin open, implant the chip just below your . . ."

"You're not as humourless as you look," I said.

"In point of fact, I am."

I took the shoes. They fitted perfectly, and when I walked on them, there wasn't a bump or a lump to suggest the thing hidden inside. Charlie beamed. "Magicians," he said brightly. "Always so busy doing the magical thing they never bother to think about technology."

*

On the third day, I got a phone call from Oda.

It went, "Where are you hiding?"

"If I told you that, it wouldn't be hiding."

"Never mind, I'll trace the call."

"You called me."

"Doesn't mean these things can't be traced."

"I'm fine."

"That wasn't really my problem."

"No. I suppose that about sums it up."

"What are you doing?"

"Waiting."

"For what?"

"To find Bakker."

"You just think sitting around on your arse is going to help you find Bakker?"

"Simmons will tell me where Bakker is."

"So you're waiting to find Simmons?"

"Yes."

"What if he doesn't? Or won't that matter?"

"It's complicated."

"You are a one-note-answer kinda guy, aren't you?"

"At the moment."

"Fair enough."

"Is that it? Fair enough?"

"Yes."

"That's not fair."

"Oh, please. I'm going to find you, remember?"

"You've made the point explicitly clear. Although, to tell the truth, it may not be such a bad thing."

"What does that mean?"

"I'm sure you'll work it out," I said. "When things get sticky, talk to Vera."

"You trust her?"

"Yes."

"Why?"

"She's not actually sworn an oath to the deity to decapitate me at the earliest available opportunity," I replied, "which is a good thing." And hung up, before she could say something offensive.

About an hour later, Charlie rang.

"Found Simmons yet?" I asked.

"Yes – you were right, about the thing following him. It's not pretty."

"Where?"

"You'll need a lift. Looks like this thing is going down in the middle of bloody nowhere."

"Let me worry about transport."

"I knew you would," he said, and gave me the address.

Just one more thing that needed to be done, before it finished. Just one.

I found a copy of the Yellow Pages on top of a bus shelter, and leafed through it until I found the number under C for Catering. I wandered back to my hotel, picked up the phone and dialled.

The voice that answered said, "Palmero Paradise, yeah?"

"I'm looking for Mrs Mikeda."

"Who's calling, like?"

"Matthew Swift."

"Right, give's a mo."

I waited. The owner of the sawing voice and grating accent could be heard in the distance beyond the receiver saying, "Hey, where's the bag gone?"

We had a feeling . . .

. . . voices in the receiver . . .

. . . we knew we could know this voice, if we wanted to. Everyone leaves something behind, in the phones.

"Hey, Swift, wasn't it?"

"Yes."

"She's just coming."

"Thank you."

. . . so easily . . .

I pinched the palm of my hand until the skin was red and lumpy. A voice came onto the phone, with a different accent that drooled across every syllable like a pot of honey. "Yes? Who's this?"

"Mrs Mikeda? It's Matthew Swift here."

"If you want money I'm not your woman, you know?"

"Money? No."

"Then piss off."

She slammed the phone down on the hook. I was surprised; but, thinking about it, I wondered how I had ever expected a better reception.

I packed up my belongings and decided to do things the old-fashioned way.

Palmero Paradise was a small, greasy sandwich shop off Smithfield meat market, where the butchers went in their lunch hour for salami sandwiches and a slosh of tea in a cardboard cup. When I arrived, it was early evening: too soon for the area's fashionable wine bars and soon-to-be-heaving clubs to have opened their doors, but late enough for the market's gates to be shuttered over the racks of mechanised hooks and the floors smelling of diluted blood and sawdust. The streets had a quiet, Sunday-afternoon feel, drained of excitement in a thin drizzle.

The lights were still on in Palmero Paradise, but they were clearly shutting up shop, moving the few wobbly metal tables back into the small shop and pulling down the covers on the fridges. I picked up the last sandwich on the shelves – Cheddar cheese and suspicious-looking pickles wrapped in cling film – and ordered a cup of coffee.

Behind the counter, the young man in the big red apron had the same nasal accent that I'd heard on the phone. He said, "We're closing, like."

"I just want a coffee."

"Sure, right, yeah, but . . ."

"We think you call telephone pornography lines," we said suddenly, feeling inspired both by his apron and the familiar drone of his voice, and irritated by his reluctance to give us something to drink. And then, because I was surprised to find both that we believed this and that his face showed it was true, I added, "You need to get yourself a girl."

He said, "Are you . . ."

"Is Mrs Mikeda around?"

"You're not the nut who phoned, are you?"

"That's me."

"Look, uh, I don't want..."

"Maybe you should see if she's still here."

"Right. Yeah. Whatever."

With that, he disappeared through the jangling plastic bead netting at the back of the café.

I waited. A moment later, to the sound of much stomping, Mrs Mikeda appeared. She had a mobile phone in one hand and a pair of scissors in the other and the words "Leave now, police soon or scissors immediately, which would you..." on her lips before she looked at me, I looked at her, and the words died.

"Mrs Mikeda," I said politely, because Mum had always taught me to be courteous to older women.

"Mr Swift!" The words were as much twisted sounds on an uncontrolled rush of air, as showing any intent to speak. "You're... not... I mean... you're..."

"How are you, Mrs Mikeda?" I asked, in an attempt to break the ice.

"I'm well, yes, fine, fine. What are you doing here?"

"Is this 'Surely you aren't after a coffee' what are you doing here or 'Why aren't you six feet under and decomposing?' what are you doing here?"

"I don't want to... but you were..."

"I wanted to talk to you about Dana."

Her face tightened. She lowered the scissors and the phone with a conscious effort that shook her little frame. "Maybe somewhere more private."

Mrs Mikeda was the daughter of a Russian émigré who, she'd always claimed, had fled the Russian Revolution in 1917 with the secrets of the Tsar's court in his head, a loyal, steadfast and cultured aristocrat who'd died of a broken heart. However, that story had always seemed a bit remote from any likelihood, and since her father had only recently died, in a council flat in Bermondsey, the chronology didn't quite make sense either.

She was of average height, and unusual width – being not so much fat as all-present, so that even in the largest of rooms there was never quite enough space for the crowd and Mrs Mikeda to coexist peacefully. Her skin had been dropped onto her frame like a curtain over a piece of treasured furniture; it was full of endless folds and hidden depths, suggested even beneath her voluminous puffed flowery shirt, and a giant navy-blue skirt from beneath which poked a pair of legs that were all kneecap. Sitting in her kitchen, she poured vodka into two plastic cups and said, "I know it's a cliché, but the English don't know how to drink."

I steeled myself and as she did, so I too downed mine in one. We were horrified by the initial shock of it, then strangely fascinated as it burnt its way into the stomach and sent a punch up through our arteries straight to the brain, as if the whole thing had instantly combusted on touching our flesh and filled our veins with vapour. We didn't know whether it would be safe to try any more; but to our relief, Mrs Mikeda didn't make the offer. Instead, the vodka out of the way, she poured coffee and said, "So . . . I suppose you must get asked this all the time?"

"Asked . . ."

"About how you were dead."

She passed a mug over to me and stood up to rummage in the back of a cupboard above a shining stainless steel sink with industrial shower attachments for cleaning purposes, until she found a packet of digestive biscuits.

"Oh. Yes. Dead," I repeated vaguely, watching as she slit the plastic open with a single titanium-razored red nail. "It's complicated."

"Sure," she said. "Always complicated. Knew it would be when I first met you."

I took the coffee and felt grateful for the distraction of it: the nice social ceremony and the hot mug into which I could peer as if it held all my troubles. She sat down again with the groan of an ageing lady who spent too much time on her feet. "So? You want to talk about my daughter."

"How is she?"

"You don't know?"

"I . . . haven't seen her recently."

"Why not? . . . Oh . . . yes. Dead."

"That's the one."

"She's all right."

"Is that it?"

"What, you were hoping for bad news?"

"No, no, not at all . . . I just . . . didn't expect it to be so brief."

"I don't see much of her these days."

"Why not?"

"Shouldn't you be asking her? Or is there something you want to tell me?"

She looked at me with her head on one side and, even though she wore an innocent, almost childish expression behind her ruddy cheeks and big, curly, metallic-red hair, her eyes still had that gleam of sharp intelligence from when I'd first met her.

I found that I couldn't answer.

"Biscuit?"

"What? . . . No, thanks."

She took a biscuit from the package, bit off a corner, dipped the rest in the coffee, waited a few seconds, then ate it in a single bite. I watched her chew and she watched the floor. When she'd finished she let out a long sigh and said, "All right, let's get through the list first. Is my daughter dead, possessed, demonically influenced or cursed in any way?"

"What? No! At least, not as far as I'm aware."

"You don't seem very far aware," she pointed out reasonably.

"I don't think she's any of the above."

"Well, that's the essentials covered. Is there anything else you need to talk to me about?" She saw my expression. "I'm a good Christian mother, you know. I like to make sure that my daughter, while clearly a vessel for some mystical forces, isn't breaking too many articles of the faith?"

"To the best of my knowledge, she's not."

"Good. Then what do you want?"

"Have you ever met Robert James Bakker?"

"Yes," she said, in the weary voice of someone who knows where this conversation is going and can't believe she has to wait at the traffic lights to get there.

"What do you think of him?"

"Nice man. Held her hand at your funeral; very nice man."

"Yes," I murmured. "I think he is."

"But you have the look of a man with something to say on that count," she added. "Come on, out with it. That's what I liked about you, Mr Swift – always very straightforward."

"Really?"

She grinned, and took another biscuit. "First thing you ever said to me: 'Excuse me, ma'am, may I have a black coffee, strong, no sugar, and is a member of your family or your household acting peculiar bordering on mystical by any chance?'"

"I said that?" I asked, surprised at myself.

"Yes."

"Just out of the blue?"

"Yes. You looked like you'd had a long day."

"It was a while back," I admitted.

"And you've probably been busy since then . . ."

"Yes . . ."

"Funerals, decomposition and so on."

I smiled patiently. "As a good Christian mother . . ." I began.

"You sure you don't want a biscuit?"

"Maybe one," we said quickly, taking it from the package offered. "Thank you. As a good Christian mother," I continued, "are you wondering about what the Bible has to say on the sanctity of resurrection when it's not our lord and saviour?"

"You know, the Old Testament . . ." she began.

"I'm really, really not dead," I said. "In fact, it's starting to get a bit of a pain having to explain it all."

"Dana thinks you're dead. Explain it to her – leave me out of it. As far as I'm concerned what happens in your world stays in your world."

"I'm sorry to come here like this . . ."

"Get on with it, Mr Swift. Bad news should at least be honest about what it wants."

"Where's Dana?"

"I don't know."

"Don't know or won't tell?"

"She went with Mr Bakker."

"Why?"

"I said. He was kind. You . . . shall we skip 'died' and go to 'disappeared'?"

"Where's Dana?"

"He's like you. He said he was your teacher."

"He was."

"Well, is it bad?" she asked sharply. "He taught you, you taught Dana, she didn't seem to become anything that I feared, any sort of..." She caught herself, then smiled, a pained twitch of the mouth. "She's fine."

"But you don't know where?"

"He gives her money for travel, her own things. She moves around a lot. You never provided money, Mr Swift. I know that's not what it's about but you have to understand... why's he successful?"

"What?"

"Mr Bakker? He came up to me at the funeral and offered me a lift, said he knew that my daughter was... well... gave me a lift home to talk about what happened next. Said she was half-trained, still needed help, but spoke highly of you. Big black car, seats made of leather."

"He's a good businessman."

"Good sorcerer?" she asked, so sharp it was almost angry.

"Yes," I said, taken aback. "Very... capable."

She snorted. "Good man?"

I didn't answer.

"Why'd you want to see Dana?"

"She was my apprentice!"

"So?"

"It's important."

"But you're not saying why."

"It's just... it *is* important."

"Come on, come on," she said, waving a hand impatiently in a circle through the air. "Get on with it!"

I took a deep breath. "She might be in danger."

"Good!"

"Good?"

"Good that you've told me; not good that it is. Why is she in danger?"

"I said might be."

"You said might be because you think I am a stupid old woman who can't cope or understand. Come on! Why is she in danger?"

"It's . . . to do with Mr Bakker."

"Ah. I thought it might be."

"Why?"

"She doesn't come home any more. She calls sometimes, but then won't talk; she says that the phones listen. She's lost a lot of weight – how can a girl who eats that much lose so much weight? Is he a good man, your Mr Bakker?"

"He was."

"But isn't any more?"

"It's . . ."

". . . complicated? Always was, Mr Swift. What do you want?"

"I . . . think I wanted to apologise."

"OK. You've apologised. Anything else?"

I shook my head, then hesitated. Mrs Mikeda waited. I said, "If you can contact her, if you can find her, tell her I'm sorry. And tell her to get out while she can."

"Why?"

"Shit and fans."

"Have you put her in danger?"

"No!"

"Will you?"

I said nothing. She smiled and asked, politely, "Vodka?"

"No thanks. Not really our thing."

"Trust me, Mr Swift?"

"Yes."

"Then tell me everything."

To my surprise, I did.

***

Second Interlude: The Sorcerer's Apprentice

In which the cost of sorcery is remembered over takeaway fish and chips.

This is how I met Dana Mikeda.

Late spring in central London; it is almost impossible to feel depressed. The trees are sprouting green leaves on every street, the sky is blue, dotted with thin white clouds, the sunlight reflects watery colours off the windows of offices and divides the street between cold shadows and burning bright rooftops. The air smells clean in the morning after it rains, and the people, who make a city what it is, start sporting bare shoulders and sunglasses almost as soon as the temperature hits double figures. It is pleasantly warm in the sun, with a breeze that isn't quite cool enough for goose bumps.

On the morning I met Dana, I was walking along the Holborn Viaduct above the busy Farringdon Road, not paying much attention to where I was going, enjoying the stroll. It was that time of the mid-afternoon when the streets in the centre of town weren't too busy, and the usual buzz of magic and urgency on the air that to a large degree dictated my daily routine was at a gentle, soft ebb.

In Smithfield I bought a sausage roll from a shop by the meat market, and sat on a bench outside the faded classical façade of Barts hospital, eating and watching people go by: young businessmen in smart suits, butchers in huge aprons and fat rubber gloves, builders in hard hats, and trendy people looking like they were designers, in fashionably torn jeans.

It was while sitting there that I became aware of being watched. I looked round; and eventually I saw the source of my unease. The rat stood on its hind legs, in a patch of shadow obscuring a narrow street that led towards the church of St Bartholomew the Great. He was quite unconcerned at the passers-by, and just staring. I was used to unusual behaviour, but even the unusual things in my life tended to have an explanation, and I couldn't muster a valid one for this, so I finished my sausage roll, brushed the crumbs off my jeans, stood up, and wandered towards the rat.

I got about halfway, when its nose twitched, its tail wiggled and it turned and scuttled away, something so normal and boringly predictable that I was startled by the fact it had happened at all. Faced with a choice between accepting normal behaviour for what it seemed to be or looking for a reason why things weren't normal at all, I did as I had been taught, and accepted the latter. Normal is unusual in this line of work, my teacher had always said. If you expect something to happen and it does, it's usually time to start looking out for the higher powers creeping your way, or the man with the knife. Sooner or later, something dangerous will happen to you, and you can never be too sure – particularly when it comes to the little things.

So I stood in the middle of the square outside the hospital, and looked for something unusual. What I found sat in a neat silent line above the row of stone urns, and the brightly coloured heraldic dragons, that ornamented the roof of the meat market. They weren't moving: not twitching, nor even hopping from one withered orange foot to the other. I shouted, "Boo!" at the top of my voice and they didn't even flap. I guessed there were over a hundred pigeons sitting there, and when I crossed through the market by the covered road, past the war memorial and the plaques detailing the history of the area, I wasn't entirely surprised to see that the birds had sat only on one side of the roof.

I crossed back the way I'd come and looked in the direction that every one of the pigeons was gazing: towards a group of shops including a pub whose sign showed a lecherous bishop, a day nursery, a launderette and a couple of sandwich bars. I picked one of the sandwich shops at random and wandered in. There weren't any customers, and neither was there any staff, but the fridge showed enough gaps in its display to suggest that this was just a mid-afternoon lull, rather than a symptom of terminal decline. I leant on the glass counter above the bowls of chicken, and tuna, and sweetcorn salad and waited.

There was a buzzing from the glass-fronted fridge, a nasty, unhealthy electric sound like a wasp trapped in a bottle, or the crack of flies hitting an electric lamp. I watched as sparks snapped out of the cabling at its back and the lights faltered along the displays of neatly packed sandwiches. Then, with a hiss, the fridge died. The bulb above my head flickered on and off a few times, and the power points in the corners of the walls spat angry electric sparks from behind the switches. After a few minutes, this too died. During this time I heard a raised voice from somewhere behind a bead curtain: the incoherent sound of a woman shouting at someone whose response was too quiet for me to hear.

My curiosity now completely engaged, I stepped round the counter, and through the bead curtain. Beyond it was a stainless-steel kitchen, and it was a mess. Pots and pans were strewn across the floor, remnants of viscous liquids were splashed up the walls, glass from shattered bulbs crunched underfoot. On the knife rack, the blades were all twisted out of shape.

I moved carefully through the wreckage towards a door at the back; as I did, the voices became louder. The woman's, shrill and frightened, babbled in a language I didn't understand but which, by its thick quality and the richness of the sound, I guessed to be eastern European. Another voice answered in the same language: male, quieter, but no less scared. I pushed open the door, onto a crooked flight of stairs. Climbing them, I emerged into a narrow corridor of scuffed paint on cracked plaster. At the far end, outside a closed door with a poster of some anonymous boy band and a sign saying "KEEP OUT!!!" in big red pen, were the owners of the voices: a short woman who seemed far too large for the space she stood in, and a man in the dark shapeless clothes of a priest, with a big black beard. In one limp hand, the priest held a crucifix; and by his gestures he was trying to pacify the woman, and failing. The place buzzed with a sparking, yellow-golden sheen that hissed like fizzy drink on my tongue as I drew it in; wild, rich, and dangerous power, emanating, I guessed, from behind the closed door.

I said, "Excuse me?"

The woman paused, looked at me, said, "We're shut," and in an instant was back to shouting at the man.

I waited a few moments; then, since she didn't seem to have any further interest in talking to me, I raised my voice and bellowed, "*Sorcery!*"

They both fell silent, more caught by surprise, I suspected, than ready to listen."Thank you," I said quickly. "Now, may I have a black coffee, strong, no sugar, and is a member of your family or your household acting peculiar bordering on mystical?"

In the kitchen, with trembling hands the woman gave me a plastic cup of vodka. She watched me down it while she clung to her own drink and said, "You police?"

"This isn't your business . . ." began the man in priest's clothes.

"Stuff you," I replied, and for her benefit I added, "No, I'm not. My name's Matthew Swift."

Mrs Mikeda introduced herself.

"A pleasure to meet you," I responded. "And this gentleman with the beard is . . . ?"

"What do you want here?" he snapped.

"A priest," replied Mrs Mikeda in a cowed voice.

"More than a priest, I'm guessing," I said, looking him over and finding myself unimpressed. "Exorcist, yes? Demonic possession, Satanic vibes, all that kind of thing?"

"Who are you?" asked Mrs Mikeda.

"You can just call me Matthew. Now, let's throw out the beardy, and why don't you tell me about your daughter?"

"How do you know about my daughter?" she demanded, her knuckles turning white around the plastic cup.

"It's the choice of boy band poster on her bedroom door," I replied. "That tells me that she's a girl. The presence of the exorcist guy tells me you haven't got a clue what's going on, and the sense of uncontrolled and raging magic tells me it's more than just hormones that gives your daughter bad period pains. So why don't you tell me what's happening here?"

Mrs Mikeda downed the vodka, scrunched up the plastic cup without thinking and dropped it in the sink. She looked from me to the priest and back again and said, "Mr Swift, I don't know why I should trust you."

"My honest face, my charming, open expression, and the fact that in the end, I'm just so damn *right*, aren't I? Nothing like a grasp of the situation to give a guy some cred."

"Can you help her?"

I thought about it. "Yes," I replied, feeling as I said it that this was absolutely the correct answer. "I think I can."

When I knocked on her door there was no answer. I called out, "Dana? You all right in there?"

No reply.

I tried the handle. The door was locked.

"Key?" I said to Mrs Mikeda.

She gave me a small brass key. I turned it in the lock and opened the door. Filthy didn't begin to cover the room beyond. It had served as bedroom, living room, kitchen and bathroom for what smelt like weeks; the heat and intensity of it slammed into my face and left no room for compromise or forgiveness. The curtains were half drawn, and at the base of the window were pigeon feathers strewn in dirty heaps. Dana Mikeda lay on the bed, her back turned to me, breathing slowly and steadily. I went over and reached out to touch her. But before I did, the hairs on the back of my hands stood up, at the same time that Mrs Mikeda gave a warning gasp.

I pulled a plug from the wall with a popping of sparks, and cut it at the top and the bottom with my penknife, exposing the metal strands beneath. Holding it by the rubber insulation I touched one end of the wire to the floor, and let the other drop onto the girl's shoulder. A white spark crawled into the carpet. When I moved my hand again over Dana, there was no longer that feel of buzzing static in the air.

I took hold of her shoulder, and rolled her over. Her eyes were shut, but when I lifted the lids they glowed underneath with the bright orange of a pigeon's iris; and as she exhaled, every breath carried with it a snort of thick black smoke and the smell of car exhaust, rattling over her lungs like a loose engine on the back of an old truck. Her skin burnt to the touch, and when I lifted up her fingers, they trailed neon scars through the air, like her nails were about to dig a hole in space itself.

"Can you do something?" whispered Mrs Mikeda.

"Maybe," I replied. "How long has she been like this?"

"A few days. But it's never been this bad before!"

"Do you own a car?"

"No."

"Have you got a friend who'll lend you one?"

Mrs Mikeda drove. I sat in the back, Dana's head in my lap. Her hair when I touched it felt like fuse wire. To escape the feelings that must have been attacking her every day and night, she'd sunk herself deep into some form of magical trance or stupor. So lost in it was she that when the pistons of the hydraulic brakes exhaled, she did too, in the same breath and tone as the car itself.

We drove west, inching past Marylebone, speeding down the Westway, and jinking about through grungy Shepherd's Bush and the genteel streets of Chiswick in the cheerful spring sun. In Chiswick

High Street, the schools were emptying, and the cafés had put seats out on the pavement under the big old plane trees to serve coffee and cakes to the locals. By the time we reached Kew Bridge, the rush hour had started; Dana's heart rate was up, so fast and strong I could see the veins moving in her neck as she responded, her blood moving at the speed of the city as its people switched direction from work to pleasure. We parked the car just beyond Kew Bridge and carried her down, each supporting her by an arm, onto the tidal mud of the Thames. Water seeped out around our feet like we were walking on a sponge, saturated so that water ran off it like oil. I pulled off my shoes, socks and jacket, and Mrs Mikeda did the same for Dana.

"This isn't . . . pagan, is it?" she asked.

"It's all relative," I replied after a moment of hesitation, reasoning that this would be the least offensive but most honest answer. Mrs Mikeda didn't look satisfied; but neither did she complain. I struggled to lift Dana up, supporting her by one arm across my shoulders and half-carrying, half-dragging her out into the biting cold river.

I walked out until the water came up to above my waist, and the mass of it had taken up most of Dana's weight. From a muddy islet in the middle of the river, a heron regarded me with something resembling bird-brained displeasure that another creature was on its patch. Beyond the little tangle of trees and birds' nests that made up the heron's home, a large white boat chugging back from Hampton Court Palace had drifted to a gentle cruise, the tourists leaning over to photograph the odd spectacle of Dana and me in the river, while the driver called out, "Hey, you OK?"

"Baptism!" I replied cheerfully; on the bank Mrs Mikeda flinched even at this much profanity.

The boat moved on by, a handful of the tourists waving and whooping cheerfully as it did. Behind the trees on the opposite bank, the sunlight was dimming to a pinkish burn across the sky, stretching out the shadow of each trunk across the water.

I risked wading a few more yards out into the river, the sediment at the bottom swirling in a gritty cloud around my toes.

"What happens now?" called out Mrs Mikeda from the bank.

"Turn of the tide!" I answered in my best optimist's voice. "Gotta have some magic in that, right?"

"Don't you know?"

"I'm trying to save your daughter's life within the tenets of the Orthodox faith. I haven't a clue!"

"If you don't know what you're doing then . . ."

"Do you have the time?"

"What?"

"The time? It's freezing out here!"

She looked at her watch. "Six forty-three."

"Near as dammit," I muttered, more for my reassurance than hers. I brushed Dana's wiry hair from her face. Her skin had a pale greyish tint, and around her chin and across the hairline were patches of dry scratchy flesh which were increasingly starting to resemble tar. I leant down so my lips were a few inches from her ear and whispered, "If you can hear me, don't be afraid. The tide'll carry it all away."

"What are you doing?" Mrs Mikeda could make her voice carry like it was a boulder tossed by a giant.

"Don't be alarmed!" I called back. "Any second . . ."

. . . a tugging around my ankles . . .

". . . any second . . ."

The heron, which had been watching the entire affair with a disinterested look on its unimaginative face, flapped into the sky . . .

"Oh, stuff it," I said, pinched Dana's nose shut with my fingers, took a deep breath and dropped both her and me under the water.

Thames water was once, so I had been told, toxic. Not just slightly unpleasant to drink, but actually lethal to fall into, a straight-to-hospital case. And although news reports still complained about disgusting messes in the water, nowadays these were more about the trash people threw in and the occasional suicide's body dragged to the surface, rather than the raw sewage defining much of the river's previous four hundred years.

So it was with a good degree of confidence that I pushed Dana down head first into the water, then let my knees bend and ducked my shoulders down after her. I let the water rush over her head and mine, let it shock my ears into an icy humming, let it tug at my hair and inflate my clothes around me to the size of a hippo as giant air bubbles crawled from under my shirt to pop and burst above my head. Dana didn't struggle, didn't squirm; all I had to do was hold her down against the bed of the river against the pressure of her natural buoyancy, and watch the bubbles roll out between her lips. As I held her down for five, ten, fifteen seconds, through the water I could hear Mrs Mikeda screaming, a strange, deep overhead rumble; also the distant *thrum thrum thrum* of some water bikes scudding past us, and a high *splishsplishsplish* of oars striking the surface somewhere downstream. Then, just as I was beginning to think I'd got the timing wrong, I heard a sound like a whale burping in the deepest part of the ocean, felt a relaxation all around, followed by a tightening, as, right on cue, the tide changed direction.

Dana exhaled. Her breath was a thick black stain in the water, slipping out to get tangled in the tide and sucked slowly past her towards the estuary, dozens of miles away. A thin metallic shimmer drifted out of her hair, whose strands started to drift loosely around her head. Grey, tarlike flakes spun away from her face, revealing clear, human skin beneath; the colour rose in her cheeks, her fingers twitched and, at the last, a moment before my lungs were going to burst, her eyes opened; and they were distinctly, irrefutably human, and just a bit beautiful.

I pitched her up out of the water just as she started to kick like a drowning person, and held her upright as the water ran off her face and out of her nose and she coughed and hacked and spat liquid, her hair tangled across her face like seaweed caught in a rudder. Mrs Mikeda was already halfway to us, up to her hips in the river, shouting incoherent curses in Russian; but at the sight of her daughter she stopped dead, hands going to her mouth and shoulders shaking. In the water around us, the clouds of trapped magic that Dana had accumulated drifted and faded into the river, and for the first time since I'd met her, she looked up at me with her own senses.

She said, "Uh . . ."

I said, "Hi."

Mrs Mikeda said something obscene.

She said, "Have we met?"

"I don't think so. Have we?"

"Did you just try to drown me?"

"Do I look like I just tried to drown you?" I asked as water dripped off the end of my nose.

"Where is this?"

"Twickenham."

"What the hell am I doing in Twickenham?"

"Do you think this is really the place to discuss it?"

"Who are you?" she demanded.

"I'm Matthew. Nice to meet you."

"Yeah," she muttered, looking round at the water flowing around us. "I guess it must be."

Mrs Mikeda's friend had left blankets in the back of her car that smelt of wet dog, but we weren't about to complain. We sat on the edge of the open car boot and ate fish and chips while Mrs Mikeda went in search of a Woolworths that might sell something warmer and fluffier to wrap around her shivering daughter. It took a while for the conversation to get going, but when it did, Dana Mikeda was pretty much to the point.

"So. Twickenham."

"Yes."

"I hate Twickenham," she said, spearing a chip with a savage thrust of her little wooden fork. "I get lost. Always end up in Isleworth, and that's like Wales."

"How is it like Wales?"

"One guy gets on a train to Swansea, one guy gets on a train to Isleworth, and you can bet the guy going to Swansea gets there first."

"I see."

We watched the sky fade to a pale cobalt blue, and the lights along the riverside start to come on.

"Some shit, huh?" she said finally.

"Does your mother know you swear?"

"Would you like to hear it in Russian?" she asked sharply.

"I'll live."

"You're . . . what? Like an exorcist?"

"Me? Hell, no. Sorcerer."

"Oh."

"You don't sound surprised."

She gave me a long sideways look. "I spent three years on antipsychotic drugs and being told by an NHS shrink that my dad had clearly abused me as a kid, and this shit still didn't stop. So I'm either mad and the medicine doesn't work, or I'm sane and there's magic out there, because I don't know what the middle ground is on this one."

"You're sane," I said quickly. "Or as sane as a hormonal teenager can be."

"I'm twenty-two," she rejoined. "Just because I live at home doesn't mean . . ."

"Sorry. My mistake."

She was eating cod, I had plaice. She had opened the tip of her ketchup and dipped each chip delicately in the end of the foil wrapping. I sprayed all of my ketchup loosely into the paper bundle of fish and chips and shook vigorously before eating."How old are you?" she asked.

"Twenty-eight," I replied honestly.

"You look, like, older. Sorcery do that for a guy?"

"No, this is just my lived-in face," I retorted. "Besides, sorry to hit you with the bad news, but you've got the sorcerous vibe bouncing off you like you could play pinball with it."

"I figured," she said.

"You did?"

"Somewhere between me being a pigeon, and reading the future in the way the litter blew outside my mum's café, I guessed something had to be up. Sorcery sounds . . . about right. Is it fatal?"

"What?"

"Like a medical condition?"

"No, not at all! There's nothing medical about it."

"What about my mum? Is she . . ."

"Doubt it."

"But if she's . . ."

"It's not a genetic thing. Forget *X-men*, *The X-Files* or anything else really at the latter end of the alphabet. It's just . . . a point of view."

She nearly dropped her fork. "A point of view? Is that what made me spend three weeks listening to the rats complaining about the butchers in the meat market and the nurse on ward three? Fuck that!"

"You're not exactly trained," I pointed out.

"Harry Potter? Three-week courses at Hogwarts, how to be a sorcerer?"

"Not like Harry Potter, no. Besides, magicians do the spells thing. Sorcery is more about... seeing magic where most people don't, and using it. Does that make sense?"

"No. Bugger it," she added, and took a large slurp from the carton of Ribena at her side. "Bugger it. Am I going to start hearing voices again?"

"Sure."

"Shit."

"The river was just a temporary thing. You go in at the changing of the tide and it just... washes it all away. But like all good launderettes, it's up to you not to spill the tomato sauce on the whites after washing, right?"

"I think I get it."

"Anyway, the whole sorcery thing, it's not that bad."

"I couldn't remember my name." There wasn't any feeling in her voice, just a flat statement of fact. When I looked at her, her eyes were lost on the river. "I was everywhere. My fingers were the streets, my toes were the wires dug into the earth, my breath was the exhaust of the cars, my..."

"You were in a trance," I said. "It's always a risk. Sorcerers draw their magic from the city around them. So much magic in one place – it's easy to get lost – to forget that you're you, and just... sort of drift off. That's what was happening to you. Your body was breaking down, your mind was just becoming absorbed. Eventually your consciousness would have become spread so thin across the city you'd probably have just popped out of existence. Something you might want to keep an eye out for, by the way."

"Oh, crap. And this happens to all sorcerers?"

"Just badly trained ones."

She gave me a thoughtful look. "So how come you're doing the sane bit?"

"I'm well trained."

"Who trained you?"

"A very good sorcerer. Very kind, very powerful."

"He dunk you in a river too?"

"No, he found me a bit earlier than that. I was about fifteen, I'd run off into the night and just run and run because I could; loved it, became lost in the streets but always found my way home. Blisters, memory loss, daydreaming, the roof practically bleached white with the pigeon shit by the time he found me. He saved my life."

"And you mine?" she asked quietly.

"Best not to think about it like that."

"How should I think about it, then?"

"Good luck and the eternal interlinked cycle of life crap."

"Cycle of life crap?"

"Ever watched *The Lion King*?"

"Sure."

"Well, think that kind of vibe, but with a fifteen certificate."

"I see." Her eyebrows were drawn together in concern. "So . . . I'm a sorcerer."

"Right now you're just a teen . . . a young woman . . . who happens to have tendencies."

"OK. Can I make it stop?"

"You could move to the countryside," I suggested.

"Is that it?"

"Probably not. Sorcerers tend to pick up on the magical thing wherever they are. It's very different outside the cities, the tone of it, the quality of the magic. But even the most stubborn sorcerers tend to adapt."

"So I'm stuck."

"Pretty much."

"How'd this happen?"

"There was probably a moment."

"A 'moment'?" she echoed. "What does that mean?"

I put my fish and chips to one side. "It goes something like this. You're walking along minding your own business, or you're on the underground or you're on a bus or something, but generally you're not paying much attention. And suddenly you look around and see all these other people and think, 'Hey, they can look at me and see me and I can see in my mind what I think they see, and when I'm gone they're going to keep on walking and they're going to go and live their lives, and their thoughts are going to be just like mine, but different, but real and solid and alive and full of feeling and confusion and colour just like life, and, hey, isn't that cool!' And it is.

"And roughly around this time you're going to notice that you can feel trains under your feet or pipes bubbling, and you can hear the sound of traffic and voices and stuff; and then you'll probably look up at the things around you and think, 'Those buildings with the lights on look almost alive, like giant trees lit up with their own constellation of stars in every window,' or maybe not if you're underground; and you'll realise that you can see the city all around, and it's so full of lives and life, and they're all buzzing around you, and every single individual is real and alive and passionate and full of mystery, and it's not just Joe Bloggs walking by who's like this, but that every part of the city is crawling with life. And you'll think, 'Hey, that's pretty damn sweet, everywhere I look there's life,' and roughly around that point you'll realise you can hear rats and pigeons and thoughts and spells and colours and electricity, and that's probably when you started going a bit mad. Am I close?"

She thought about it. Then, "They said you were coming."

"Who said?"

"Them. In the phones."

"I'm still curious about who 'them' is."

"They said life wasn't worth living unless you lived it to the full, that it was all right to catch fire and burn for ever, and that all I had to do to be free was to light up the sky. Forget the laws, forget what people tell you you should or should not be able to achieve. They said, 'We be light, we be life, we be fire – come be me and be free.' You still think I'm not mad?"

"Oh. *Them*. They're not worth paying much attention."

"What are they?"

"They live in the telephone lines. Bits of life that got left behind. They're just after kicks."

"They said you were coming."

"They're good at spooking people. Don't pay any attention."

"What did they mean?"

"They want to know what it's like to be human. Some people say that they'll eat up your dying breath, your soul, gobble you up in order to find out what it is that makes you tick. Theory also goes the other way, though. If they breathed, that is. I used to . . . but it's not safe."

"That doesn't answer my question."

"Best not to think about it."

"I should just ignore it?"

"Yup."

"Why?"

"They're dangerous."

"Is this a sorcery thing?"

"What do you think?"

She grunted. We sat in silence for a while longer, the grease from the fish-and-chip paper congealing on my fingers. Finally she added, "They said they were angels."

"They lied."

"You've heard them?"

"Yes. All sorcery is, is about spotting life in unusual places. Not to wax metaphysical about things, but it's not just the sky, sea, mountains and so on; it's the light from the street lamps and the buzz in the telephone. You can spot these things where others don't. The blue electric angels sing a very seductive song. 'Forget the confines of your own world, forget your flesh, your feelings, your friends, your laws. You are a sorcerer – you could blaze so brightly if only you thought you could.' They want that, freedom and fire and bright lives; it's all they're about. Keep away from them."

"Are there more things like that?"

"Sure. Demons and monsters and all that palaver. Easy enough to avoid though, if you're careful."

"Right." She let out a long, shuddering breath. "My mum's going to do her nut over this."

"I think she's so chuffed that you're not currently exhaling lead, she won't really care."

"But it'll happen again, right?" I looked up to find her eyes fixed on me. "You said – all this stuff, it'll happen again."

I shrugged.

"Why'd you get involved?" she asked sharply.

"Happened to be passing."

"Coincidence?"

"Dodgy word, but short of a discussion on the merits of higher powers and the uncomfortable prospect of fate, destiny and so forth, yes. Coincidence."

"Don't suppose the guy who taught you wants another student?"

"Maybe."

"You got his number?"

"Sure."

She waited. When I didn't move she said, "Well, can I have it?"

I hesitated. "There is . . ."

"Yes?"

". . . the way it usually works is . . ."

"You teach me?"

"Pretty much."

She nodded slowly then said, "There's no nudity or blood, right?"

"What? No!"

"Good. How about living sacrifices and ceremonial dancing?"

"I don't know if you're really taking this seriously enough . . ."

"I am," she said quickly. "Believe me, I just want to know what it is I'm getting into."

"You're already there," I pointed out.

"Yeah. I guess so." She looked up at the sky then back down at the river. "Are you a psychopathic murdering bastard?" she asked casually, no tone of offence in her voice or on her face.

"No," I answered with a sigh.

"Well then," she said. "Maybe we should talk."

***

I left Mrs Mikeda in Smithfield around the time that the local clubs were starting to build up their queues of barely clad trendy young things ready to dance until the buzz in their heads had worn itself away. I didn't know what the lady made of me or my story – her face had shut down to an impassive wall almost before I'd begun. But it was something that I felt had needed to be done.

I packed my bag, paid my hotel bill and, feeling there wasn't much else left to do, caught the first bus I could find to Willesden.

Blackjack was at home, but only at the third time of knocking on the door to his shed. He was jumpy. No lights went on, no sounds were made from inside the wobbly, lopsided stack of iron that he called home, but he opened the door with a single tug and, the instant the door was wide enough, swung a double-barrelled shotgun up into my face that would have made the Metropolitan Police swoon on the spot.

On seeing my expression, he hesitated a moment too long before swinging it down to his hip and muttering, "You any idea what time it is?"

"Witching hour of night?" I suggested.

"You alone?" he asked, peering past me into the darkened scrapyard. Even though it was late, he still wore his leather jacket and big black boots, with a red spotty scarf tied around his neck; he'd pulled a thick pair of gloves up over his hands, so that his finger barely fitted into the trigger guard of the gun.

"Can I come in?" I asked.

He indicated that I should, and turned up a paraffin lamp as I stepped into the gloom of the shed. "You want coffee?" he asked, turning towards the low stove and slotting the shotgun down by a shelf full of spray-paint.

"Thanks, that'd be good."

He put the kettle onto the stove, turned the nozzle on a cylinder of camping gas and struck a match to the hob, which belched its way into low blue life.

"Haven't seen you for a while, what've you been doing, sorcerer?" he asked in a single breath as I settled down on a pile of least suspiciously stained blankets.

"Not a great deal," I admitted.

"Heard you got hurt at the Exchange."

"I'm fine."

"Shit, like you're ever really fine." At the humourless chuckle in his voice, we looked up. He flapped a hand. "Never mind. Times are changing, you know, like the bard said?"

"The bard?"

"Jesus Christ, you need to get a life."

"That's the whole point of the exercise," we replied. "You doing anything in the next few hours?"

"You want my guide to healthy living?"

"I want a lift."

"Take the fucking train!"

"The lord of the lonely travellers probably isn't my friend right now."

"The what?"

"You should probably rethink your place in the grand picture sometime soon," I said. "Can I have that lift, please?"

Blackjack grinned. "You've gotta get somewhere in a hurry?"

This is the biker's magic. It is the melding of places into one. In every city, on every road, there is always a loose spot where things seem transient, where for a moment north doesn't seem to make sense to be in the north, where in the instant before recognition that pub on the corner seems to be exactly like another which you visited some years back, in a different place. There are streets where you wake after sleeping in the back of a car and for a second, no matter how many years you've lived here or worked here or travelled this way, you have no idea where you are. In those places, if you know what you're doing, it's sometimes possible to slip through the gaps and cover, in a very short time, very large distances.

We were curious to see the biker's magic at work, and found the thrill of the ride on the back of his bike an excitement that made our heart race as he spun through the empty streets. Nevertheless, inside the confines of the biker's spare helmet, passing from light to shadow in an endless dazzle under the street lights, the whole thing made us feel rather motion-sick.

A flickering of anonymous streets. He didn't take us south, despite the fact that this was where we needed to go, but drove north, until the streets faded into one long blur of semi-detached mock-Tudor houses that in my imagination defined so much of outer London suburbia. The roar of his bike's engine was the loudest thing on the streets, startling the foxes as they rummaged in the bins, and echoing off the sleeping houses. I watched the names run by: Harlesden, Dollis Hill, Neasden, Queensbury, Stanmore; and then, out of nowhere, we turned left and roared into a housing estate, swinging round into an area of locked garages graffitoed over by a mixture of kids and the odd magician, one of whom had covered a whole wall with the image of flowing white horses. Blackjack took us off the road, over a patch of grass that spattered soggy mud and limp grass up around our ankles, and through an alleyway surrounded by dumpsters.

There was a moment of sickness, a tightening in our stomach, and all we could see was an endless dark alley, illuminated by the succession of white, stuttering long-life lamps.

Then we emerged at the other end, and swung into a street that looked exactly like all the others we'd passed through so far on our journey north. But now, when we reached the end of it and Blackjack passed straight through the red traffic light onto the empty curving road beyond, the signs were no longer for the M1, the Midlands and the North, but offered to show the way to Dover, Folkestone and the south-east. In a single cut through a council estate we'd covered over twenty miles of urban sprawl, and were on the other side of the river.

More cuts. Blackheath turned into the green belt with a sickening twist between a pair of trees; a service station's endless winding internal roundabouts just before Rochester led out into the endless winding roundabouts of an equally depressing service station near Faversham; the monotonous street lights overhead seemed to dissolve into each other faster than a mere failure of eyesight to keep track would have suggested. When we reached the ring road above Dover's white cliffs, I guessed that no more than forty-five minutes had passed between us leaving Willesden and arriving at the English Channel.

Blackjack took things easily down the long, steep road cut into the cliff's edge below the castle. Dover sat below all that chalk like a stubborn stain on a perfect white tablecloth, caught between cliff and sea, a thin beady line of orange glow that mixed a history longer than the sea wall around the ferry port with 1950s lumps pretending to be architecture, from when much of the town had been levelled during the war.

Blackjack parked the bike in the ferry terminal's car park. I staggered off the rear seat, back aching, knees wobbling, and legs hot from being so close to the engine, and sniffed the air. I smelled oil, diesel, seagull and the salt of the sea, whose cleansing rhythm washed against the buzz and flow of magic in the air. We tasted strange, thin magic that hinted at layers beneath it, but which were too unfamiliar to touch. I imagined that a druid would feel as uneasy as I did in that place, where so many different kinds of magic – traditional sea sorcery, the natural magic of the countryside around, the weighty history of the place and lastly the imposed bustle of life and business around the port – collided.

Blackjack said, "You been here before?"

"No," we answered.

"And what about you?"

"Give it a rest," I replied. "Come on."

"Where now? France?" he asked, swinging a heavy sports bag over his shoulder and shoving my helmet into a plastic compartment on the back of the bike. "Holiday time?"

"You'll feel embarrassed about those words when you're finished with them." We walked on into the port.

Tucked behind the maze of ramps and causeways and car parks that made up most of Dover's ferry port was a small and mostly makeshift customs area, full of little offices, confiscated goods and demolished cars that suspicious customs officers had literally taken apart piece by piece. Beyond that, a small red-brick building was almost built into the cliff itself, with a black metal door and a single buzzing light that sounded like a fly was trapped inside the bulb. I dug into my bag for my set of blank keys and fitted one into the lock.

The magic was slow coming here, even though we could hear the splashing of the sea and smell petrol fumes. We knew there was potential in this place for all sorts of wonders; but it was so unfamiliar to us that we struggled to access it, as if we were caged in walls of perfect glass.

"You OK?" asked Blackjack as I tried to make the key work.

"Fine," I muttered through gritted teeth. "Give me a moment. It's just..."

The key sprung in the lock, the door slipped open.

Inside was a long white corridor that smelt of disinfectant. The tiles were chipped and the lino-covered floor, despite regular cleaning, was so ingrained with dirt that its former blue colour had been reduced to speckled brown. Suddenly we were sure that of all the places we didn't want to be, all the parts of life we didn't want to explore, this topped the list. I made us step forward carefully, as calmly as I could, in my new shoes. Blackjack hadn't noticed them. That could be useful.

Off the corridor on either side were small offices, the walls covered by pin-boards dotted with pictures, notes and departmental memos, the chairs small, grey swivel jobs for rocking in when bored after lunch; the whole place lifeless, cold, and hard. It cast a sickly, overwhelming muddy stench across our senses that blotted out our usual perceptions, reduced what we felt, and dared to feel, down to a minimum, swamped us with nothing. Horrid, magicless nothing.

"Hey – you sure you're all right?"

"Let's get it over with," I muttered.

"Get what over with?"

I pushed back the door at the end of the corridor and walked down a metal staircase. In the basement were stainless-steel beds, trays, tables and knives, and on one wall a bank of steel doors, like a baker's oven, but too small and too cold.

"Sorcerer?" There was a note of caution in Blackjack's voice. "What the hell are we doing here?"

"Things must end," we replied. "And we are all about now."

I scanned the labels on the steel doors until I found the one I was looking for, swung the handle back and opened it up, pulled the steel handle inside and dragged it out, pulled the sheet back from the face of the corpse and saw . . .

Once Harris Simmons.

There was still enough of the face left to tell that much.

It had once been Harris Simmons. But they'd probably need to use fingerprinting, just to make sure.

"Oh, God," muttered Blackjack.

"Things must end," we repeated quietly, pulling the sheet back over the remnants of Harris Simmons's face and leaning against the cold steel wall. "So why not now?"

"What the hell happened to him?"

"He ran. He was afraid of . . . us. The shadow killed him. When I spoke to the lord of the lonely travellers, he said a shadow was hunting Simmons. It was always going to find him before I could, and it only really has one solution to any problem."

"You knew Simmons was dead?"

"Yep."

"Then what the fuck are we doing here? Séance?"

"No," I sighed. "Something much worse."

The lights dimmed in the ceiling. Blackjack backed towards the wall. "Sorcerer!" His voice was a warning growl, his hand already going into his big sports bag. "What is this?"

A laugh started somewhere at the back of my throat and spread uncontrollably, we held in our sides with the force and pain of it. I rubbed my eyes as they ran with tears, wiped my nose on my sleeve. All around I could hear the slow snap of the lights going out, see my shadow stretching thin. "Bakker knows I'm looking for Simmons. So why shouldn't his shadow know too?" Blackjack had a hand out of his bag holding a fistful of chain. I looked straight into his eyes, and there was something more than fear on his pale – unusually pale – face. "Simmons is going to lead me to Bakker," I said gently. "He was always going to be a trap. But I wanted to know if you'd be the one to spring it."

For a moment, he hesitated.

Then the shadow at his feet reached up, stretched one long, clawed hand out of the floor, clung onto the edge of a steel bed, and pulled. It pulled out a shoulder, pulled out the top of a head, tilted backwards towards the dying light of the bulb, and as its eyes started to form out of the darkness it turned to me and hissed, "There you are!"

"Charmed," I said, and threw ourself nails first at Blackjack, stepping straight through the half-formed shadowy shape of Hunger as he pulled himself up from the darkness on the floor. Blackjack was fast, but, off-guard and big, he lumbered to one side as we hurled ourself at him, reaching up for his eyes. The lights above us popped, and sprinkled burnt glass, and Hunger lashed out at our passing ankle with still only half-formed claws that passed straight through us like ice-crystal fog. Our fingers scraped the side of Blackjack's face, and our teeth sunk into the corner of his ear, drawing blood which tasted of nothing but burnt ash and salt.

Then something landed across our back, heavy and fast, and through his own grunting Blackjack caught us by the scruff of the neck like we were a dog and threw us back, snarling, anger in his eyes, and the chain in his hand didn't so much move through the air as suddenly go from being in his hand to being round our throat with nothing in the middle to justify the journey. We gagged and clawed at our neck even as he tugged on the other end of the chain and dragged us down to our knees, his eyes burning, blood rolling down the side of his face and staining his necktie purple red.

"Bastard!" he screamed; "Bastard!" but that didn't really seem enough, just empty sound with no meaning in the noise.

Then Hunger rose up in front of me and smiled a mouth full of rotten gum. "Hello, fire!"

That seemed to put an end to Blackjack's swearing. His face turned grey.

Hunger leant down in front of me, grabbed my hair with one now solid, snow-white hand, and tilted my chin up with his other, its black nails digging deep. Turning my head so that all I could see were his dead eyes, he whispered, "Where is Matthew's fire now?"

"It's a better question than you know," I replied.

A glimpse of doubt behind Hunger's empty eyes?

Possibly. I looked at him and saw Bakker, and perhaps I only thought I saw feeling, in the replication of my old teacher's body language on Hunger's empty form. Hunger's nails under my chin dug in deeper, drawing blood.

"Matthew..." and for a moment it was Bakker's voice from Hunger's lips, just for a moment, then gone, snatched away back into the depths of the creature's belly. "Will you sing for me?" he asked. "Your old, favourite song?"

"'Ten Green Bottles'?" I wheezed, feeling my blood start to run freely across my skin.

"The one that the angels sing. We be light, we be life, we be fire..."

"Shouldn't trust what you hear on the telephone," I replied. "You never know whether they're laughing as they lie."

He snarled, and then his hands became shadow across my head, and reached into me, curled around my heart and in that place, that dead place with the biker's chain around my throat ready to strangle, I didn't have anything to fight back with, and we were too afraid to try.

We were aware of...

. . . weaknesses . . .

. . . that we would not describe.

When the lights went out in the waking parts of our mind, we were secretly glad.

Journey with spaces and motion sickness.

Jumping from A to C without bothering to ask B if it wanted a look-in.

Incoherent vagaries. Flickering lights, burning around our neck, darkness in our blood, and always his voice. Give me life, he said, give me life.

We know that they drugged us.

We know that they tapped our blood. It wasn't anything too unhygienic; they wanted us alive. They took a pint that Hunger licked at with his fingertips as if it were hot curry sauce. Then they took another because he could not understand why it tasted human. Then he shook us where we lay, and screamed, "I don't want the sorcerer's blood; I've tasted it before and it isn't enough: boring, human, boring and grey! Where are the angels?"

It would have been easy for us to ignite my red blood in its plastic packages to our burning blue fire. It would have been so easy it would have made dying look complicated.

We stayed in darkness, and tried to stay that way, for as long as we could manage.

We had a dream. I've never been a big fan of the mystical interpretation of dreams, but say what you will for the implausibility of prophecy, as well as its uncomfortable metaphysical curiosity, this dream had something going for it. In it, we found ourselves drifting in a bright blue wire, while around us danced the distant humdrum sound of voices saying,

hello?

hello?!

HELLO?

Hi, your call has been forwarded to...

press one for damnation

two for enlightenment

three to alter your account details
or press the star key to listen to the menu again . . .

HELLO!

and to our surprise, we weren't alone. We turned in the dancing space of the telephone line and looked at the stranger who'd surprised us. I was crouching on a drifting Microsoft Windows sign, face covered in blood, trailing my fingertips casually in the wake of a passing computer virus, watching the tendrils of flaky white malignancy tumble into nothing around my fingers, and we realised that I knew, even in this place, *especially* in this place, even the computers were alive.

We said, "Who are you?"

I looked up at the sound of our voice, a strange sparkling thing that, I realised, wasn't just one voice but thousands, a burst of interference clubbed together from the myriad of human voices passing through the system at that instance to form a sound, where we had no mouth to do so, of speech. We stood in front of me, the blue electric fire of the wires passing straight through us like it was fog, or perhaps we were fog, it was hard to tell the difference, coalescing in and out of existence, staring at me through a face covered in flame.

"Matthew Swift," I replied. "What the bloody hell is going on?"

"We remember you," we said. "You gave us life!"

"I did? That's nice."

Round about this point, as is so often the case with dreams, I became confused, nagged by the sense that something about this whole picture wasn't quite right.

"Have we met?" I asked, as we grew a hedgehog on our head and a small bendy bus drove across the Eiffel Tower beneath us.

"We are . . ." we began.

". . . I'm sure there's something . . ." I suggested, surprised to discover that my hands were purple and had three fingers each.

"Is this . . . ?" we tried.

"Definitely something up," I agreed. "Perhaps if . . ."

Then we heard a sound, a deep dark rumble sound that shouldn't have been there, that rose up into a hacking boom, that became, filling the wire with its presence, laughter. We cowered behind me, instinctively feeling that I offered better protection against this very human sound in our domain, although surprised at ourself for feeling so immediately drawn to shelter behind a creature that was as clearly weak and alien as myself. In a turn in which our toes trailed across the mobile phones of Africa and our nose bumped the firewalls of Washington, we spun in the blueness until we saw the source of the laugh.

The source was, predictably enough, a mouth, full of pointed, rotting teeth, and that was all it was. The mouth filled our world, rose up over and above the scattering voices and dancing fire of our home, revealing a deep black gullet behind, and from between its lips came the stench of rotting flesh and the sound of giggling ball-bearings as it spread, swallowing our world whole in a single bite, blocking out all light around us, as we felt the fire on which we stood, the electricity in which we swam sink into the black hole of its throat, sliding down like its tongue was greased with thin oils, until all we could see was mouth and teeth and tongue and dead once-pink tissue that with a single gulp swallowed us whole.

As we fell into darkness, we looked back.

I watched the fire of the blue angels die out in the encroaching shadow, dislodging the cheetah that had decided to attach itself to my shoulders in order to keep warm, and said, "Don't look at me. I was dead to begin with."

Then even I was swallowed up into darkness.

Whiteness, whiteness, everywhere.

I looked to my left; I looked to my right. This was about as much physical movement as I could manage.

My eyes fell on the needles plugged into my left arm. If I hadn't already seen most of my own internal organs up close and personal the last time something bad happened, we would probably have fainted. I held us to consciousness, and tried to think calmly.

The whiteness was from the walls, and the ceiling, and the buzzing strip light overhead, so bright that it hurt. Our eyes were gummy and dry, our lips were chafed, our tongue felt like leather in our mouth. Lifting my head was the extent of what I could manage; everything else seemed firmly strapped to the bed I lay on. I squinted at the bags suspended above where someone had rolled up my shirt sleeve to put in the needles. One held blood, type O, flowing at a steady rate; I noticed that my veins stood out thin and blue like an addict's. Another plastic bag, dripping its contents into me, looked like it held glucose and minerals. Further up my arm, there was a pink plaster over the bulging veins in the crook of my elbow; clearly the relationship I was now in was one of give, as well as take. Someone had taken our blood.

We bit back on anger and nausea.

I wondered why I was still alive, and looked down further. My feet were bare. I wiggled my toes in an attempt to distract myself from the sudden grip of fear in my stomach. Where had they taken my shoes? More importantly, perhaps, *when* had they taken my shoes? I had no way of telling and for a moment we almost considered lashing out with what strength we could feel inside ourself and incinerating everything that came within the radius of our limited perceptions, so that at least if all things had to end, they could end with a bit of glory.

I resisted, forcing us to breathe in and out with a slow, steady rhythm and consider our situation. By rubbing my chin against my shoulder I got the impression of a few days' growth of beard. By my light-headed state after even that small excursion, I guessed that they'd taken several pints of blood from me during this time; the administration now of type-O blood was for no better purpose than to keep us alive a bit longer, for their own benefit, rather than ours. By the fact that all our internal organs were where they should have been and our heart rate steady, we guessed that they still needed us, and felt for a moment a thrill of optimistic heat in our skin.

There was no hurry.

I could wait.

I lay back and closed my eyes, and let the blood fill my veins again.

"Matthew?"

I said nothing.

"Oh, Matthew. How did things ever come to this?"

"You know," I replied, "I'm only two restraints, a cramp and a cocktail of drugs away from shrugging contemptuously in answer to that one."

The squeak of a wheelchair on rubber flooring; a sigh. "Matthew," chided the voice, "this is for the best."

"Uh-huh."

"I still don't understand how you ended up like this! How it became so... rooted... in you. I know they drove you to do the things you did, and I promise you, I will free you from their curse."

We opened our eyes. "Our what?"

Bakker leant forward in his chair, hands clasped together in front of him, face concerned. "I understand that... despite the terrible things you've done... it was for them. The angels hunger for life; of course they do; what wouldn't? They feed on it, long for it, for experience, sense, freedom – it only makes sense that they would... well. Enough of what they would. It's too late now for San and Guy and Harris and all those other poor souls who I'm sure they've dragged down, while wearing your body. I am sorry for it, and for the things that you will feel, if I should ever manage to free you from the angels' snare."

I stared at him, his pale, ageing face made more so by the gaunt contrasts of the room. "I'm sorry," I said, "but can I just clarify this? You think *I* killed San Khay and Harris Simmons? You think that Guy Lee was even capable of dying? You think the angels have possessed me? Are you really that lost?"

He shook his head in dismay; began to turn the chair.

"Mr Bakker!" I called out after him. "I do not believe you can't in your heart of hearts sense the things that have been done, guess at the crimes committed in your name! Look in the mirror and tell me where your shadow goes when you are so happily dreaming of good deeds; look at your own reflection and tell me why, in a bright light, the darkness we all cast isn't lying at your feet!" He gave no response. I screamed after him, "You can't be so blind as to not know! A part of you *must* know!"

He didn't answer, and wheeled his way out of the room without once looking back.

No more dreams.

We wanted no more dreams.

Make me a shadow on the wall...

can you keep control?

a few pearls of wisdom

. . . you're kinda stuffed, sorcerer!

come be me

we be light, we be life, we be fire

make me a shadow on the wall

burn for ever

. . . not worth paying much attention to

You're a nit when not them, aren't you?

we sing electric flame, we rumble underground wind, we dance heaven!

come be me and be free

we be . . .

I be . . .

be free

I'm sorry there's no one to take your call right now, please leave your message after the dialling tone!

Beeeeeeeeee . . .

. . . me . . .

And be free.

.-.-.

No more dreams.

We couldn't stand them any more.

A tickle in our nose?

A rumble somewhere far off, like the hot sigh of underground wind coming up from the tube.

I opened my eyes, since we were too afraid to, and looked around. Somewhere in the distance, there was a deep, polite *whumph*.

A tickle in my nose.

A trickle of mortar dust drifted down from the ceiling. We licked it off our lips, curious. It made our dry tongue, if possible, drier, and tasted of nothing much, with a hint of salt.

I croaked, "Dana?"

From the corner behind my head, out of my line of sight, she said, "That's a spooky thing you've got going there."

"What is?"

"The way you knew I was here."

"I was faking being asleep."

"Then the blue eyes are spooky instead."

"We can't really do anything about that."

"Another spooky thing."

"What is?"

"The way you sound human when you speak."

"That's got a better explanation, all things considered. What's going on?"

She shrugged. "There's an underground line beneath us."

"Which one?"

"Northern."

"Oh. That's what the rumbling is."

"Perhaps."

"You don't sound convinced."

"I'm not buying into any new faith systems."

"I wasn't asking for you to . . ."

"I think we're going to die," she said quietly.

We thought about this, then smiled. "All things must end," we said. "So, in the long-term perspective, you may be right. But what's the point of living, unless you have an end to live for?"

She grunted. I heard the sound of her shoes plodding flatly on the carpet, of something moving on a table beyond my vision. The needles in my arm were gone, the pinpricks covered with small plasters, but I didn't feel any better for it. Her hand brushed the back of our head, tilted it up carefully. She put a plastic cup next to our lips and said, "Go on. Have some."

We hesitated, and looked up into her face. She looked pale, thin, but her eyes were still alert, if no longer bright. I sipped. The touch of the water was absolute balm; it rolled across our tongue as if the muscles in our mouth had cracked and dried like a desert, so solidly baked it was almost incapable of absorbing the moisture. When I'd drunk, she said, "I read somewhere that it just goes straight through you, if you're too dehydrated, like a brick."

"Cheering," I said.

"Would you like some more?"

I licked my lips and nodded. She disappeared somewhere behind me. Water ran. She reappeared and helped me drink. Then she said, "You haven't asked me to help you yet."

"I didn't want to rush things."

"They say you're possessed."

"Who 'they'?"

"Mr Bakker." The same tone of respect was in her voice that still, even now, instinctively filled mine.

"I'm not."

"But you're not quite yourself, are you?"

"No. Not entirely."

"He said you killed Khay, Lee, Simmons."

"I didn't."

"But you did see my mother."

I looked up and she was right there, staring down at me, face impassive, voice so cold and empty I half-imagined she hadn't spoken at all. I licked the last drops of water off my lips, and she didn't offer to get any more. "I saw Mrs Mikeda. She's worried about you."

"Did you do anything to her?"

"You know I didn't."

She nodded slowly. Then, "If I help you, promise me you'll leave. Just get up and go, run. Just run and don't stop running and move east faster than the night-time and keep going. I know you can do that. I know you know how. Just . . ." She stopped. I waited. She took a deep breath, steadied herself. "He watches me, all the time," she murmured. "He'll find out."

"Bakker?" I asked.

She shook her head. "He is kind. He tried to help me."

"Hunger?" I said.

Her eyes turned to me, uncertainty giving them a certain light, for a moment. "You . . ." she began, a question trailing off in her voice.

"Tall, dark, wears Mr Bakker's face?" I asked. "He who watches you?"

She nodded.

"Wears my old coat?"

Slowly, nodding.

"What does he want?"

"He said he'd let me live if I helped him."

"Help him do . . .?"

"Summon the angels. He said . . ."

Realisation dawned slowly. "You called us back," we murmured. "You brought us here!"

There it was, a spasm of fear on her face. "Yes," she said.

"You brought us back!" we repeated, louder. "It was you, you dragged us out of the lines because we've always spoken to you, always known you, always been there for you and you knew where we would hide and you brought us back! We have loved you your whole life, we have whispered to you of freedom and the brightness of life and you, *you* brought us back! You summoned us!"

"Yes," emotion now in her voice, trembling on the edges.

"Why?" we asked.

"So many dead," she replied. "He killed them – Akute, Pensley, Foster, all the sorcerers who you told me to run to if things got bad – he killed them all! Not just because they were his enemies, but because they were *your* friends! To have his revenge on you even once you were dead because *you* wouldn't help him; wherever I went he killed! And you left me!"

Talking to me, I guessed, not us; we had never entirely left her.

"You left me half-trained, unprepared, what was I supposed to do when you were dead?" Her voice was rising in anger and fear and, perhaps, something else. "He said he'd kill everyone I knew, everyone I touched, everyone I . . . but I'd be alive because they'd never found your body, because he saw you the night you died, he saw you breathe your life into the telephone lines, saw your flesh eaten away in a second by a mountain of blue electric maggots that fed on you until there was nothing but blood left, and I hoped, I thought, that perhaps . . . *what was I meant to do?*"

We stared at her, and there were the beginnings of tears in her eyes, although she was fighting with all her pride to hold them back, daring me to disagree. We said, "We're sorry."

She grunted, half-turned away from us to wipe her eyes with her sleeve, snuffled and turned back, as if somehow we hadn't noticed the gesture.

I said, "I'm sorry. Dana – I'm sorry."

She swallowed and nodded. "Run away," she said. "You can't stop him. Please. Run away."

"It may be a bit too late for that," we answered. "Dana?"

"Yes?"

"What did your mother have to say?"

Dana half-laughed, a choked-off, failed sound. "She said you were an arrogant bastard and probably in league with the Devil."

"Really?" I asked, not too surprised.

"She said you told her everything. She said you apologised."

"That's true."

"In all the years since you've been gone, with all the things that have happened," murmured Dana, "Bakker has never apologised. He doesn't know that he needs to."

A distant thud, another trickle of mortar dust from the ceiling. I said, "That's not the Northern line."

A flash of a grin on her face, wry and familiar. "Central line around here too."

"Really?"

"Sure."

I thought about it, then started to laugh.

"What's so funny?" she asked.

"I know where we are. Christ, the guy's got some cheek," I muttered. "Dana?"

"Yes, Matthew?"

"Will you help me?"

"He'll kill us."

"I can handle Bakker."

"It's not him I'm talking about."

"We know. We can handle him."

"Mum said you were possessed. Mr Bakker said you were possessed too."

"It's too short a word for the relationship," I murmured. "Please, Dana. You wouldn't be here at all if you weren't going to help me. So I'm sorry to rush this, but please, *please* do what you had to, sooner rather than later?"

"Why'd you see my mum?"

"I was worried!"

"About me?"

"Of course about you!"

"But you thought she might call me. Say you came by. You counting on me to help you out? You were dead until a few weeks ago. You've got the wrong colour eyes."

"Please," I said. "Please, you know that this is still me. Help me."

She thought about it. "Maybe we should talk," she said.

We talked.

She told me about being Mr Bakker's apprentice. That he had shown her the wonders of the city, taught her to find beauty in all the brightest things, taught her that everything was alive, and bright and full of potential and wonder if you just bothered to see, and that this was good, this was how sorcery felt it should be.

Then she told me that he'd told her that magic was life. That there would be no life if there wasn't magic, that the study of magic, the pursuit of it, the analysis of it, the understanding of it, all these things were key to understanding life.

Then he'd told her to listen to the voices in the wire, the angels that had always talked to her in her childhood, because we'd always sensed that she had a love for life and could live it so fully, we were drawn to that delight in all things that she had in her voice even over the phone. Even when speaking to a faceless machine her words had been full of feelings and thoughts and honest truths, even in the wire we had sensed the expressions on her face, she had given us so much life.

Then he'd told her to talk back to the angels.

Then he'd told her that they were another form of magic, and that as such, they could give life.

Then he'd told her to summon them.

And after the shadow had appeared in her room at night and all the spells she'd thrown at it had been for nothing, she had. After it had told her that it was hungry, so hungry, that it wanted to drink the blue fire of the angels and, if it could not, it would have to feast on the meagre blood of sorcerers – or sorceresses – so, instead, she had.

We were going to say something rude, but I bit it back. Thinking about it, I pointed out a few basic flaws. It wasn't about talking; all I had to do was listen, and I wasn't going anywhere until the story was done.

Then she let us go.

We were surprised how weak we were. We did not understand how I could bear it; but then, I wasn't in the mood to consider what could go wrong for us next.

Dana helped us to the door of the white room, and pushed it open. There was nothing outside but an empty corridor, with strip lights buzzing quietly overhead, and the humid hotness of water pipes running through the ceiling. There was also, however, the familiar smell of…

rich deep blue magic rising up from the underground lines
rumbling reddish-brown tints of the traffic overhead
silvery sparkle from the water pipes
flashing blue fire from the electricity!

…enough magic to grasp hold of and tangle in our fingers, a remembrance of our power, thick and compelling.

We let out a sigh of relief.

"I know where we are," I repeated, pressing my fingers into the dry, unadorned concrete of the walls. More than just the ordinary hodgepodge of sensation, I knew why Bakker chose this place for his home. It buzzed with something more, a deeper line of power that in the good old days of naked dances and ritual sacrifice would probably have been worshipped at dawn.

"You've been here before?" she asked.

"No. But, Central line, Northern line, the Tower; and Mr Bakker always had a sense of the ironic. You didn't need to tell me anything more."

"I don't like this dark," she muttered. "*He* keeps on popping out of it."

"It's all right," we answered. "We can protect you."

"I'd rather Matthew did," she replied.

"I'll do my best," I said. "Tell me: when I was brought here, was I wearing shoes?"

"What?"

"It's important."

"Yes. Why?"

I smiled, standing on tiptoe to brush the ceiling, feeling the warmth seep into my fingers from the cables clustered within it. "Friends are coming. We need to get you out."

"Me? Why?" Then she thought about it some more and added, "Friends? How?"

"Because they're not very sympathetic," I replied. "And you've been keeping bad company. What were the other questions?"

"Is this about your shoes?"
"Yes."
"Thought it might be."
"Good. Which way to out?"

The map of the London underground system was an elegant bit of design by any standard. In other cities, the equivalent looked like a faded imitation, full of implausible destinations highlighted in unsuitable colours, and confusing junctions between overlapping stations, where dotted lines were indistinguishable from coloured blobs meant to inform the viewer that here you could get three escalators, or just walk between stops without violating the terms and conditions of your ticket.

Be that as it may, on the map of the London underground there were only two places where the Central and the Northern lines met, as they ran through the city nearly at right angles to each other. The first was the strange vortex of direction-distorting tunnels, platforms and winding white-tiled stairways that made up Bank station, a place in which even the shrewdest geographers armed with compass and map could get lost while trying to track their way between DLR and Circle line platforms. A place indeed, so some practitioners said, where the borders between spaces were more flexible than usual, and where the bikers swore that, even at the slowest speed, it was possible to find those weak points and slip through to a destination entirely different from any on the map.

But the buzz of magic in the place where I stood, feeling the warm, familiar rumble of the trains under my feet, wasn't that of Bank. That left one other station: Tottenham Court Road, serving an area of suspicious computer shops, hi-fi warehouses and dodgy second-hand dealers, together with the megastores and brothels of Oxford Street and Soho.

And there was a tower. It amazed me that I hadn't thought of it before; there was a tower, and it wasn't just a giant building stretching up into the sky, it wasn't just an expression of power or, as some feminists would have it, a symbol of masculine insecurity, as so many tower blocks in so many cities seemed to be. It was the Tower; it featured on postcards; and the air inside it buzzed with all the magic that such a position entailed.

If I hadn't been certain before, I was by the time Dana helped me up a flight of stairs, pushed back a door with the words "Danger!! High Voltage!!" plastered in big yellow letters on it, and led me out into a concourse that smelt of sweat and chlorine. Opposite me was a sign. It read:

Men's Toilets ⇒
⇐ Women's Toilets
** *Centre Point is a Non-Smoking Zone* **

Dana said, "What d'you think?"

I laughed.

"Thought you'd say that," she grunted.

"Bakker lives here?"

She shook her head. "He moves around."

"But he's here, tonight." It wasn't a question.

"Yes. How'd you know?"

"He wants our blood," we replied. "He's trying to make it catch fire, he wants us to give him life. I knew he wouldn't want to be too far from us, once he found us."

"You . . . wanted to be found?"

"I knew Simmons was most likely dead. I knew Bakker wanted us alive. I knew that, with San Khay and Guy Lee both gone, the shadow would have to deal with me myself. I knew I was going to be betrayed, and a process of elimination led me to think it would be by my friend. With such a wonderful array of information at your fingertips, what would you have done?"

"But . . . you were . . . there were needles and . . ."

"I was keeping my fingers crossed that you might let me go."

"You didn't know?" she asked sharply.

"Didn't seem good manners to presume."

She scowled. Then, sharply, out of nothing asked, "Can you?"

"What?"

"Give him life? Can you cure Bakker?"

We shook our head. "Not as he'd see it."

"He said that you could save his life. He's dying," she added, with reproach in her voice.

"I know, and no one can," I replied gently. "Least of all us."

"Then what can you do? Sorry to sound like the naive one, but wouldn't it have saved a lot of trouble if you'd told him this?"

"We are creatures of the life you leave behind. We feed off the feelings you forget, we were born of the thoughts that faded the moment they were spoken, of the unseen things, of the unspoken things that got trapped in the wire when the phone was cut off or the words lost in interference, or when the mouth that spoke them lied, but on the other end of the line they couldn't see their faces. We *are* all this, and he thinks that if he takes it, for himself, takes that which makes us alive, he will live for ever."

"Forever doesn't sound so bad; I mean, if you're not such a bad man. What's the catch?"

"Apart from the fact that he's been leeching my blood?" I asked.

"Apart from that."

"It's complicated."

"Oh, please. I think I got way past that lesson on day one."

"Which way?" I asked.

She nodded round the curve of the dimly lit passageway. I grinned.

"What?" she asked, seeing my expression. "What's so funny?"

"I've always liked this place."

"You know that it's a disgraceful example of the greed of the property industry, a crappy piece of planning and, until dead recently, a dive for druggies, right?"

"Yeah," I said. "It fits the vibe."

"Is this the right time to criticise some of your teaching techniques?"

A rumble somewhere not too far off, a ripple of sensation, a shudder of the lights, a moment where we thought we heard

hello Matthew's fire . . .

"No," I said firmly. "Come on."

The tower's foundations had been set deep, and there were more than on the official map; tunnels spread around the water mains, and between the passages of the underground station almost immediately beneath it. We seemed to walk, stagger, jog on our irregular progress through the maze of seemingly identical passageways under Centre

Point, the smell of the underground gym – all body odour and chemicals – being replaced by the stench of urine that defined the subways passing beneath its concrete struts, which in turn faded down to the distant *thrumthrumthrum* of pounding club music humming through the walls.

We found a service lift, its panels rusted, its floor uneven, its wall of cardboard stuck on with gaffer tape. Dana pressed the ground-floor button and I didn't argue, leaning against her and watching my world steady itself as we rose up with a slow cranking sound through the lift shaft. I didn't know how much blood they'd taken or how much they'd put in me, but by the lightness of my head I was willing to guess that it hadn't been a proportionate ratio.

We had passed the grid to the basement exit when the lift lurched, the lights went out and everything stopped.

Dana said, her breath coming fast and ragged, "What the hell?"

"Friends are coming," I replied, straining to hear something through the dull echoes of the shaft. "It'll be all right."

"Is this something to do with your bloody shoes?"

"Yes. Magicians are always so hung up on magic, they never bother to check for technology."

"You . . . were followed?"

"Pretty much. I'm not the only one capable of tricksy planning and cunning insight, you know."

She scowled, staring round the tight confines of the lift, uneasy at the small space. "We're going to sit here?"

"Too many shadows," I answered.

"You had to say it, just when I was being steely with self-control, you had to say it!"

We took a deep breath and rubbed our hands together, searching for warmth between our fingers. The magic was easy in this place, we didn't need much to work with. I opened up the palm of my hand and let the bubble of pinkish-orange neon light float up above our heads, illuminating the tight space of the lift. Dana's face was pale, the fixed smile scared, but refusing to sink into any more honest expression. "He's going to kill me, isn't she?" she said, not bothering to raise her voice or let the terror fill it. "He's going to kill me."

"He hasn't yet."

"So?"

"The shadow . . . is part of Bakker," I answered, thinking about my argument a word at a time. "Perhaps there's a part of him – both the man and his creature – which doesn't want you dead?"

"You've always got a way with the implausible."

"I'm just theorising."

"What now?"

The lift jerked, and started moving again, of its own accord, tossing us to the sides to cling on for support.

"Good?" asked Dana breathlessly.

"Buggered if I know."

"You know, for a man possessed – sorry – in a complicated relationship with mystical entities of bloody magic and forgotten life – you're pretty useless when it comes to a tight situation, aren't you?"

"This isn't a tight situation yet."

"Tell that to the white room and the operating table," she retorted sharply. "Looked pretty tight from where I was."

"Yes," I replied, "but you *did* help me, didn't you?"

She opened her mouth to speak, then hesitated, thought about it, then opened her mouth again. "You are a total . . ."

The lift jerked to a stop. The door slid open with inexorable slowness. Beyond was a single cream-coloured corridor, lined with tinted glass windows that obscured the light and darkened even the shadows beyond it. Outside it was night; inside it was harsh strip-light day, the floor cold and the air dry, unstirred. I stepped out of the lift cautiously and looked around. Dana said, "This isn't the ground floor."

Behind us, the lift door slid shut.

I walked to the window and looked down. Some distance below I saw the shape, tinted brown, of what in real life was a bright blue, floodlit fountain of three treble-pronged stone nozzles that squirted water into the pool around them and, chaotically, over the narrow pavement beyond. I guessed it to be about four floors down. Dana said, "I'm sure I pressed ground."

"I'm sure you did too," I answered, looking around the corridor. There was no feature in it except a red fire extinguisher next to a closed door. "But lifts can be subject to other people's control."

"I didn't feel we moved that many floors..." she began again, a note of urgency entering her voice.

"Moving without covering all the distances involved," I answered cheerfully. "It's been known. Dana?"

"Yes?"

"If Mr Bakker got round to teaching you any sort of protective magics, now might be the time to practise them." I could hear a humming, a sound like an angry beehive, or perhaps a very expensive, very badly treated car engine caught in traffic...

"Is this where the lights go out?" she asked.

I wandered over to the fire extinguisher and tugged it out of its rack on the wall. "Deep breaths," I said, and kicked open the door.

On the other side was another long white corridor. Standing in it were at least half a dozen men and women, armed variously with grenades, handguns, and rifles, and assorted magical baubles that floated and drifted, or had just been slung down casually at the owner's feet. In front of them a huge motorbike dominated the corridor, black tyre marks skidded all around it. Sitting on it, mirrored visor lowered over his face, was the wide form of the biker. He revved his engines.

Dana said, "Um..."

He put his foot down on the pedal, kicked the bike off the stand and, with a roar of engine that filled the whole corridor with an angry thrum, and a burst of black fumes that darkened the faces of the people around him, charged straight for us.

I pressed down on the fire extinguisher.

From its end came thick white billowing gas. I pressed down harder, caught a fistful of gas between my fingertips, spun it into a tornado of whiteness and threw it down the corridor, straight at Blackjack and his friends as they ran towards us. It spread out as it moved, rattling the windows and splattering the walls with patches of pale foam, thickening in an instant to the consistency of froth on hot cappuccino, blinding the eyes of the men with the guns and the women with the bombs as they ran at us, choking them and filling their noses with the stench of chemical suppressants. But not Blackjack. Behind his empty-faced helmet he just kept coming. I grabbed Dana's hand, pulled her away from the door and said, as calmly as I could, "Run."

Bakker had taught her as he had taught me, because she did as I said without question.

We ran.

Corridors, offices. The offices sat behind dull plywood doors. Most of them were empty. Some were missing panels on their ceilings, through which wires drooped and odd foil-covered pipes poked. Some had water coolers, the gossip-corner of any workplace; some had long rows of endless boring desks lined with endless boring computers that were probably capable of making phone calls to innocent bystanders, but had almost certainly had all the games wiped before installation, with no opportunity to install any more.

We ran into another office of neglected desks and the odd revolving chair. Right behind us, the biker burst through the doors, smashing them apart with the front wheel of his bike. Dana dove left, I dove right and the biker tore between us, spinning around a few metres beyond with a screech of burning tyre that tore a gash in the carpeted floor. He revved his engine a few times, like the challenge a knight gives before the joust, and the sound was so loud that the windows tinkled, the loose wires in the roof swayed, and the chairs creaked and rocked; the noise went straight through the eardrum and made the inside of our nose ache, shook into our stomach and blurred the edges of our vision. From the back of the bike, a cloud of noxious black smoke whirled up around him; its instant taste in our throat was like the stench from a garage forecourt, which could penetrate even the thickest glass and suck moisture from our mouth.

The lights faltered around us and, for a panicked moment, I looked down at the floor to see my own shadow; it was not turning. I looked over to Dana and saw that she had one hand raised towards the ceiling, and was dragging crackling jagged arcs of blue electricity out of the wires above us, causing the lights to dim as she spun it between her fingers. The motorbike roared into life, and went straight for her. She threw her bundle of voltage at the biker, but at the last instant he swerved; and for a moment, there were two of him, one swooping straight into the oncoming blast of Dana's spell, the other spinning away from it, behind her already, the two images flickering for a moment as Blackjack worked his magic and moved from A to C, without calling in at B.

He disappeared from in front of Dana.

Instantly, he reappeared, a few feet behind her, and his front wheel was still headed straight for her. I called out a warning and swatted a wave of pressure through the air that wasn't nearly enough to dislodge something as heavy and as fast as the motorbike, but knocked Dana aside enough so that the front wheel missed her. It slammed on past, pounding through a plywood desk that didn't even slow the bike down, but splintered right through the middle without the biker losing an instant of speed. I ran to Dana, grabbed her by the wrist, dragged her up and pulled her through the nearest door. A corridor away there was a flight of stairs, winding round one corner of the building; below I could see a theatre and the bright lights of the crossroads outside it, the evening's crowd pouring out after a performance, the buses struggling round the tight corners and the taxis lining up for their fares in the narrow bus lanes of New Oxford Street to the indignant tooting of other traffic.

We wanted to go up; up would be where he was – but with Dana I didn't dare risk it, didn't want her in the same building as that man and his shadow for a second longer than necessary, so we went down, winding round the narrow confines of the stairwell, third floor, second –

– just after the second floor, we felt a tugging of sickness in our stomach, a moment of dislocation, and looking down, we saw that below us was the third floor. We tried again, reached the second floor, dropped down another flight of stairs and were instantly back at the third floor. We could taste Bakker's magic in this, we could feel the familiar taste of his spells, the unique craft and skill of them, but under it, too, a faltering of the lights, a pulling in our stomach.

We looked down at the floor and saw our shadow starting to stretch long, even though we weren't moving. Dana followed our gaze, and her hand tightened around ours.

"He's coming," she whispered.

The lights dimmed in the stairwell, and this time it wasn't our doing. I turned to the window and started kicking at it. Dana, realising what I was doing, joined in, but the glass just went *bonk*, as if it was a solid plastic sheet. I cursed in frustration, looking around for some sort of inspiration; Dana got there first. She dug the nails of her right hand into the palm of her left, flinching as she did, until the skin tore and a thin line of blood crawled out. She dipped a finger into the blood and drew, on the glass, the image of a keyhole. For a few moments the shape was nothing more than a dark stain on a dark surface; then it began to hiss and smoke. She clenched her right hand into a fist and punched the glass as hard as she could in the heart of the keyhole.

The glass cracked. She punched again. Little fault lines spread out, thickened; the whole thing started to creak. She drew her fist back for one more punch, and a fist emerged out of the darkness of the glass, and caught her by the wrist, black nails digging into her skin. She screamed, a sound of genuine terror that was the product of I couldn't imagine how many months of fear. I grabbed her by the shoulders and pulled her back, and the arm that held hers reached out of the glass, the blackness of its shape growing sickly white flesh, and her blood trickling around his fingertips as he became real.

We snarled, and lashed out at the forming flesh of Hunger, our fingers trailing sparks through the air; and our nails drew three parallel lines of black blood through his flesh. His hand spasmed around Dana's arm and she whimpered again, cowering away and shaking her head in numb horror, every instinct she had shut down behind the fear. Then out of the dark glass the head appeared, and leaned forward with its mouth already open, teeth sparkling, tongue licking its blue lips as it reached out for Dana's blood, its eyes, nose, skin gradually becoming solid.

I waited for its ears to become real and, though it was probably only moments, that waiting seemed to take for ever. Then I put my hands over Dana's ears, drew my foot back and kicked the metal banisters of the stairwell with the sole of my bare heel.

The metal went *booooiinnnnggg*.

Hunger flinched.

He *was* scared of us.

We grinned and kicked it again.

The rails responded with a hollow, long, resounding *boooooii innnngggggooinnggggoinnnggg* . . .

Bakker had taught me this spell, and knew how it would end. And, because Hunger was, in the end, Bakker's shadow, so did he; even before I levelled a final kick he was retreating, drawing back into the shadows while the lights around us brightened. But just to make sure, to finish him off, I aimed one final kick, and drove my heel as hard as I could against the metal banister.

The stairwell shook. The sound was the sound of hollow metal vibrating, but rising up through more than just a single long rail. It filled the stairwell, hummed up every banister, and the sound fed off itself, the hum in one setting off a vibration in another which set off resonance in the next, filling the whole stairwell with such a clamour of magically enhanced ringing that the cracks in the windows spread of their own accord, that the light fixtures tingled, that dust shimmered down from the plastic-padded walls, that the edges of the black rubber sheath over the top of the banister started to warp under the strain, that the whole world seemed to quake. In the street outside, car alarms sounded; in the blue pool of the three ugly fountains, water sloshed against its sides and one fountain spurted the half-hearted residue left in its pipes over a passing tourist who clung to a lamp-post as the hum rippled through the street.

Hunger's fingers uncurled in an instant, his face stretching with pain; and he was gone, retreating into the window. Dana's bloody hands were pressed over mine, which were covering her ears; her eyes were shut and her face a twisted mass of confusion and distress. I felt my ears pop and my nose start to run with hot blood – something we didn't feel we could afford to lose right now. I staggered up the stairs, pulling Dana along with me by her head, kicked open the nearest door and, blind to which floor or what spell we were trapped on or in this time, fell onto the carpet beyond, pulling Dana down with me, and shoving the door shut behind us.

The echoes slowly faded. I sat up, my ears ringing. Dana pulled herself up and experimentally lifted her hands over and away from her ears. Then she turned to me, her voice shaking, and said, "You never taught me that."

"It was luck," I replied. "Damn things could have been solid, for all I knew."

"In this building?" Her voice was distant and slightly too low, as if heard through a thin sheet of water. I wiped the blood from my nose and shook my head, as if that would be enough to banish the tinnitus buzzing just behind my eardrums.

"Fair point," I conceded. "Where are we?"

She staggered onto her feet and pulled me up with her. "It all looks the same to me," she admitted. "But I'm pretty sure we should have hit the ground floor by now."

"Good old-fashioned spells to confuse, baffle and bewilder," I groaned. "We *are* starting to lose patience with this game."

"Is that what it is?"

"For *him*," we replied, and felt that we didn't need to specify for who.

"You hear that?" she asked.

We put our head on one side, not sure if the tinnitus was fading or if we were simply getting used to it. Perhaps a hint of...

"Motorbike," said Dana.

"Now we really *are* out of patience," we announced.

The door at the end of the corridor burst open, and this time, the motorbike was trailing fire. Dana threw herself through the nearest door and I followed. A female toilet, somewhere neither I nor we had ever been before, and which disappointed us in its plainness.

Dana slammed the door shut behind us and pressed a large metal bin against it as the bike swept by. The sound of it stopped too suddenly for it to have gone into the stairwell; the engine noise just winked out, leaving us in sudden and uncomfortable silence.

Dana looked at me, I looked at her. She rolled her eyes, marched over to the bank of low, cracked metal taps and started running every single one, putting in the plugs and dipping her hands into every basin as they started to fill. I groaned as I saw what she was doing; but, not having a better idea, I picked up the lid of the bin lodged against the door, and smashed it against the long mirror above the sinks. I carefully picked out a shard of glass from the cracked spider's web clinging to the wall, curling my fist around it until it bit into my skin, drawing blood. Dana raised her hands from the final basin, water pouring off them, and grinned. "Right," she said. "Not so useless!"

She started to spin her hands through the air, with a beckoning, gentle gesture. The water pouring out of the taps started to turn, twist up away from the basins it was filling and spin towards her, circling around her like clear silk scarves, winding around her legs and arms without ever actually touching her skin, the taps still running so that she seemed to be almost attached by liquid placentas to the sinks, by lines of still-flowing, thickening water that constantly spun and moved around her as the taps poured more and more into the spell, and kept on pouring. I'd heard of sorcerers who'd sucked whole reservoirs dry doing spells like this; unless someone actually, physically turned off the taps, there was no reason to stop.

And she was good at it. The spell flowed around her, and the way she spun it, the way she let the growing swirls of water dance and mingle into thicker strands of sparkling translucence across her – she knew the effect was beautiful, and in many ways, that sense of the elegance of the thing was what let her craft the spell so well. She'd always said she'd found the sight of still waters to be calming; and watching her then, entirely in control, I felt for a moment that, perhaps, everything would be all right after all.

I raised my fist, the glass clenched inside it, towards the mirror and spun my own version of the same magic. The cracks spread from where I'd smashed it with the lid of the bin, rippling out towards the edges in ever-splitting streams like the passage of water across uneven dry soil, until, with a single heave, the entire thing shattered. The glass fragments, however, did not fall. They drifted at my command; I could feel every one like the skin on my back, taste them in my mouth, a sharp metallic feel on the tip of my tongue, and when I moved, they moved with me, wrapped themselves around me like a reflective blanket, each one shimmering back the brightness of my eyes

our eyes

bright blue

a moment to remember that our eyes are blue now, a thousand, thousand pieces of blue brightness looking back

beautiful brightness too

before I turned to the door, painfully aware of the silent nothing outside, and said to Dana, "Right. Sorcery."

I kicked open the door, as much for the drama as anything else.

The corridor outside was empty, except for a trail of burning tyre marks along its length that finished as suddenly as it had begun. Dana gestured, and a slender filament of water still drawing its life from the running taps in the bathroom, and snaking out from the door behind her as she moved, now slithered through the flames, extinguishing them in front of us. I walked ahead, careful, in case I cut her, to keep my distance as the shards of shattered glass and mirror danced and dazzled around me in a standing wave of silver. Moving slowly behind, Dana trailed the umbilical cords of water like the tails of a kite.

We passed through another office. A post room, full of empty sacks and bags; a small kitchen; a canteen, the shutters drawn across the windows. Our shadows stayed obeying the laws of physics, turning and bending with the light. Another office. Another flight of stairs.

Dana said, "Can we break his spell? Can we get out?"

"Sure," I answered. "But it'd be easier with a motorbike."

Shouting somewhere below; sounds of battle somewhere above.

"Guns?" asked Dana.

"Yes; my friends don't have much imagination," I replied. "Come on."

"Can't we find them?"

"Sure," I said. "Bakker's ex-apprentice and his current apprentice together at last in front of an angry mob of people come here for the express purpose of destroying the Tower, bloody sorcerers and all their works. What a happy meeting that would be."

"No need to get sarky."

"Sorry."

We started descending, slowly, one step at a time. We turned the corner of the stairwell and I could see the door to the second floor and felt a tight tugging in my belly and we stopped.

Putting our head on one side we leaned gently forward, then back on our heels, feeling the sickness grip us as we did. "It's here," we whispered, eyes half shut as we tried to pinpoint the source of our unease. "Right here."

We looked round. The floor we stood on was uncarpeted, the walls clean. We looked up. The ceiling consisted of plastic panels set into concrete. Dana threw a fistful of tight, high-pressure water at the most central one, which wobbled, came loose, and flopped onto the floor.

I bent to pick it up, letting my glass shroud drift above me for a while. On the back, someone had drawn, very carefully in thin black ink, a picture of a stairwell, all odd angles and strange dimensions, that seemed to feed inexorably into itself. I touched it with a fingertip. The hot magic of it burnt; we snatched our hand away and for a moment heard

Matthew's fire!

We dropped the panel. Then, with a scowl, we directed a handful of shattered glass at it, tearing the thin plastic to shreds in an instant.

"You OK?" asked Dana.

"Children's games," we snapped, louder than we'd meant. "We have no patience with these tricks of the light!"

I grabbed back my handful of glass, tossing it into the whirling mêlée around my head, and kept descending. This time, the second floor stayed the second floor, and the first floor was the first. The door to the ground floor was locked, but Dana leant out of her watery cloak for a moment to stroke it, whispering gentle invocations into the bars on the door, which eventually, reluctantly, clicked loose. The doors swung back.

There was a foyer beyond, high-ceilinged, full of odd alcoves and strange shapes, along with the occasional neglected potted plant, a battered reddish carpet and an abandoned reception desk. Beyond that were a pair of large, black glass doors.

In front of them sat the motorbiker, and there too, its long tail curled round the back of him, was a dragon.

There was no mistaking the creature. The tail was the signs of street names that had been changed by the local council; its claws were the bent pipes of signposts that had been smashed into by speeding cars; its spine rippled with the reflective Catseyes of the motorways; its belly was plated with speed warnings; its haunches were tense with the triangular fluorescent warning signs of "DANGER!" or "SLOW – CHILDREN CROSSING", bent and twisted to fit the curves of its hulk. Unlike the litterbug, this creature was at least fifteen feet end to end, and all metal; no vulnerable cardboard underbelly here, nor beating recyclable heart. It didn't so much blink as that the reflective coating of its eyes – the battered lenses of smashed speed cameras – glinted with the slightest movement of its head, capturing the shimmer of the white lamps dangling high overhead like suspended jellyfish.

If there was an expression on the biker's face, it was hidden under his shiny helmet, and the impassive curling dragon showed no inclination towards feeling across its twisted metal snout, buckled together by the reflective neon yellow bands of cyclists' warning straps.

Dana said through the corner of her mouth, wisely keeping perfectly still as we surveyed the creature and the dwarfed shape of the biker beneath it, "You didn't mention dragons."

"Oh, come on. I must have."

"Pretty sure I would have remembered."

I considered the beast. There was a familiarity in its shape and form. I said, "I don't suppose you've ever lived in the City of London?"

"Not my kind of rent," she admitted. "Is this going to be relevant?"

"Perhaps." We looked down at the biker, cleared my throat and raised my voice. "Bakker still needs us," we said. "The shadow still wants us."

Blackjack reached up, and slowly pulled off his helmet. Underneath, his face was blistered, red, eruptions of pus around his throat and chin, and thick infected arteries standing out across his forehead. "I know," he said, staring straight at me, his voice hoarse and weak. "He told me."

The lights shuddered, dimmed overhead. The dragon stirred. I murmured to Dana, for her ears only, "Legally the City of London is a historical anomaly; it's been almost unchanged for centuries. They say the Mayor has the power to exclude even the sovereign from entering the city, not that anyone's tried for a while."

"If it's not relevant I will actually chain you back up in that damn room myself," sung out Dana in a fluty, frightened voice. The shadows stretched, bent at our feet.

"The city's symbol," I replied, keeping my voice as low and as calm as I could, "is a dragon, holding the cross of St George. And its motto..."

...darkness thickening in front of the dragon, tightening to a spot, warping, rising...

"...is *Domine dirige nos*."

"Nice," squeaked Dana. "Catchy."

. . . rising up from the floor, forming a head, a chest, arms, a face . . .

"Let me handle the dragon," I muttered.

Hunger emerged from the shadows. He stood in front of the dragon, which seemed quite content to have him there, and stretched, the darkness swirling around him. I saw Blackjack flinch in his presence, but he didn't otherwise move. Hunger looked at the biker, like a snake drawn by movement, and grinned, exposing rotten teeth. "Poisons in your blood?" he murmured.

Blackjack looked away, and for a moment it occurred to me that the expression on his face wasn't anger, but shame.

Hunger turned to me, still grinning; then his attention moved to Dana. "I always knew you'd betray me, to him," he whispered, voice carrying like the hiss of a serpent. "I hoped that the pain of you betraying him would be enough to kill his heart, and let them take over what was left; but you didn't. Little child, running back for safety."

Dana didn't answer.

Hunger's empty black eyes settled on my face. "Ever killed a dragon, sorcerer?"

"Not lately," I replied.

Behind him, the dragon flexed its claws.

"This is a beast of forgotten and disobeyed things," said the shadow. "He is summoned from the broken street sign, from the smashed order and the bent commands, vulnerable to being summoned because so much of what he is has simply been ignored."

A hand stroked the dragon's metal flank, nails scraping across the rusted remains of a one-way street sign. "Little humans always think they know best. Forget the past, forget the rules, forget humility – that is their natural place, being petty things. It is why he is angry."

I licked my dry lips and risked staring into the cracked camera lens of the dragon's eye. It shimmered back at me.

"I hoped that she would free you," explained Hunger. "Does that surprise you?"

"You wanted what?" Dana's voice was a bare breath on the air.

"We thought you would let her help us," we replied coldly.

"And why?" he asked, enjoying his moment.

"To make us fight to escape. To make me fight to protect her."

"To make your blood burn blue!" He almost laughed it, practically clapped his hands together with childish delight. "When you are the sorcerer your blood is nothing to me. I have drunk my fill of it already and it tastes like the others, like all the other dead old men and frail little women; it barely touches a corner of my belly, it is tepid in my throat! When you are the angels, your blood burns so brightly it... it..." A whine entered in his voice, he seemed to constrict, shrink into himself like a petulant child. "Hungry." The words rattled out thin across his teeth. "So hungry..."

"We can beat you," we said easily.

"You've never killed a dragon," explained Hunger, eyes burning bright.

I grinned. "Life is full of... well, a lot *more* life."

And, because we had it to hand, we threw a wall of glass towards Hunger and Blackjack; Hunger melted into the shadows in a second, Blackjack threw himself down under the blast and the glass shattered lightly off the dragon's metal sides. Its nostrils flared with the clanging of tempered metal, and it raised itself up, shaking its bulk with a deafening clamour. I grabbed Dana's wrist and hissed, "You worry about the biker."

Dana opened her mouth to complain, looked into our eyes and changed her mind. She nodded, turned and threw a head-sized ball of water at Blackjack, wrapping it around his nose and mouth as he struggled to his feet. I focused my attention on the dragon.

It raised itself up on its back legs, the slashed wreckage of a speed-humps sign warping around its thighs as it did, the bent remnants of a "dog fouling" notice cracking under the strain, and roared. The sound severed the lamps in the ceiling, which smashed down on the floor in front of it and around it; it shattered the glass of the foyer and knocked Dana off her feet. We dropped to a crouch, ready to pounce, and I dug my nails into the palm of my hand without even thinking about it, digging them deep until the blood ran. I dipped two fingers in the pool of red liquid accumulating in my hand and, the blood sloshing thinly, drew a crude cross on the floor in front of me, and another, smaller cross in the left-hand corner of the shape. The dragon lumbered towards me with surprising ease and grace, its form shimmering across the floor. It didn't even need to claw me to death; a single swipe of its neck would break every bone in my body.

I heard the cracking of metal and saw that Blackjack had crawled away from his bike. He had a chain in his hand, which was lashing out towards Dana's face; but she ducked, and hurled tall funnels of water at him. They spattered his face, then knocked him off his feet, and bowled him backwards like they were ocean waves breaking from a storm. The tendrils of her spell, winding around her and back through the doorway to the stairwell, led from where the taps were still running, some floors above.

Above me, meanwhile, the dragon raised a paw. Its palm, ready to smash down on my head, was a blackened "STOP" sign, graffitoed over in big green letters by some wag with the comment "Caliper Boy SMELLS". I dropped instinctively to one knee, raising my hands above my head, and, from under this metallic death, in the second before the lights went out I shouted, "Lord lead us!"

The paw hesitated, hovering a few inches above my head, so wide that I couldn't see the ceiling above it.

Somewhere on the foyer floor, I heard a hacking and spluttering as Blackjack tried to spit water out of his lungs; and the sloshing of Dana preparing another twist to her spell.

The paw trembled in the air above me.

"*Domine dirige nos!*" I repeated, shouting the words up at it. "Lord lead us! Lord lead us!"

The paw drifted to one side. A pair of camera-lens eyes stared down at us.

"You are the dragon that guarded the city of London," we whispered frantically. "We recognise you, we know you; you are the dragon on all the old gates at the city walls, you are the symbol of the old part of the city; *Domine dirige nos* is your motto: Lord lead us; we know you . . ."

A rumbling sound from somewhere inside the monster like the passing of a distant train.

"No!" The voice came from the shadows, where Hunger emerged. "No! I summoned you. Obey *me*!"

"Lord lead us," I whispered again. "We know you; Lord lead us. 'The city of London shall have all its ancient liberties and free customs, as well by land as by water; furthermore, we decree . . .'"

"I summoned you!" shrieked Hunger. "You are mine! I summoned you out of the city; you will . . ."

"' . . .know that I have granted to my citizens of London for themselves and their heirs, the citizens may appoint as sheriff whomever they want from among themselves and as judge whomever they want from among themselves to take charge please of the crown and supervise their conduct; no one else shall be judge over the men of London . . .'"

"They are the blue electric angels, they do not know these laws!" shrieked Hunger.

"You are the dragon of the city of London," I whispered. "Listen to me! I'm from this city, I know its laws, I know what makes it alive, I understand it. *Domine dirige nos;* I know your history, I understand *how* the shadow summoned you, but you don't have to listen, I know the history, duty, humility, laws, time . . ."

"No!"

The scream came from somewhere other than the shadows. I looked round and saw that the shadow had moved; he now stood behind Dana, one black arm across her throat, claws pressed against-her eyelids, his eyes burning. "Stop it, sorcerer," he muttered, and then, in a voice that wasn't quite his, not quite, "Stop it, Matthew."

I stayed absolutely still, while the dragon coiled back in on itself, watching with empty eyes. "You know the Magna Carta, you know the rights of the city; you may even know how to unsummon an urban dragon," not Hunger's voice, coming from Hunger's mouth, "but if you push me, I *will* kill her!"

Blackjack was on his knees, throwing up water through his nose and mouth. Dana's trailing spirals of tap water were now flooding pools splashed across the floor, her eyes shut and breath coming in-little wheezes as Hunger held her close to his frozen skin. "I kept-her-alive for this," he whispered. "Just like my sister. I kept her alive."

I started forward, but his fingers pressed harder into her face, pushing the blood out of it. Hunger grinned. "Where's Matthew's fire now?"

"You didn't know I'd come back!"

"But I never found a body either," he replied. "And the angels always loved to talk to you. Come be me, they said, and be free, and you've always wanted to be free, Matthew. You've always dreamed of turning yourself into dancing blue fire and spinning across the sky, you've always wanted to be a rumble on the wind, a dancer in the clouds; what creature of flesh would want less? The chance to fly and be free, to forget the poor, constructed laws of humanity, the pain, the fear, the feeling, the ageing, the dying. The angels have always loved you, because you've loved them, you've always wanted their message to be real, you've always wanted to be fire and light and life and now that you are . . . you will not share. So I kept her alive, and maybe, just maybe, the sorcerer has enough control over the angels to not let her die?"

"Robert . . ." I began.

"I am Hunger!" he screamed. "I am not bound by the laws of flesh! I am hungry! You are so alive when you burn – I will have that life!"

The dragon's tail twitched, scraping along the floor.

"We can't . . ." we whimpered. "Please . . . I . . ."

"Which one? Which one can't? Which one can't bear it if she is dead?"

"We are . . ." we stuttered.

". . . almost . . ." I began.

". . . the same."

"Please," we said.

"Please . . ." I added.

Then Hunger grinned. "I will understand these things when I am alive again," he said, and raised one fist of black claws towards Dana's face.

We screamed.

The bloody cross within a cross that we had drawn on the floor at our feet caught fire. The fire was bright blue flashing sparks that wriggled and writhed by themselves.

And because we didn't know what to do, couldn't cope
not this
my feelings
such feelings
not this

because we couldn't understand
this feeling
too much
—-because we couldn't
I couldn't-—

we screamed

"Domine dirige nos! **Domine dirige nos!**"

And the dragon of broken and disobeyed signs was, in the end, an urban creature, summoned out of the city itself; and the city's dragon, the lord of the city's gates, did so very much like to lead, and be obeyed, and have its own rules that could, so rumour went, stop the king or queen entering the city, if it was felt that Londoners didn't need them inside their walls. Hunger had told me the key himself: time, law, humility, a recognition that in the eyes of the city, we were nothing, and the dragon was the lord.

Without a moment's hesitation, it swiped its tail in an easy gesture that took the head off Hunger where he stood, slashing it from his shoulders with a single razored edge of broken signpost.

Hunger disintegrated into nothing, black wisps of darkness crawling away into the corners of the room, where they melded into the shadows.

We looked at the dragon, it looked at us, as the blue fire of our blood gently retreated back down to dull redness. Then, without a sound, it started to melt. Scales of reflective plastic drifted off its skin, in flashes of bright white, yellow and red. The traceries of a thirty-mile-an-hour warning sign, the remnants of a school crossing notice, part of a placard welcoming you to a council estate, a shard of post office notice, a chipped blue piece of a notable's plaque, a warning about temporary lights. They slipped off it like seeds from a dandelion as the spell that had sustained it slowly disintegrated.

Last of all, flopping to the ground with a single dull thunk, was a small rounded piece of stone that rolled towards our feet. We picked it up. Its edges were smooth and surface warm; it felt old in our hands. On one side were the words:

n this day in 167
derman of the city
in honour o

Domine dirig

and that was all.

"Matthew?"

I turned to look at Dana, who, without a sound, slipped to the floor in a rapidly growing circle of her own blood.

We dragged our nails into our hand to draw blood, and put all our strength and heat and warmth into it until it burned so brightly that the walls were blazing blue. We rubbed it into her wounds but she didn't speak, didn't stir.

We screamed for help, shook her, shouted her name, pressed the heat of our flesh into her cold skin, pressed our hands as hard as we could into the gashes in her chest and neck but the blood just seeped out around our fingers and mingled with our own until we couldn't tell what was ours and what was hers and the burning of ours was muted in the medley.

I couldn't

not Dana

I couldn't

so we had to. We held her in our arms, and every joint seemed to have just broken, every limb hanging so heavy, we were amazed she had been able to lift them, even her fingers were so heavy when we tangled them in ours, and because I knew and couldn't cope, we screamed.

We screamed until the glass that had shattered on the floor danced again with our voice, until the wires under the floor grew up like ivy through soil and tangled themselves around every railing and buried themselves in every wall, until the foundations warped and the ceiling shook, until the electricity danced around us in a tornado, until the gas pipes burnt inside their casings and the water pipes burst in geysers around our head, erupting towards the ceiling and boiling away in clouds of billowing steam. We screamed until the fire extinguishers burst, until plastic melted, until the thinnest wires started to melt and drip with their own heat, until our voice wasn't human, but the roar of the traffic and the screech of brakes and rattle of engines and rumble of an underground wind and

come be we

and until our hair danced with electric flame and our breath was black carbon on the air in front of us, bursting through our nostrils, and our fingers had the metallic gleam of a penknife and our heart raced in time to the *dedumdedumdedum* of the speeding train racing across old tracks deep in the earth and the rats clustered in the gutters and the pigeons scattered to the sky and, all around us, every telephone started to ring.

If we had known how, that would have been when we crawled back into the telephones.

We would have forgotten that moment, would have said goodbye to being human, if this was what it was like. I'd have done it in an instant, if I'd known how. But we'd burnt out the telephones around us, and the lights in the street, so we sat and rocked the body of Dana Mikeda, and whispered the dead sounds that people make at corpses, like the soothing words of a mother to her baby, telling them it'll be all right, after all.

We became conscious of Blackjack's wheezing by slow degrees. We looked up. Part of his leg was open and torn, and one arm hung oddly, but he was still alive, for what it was worth. His jacket had been slashed to ribbons and under it I could see the bare flesh of his infected veins. He had found his bag crushed under the remains of his bike and from it, pulled a gun, which he pointed at us. We felt...

...not quite nothing...

He found it hard to speak, but we weren't going anywhere.

"You..." he began, then spat blood and a piece of tooth, and tried again. "You...knew I was the traitor."

We said nothing.

"Used me!" he rasped. "Used me to find Bakker, find her. Knew I'd betray, knew you had to be alive. They followed...you were followed...so that the others could come here, destroy the Tower."

Still we said nothing. There wasn't anything that seemed to need saying.

"Used me," he repeated, nodding a quick, frantic nod. "Respected that, sorcerer. Respected it." He flicked back the safety on the gun. "I'm dying," he said.

Nothing.

"Blood curse. I swore and I betrayed. Knew it'd happen. Knew I'd die when I swore. Gotta be done. Gotta...gotta keep moving...gotta... find speed...enough...it's gotta be real. Life has to be lived on the edge, you have to see how it ends, to know that you're living it. I was so fast...you gotta be different, you know? To know you're alive? The whole clan they fucking said...gotta fight the Tower. Gotta work as one. Gotta work with others, say the right fucking thing, walk the right fucking walk, talk the right...you gotta bleed and burn and die and do what is right, because that's what's expected. You gotta do right. Because that's what a normal guy is meant to do. I ain't never going to be that normal guy. I ain't never going to be what they told me to be. When the shadow killed the head of my clan...he set us free. Do you understand, Matthew? The chaos? The speed? Do you understand being free? It's... it's all about...it's...no one tells me who I'm going to be. No one."

We said nothing.

He levelled the gun. "Don't you want to hear the rest?"

We thought about it. We shook our head.

He closed his finger over the trigger.

There was a single, sharp gunshot. Then another. It echoed across the flooded, shattered debris of the room. Blackjack staggered forward, the curse-ridden, battered remnant of his body barely able to support even that movement, then slid into a puddle on the floor.

From the stairwell, Vera said, "Psycho-bitch can shoot, can't she?"

We heard the clicking of a rifle, and footsteps coming towards us. We looked up. Oda looked back at us, behind her Vera, and behind that, a dozen or so Whites stinking of various destructive magics.

Oda said, "You look shit. Need a hand?"

We thought about it. Then we nodded, took hold of the hand that she offered us, and let her pull us back onto our feet, carefully laying down the body of Dana Mikeda on the floor behind us as we did.

There were Whites scattered on every floor. Vera said they'd lost the signal from the tracker in my shoe just outside the tower, but it hadn't taken much guessing to work out where I'd gone. She said there'd been confusion about why they kept on arriving at the same floor over and over again, no matter how many times they went upstairs, but it was nothing a lot of shooting and a dash of magic couldn't solve.

She agreed that we looked like shit.

It almost sounded like a compliment, coming from her.

We took the lift up to the tenth floor, where it stopped working. At the twelfth we found another dozen Whites and a lot of bodies; on the seventeenth a group of weremen dropped in; on the twenty-third we found a gaggle of warlocks; on the twenty-seventh, Oda greeted stony-faced Order men, laden with more weapons than we had ever seen.

At the thirty-fifth, the very top floor, Oda pressed a gun in our hand.

I said, "I don't know if I can . . ."

Vera, standing behind us, said, "Arseholes, we've come this bloody far!"

Oda thought about it, looked us straight in the eyes and said, "You came here for revenge. Now you've got a real reason for it."

"I . . . I was . . . it . . ." I couldn't really explain.

She thought about it, then said, lowering her voice, "Bakker is alone up there. No one is coming for him, not Amiltech, not Lee, not Simmons. You destroyed them all to get to him. Even the *shadow* is gone . . ."

"Not yet," I replied, "not quite."

". . . if you can't finish this," she said, firmer, "then maybe you should let *them* do it for you."

We stared at her in surprise. "Oda?" we said.

"Well?"

"We don't know if we can do it either."

"This is the only thing you have."

We took the gun, left the Whites in the stairwell, and went alone to meet Mr Bakker.

There is a magazine, published irregularly in the UK, and distributed occasionally in the US, Australia, South Africa and among a specialist English-speaking market, whose imaginative founding editor dubbed it *Urban Magic*. Students sometimes read it when they're bored and listless, in case they can get useful hints about sex out of it; fluffy ladies who care about gardening sometimes read it in case it can advise them on how to read their own palms; sinister men with an unhealthy interest in rabbit's blood sometimes read it, in case they can find clues in its-pages to a conspiracy. All of these people tend to be disappointed. If you ignore the occasionally garish covers designed to entice readers of just this sort into paying the £1.60 required per issue, the contents tend to be rather dry – essays on the various applications of ultraviolet light in binding spells; studies on the effect of different kinds of road paint in summoning circles, with excruciatingly detailed footnotes and usually a URL link to online case notes as supporting evidence; an assessment of how the wave–particle theory of light might be connected to the manipulation of pure elemental forces, and so on. It is the magazine of the professional urban magician, and a fairly specialist one at that. I first started reading it when I was in my twenties, a while after the first issue was published, and borrowed the back copies from the local library, because my teacher told me to. When I couldn't find the more obscure issues, I joined the British Library and went through their archives. There, after much scrutiny, I found an article very well received at the time, entitled "The Changing Concept of Magic", written for one of the earlier issues by my very own teacher. I read it, took notes and reported back favourably enough; but it took me a long while to work out what it was about the thing that bugged me so much.

It said: magic is life.

And there, quite simply, should have been the warning.

There was a pair of double doors at the end of a hall, and an empty reception desk in front of them. The doors were locked. We kicked them until they opened, no strength left for subtlety, and marched into the room beyond.

The room was gloomy, the lights switched off; but more than enough street light drifted through, reflected down from the orange clouds outside, drawing long shadows within shadows across the carpeted floor. Spread out beyond the windows, on every side except the one I'd come from, was the city. It ran away as far as the eye could see, a chaotic pattern of orange, white and pinkish stars across an uneven black floor, gleaming off the Thames, catching the flashing yellow indicator lights of the cars in the streets below, the glare of headlights where the streets aligned with our point of view, the glint of bedroom lights as they were turned out for the night, or the neon glow of the signs above the restaurants, clubs and bars.

And it was beautiful. No getting round the fact. It was simply and utterly beautiful.

And sitting in front of it, looking south towards the high red lights of Crystal Palace and the distant blackness of the North Downs where they cut off the orange sky, his back turned to the door, was Mr Robert Bakker.

He sat utterly still in his wheelchair, head forward, breathing slow and steady. Tubes were attached to his arms. On one side was a bag of some clear fluid that we couldn't guess at, leading into a drip. On the other side was a bag of bright red blood. I could guess whose. We felt the weight of the gun in our hand, the sticky hotness of our palm, and noticed in the light of the moon peeking out occasionally between the scudding clouds that he was casting a very respectable black shadow.

"Mr Bakker?" I said.

He stirred slightly in the wheelchair. "Matthew?" he asked, in a distant, confused voice.

We moved forward. "Mr Bakker?" we repeated, louder.

"Matthew, is that you?"

I stepped round so that I was next to him. He looked up, confused, then smiled. "Come to admire the view?"

I nodded and looked out across at it. "It's a good view," I said finally.

"One of the best. I had this whole floor cleared out so I could see it better." His eyebrows tightened. "How'd you get here? Not that I'm not pleased to see you . . ."

"I was kidnapped, drugged, tied up and left in a basement thirty-something floors beneath this," I replied cordially. "I then had a large amount of my blood taken out of my body for what I can only assume were experimental purposes, before my friends, having followed me here with foreknowledge of my imminent kidnapping and likely fate, attacked, and I escaped."

He thought about it, then said, "That's not what I expected to hear, I'll admit."

"Would you like to hear the rest?"

"Yes," he said. "I would." And by now, his eyes had clocked the gun in my hand, and the blood on my clothes and skin, and his voice was level and tense.

"Your shadow is alive."

"What?"

"Your shadow is alive," we repeated, struggling not to raise our voice. "It's been alive for several years. It killed Patel, Pensley, Dhawan, Akute, Foster, Awan . . ."

"Matthew, are you quite all right?"

". . . Koshdel, Khay, Dana, and me, to name a few. It is you. No getting round it. And it won't be killed until you are."

His fingers tightened on the arms of his chair. "You . . . believe this to be true?"

"Yes."

"What did you mean by Dana?"

I met his eyes squarely, and saw him flinch. "It killed her. It held her, and I said, *'Domine dirige nos'* . . ."

"The blessing of the city?"

"The very same, just like you taught me, the invocation of all its guardians and its spirits. And it killed her. I held her and I couldn't stand it, so I just . . . we were . . . anyway. It killed her. It wants to be alive – really alive. It is hungry. Nothing will ever sate its appetite, it is so hungry for life. It has no pleasure in anything, it cannot understand delight or feeling or pain, but it tries; it feasts on the blood and the fire of others, kills in order to see how people die, is fascinated by death and feasting and life. And it is a he; and he is you. That's how it is, I'm afraid. How it's going to go."

"Matthew . . ." he began.

"It came alive when you had the stroke. You were a good man – a brilliant sorcerer. You had always delighted in life, seen beauty in it; that's what sorcery is. The ability to see something wonderful, magical, where other people see just mundane and boring nothing. A point of view. You taught me that. Then you started dying and you couldn't cope. You couldn't reconcile the loss of your faculties, your abilities, your strength, your life, to how you'd lived it in the past. You were a healthy and active man and suddenly you're trapped in this dying carcass. But you've still got those scruples. The moral part of your brain says, "Oh, well, such is life, et cetera et cetera, better make the most of it and not cause any fuss." Then there's this other part, the part that everyone has anyway, that screams and fights and kicks against the idea of dying, that is terrified of it, can't cope with it, refuses to accept it and longs, above all other things, to live. That can find nothing in this life that doesn't lead to death, can see nothing in this life that it doesn't think is destructible or must have an end. I'm sure you see where this is leading."

"You're wrong," he said simply.

"Because you're a sorcerer," I went on, drained, empty. "Because you have a certain view on life, this other part comes alive. Perhaps it's harmless for a while, but then its thoughts seep into your own, its dreams infect your own, and you start thinking, 'Hey, let's see if I can stay alive, I'm sure it wouldn't cause anyone any trouble, where to start?' And you think of the blue electric angels and go, 'They're just surplus life waiting to be tapped, I wonder if they'd like to give some of their power to me?' And somehow in this process you forget the rules. You forget that the angels are about freedom from restraint and laws and all the earthly things, and you forget that they are not just life, they are *power*. And the hungry part of your brain might be thinking, 'I shall be a burning blue fire across the sky,' but you sure as hell don't say it. You could steal the electric angels' power and be a god, without flesh, form, feeling, substance, without restraint by the laws of man. And you're already halfway there, as we've established, because there's your shadow doing its thing. So you ask your apprentice round. And I said no. Probably didn't explain it well at the time – sorry – but no was the answer and it was the right answer. And you're a bit pissed at that."

"Matthew, I didn't..." he tried again.

"Let me finish," I snapped. "I need to get it right this time. You're a bit pissed off and, whether you like it or not, there's a part of you going, 'Little bastard betrayed me! The angels always talk to him, why not to me, little shit!' or words to that effect and, Bob's your uncle, I am surprised to find myself dead at the claws of a creature that wears your face but is distinctly, definitely not alive, merely hungry. So very, very hungry."

We clicked off the safety on the gun, and turned it this way and that in our grip, wiggling a finger into the trigger guard. "So there's really two things, as far as we see, which need explaining on our part, us to you. The first thing is why we didn't talk to you, when you listened for us in the phone lines. And the short answer is this – you are a great sorcerer, a brilliant master of your arts, you see magic wherever you go. But you said, 'Magic is life,' and that's not quite right. You think that the study of magic, the understanding of it, gives you some sort of better grasp of life. Unfortunately, even I worked out that this isn't quite true; it's a bit skewed, see? We understand this. Magic is not life. Life *is* magic. Even the boring, plodding, painful, cold, cruel parts, even the mundane automatic reflexes, heart pumping, lungs breathing, stomach digesting, even the uninteresting dull processes of walking, swinging the knees and seeing with eyes, *this* is magic. This is what makes magic. Understand that, and you are some way to understanding why we are what we are.

"And I guess that covers point the second – why I didn't help you summon the angels. It pretty much boils down to this: a man who looks at everything and sees a tool to be used, a force to be manipulated, rather than just good, old-fashioned stuff doing its thing, should not be free of the restraints of humanity. Have we missed anything?"

He thought about it a while, then smiled. "I don't think so."

"You don't seem particularly surprised."

"I knew you had to believe something like this."

"You don't seem particularly surprised that Dana's dead." He didn't answer. "Why did you keep her alive?"

He thought about it a long while, then said, "I doubt you'd really care for the reasoning. And it really is worth staying alive, however you can."

I saw it coming a second before it happened, a flick of his wrist. I raised the gun, swinging it up instinctively towards his head, but he'd already opened his fingers. The wall of twisted air slammed into me and picked me off my feet, knocking me back and wrenching my wrist as I skidded across the floor. The barrel of the gun smoked and burnt red-hot. I threw it aside and crawled back onto my feet, spinning my fingers through the air to catch a fistful of the magic of that place, dragging the reflected orange light in the clouds around me like a fluffy blanket to ward off the cold, until my skin burnt with its dull gleam. Bakker hadn't moved from his chair, hadn't stood; his back was half-turned to me. But as I watched and prepared a spell, he reached over and slipped out from his skin the needles carrying blood and other fluids, put them to one side and, very carefully, stood up. His legs buckled, but he caught himself on the handles of the chair, and rose nonetheless. He steadied himself and turned to look at us, standing on his own two feet, unsupported; and his face was white, his eyes empty, his teeth rotten, he trailed darkness as he moved, and he cast no shadow.

"There you are," we said.

Hunger/Bakker grinned. "And we are so *hungry*!"

"No, really?"

He opened his mouth and the darkness poured out like he had swallowed a bellyful of black, breeding locusts. It buzzed on the air and filled the room, expanding into every corner to block out the moonlight. Its touch was ice on our skin, but we drew our neon blanket tighter around us and half-closed our eyes, letting the bite of it settle down on us like a winter's wind after leaving the confines of a warm house. We couldn't see anything other than our own hands, lit in neon; the windows, the walls and even the floor were obscured by the almost liquid dark that swirled around us as we drew our hands through the air.

We heard, very faintly, an electric crackle. Unwilling to trust to chance, we threw up our hands to catch the bolt of mains-powered lightning that lashed out of the darkness in a burst of blinding white fire, snatching it into our fingers and spinning it towards the floor before it had more than a chance to singe our sleeves. Beneath us, the floor itself started to spout barbed wire that crawled up around our ankles. We ignited a gas pipe overhead and spilled the roiling liquid fire around our feet until the wires melted and withered away, before batting out blobs of smelly flame into the darkness all around where, to one side, briefly, they illuminated a flash of white skin before it was eaten up again by the dark.

He spat a billow of hot ashes at our face; we burst the pipes under our feet to smother it in backwards-falling rain. He shattered a window, letting in a dragging blast of wind that pulled and clawed at us both, then sent the jagged glass flying towards us. We spun the wind from the smashed window into a tornado around us, calm at the centre, that snatched each shard of glass and reduced it in a second to sand; he pulled the steel skeleton of the building up from beneath our feet, jagged rods lashing at us from the floor we stood on; but we simply jumped aside, weaving our way through them as they danced. He pulled the wires down from the ceiling cavity and wound them round our wrists and throat, choking us and dragging us off our feet in their snare; we pumped electricity through them until they melted and burnt through, dropping us back down onto our knees in the whirling darkness.

We felt him prepare another spell, sensed the tug of his magic in the air, and this time we struck instead. We put the warmth of our skin into the sodium-coloured neon light that blanketed us, then the touch of our breath, then the beating of our heart, so that in each second it grew brighter, and brighter. It burnt into the dark like a Mediterranean sun, it boiled off our skin like a corona, it made our hair stand on end, it scalded the floor and blackened the ceiling, and we put more and more and more into it, filled it with ourself until the flames started to turn blue and our feet no longer touched the ground and we opened our arms like the angel, ready to embrace any enemy who came towards them, and opened our mouth to let out the buzzing blue locusts in our belly, the flaring blue sparks that danced like living light, let them roll across our tongue in a glittering icy sea that gnawed into the darkness and congregated in dizzying hordes, like the lights that magicians had once called will-o'-the-wisps, and we blazed

so cold

because we could, we let our skin turn white with the ice of it, let our bones shiver, let our feet drift up off the floor and the eddy of our own breath spin us round, let the blue electric fire shatter every last window, and blast holes in the roof that lashed up towards the moonlight, let it burrow deep black burns in the floor and melt the walls; we let it consume every last vestige of warmth and anger and pain and fear inside me

inside me!

inside us, we let it eat up every feeling inside us

inside me!!

and through the burning we saw the shadow staggering, struggling to stay upright as the fire ate at his flesh, burnt his hair, dissolved the darkness of his coat, ate at his fingers, his nose, until black blood ran across him and until even that blood started to bubble and burn, steam and boil on his skin and he screamed and screamed and

was for a moment

as he screamed

just a frail old

His knees buckled.

His legs gave way.

His blood was bright red, his shadow a tiny pinprick under him.

And we were laughing.

because we were so bright and so powerful and no one could control us because we were

I was

unstoppable, untameable, so alive that we could burn for ever, light and life and fire and

laughing at his screaming

our skin cracking and the blue light blazing through underneath it

through our mouth and eyes and under our nails

because

I was

we were

blue light pouring out under our clothes, bursting out of us with every breath and we couldn't inhale there was so much of it

because I was . . .

because

we am

so much power . . . we were light, we were fire, we were life, we were the slithering underground wind, we were dancing heaven, we were blazing blue fire and

we were the angels!

. . .

Then he said my name.

And we were surprised to realise that I could still remember it. And we screamed and kicked and struggled as I forced us to breathe in, we screamed and punched and tore at our own skin, trying to pull the light out of us so that we would dissolve our flesh and be nothing but a blazing comet in the sky as I made us close our eyes against the blue blanket across our vision, we punched and bit and tore as I dragged our arms back down and clenched our fingers into fists and we screamed

WE BE LIGHT, WE BE LIFE, WE BE FIRE
COME BE WE AND BE FREE
WE BE
WE BE
WE BE . . .!

"Matthew?" His voice was weak, old, frail and dying.

WE BE BL . . . WE BE . . . WE BEEEEEEE . . .

And blood started running out of the cracks in my skin instead of our light, started seeping into our clothes and I was so weak, so small inside of us and we said

weeee beeeeeee . . .

but I am

come be . . .

Sinking to our knees, pain, so much pain

we can make you free!

from so much pain

come be we . . . we blaze for ever across the sky . . .

so weak

we set you free

nothing but ice left inside.

come be we and be free . . .

I shook my head. "Not today," I said. "Not yet!"

a fading remnant of fire worming its way beneath our fingers. We whispered, "So bright, so bright . . ." our fingers scuttling after it as it disappeared into the floor, "so beautiful . . ."

"Matthew?"

I looked up.

Just me.

He lay in a growing pool of his own blood, awkward, on one side, head towards the window. He coughed, spittle and blood mixing around his lips. I crawled on hands and knees towards him, knelt next to him and murmured, "Sorry, Mr Bakker."

A glimpse of a smile. "What's there . . . to be sorry?" he croaked.

"It's complicated."

"Always is. You're a sloppy sorcerer, Matthew Swift."

I shrugged, and even that was agony. "Could be worse," I replied.

His fingers closed around my wrist, and I noticed that, even though the face was Bakker's, the nails were still long and black. "Dying," he said. I stared down into his watery eyes. "Dying," he added, and his nails dug deeper into my skin, long, black nails. "Something we never understood about life," he explained and in that instant there was a pallor on his skin, more than just blood loss.

We snatched our wrist away, and threw ourself back even as his other hand reached up for our neck, nails gouging a slash just in front of our jugular vein, and his blood was still black as it came out of his skin, and his tongue licked rotten teeth and he screamed, "Want it! Want it now!" and he raised his head up on a shattered old body, ready to bite with yellow teeth, seizing my head by the hair and dragging it towards his with a strength that no one should have had, screaming, "Want it! Want to burn!"

I wound my fingers together, pressed electricity into them, drew them back, and slammed them as hard as I could into his chest. At least, I think I did it. In that moment, it was hard to tell.

The shock knocked him backwards, picking his feet up off the floor as he went, snapping his head back with a loud crack of bone on bone, and thrust him shoulders first out of the remnants of the window. I heard the screaming fade, and then stop abruptly with a splash, thirty-five floors below.

Epilogue: The Brief Act of Living

In which things, having ended, continue pretty much the same, despite all probable circumstance.

There was a hospital intensive-care ward.

Then there was a less intensive ward.

Then there was outpatients.

Then there was the street with a discharge notice, a single change of clothes, my old coat, my bag and a new pair of shoes; everything, in short, that I owned in the world.

I had no way to prove that I was alive, no home address and no money of my own. Sinclair gave me ten grand in a brown paper bag and said that the concerned citizens were grateful for my assistance.

In a way, the absence of these things seemed liberating.

I stayed with the Whites for a few weeks, in order to get my bearings. Then I stayed with a couple of friends in the countryside, who were close enough to put me up but not so close as to have realised that I was ever dead to begin with. I went walking in the hills, sploshing through mud and after a few weeks of it, despite the unfamiliarity of the place, I was beginning to understand how the countryside too could produce sorcerers, who summoned ivy instead of barbed wire.

But my heart was still in the city, and eventually I drifted back.

I took casual work in odd places here or there. My skills weren't necessarily that useful, but I supervised a few exorcisms and blessed the odd business about to set up shop, scratching very carefully into the walls of one or two abodes, *Domine dirige nos*, just for good luck.

I was leaving the swimming pool when she found me. I'd taken to making regular visits, partially because we enjoyed the act of swimming so much, but mostly because there was the promise of a hot shower afterwards, to keep me clean. It was in Highbury Fields, at that cool time of the evening on an overcast day when the sun is already below the horizon but its reflection is still bright enough to see without the street lamps' sodium glow. I walked away from the swimming pool, turned towards my regular bus stop, and she was there, emerging without a sound from the shadows of a shrubbery, pressing the gun to the back of my head and grabbing me by the shoulder to stop me flinching from its metal.

"Bang," she said.

"Oda," I replied breathlessly. "We wondered."

"Bang," she repeated. "Two in the head, and then three to the chest. Bang bang bang. No coming back from that; no phone boxes to hand either, just to make sure. Lights out, game over, good night the sunny time and so on."

"I didn't think you'd be the kind of person to go on about it," I said reproachfully. "If you're really going to do it, then just do it."

"You don't seem too freaked?"

"I'm not."

"What about them?"

"What is life, if it doesn't end?" we said.

"That's a really unhealthy attitude you've got there," she pointed out. "And I thought the Order was all about the spiritual things?"

Oda grunted, gently lifted her hand from my shoulder, and removed the gun from my head. She stepped back. I turned to look at her, curious. She met my gaze easily and said, "I wanted you to know. Any time, at any moment, wherever you are, whatever you do, I can do it. I can. I'm really that good."

"I believe you."

"Good. Think about it if you should be feeling Satanic."

She turned, swept her bag up off the pavement, and started to walk away. "Wait!" we called out.

She stopped, turned, looked back, eyebrows raised.

"We were informed that you'd kill us anyway," we said.

"I'm sure I will, some day. When you lose control or start sacrificing kiddies or eating rabbits' skulls for kicks, I'll be there. But as it is, right now . . ." She hesitated, half-turning her head up to the street lamp as if looking for it to click on in a moment of inspiration. Then she shook her head. "Right now, you're still on the side of the angels."

"Oh, the irony."

"Isn't it just?"

"Did you think of that now, or was it a pre-planned kinda thing?"

"See you around, Matthew Swift," she said in reply.

"You too, Oda. I'll see you around."

And she walked away.

Using Sinclair's money, I bought a PO Box at Mount Pleasant Post Office, and kept the rest in a small metal box buried in Abney Park Cemetery, since I didn't really know what else to do with it. A few days later, leafing through a copy of the Yellow Pages left on top of a bus shelter, I found under S the following entry:

"Swift, M. (sorcerer): PO Box 134B, Mount Pleasant, Rosebery Avenue, London, EC1R 2JA."

Since I hadn't put it there, I dismissed it as being down to damn mystical forces again, and tossed the fat yellow document back up on top of the shelter. I slung my bag over my shoulder, stretched my legs, patted down my pockets to make sure I hadn't dropped anything and, not knowing where I was going, or how I was going to get there, started walking. In the distance, we could hear the rumble of buses, the honking of cars, the shriek of a scooter's brakes, the tinging of the bicycle bells, the flapping of the pigeons, the scuttling of the rats, the shouting of the children, the mumbling of the old bag ladies, the cursing of the young men, the flirting of the pretty women, the slamming of windows, the venting of pipes, the dripping of taps, the hissing of televisions, the pinging of ovens and the ringing of the telephones, all around on every side, at every hour of every day, every day of every week, for ever, unending, an infinity of sound, sight, smell, life, light, wonder, a quiet endless mundane magical clamour that filled every corner of every street with the promise of adventure; a world too big for mortals, immortals and all the creatures in between.

We kept on walking.

Whatever happened next, good or bad, it would be wonderful finding out.